THE
BOURNE
LEGACY

BY ROBERT LUDLUM

The Tristan Betrayal
The Janson Directive
The Sigma Protocol
The Prometheus Deception
The Matarese Countdown
The Apocalypse Watch
The Road to Omaha
The Scorpio Illusion
The Bourne Ultimatum
The Icarus Agenda
The Bourne Supremacy
The Aquitaine Progression
The Parsifal Mosaic
The Bourne Identity
The Matarese Circle
The Gemini Contenders
The Holcroft Covenant
The Chancellor Manuscript
The Road to Gandolfo
The Rhinemann Exchange
The Cry of the Halidon
Trevayne
The Matlock Paper
The Osterman Weekend
The Scarlatti Inheritance

ROBERT LUDLUM'S
Jason Bourne
in

THE
BOURNE
LEGACY

A Novel by
Eric Van Lustbader

ST. MARTIN'S PRESS ❧ NEW YORK

www.stmartins.com

ISBN 0-312-33175-4
EAN 978-0312-33175-7

First Edition: June 2004

10 9 8 7 6 5 4 3 2 1

In memory of Bob

THE
BOURNE
LEGACY

PROLOGUE

Khalid Murat, leader of the Chechen rebels, sat still as a stone in the center vehicle of the convoy making its way through the bombed-out streets of Grozny. The BTR-60BP armored personnel carriers were standard Russian military issue and, as such, the convoy was indistinguishable from all the others rumbling through the city on patrol. Murat's heavily armed men were crammed into the other two vehicles—one in front and one behind his own. They were heading toward Hospital Number Nine, one of six or seven different hideouts Murat used to keep three steps ahead of the Russian forces searching for him.

Murat was darkly bearded, close to fifty, with a bear's broad stance and the fire-lit eyes of the true zealot. He had learned early on that the iron fist was the only way to rule. He had been present when Jokhar Dudayev had imposed Islamic Shariah law to no avail. He had seen the carnage wreaked when it had all begun, when the Chechnya-based warlords, foreign associates of Osama bin Laden, invaded Daghestan and executed a string of bombings in Moscow and Volgodonsk that killed some two hundred people. When the blame for the foreigners' actions was falsely put on Chechen terrorists, the Russians began their devastating bombing of Grozny, reducing much of the city to rubble.

The sky over the Chechen capital was blurred, made indistinct by a constant flux of ash and cinder, a shimmering incandescence so lurid it seemed almost radioactive. Oil-fueled fires burned everywhere across the rubble-strewn landscape.

Khalid Murat stared out the tinted windows as the convoy passed a burned-out skeleton of a building, massive, hulking, the roofless interior filled with flickering flames. He grunted, turned to Hasan Arsenov, his second in command, and said, "Once Grozny was the beloved home to lovers strolling down the wide tree-lined boulevards, mothers pushing prams across the leafy squares. The great circus was nightly filled to overflowing with joyous, laughing faces, and architects the world over made their pilgrimage to tour the magnificent buildings that once made Grozny one of the most beautiful cities on earth."

He shook his head sadly, slapped the other's knee in a comradely gesture. "Allah, Hasan!" he cried. "Look how the Russians have crushed everything that was good and fine!"

Hasan Arsenov nodded. He was a brisk, energetic man fully ten years Murat's junior. A former biathlon champion, he had the wide shoulders and narrow hips of a natural athlete. When Murat had taken over as rebel leader, he was at his side. Now he pointed out to Murat the charred husk of a building on the convoy's right. "Before the wars," he said with grave intent, "when Grozny was still a major oil-refining center, my father worked there at the Oil Institute. Now instead of profits from our wells, we get flash fires that pollute our air and our water."

The two rebels were chastened into silence by the parade of bombed-out buildings they passed, the streets empty save for scavengers, both human and animal. After several minutes, they turned to each other, the pain of their people's suffering in their eyes. Murat opened his mouth to speak but froze at the unmistakable sound of bullets pinging against their vehicle. It took him but an instant to realize that the vehicle was being hit by small-arms fire too weak to penetrate their vehicle's sturdy armor plate. Arsenov, ever vigilant, reached for the radio.

"I'm going to order the guards in the lead and tail vehicles to return fire."

Murat shook his head. "No, Hasan. Think. We're camouflaged in Russian military uniforms, riding in Russian personnel carriers. Whoever is firing on us is more likely an ally than a foe. We need to make sure before there's innocent blood on our hands."

He took the radio from Arsenov, ordered the convoy to a halt.

"Lieutenant Gochiyayev," he said into the radio, "organize your men into a recon. I want to find out who's shooting at us, but I don't want them killed."

In the lead vehicle, Lieutenant Gochiyayev gathered his men and ordered them to fan out behind the cover of the armored convoy. He followed them onto the rubble-strewn street, hunching his shoulders against the bitter cold. Using precise hand signals, he directed his men to converge from the left and right onto the place from which the small-arms fire had come.

His men were well trained; they moved swiftly and silently from rock to wall to pile of twisted metal beams, scrunched down, presenting as small a target as possible. However, no more shots were heard. They made their final run at once, a pincer move, designed to trap the enemy and crush them in a blistering cross-fire.

In the center vehicle, Hasan Arsenov kept his eye on the place where Gochiyayev had converged the troops and waited for the sounds of gunfire that never came. Instead, the head and shoulders of Lieutenant Gochiyayev appeared in the distance. Facing the center vehicle, he waved his arm back and forth in an arc, signaling that the area had been secured. At this sign, Khalid Murat moved past Arsenov, stepped out of the personnel carrier and without hesitation walked through the frozen rubble toward his men.

"Khalid Murat!" Arsenov called in alarm, running after his leader.

Clearly unperturbed, Murat walked toward a low crumbling stone wall, the place where the gunfire had emanated. He caught a glimpse of the piles of garbage; on one was a waxy white-skinned corpse that had some time ago been stripped of its clothes. Even at a distance the stench of putrefaction was like being hit with a poleax. Arsenov caught up with him and drew his sidearm.

When Murat reached the wall, his men were on either side, their arms at the ready. The wind gusted fitfully, howling and whining through the ruins. The dull metallic sky had darkened further and it began to snow. A light dusting quickly coated Murat's boots, created a web in the wiry jumble of his beard.

"Lieutenant Gochiyayev, you've found the attackers?"

"I have, sir."

"Allah has guided me in all things; he guides me in this. Let me see them."

"There's only one," Gochiyayev replied.

"One?" Arsenov cried. "Who? Did he know we're Chechen?"

"You're Chechen?" a small voice said. A pallid face emerged from behind the wall, a boy not more than ten years old. He wore a filthy wool hat, threadbare sweater over a few thin plaid shirts, patched trousers and a pair of cracked rubber boots far too big for his feet, which had probably been taken off a dead man. Though only a child, he had the eyes of an adult; they watched everything with a combination of wariness and mistrust. He stood protecting the skeleton of an unexploded Russian rocket he had scavenged for bread money, likely all that stood between his family and starvation. He held a gun in his left hand; his right arm ended at the wrist. Murat immediately looked away but Arsenov continued to stare.

"A land mine," the boy said with a heartbreaking matter-of-factness. "Laid by the Russian scum."

"Allah be praised! What a little soldier!" Murat exclaimed, directing his dazzling, disarming smile at the boy. It was this smile that had drawn his people to him like filings to a magnet. "Come, come." He beckoned, then held his empty palms up. "As you can see, we're Chechen, like you."

"If you're like me," the boy said, "why do you ride in Russian armored cars?"

"What better way to hide from the Russian wolf, eh?" Murat squinted, laughed to see that the boy held a Gyurza. "You carry a Russian Special Forces gun. Such bravery must be rewarded, yes?"

Murat knelt next to the boy and asked his name. When the boy told him, he said, "Aznor, do you know who I am? I am Khalid Murat and I, too, wish to be free of the Russian yoke. Together we can do this, yes?"

"I never meant to shoot at fellow Chechens," Aznor said. With his mutilated arm, he pointed to the convoy. "I thought this was a *zachistka*." He meant the monstrous clean-up operations perpetrated by Russian soldiers who searched for suspected rebels. More than twelve thousand Chechens had been killed during the *zachistkas*; two thousand had simply disappeared, countless others injured, tortured, maimed and raped. "The Russians murdered my father, my uncles. If you were Russians I would've killed you all." A spasm of rage and frustration played across his face.

"I believe you would've," Murat said solemnly. He dug in his pocket for some bills. The boy had to tuck the gun into his waistband in order to take them in his remaining hand. Leaning toward the boy, Murat said in a collusive whisper, "Now listen to me—I'll tell you where to buy more ammunition for your Gyurza so you'll be prepared when the next *zachistka* comes."

"Thank you." Aznor's face cracked open in a smile

Khalid Murat whispered a few words, then stepped back and ruffled the boy's hair. "Allah be with you, little soldier, in everything you do."

The Chechen leader and his second in command watched the small boy as he clambered back over the rubble, pieces of an unexploded Russian rocket tucked under one arm. Then they returned to their vehicle. With a grunt of disgust, Hasan slammed shut the armor-plated door on the world outside, Aznor's world. "Doesn't it bother you that you're sending a child to his death?"

Murat glanced at him. The snow had melted to trembling droplets on his beard, making him seem in Arsenov's eyes more like a liturgical imam than a military commander. "I've given this *child*—who must feed and clothe and, most important, *protect* the rest of his family as if he were an adult—I have given him hope, a specific objective. In short, I've provided him with *a reason to live.*"

Bitterness had turned Arsenov's face hard and pale; his eyes had a baleful look. "Russian bullets will tear him to ribbons."

"Is that what you truly think, Hasan? That Aznor is stupid or, worse, careless?"

"He's but one child."

"When the seed is planted, the shoots will rise out of even the most inhospitable ground. It's always been this way, Hasan. The belief and courage of one inevitably grows and spreads, and soon that one is ten, twenty, a hundred, a thousand!"

"And all the while our people are being murdered, raped, beaten, starved and penned like cattle. It's not enough, Khalid. Not nearly enough!"

"The impatience of youth hasn't yet left you, Hasan." He gripped the other's shoulder. "Well, I shouldn't be surprised, yes?"

Arsenov, catching the look of pity in Murat's eyes, clenched his jaw and turned his face away. Curls of snow made visible wind devils along the street, whirling like Chechen dervishes in ecstatic trance. Murat took this as a sign of the import of what he had just done, of what he was about to say. "Have faith," he said in hushed, sacramental tones, "in Allah and in that courageous boy."

Ten minutes later, the convoy stopped in front of Hospital Number Nine. Arsenov looked at his wristwatch. "Almost time," he said. The two of them were riding in the same vehicle, against standard security precautions, owing to the extreme importance of the call they were about to receive.

Murat leaned over, pressed a button, and the soundproof barrier rose into place, cutting them off from the driver and four bodyguards sitting forward. Well-trained, they stared straight ahead through the bullet-proof windshield.

"Tell me, Khalid, as the moment of truth is upon us, what reservations you have."

Murat raised his bristling eyebrows in a display of incomprehension that Arsenov thought rather transparent. "Reservations?"

"Don't you want what's rightfully ours, Khalid, what Allah decrees we should have?"

"The blood runs high in you, my friend. I know this only too well. We've fought side by side many times—we've killed together and we owe each other our very lives, yes? Now, listen to me. I bleed for our people. Their pain fills me with a rage I can barely contain. You know this better, perhaps, than anyone. But history warns that one should beware what one wants the most. The consequences of what's being proposed—"

"What we've been planning for!"

"Yes, planning for," Khalid Murat said. "But the consequences must be considered."

"Caution," Arsenov said bitterly. "Always caution."

"My friend." Khalid Murat smiled as he gripped the other's shoulder. "I don't want to be misled. The reckless foe is easiest to destroy. You must learn to make patience a virtue."

"Patience!" Arsenov spat. "You didn't tell the boy back there to be patient. You gave him money, told him where to buy ammunition. You set him against the Russians. Each day we delay is another day that boy and thousands like him risk being killed. It's the very future of Chechnya that will be decided by our choice here."

Murat pressed his thumbs into his eyes, rubbing with a circular motion. "There are other ways, Hasan. There are *always* other ways. Perhaps we should consider—"

"There's no *time*. The announcement has been made, the date set. The Shaykh is right."

"The Shaykh, yes." Khalid Murat shook his head. "Always the Shaykh."

At that moment, the car phone rang. Khalid Murat glanced at his trusted companion and calmly clicked on the speakerphone. "Yes, Shaykh," he said in a deferential tone of voice. "Hasan and I are both here. We await your instructions."

High above the street where the convoy was idling, a figure crouched on a flat rooftop, elbows atop the low parapet. Lying along the parapet was a Finnish Sako TRG-41 bolt-action sniper rifle, one of many he had modified himself. Its aluminum and polyurethane stock made it as light as it was deadly accurate. He was dressed in the camouflage uniform of the Russian military, which did not look out of place with the Asian caste of his smooth features. Over the uniform, he wore a lightweight Kevlar harness from which hung a metal loop. In his right palm, he cradled a small matte-black box, no larger than the size of a pack of cigarettes. It was a wireless device in which were set two buttons. There was a stillness about him, a kind of aura that intimidated people. It was as if he understood silence, could gather it to him, manipulate it, unleash it as a weapon.

In his black eyes grew the world entire, and the street, the buildings upon which he now gazed were nothing more than a stage set. He counted the Chechen soldiers as they emerged from the guard vehicles. There were eighteen: the drivers still behind the wheels and in the center vehicle at least four guards as well as the principals.

As the rebels entered the main entrance of the hospital on their way to secure the site, he depressed the top button of the wireless remote and C4 charges went off, collapsing the hospital entrance. The percussion shook the street, set the heavy vehicles to rocking on their oversized shocks. The rebels caught directly in the blast were either blown to bits or crushed beneath the weight of falling rubble, but he knew that at least some of the rebels could have been far enough inside the hospital lobby to have survived, a possibility he had factored into his plan.

With the sound of the first explosion still ringing and the dust not yet settled, the figure looked down at the wireless device in his hand and depressed the lower button. The street in front and back of the convoy erupted in a deafening blast, collapsing the shell-pocked macadam.

Now, even as the men below struggled to come to grips with the carnage he had visited upon them, the assassin took up the Sako, moving with a methodical, unhurried precision. The rifle was loaded with special non-fragmentation bullets of the smallest caliber the rifle could accommodate. Through its IR-enabled scope, he saw three rebels who had managed to escape the blasts with only minor injuries. They were running toward the middle vehicle, screaming at the occupants to get out before it was destroyed by another blast. He watched as they yanked open the right-hand doors, allowed Hasan Arsenov and one guard to emerge. That left the driver and three remaining bodyguards inside the car with Khalid Murat. As Arsenov turned away, the figure sighted on his head. Through the scope, he noted the expression of command plastered on Arsenov's face. Then he moved the barrel in a smooth, practiced motion, this time sighting on the Chechen's thigh. The figure squeezed off a shot and Arsenov grabbed his left leg, shouting as he went down. One of the guards ran to Arsenov, dragged him to cover. The two remaining guards, swiftly determining where the shot had come from, ran across the street, entering the building on whose roof the figure crouched.

As three more rebels appeared, racing out a side entrance to the hospital, the assassin dropped the Sako. He watched now as the vehicle containing Khalid Murat slammed into reverse. Behind and below him, he could hear the rebels pounding up the stairs leading to his rooftop perch. Still unhurried, he fitted titanium and corundum spikes to his boots. Then he took up a composite crossbow and shot a line into a light pole just behind the middle vehicle, tying off the line to make sure it was taut. Shouting voices reached him. The rebels had gained the floor directly below him.

The front of the vehicle was now facing him as the driver tried to maneuver it around the huge chunks of concrete, granite and macadam that had erupted in the explosion. The assassin could see the soft glint of the two panes of glass that comprised the windshield. That was the one problem the Russians had yet to overcome: Bullet-proofing the glass made the panes so heavy it required two of them for the windshield. The personnel carrier's one vulnerable spot was the strip of metal between the two panes.

He took the sturdy metal loop attached to his harness and snapped himself to the taut line. Behind him, he heard the rebels burst through the door, emerging onto the roof a hundred feet away. Spotting the assassin, they swung around to fire on him as they ran toward him, setting off an unnoticed trip wire. Immediately, they were engulfed in a fiery detonation from the last remaining packet of C4 the assassin had planted the night before.

Never turning around to acknowledge the carnage behind him, the assassin tested the line and then launched himself from the rooftop. He slid down the line, lifting his legs so that the spikes were aimed at the windshield divider. Everything now depended on the speed and the angle with which he would strike the divider between the bullet-proof panes of the windshield. If he was off by just a fraction, the divider would hold and he had a good chance of breaking his leg.

The force of the impact ran up his legs, jolting his spine as the titanium and corundum spikes on his boots crumpled the divider like a tin can, the panes of glass caving in without its support. He crashed through the windshield and into the interior of the vehicle, carrying with him much of the windshield. A chunk of it struck the driver in the neck, half-severing his head. The assassin twisted to his left. The bodyguard in the front seat was covered in the driver's blood. He was reaching for his gun when the assassin took his head between his powerful hands and broke his neck before he had a chance to squeeze off a round.

The other two bodyguards in the jumpseat just behind the driver fired wildly at the assassin, who pushed the bodyguard with the broken neck so that his body absorbed the bullets. From behind this makeshift protection, he used the bodyguard's gun, fired precisely, one shot through the forehead of each man.

That left only Khalid Murat. The Chechen leader, his face a mask of hatred, had kicked open the door and was shouting for his men. The assassin lunged at Murat, shaking the huge man as if he were a water rat; Murat's jaws snapped at him, almost taking off an ear. Calmly, methodically, almost joyously he seized Murat around the throat and, staring into his eyes, jabbed his thumb into the cricoid cartilage of the Chechen leader's lower larynx. Blood immediately filled Murat's throat, choking him, draining him of strength. His arms flailed, his hands beating against the assassin's face and head. To no avail. Murat was drowning in his own blood. His lungs filled and his breathing became ragged, thick. He vomited blood and his eyes rolled up in their sockets.

Dropping the now-limp body, the assassin climbed back into the front seat, hurling the driver's corpse out of the door. He slammed the vehicle into gear and stepped on the gas before what remained of the rebels could react. The vehicle leaped forward like a racehorse from the gate, hurtled over rubble and tarmac, then vanished into thin air as it plummeted into the hole the explosives had made in the street.

Underground, the assassin upshifted, racing through the tight space of a storm drain that had been widened by the Russians, who had intended to use them for clandestine assaults on rebel strongholds. Sparks flew as the metal fenders now and again scraped against the curving concrete walls. But for all that, he was safe. His plan had concluded as it had begun: with perfect clockwork precision.

After midnight the noxious clouds rolled away, at last revealing the moon. The detritus-laden atmosphere gave it a reddish glow, its lambent light intermittently disturbed by the still burning fires.

Two men stood in the center of a steel bridge. Below them, the charred remains of an unending war were reflected in the surface of the sluggish water.

"It's done," the first one said. "Khalid Murat has been killed in a manner that will cause maximum impact."

"I would expect nothing less, Khan," the second man said. "You owe your impeccable reputation in no small part to the commissions I've given you." He was taller than the assassin by a good four inches, square-shouldered, long-legged. The only thing that marred his appearance was the strange glassy utterly hairless skin on the left side of his face and neck. He possessed the charisma of a born leader, a man not to be trifled with. Clearly, he was at home in the great halls of power, in public forums or in thuggish back alleys.

Khan was still basking in the look in Murat's eyes as he died. The look was different in every man. Khan had learned there was no common thread, for each man's life was unique, and though all sinned, the corrosion those sins caused differed from one to the next, like the structure of a snowflake, never to be repeated. In Murat, what had it been? Not fear. Astonishment, yes, rage, surely, but something more, deeper—sorrow at leaving a life's work undone. The dissection of the last look was always incomplete, Khan thought. He longed to know whether there was betrayal there, as well. Had Murat known who had ordered his assassination?

He looked at Stepan Spalko, who was holding out an envelope, heavy with money.

"Your fee," Spalko said. "Plus a bonus."

"Bonus?" The topic of money refocused Khan's attention fully on the immediate. "There was no mention of a bonus."

Spalko shrugged. The ruddy moonlight made his cheek and neck shine like a bloody mass. "Khalid Murat was your twenty-fifth commission with me. Call it an anniversary present, if you wish."

"You're most generous, Mr. Spalko." Khan stowed the envelope away without looking inside. To have done otherwise would have been very bad manners.

"I've asked you to call me Stepan. I refer to you as Khan."

"That's different."

"How so?"

Khan stood very still, and the silence flowed toward him. It gathered in him, making him seem taller, broader.

"I'm not required to explain myself to you, Mr. Spalko."

"Come, come," Spalko said with a conciliatory gesture. "We're far from strangers. We share secrets of the most intimate nature."

The silence built. Somewhere on the outskirts of Grozny an explosion lit up the night, and the sound of small-arms fire came to them like strings of children's firecrackers.

At length, Khan spoke. "In the jungle I learned two mortal lessons. The first was to trust absolutely only myself. The second was to observe the most minute proprietaries of civilization, because knowing your place in the world is the only thing standing between you and the anarchy of the jungle."

Spalko regarded him for a long time. The fitful glow from the firefight was in Khan's eyes, lending him a savage aspect. Spalko imagined him alone in the jungle, prey to privations, the quarry of greed and wanton bloodlust. The jungle of Southeast Asia was a world unto itself. A barbarous, pestilential area with its own peculiar laws. That Khan had not only survived there, but flourished, was, in Spalko's mind at least, the essential mystery surrounding him.

"I'd like to think we're more than businessman and client."

Khan shook his head. "Death has a particular odor. I smell it on you."

"And I on you." A slow smile crept across Spalko's face. "So you agree, there is something special between us."

"We're men of secrets," Khan said, "aren't we?"

"A worship of death; a shared understanding of its power." Spalko nodded his assent. "I have what you requested." He held out a black file folder.

Khan looked into Spalko's eyes for a moment. His discerning nature had caught a certain air of condescension that he found inexcusable. As he had long ago learned to do, he smiled at the offense, hiding his outrage behind the impenetrable mask of his face. Another lesson he had learned in the jungle: Acting in the moment, in hot blood, often led to an irreversible mistake; waiting in patience for the hot blood to cool was where all successful vengeance was bred. Taking the folder, he busied himself with opening the dossier. Inside, he found a single sheet of onionskin with three brief close-typed paragraphs and a photo of a handsome male face. Beneath the picture was a name: David Webb. "This is all of it?"

"Culled from many sources. All the information on him anyone has." Spalko spoke so smoothly Khan was certain he had rehearsed the reply.

"But this is the man."

Spalko nodded.

"There can be no doubt."

"None whatsoever."

Judging by the widening glow, the firefight had intensified. Mortars could be heard, bringing their rain of fire. Overhead, the moon seemed to glow a deeper red.

Khan's eyes narrowed and his right hand curled slowly into a tight fist of hate. "I could never find a trace of him. I'd suspected he was dead."

"In a way," Spalko said, "he is."

He watched Khan walk across the bridge. He took out a cigarette and lit up, drawing the smoke into his lungs, letting it go reluctantly. When Khan had disappeared into the shadows, Spalko pulled out a cell phone, dialed an overseas number. A voice answered, and Spalko said, "He has the dossier. Is everything in place?"

"Yes, sir."

"Good. At midnight your local time you'll begin the operation."

PART ONE

CHAPTER ONE

David Webb, professor of linguistics at Georgetown University, was buried beneath a stack of ungraded term papers. He was striding down the musty back corridors of gargantuan Healy Hall, heading for the office of Theodore Barton, his department head, and he was late, hence this shortcut he had long ago discovered using narrow, ill-lighted passageways few students knew about or cared to use.

There was a benign ebb and flow to his life bound by the strictures of the university. His year was defined by the terms of the Georgetown semesters. The deep winter that began them gave grudging way to a tentative spring and ended in the heat and humidity of the second semester's finals week. There was a part of him that fought against serenity, the part that thought of his former life in the clandestine service of the U.S. government, the part that kept him friends with his former handler, Alexander Conklin.

He was about to round a corner when he heard harsh voices raised and mocking laughter and saw ominous-seeming shadows playing along the wall.

"Muthfucka, we gonna make your gook tongue come out the back of your head!"

Bourne dropped the stack of papers he had been carrying and sprinted around the corner. As he did so, he saw three young black men in coats down to their ankles arrayed in a menacing semicircle around an Asian, trapping him against a corridor wall. They had a way of standing, their knees slightly bent, their upper limbs loose and swinging slightly that made their entire bodies seem like blunt and ugly aspects of weapons, cocked and ready. With a start, he recognized their prey was Rongsey Siv, a favorite student of his.

"Muth*afucka*," snarled one, wiry, with a strung-out, reckless look on his defiant face, "we come in here, gather up the goods to trade for the bling-bling."

"Can't ever have enough bling-bling," said another with an eagle tattoo on his cheek. He rolled a huge gold square-cut ring, one of many on the fingers of his right hand, back and forth. "Or don't you know the bling-bling, gook?"

"Yah, gook," the strung-out one said, goggle-eyed. "You don't look like you know *shit*."

"He wants to stop us," the one with the tattooed cheek said, leaning in toward Rongsey. "Yah, gook, whatcha gonna do, *kung-fuckin-fu* us to death?"

They laughed raucously, making stylized kicking gestures toward Rongsey, who shrank back even farther against the wall as they closed in.

The third black man, thick-muscled, heavyset, drew a baseball bat from underneath the voluminous folds of his long coat. "That right. Put your hands up, gook. We gonna break your knuckles good." He slapped the bat against his cupped palm. "You want it all at once or one at a time?"

"Yo," the strung-out one cried, "he don't get to choose." He pulled out his own baseball bat and advanced menacingly on Rongsey.

As the strung-out kid brandished his bat, Webb came at them. So silent was his approach, so intent were they on the damage they were about to inflict that they did not become aware of him until he was upon them.

He grabbed the strung-out kid's bat in his left hand as it was coming down toward Rongsey's head. Tattoo-cheek, on Webb's right, cursed mightily, swung his balled fist, knuckles bristling with sharp-edged rings, aiming for Webb's ribs.

In that instant, from the veiled and shadowed place inside Webb's head, the Bourne persona took firm control. Webb deflected the blow from tattoo-cheek with his biceps, stepped forward and slammed his elbow into tattoo-cheek's sternum. He went down, clawing at his chest.

The third thug, bigger than the other two, cursed and, dropping his bat, pulled a switchblade. He lunged at Webb, who stepped into the attack, delivering a short, sharp blow to the inside of the assailant's wrist. The switchblade fell to the corridor floor, skittering away. Webb hooked his left foot behind the other's ankle and lifted up. The big thug fell on his back, turned over and scrambled away.

Bourne yanked the baseball bat out of the strung-out thug's grip. "Muthafuckin' Five-O," the thug muttered. His pupils were dilated, unfocused by the effects of whatever drugs he'd taken. He pulled a gun—a cheap Saturday-night special—and aimed it at Webb.

With deadly accuracy, Webb flung the bat, striking the strung-out thug between the eyes. He staggered back, crying out, and his gun went flying.

Alerted by the noise of the struggle, a pair of campus security guards appeared, rounding the corner at a run. They brushed past Webb, pounding after the thugs, who fled without a backward glance, the two helping the strung-out one. They burst through the rear door to the building, out into the bright sunshine of the afternoon, with the guards hot on their heels.

Despite the guards' intervention, Webb felt Bourne's desire to pursue the thugs run hot in his body. How quickly it had risen from its psychic sleep, how easily it had gained control of him. Was it because he wanted it to? Webb took a deep breath, gained a semblance of control and turned to face Rongsey Siv.

"Professor Webb!" Rongsey tried to clear his throat. "I don't know—" He seemed abruptly overcome. His large black eyes were wide behind the lenses of his glasses. His expression was, as usual, impassive, but in those eyes Webb could see all the fear in the world.

"It's okay now." Webb put his arm across Rongsey's shoulders. As always, his fondness for the Cambodian refugee was showing through his professorial reserve. He couldn't help it. Rongsey had overcome great adversity— losing almost all his family in the war. Rongsey and Webb had been in the same Southeast Asian jungles, and try as he might, Webb could not fully remove himself from the tangle of that hot, humid world. Like a recurring fever, it never really left you. He felt a shiver of recognition, like a dream one has while awake.

"*Loak soksapbaee chea tay?*" How are you? he asked in Khmer.

"I'm fine, Professor," Rongsey replied in the same language. "But I don't . . . I mean, how did you . . . ?"

"Why don't we go outside?" Webb suggested. He was now quite late for Barton's meeting, but he couldn't care less. He picked up the switchblade and the gun. As he checked the gun's mechanism, the firing pin broke. He threw the useless gun in a trash bin but pocketed the switchblade.

Around the corner, Rongsey helped him with the spill of term papers. They then walked in silence through the corridors, which became increasingly crowded as they neared the front of the building. Webb recognized the special nature of this silence, the dense weight of time returning to normal after an incident of shared violence. It was a wartime thing, a consequence of the jungle; odd and unsettling that it should happen on this teeming metropolitan campus.

Emerging from the corridor, they joined the swarm of students crowding through the front doors to Healy Hall. Just inside, in the center of the floor, gleamed the hallowed Georgetown University seal. A great majority of the students were walking around it because a school legend held that if you walked on the seal you'd never graduate. Rongsey was one of those who gave the seal a wide berth, but Webb strode right across it with no qualms whatsoever.

Outside, they stood in the buttery spring sunlight, facing the trees and the Old Quadrangle, breathing the air with its hint of budding flowers. At their backs rose the looming presence of Healy Hall with its imposing Georgian red-brick facade, nineteenth-century dormer windows, slate roof and central two-hundred-foot clock spire.

The Cambodian turned to Webb. "Professor, thank you. If you hadn't come . . ."

"Rongsey," Webb said gently, "do you want to talk about it?"

The student's eyes were dark, unreadable. "What's there to say?"

"I suppose that would depend on you."

Rongsey shrugged. "I'll be fine, Professor Webb. Really. This isn't the first time I've been called names."

Webb stood looking at Rongsey for a moment, and he was swept by sudden emotion that caused his eyes to sting. He wanted to take the boy in his arms, hold him close, promise him that nothing else bad would ever happen to him. But he knew that Rongsey's Buddhist training would not allow him to accept the gesture. Who could say what was going on beneath that fortresslike exterior. Webb had seen many others like Rongsey, forced by the exigencies of war and cultural hatred to bear witness to death, the collapse of a civilization, the kinds of tragedies most Americans could not understand. He felt a powerful kinship with Rongsey, an emotional bond that was tinged with a terrible sadness, recognition of the wound inside him that could never truly be healed.

All this emotion stood between them, silently acknowledged perhaps but never articulated. With a small, almost sad smile, Rongsey formally thanked Webb again and they said their good-byes.

Webb stood alone amid the students and faculty hurrying by, and yet he knew that he wasn't truly alone. Despite his best efforts, the aggressive personality of Jason Bourne had once again asserted itself. He breathed slowly and deeply, concentrating hard, using the mental techniques his psychiatrist friend, Mo Panov, had taught him for pushing the Bourne identity down. He concentrated first on his surrounding, on the blue and gold colors of the spring afternoon, on the gray stone and red brick of the buildings around the quad, of the movement of the students, the smiling faces of the girls, the laughter of the boys, the earnest talk of the professors. He absorbed each element in its entirety, grounding himself in time and place. Then, and only then, did he turn his thoughts inward.

Years ago he had been working for the foreign service in Phnom Penh. He'd been married then, not to Marie, his current wife, but to a Thai woman named Dao. They had two children, Joshua and Alyssa, and lived in a house on the bank of the river. America was at war with North Vietnam, but the war had spilled over into Cambodia. One afternoon, while he was at work and his family had been swimming in the river, a plane had strafed them, killing them.

Webb had almost gone mad with grief. Finally, fleeing his house and Phnom Penh, he'd arrived in Saigon, a man with no past and no future. It had been Alex Conklin who had taken a heartsick, half-mad David Webb off the streets of Saigon and forged him into a first-rate clandestine operative. In Saigon, Webb had learned to kill, had turned his own self-hatred outward, inflicting his rage on others. When a member of Conklin's group— an evil-tempered drifter named Jason Bourne—had been discovered to be a spy, it was Webb who had executed him. Webb had come to loathe the Bourne identity, but the truth was that it had often been his lifeline. Jason Bourne had saved Webb's life more times than he could remember. An amusing thought if it hadn't been so literal.

Years later, when they had both returned to Washington, Conklin had given him a long-term assignment. He had become what amounted to a sleeper agent, taking the name of Jason Bourne, a man long dead, forgotten by everyone. For three years Webb *was* Bourne, turned himself into an

international assassin of great repute in order to hunt down an elusive terrorist.

But in Marseilles, his mission had gone terribly wrong. He'd been shot,
cast into the dark waters of the Mediterranean, thought dead. Instead, he
had been pulled from the water by members of a fishing boat, nursed back
to health by a drunkard doctor in the port they'd set him down in. The
only problem was that in the shock of almost dying he'd lost his memory.
What had come slowly back were the Bourne memories. It was only much
later, with the help of Marie, his wife-to-be, that he had come to realize the
truth, that he was David Webb. But by that time the Jason Bourne personality was too well ingrained, too powerful, too cunning to die.

In the aftermath, he'd become two people: David Webb, linguistics professor with a new wife and, eventually, two children, and Jason Bourne, the
agent trained by Alex Conklin to be a formidable spy. Occasionally, in some
crisis, Conklin called on Bourne's expertise and Webb reluctantly rose to
duty. But the truth was that Webb often had little control over his Bourne
personality. What had just happened with Rongsey and the three street
thugs was evidence enough. Bourne had a way of asserting himself that was
beyond Webb's control, despite all the work he and Panov had done.

Khan, having watched David Webb and the Cambodian student talking
from across the quad, ducked into a building diagonally across from Healy
Hall, mounted the stairs to the third floor. Khan was dressed much like all
the other students. He looked younger than his twenty-seven years and no
one gave him a second look. He was wearing khakis and a jeans jacket, over
which was slung an outsize backpack. His sneakers made no sound as he
went down the hallway, past the doors to classrooms. In his mind's eye was
a clear picture of the view across the quad. He was again calculating angles,
taking into account the mature trees that might obscure his view of his intended target.

He paused in front of the sixth door, heard a professor's voice from
inside. The talk about ethics brought an ironic smile to his face. In his
experience—and it was great and varied—ethics was as dead and useless as
Latin. He went on to the next classroom, which he had already determined
was empty, and went in.

Quickly now, he shut and locked the door behind him, crossed to the line of windows overlooking the quad, opened one and got to work. From his backpack, he removed a 7.62-mm SVD Dragunov sniper rifle with a collapsible stock. He fitted the optical sight onto it, leaned it on the sill. Peering through the sight, he found David Webb, by this time standing alone across the quad in front of Healy Hall. There were trees just to his left. Every once in a while, a passing student would obscure him. Khan took a deep breath, let it out slowly. He sighted on Webb's head.

Webb shook his head, shaking off the effect his memories of the past had on him, and refocusing on his immediate surroundings. The leaves rustled in a gathering breeze, their tips gilded with sunlight. Close by, a girl, her books clutched to her chest, laughed at the punchline of a joke. A waft of pop music came from an open window somewhere. Webb, still thinking of all the things he wanted to say to Rongsey, was about to turn up the front steps of Healy Hall when a soft *phutt!* sounded in his ear. Reacting instinctively, he stepped into the dappled shadows beneath the trees.

You're under attack! shouted Bourne's all-too-familiar voice, reemerging in his mind. *Move now!* And Webb's body reacted, scrambling as another bullet, its initial percussion muffled by a silencer, splintered the tree bark beside his cheek.

A crack marksman. Bourne's thoughts began to flood through Webb's brain in response to the organism finding itself under attack.

The ordinary world was in Webb's eyes, but the extraordinary world that ran parallel to it, Jason Bourne's world—secret, rarefied, privileged, deadly—flared like napalm in his mind. In the space of a heartbeat, he had been torn from David Webb's everyday life, set apart from everyone and everything Webb held dear. Even the chance meeting with Rongsey seemed now to belong to another lifetime. From behind, out of the sniper's sight, he gripped the tree, the pad of his forefinger feeling for the mark the bullet had made. He looked up. It was Jason Bourne who traced the trajectory of the bullet back to a third-floor window in a building diagonally across the quad.

All around him, Georgetown students walked, strolled, talked, argued and debated. They had seen nothing, of course, and if by chance they had heard anything at all, the sounds meant nothing to them and were quickly forgotten. Webb left his protection behind the tree, moving quickly into a knot of students. He mingled with them, hurrying, but as much as possible keeping to their pace. They were his best protection now, blocking Webb from the sniper's line of sight.

It seemed as if he was only semiconscious, a sleepwalker who nevertheless saw and sensed everything with a heightened awareness. A component of this awareness was a contempt for those civilians who inhabited the ordinary world, David Webb included.

After the second shot, Khan had drawn back, confused. This was not a state he knew well. His mind raced, assessing what had just happened. Instead of panicking, running like a frightened sheep back into Healy Hall as Khan had anticipated, Webb had calmly moved into the cover of the trees, impeding Khan's view. That had been improbable enough—and totally out of character for the man briefly described in Spalko's dossier—but then Webb had used the gash the second bullet had made in the tree to gauge its trajectory. Now, using the students as cover, he was heading toward this very building. Improbably, he was attacking instead of fleeing.

Slightly unnerved by this unexpected turn of events, Khan hurriedly broke down the rifle, stowed it away. Webb had gained the steps to the building. He'd be here within minutes.

Bourne detached himself from the pedestrian flow, raced into the building. Once inside, he leaped up the stairway to the third floor. He turned left. Seventh door on the left: a classroom. The corridor was filled with the buzz of students from all over the world—Africans, Asians, Latin Americans, Europeans. Each face, no matter how briefly glimpsed, registered on the screen of Jason Bourne's memory.

The low chatter of the students, their fitful bursts of laughter, belied the danger lurking in the immediate environment. As he approached the classroom door, he opened the switchblade he had confiscated earlier, curled his fist around it so that the blade protruded like a spike from between his second and third fingers. In one smooth motion, he pushed open the door, curled into a ball and tumbled inside, landing behind the heavy oak desk, some eight feet from the doorway. His knife hand was up; he was ready for anything.

He rose cautiously. An empty classroom leered at him, filled only with chalk dust and mottled patches of sunlight. He stood looking around for a moment, his nostrils dilated, as if he could drink in the scent of the sniper, make his image appear out of thin air. He crossed to the windows. One was open, the fourth from the left. He stood at it, staring out at the spot beneath the tree where moments ago he had been standing, talking with Rongsey. This is where the sniper had stood. Bourne could imagine him resting the rifle barrel on the sill, fitting one eye to the powerful scope, sighting across the quad. The play of light and shadow, the crossing students, a sudden burst of laughter or cross words. His finger on the trigger, squeezing in an even pull. *Phutt! Phutt!* One shot, two.

Bourne studied the windowsill. Glancing around, he went to the metal tray that ran below the wall of blackboards, scooped out a measure of chalk dust. Returning to the window, he gently blew the chalk dust from his fingers onto the slate surface of the sill. Not a single print appeared. It had been wiped clean. He knelt, cast his gaze along the wall beneath the window, the floor at his feet. He found nothing—no telltale cigarette butt, no stray hairs, no spent shells. The meticulous assassin had vanished just as expertly as he had appeared. His heart was pounding, his mind racing. Who would try to kill him? Surely, it was no one from his current life. The worst that could be said about it was his argument last week with Bob Drake, the head of the ethics department, whose penchant for droning on about his chosen field was both legendary and annoying. No, this threat was coming from Jason Bourne's world. Doubtless, there were many candidates from his past, but how many of them would be able to trace Jason Bourne back to David Webb? This was the real question that worried him. Though part of him wanted to go home, talk this through with Marie, he knew that the one person with sufficient knowledge of Bourne's shadow existence to be able to help was Alex Conklin, the man who like a conjurer had created Bourne out of thin air.

He crossed to the phone on the wall, lifted the receiver and punched in his faculty access code. When he reached an outside line, he dialed Alex Conklin's private number. Conklin, now semiretired from the CIA, would be at home. Bourne got a busy signal.

Either he could wait here for Alex to get off the phone—which, knowing Alex, could be a half hour or more—or he could drive to his house. The open window seemed to mock him. It knew more than he did about what had taken place here.

He left the classroom, heading back down the stairs. Without thinking, he scanned those around him, looking to match up anyone he had passed on his way to the room.

Hurrying across the campus, he soon reached the car park. He was about to get into his car when he thought better of it. Making a quick but thorough inspection of the car's exterior and its engine, he determined that it had not been tampered with. Satisfied, he slid behind the wheel, turned on the ignition and drove out of the campus.

Alex Conklin lived on a rural estate in Manassas, Virginia. Once Webb reached the outskirts of Georgetown, the sky took on a deeper radiance; an eerie kind of stillness had taken root, as if the passing countryside was holding its breath.

As with the Bourne personality, Webb both loved and loathed Conklin. He was father, confessor, coconspirator, exploiter. Alex Conklin was the keeper of the keys to Bourne's past. It was imperative he talk to Conklin now because Alex was the only one who would know how someone stalking Jason Bourne could find David Webb on campus at Georgetown University.

He'd left the city behind him, and by the time he'd reached the Virginia countryside, the brightest part of the day had slipped away. Thick banks of clouds obscured the sun, and gusts of wind swept through the verdant Virginia hillsides. He pressed down on the accelerator and the car leaped forward, its big engine purring.

As he followed the banked curves of the highway, it suddenly occurred to him that he hadn't seen Mo Panov in over a month. Mo, an Agency psychologist recommended by Conklin, was trying to repair Webb's fractured psyche, to suppress the Bourne identity for good and help Webb recover his lost memories. Through Mo's techniques, Webb had found chunks of memory he had assumed lost floating back up to his conscious mind. But the work was arduous, exhausting, and it wasn't unusual for him to halt the sessions during ends of terms when his life became unbearably hectic.

He turned off the main highway and headed northwest on a two-lane blacktop road. Why had Panov come into his mind at just this moment? Bourne had learned to trust his senses and his intuition. Mo popping up out of the blue was a kind of signpost. What meaning did Panov have for him now? Memory, yes, but what else? Bourne thought back. The last time they had been together, he and Panov had been talking about silence. Mo had told him that silence was a useful tool in memory work. The mind, needing to be busy, did not like silence. If you could induce a complete enough silence in your conscious mind, it was possible that a memory lost to you would appear to fill the space. *Okay*, Bourne thought, *but why think about silence just at this moment?*

It wasn't until he had turned into Conklin's long, gracefully curving drive that he made the connection. The sniper had used a silencer, the main purpose of which was to keep the shooter from being noticed. But a silencer had its drawbacks. In a long-range weapon, like the one the sniper had been using, it would significantly impair the accuracy of the shot. He should have been aiming at Bourne's torso—a higher-percentage shot because of body mass—but instead, he'd fired at Bourne's head. That wasn't logical, if you assumed the sniper was trying to kill Bourne. But if he was only attempting to frighten, to give warning—that was another matter. This unknown sniper had an ego, then, but he was not a showboat; he had left no token of his prowess behind. And yet he had a specific agenda—that much was clear.

Bourne passed the looming misshapen hulk of the old barn, the other smaller outbuildings—utility facilities, storage sheds and the like. Then the main house was in sight. It stood within stands of tall pines, clumps of birch and blue cedars, old wood that had been here for close to sixty years, predating the stone house by a decade. The estate had belonged to a now-deceased army general who had been deeply involved in clandestine and rather unsavory activities. As a result, the manor house—the entire estate, actually—was honeycombed with underground tunnels, entrances and egresses. Bourne imagined it amused Conklin to live in a place filled with so many secrets.

As he pulled up, he saw not only Conklin's BMW 7-series but Mo Panov's Jaguar parked side by side. As he walked across the bluestone gravel, his heart felt suddenly lighter. The two best friends he had in the world—both in their own ways the keepers of his past—were inside. Together, they would solve this mystery as they had all the others before. He climbed onto the front portico, rang the bell. There was no answer. Pressing his ear to the polished teak door, he could hear voices from within. He tried the handle, found the door unlocked.

An alarm went off inside his head and, for a moment, he stood behind the half-open door, listening to everything inside the house. No matter that he was out here in the countryside where crime was practically unheard of—old habits never died. Conklin's overactive sense of security would dictate locking the front door whether or not he was home. Opening the switchblade, he entered, all too aware that an attacker—one of a termination team sent to kill him—could be lurking inside.

The chandeliered foyer gave out onto a wide sweep of polished wood stairs leading up to an open gallery that ran the width of the foyer. To the right was the formal living room, to the left the denlike media room with its wet bar and deep, masculine leather sofas. Just beyond there was a smaller, more intimate room that Alex had made into his study.

Bourne followed the sound of the voice into the media room. On the large-screen TV a telegenic CNN commentator was standing outside the front of the Oskjuhlid Hotel. A superimposed graphic indicated that he was on location in Reykjavík, Iceland. ". . . the tenuous nature of the upcoming terrorism summit is on everyone's mind here."

No one was in the room, but there were two old-fashioned glasses on the cocktail table. Bourne picked one up, sniffed. Speyside single-malt, aged in sherry casks. The complex aroma of Conklin's favorite Scotch disoriented him, brought back a memory, a vision of Paris. It was autumn, fiery horse-chestnut leaves tumbling down the Champs-Elysées. He was looking out the window from an office. He struggled with this vision, which was so strong he seemed to be pulled out of himself, to actually be in Paris, but, he reminded himself grimly, he was in Manassas, Virginia, at Alex Conklin's house, and all was not well. He struggled, trying to maintain his vigilance, his focus, but the memory, triggered by the scent of the single-malt, was overpowering, and he so yearned to *know*, to fill in the gaping holes in his memory. And so he found himself in the Paris office. Whose? Not Conklin's—Alex had never had an office in Paris. That smell, someone in the office with him. He turned, saw for the briefest instant the flash of a half-remembered face.

He tore himself away. Even though it was maddening to have a life you remembered only in fitful bursts, with all that had happened and things here feeling just slightly off-kilter, he couldn't afford to get sidetracked. What had Mo said about these triggers? They could come from a sight, a sound, a smell, even the touch of something, that once the memory was triggered he could tease it out by repeating the stimulus that had provoked it in the first place. But not now. He needed to find Alex and Mo.

He looked down, saw a small notepad on the table and picked it up. It seemed blank; the top leaf had been ripped off. But when he turned it slightly, he could see faint indentations. Someone—presumably Conklin— had written "NX 20." He pocketed the pad.

"So, the countdown has begun. In five days' time, the world will know whether a new day, a new world order will emerge, whether the law-abiding peoples of the world will be able to live in peace and harmony." The anchor continued to drone on, segueing into a commercial.

Bourne switched off the TV with the remote and silence descended. It was possible that Conklin and Mo were out walking, a favorite way for Panov to let off steam while in conversation, and he, no doubt, would want the old man to get his exercise. But there was the anomaly of the un-locked door.

Bourne retraced his steps, reentering the foyer and going up the stairs two at a time. Both guest bedrooms were empty, devoid of any sign of re-cent habitation, as were their en suite bathrooms. Down the hall, he went into Conklin's master suite, a Spartan space befitting an old soldier. The bed was small and hard, not much more than a pallet. It was unmade, clear that Alex had slept there last night. But as befitted a master of secrets, there was very little in the way of his past on display. Bourne picked up a silver-framed snapshot of a woman with long wavy hair, light eyes and a gently mocking smile. He recognized the regal stone lions of the fountain at Saint-Sulpice in the background. Paris. Bourne put the photo down, checked the bath. Nothing there of interest.

Back downstairs, two chimes sounded the hour on the clock in Con-klin's study. It was an antique ship's clock, its note bell-like, musical. But for Bourne the sound had unaccountably taken on an ominous cast. It seemed to him as if the tolling of the bell was rushing through the house like a black wave, and his heart beat fast.

He went down the hallway, past the kitchen into whose doorway he momentarily poked his head. A teakettle was on the stove, but the stainless-steel counters were spotlessly clean. Inside the refrigerator, the ice machine ground out cubes. And then he saw it—Conklin's walking stick, polished ash with the turned silver knob at its top. Alex had a bum leg, the result of a particularly violent encounter overseas; he would never have gone out on the grounds without the stick.

The study was around to the left, a comfortable wood-paneled room in a corner of the house that looked out onto a tree-shaded lawn, a flagstone terrace in the middle of which was sunk a lap-pool and, beyond, the beginning of the pine and hardwood forest that ran for most of the property. With a mounting sense of urgency, Bourne headed for the study. The moment he entered, he froze.

He was never so aware of the dichotomy inside himself, for part of him had become detached, an objective observer. This purely analytic section of his brain noted that Alex Conklin and Mo Panov lay on the richly dyed Persian carpet. Blood had flowed out of their head wounds, soaked into the carpet, in some places overflowing it, pooling on the polished wood floor. Fresh blood, still glistening. Conklin was staring up at the ceiling, his eyes filmed over. His face was flushed and angry, as if all the bile he had been holding deep inside had been forced to the surface. Mo's head was turned as if he had been trying to look behind him when he was felled. An unmistakable expression of fear was etched on his face. In the last instant, he had seen his death coming.

Alex! Mo! Jesus! Jesus! All at once, the emotional dam burst and Bourne was on his knees, his mind reeling with shock and horror. His entire world was shaken to its core. Alex and Mo dead—even with the grisly evidence before him it was hard to believe. Never to speak to them again, never to have access to their expertise. A jumble of images paraded before him, remembrances of Alex and Mo, times they had spent together, tense times filled with danger and sudden death, and then, in the aftermath, the ease and comfort of an intimacy that could only come from shared peril. Two lives taken by force, leaving behind nothing but anger and fear. With a stunning finality, the door onto his past slammed shut. Both Bourne and Webb were mourning. Bourne struggled to gather himself, swept aside Webb's hysterical emotionalism, willed himself not to weep. Mourning was an indulgence he could not afford. He had to think.

Bourne got busy absorbing the murder scene, fixing details in his mind, trying to work out what had happened. He moved closer, careful not to step in the blood or to otherwise disturb the scene. Alex and Mo had been shot to death, apparently with the gun lying on the carpet between them. They had received one shot each. This was a professional hit, not an intruder break-in. Bourne's eye caught the glint of the cell phone gripped in Alex's hand. It appeared as if he had been speaking to someone when he was shot. Had it been when Bourne was trying to get through to him earlier? Quite possibly. By the look of the blood, the lividity of the bodies, the lack of rigor mortis in the fingers, it was clear the murders had happened within the hour.

A faint sound in the distance began to intrude on his thoughts. Sirens! Bourne left the study and raced to the front-facing window. A fleet of Virginia State Police cruisers was careening down the driveway, lights flashing. Bourne was caught in a house with the bodies of two murdered men, and no plausible alibi. He had been set up. All at once, he felt the prongs of a clever trap closing around him.

CHAPTER TWO

The pieces came together in his mind. The expert shots fired at him on campus had not been meant to kill him but to herd him, to force him to come to Conklin. But Conklin and Mo had already been killed. Someone was still here, watching and waiting to call the police as soon as Bourne had shown up. The man who'd shot at him on campus?

Without a second thought, Bourne grabbed Alex's cell phone, ran into the kitchen, opened a narrow door onto a steep flight of stairs down into the basement and peered down into pitch blackness. He could hear the crackling of the police radios, the crunch of gravel, the pounding on the front door. Querulous voices raised.

Bourne went to the kitchen drawers, scrabbled around until he found Conklin's flashlight, then went through the basement door; for a moment he was in utter darkness. The concentrated beam of light illuminated the steps as he descended quickly, silently. He could smell the scents of concrete, old wood, lacquer and oil from the furnace. He found the hatch underneath the stairs, pulled it out. Once, on a cold and snowy winter's afternoon, Conklin had shown him the underground entrance the general had used to get to the private heliport near the stables. Bourne could hear the boards creaking above his head. The cops were inside the house. Possibly they had already found the bodies. Three cars, two dead men. It would not be long before they traced the license tags to his car.

Ducking down, he entered the low passageway, fitted the hatch back into place. Too late he thought of the old-fashioned glass he had picked up. *When the forensics people dust, they'll find my prints. Those, along with my car parked in the driveway . . .*

No good thinking about that now, he had to move! Bent over, he made his way along the cramped passageway. Within ten feet it opened up so that he was able to walk normally. There was a new dampness in the air; from somewhere close at hand he could hear the slow drip of water seeping. He determined that he had gone beyond the foundation of the house. Bourne quickened his pace and, not three minutes later, came upon another set of stairs. These were of metal, military in nature. He mounted them and, at the top, pushed up with his shoulder. Another hatch opened. Fresh air, the hushed and tranquil light at the end of the day, the droning of insects washed over him. He was at the edge of the general's heliport.

The tarmac was littered with twigs and bits of dead branches. At some point, a family of raccoons had made their way into the small ramshackle shingle-roofed shed at the edge of the tarmac. The place bore the unmistakable air of abandonment. The heliport was not, however, his objective. He turned his back on it and plunged into the thick pine forest.

His goal was to make a long sweeping curve away from the house, the entire estate, eventually ending up on the highway far enough away from any cordon the police threw around the estate. However, his immediate objective was the stream that ran more or less diagonally through the property. It would not be long, he knew, before the police brought in dogs. He could do very little about leaving his scent on dry land, but in the moving water even the dogs would lose his trail.

Snaking through the thorny snarl of underbrush, he crested a small ridge, stood between two cedars, listening intently. It was vital to catalog all the normal sounds of this specific environment so that he would instantly be alerted to the sound of an intruder. He was keenly aware that an enemy was in all likelihood somewhere close by. The murderer of his friends, of the moorings of his old life. The desire to stalk that enemy was weighed against the necessity of escaping from the police. As much as he wanted to track down the killer, Bourne knew it was crucial for him to be outside the radius of the police cordon before it was fully set up.

The moment Khan had entered the dense pine and hardwood forest on Alexander Conklin's estate he felt as if he had come home. The deep green vault closed over his head, plunging him into a premature twilight. Overhead, he could see sunlight filtering through the topmost branches, but here all was murk and gloom, the better for him to stalk his prey. He had followed Webb from the university campus to Conklin's house. During the course of his career, he had heard of Alexander Conklin, knew him for the legendary spymaster he had been. What puzzled him was why David Webb should come here? Why would he even know Conklin? And how was it that so many police had shown up at the estate mere minutes after Webb himself?

In the distance, he could hear baying, and he knew the police must have let loose their tracking dogs. Up ahead, he saw Webb moving through the forest as if he knew it well. Another question without an obvious answer. Khan picked up his pace, wondering where Webb was headed. Then he heard the sound of a stream and he knew precisely what his quarry had on his mind.

Khan hurried on, reaching the stream before Webb. He knew his prey would head downstream, away from the direction in which the hounds were headed. That was when he saw the huge willow and a grin captured his face. A sturdy tree with a network of spreading branches was just what he needed.

The ruddy sunlight of early evening threaded itself like needles of fire through the trees, and Bourne's eye was caught by the splotches of crimson that fired the edge of the leaves.

On the far side of the ridge, the land fell away rather steeply, and the way became more rocky. He could pick out the soft burbling sound of the nearby stream, and he headed for it as quickly as he could. The winter's snowpack had combined with the early spring rains to leave the stream swollen. Without hesitation, he stepped into the chill water, wading downstream. The longer he stayed in the water the better, as the dogs would lose all scent of him and become confused, and the farther away he emerged, the harder it would be for them to pick up his scent again.

Safe for the moment, he began thinking of his wife, Marie. He needed to contact her. Going home was out of the question now; doing so would put them in immediate jeopardy. But he had to contact Marie, warn her. The Agency was sure to come looking for him at home, and not finding him there, they were certain to detain Marie, interrogate her, assuming she would know his whereabouts. And there was the even more chilling possibility that whoever had set him up would now try to get to him through his family. In a sudden sweat of anxiety, he pulled out Conklin's cell phone, dialed Marie's cell phone, input a text message. It was one word only: *Diamond*. This was the code word he and Marie had previously agreed upon, to be used only in dire emergencies. It was a directive for her to take the kids and leave immediately for their safe house. They were to stay there, incommunicado, secure, until Bourne gave Marie the "all clear" signal. Alex's phone rang and Bourne saw Marie's text: *Repeat please*. This was not the prescribed response. Then he realized why she was confused. He had contacted her on Alex's cell phone, not his. He repeated the message: *DIAMOND*, this time typing it in all capital letters. He waited, breathless, and then Marie's response came: *HOURGLASS*. Bourne exhaled in relief. Marie had acknowledged; he knew the message was real. Even now, she would be gathering up the kids, bundling them into the station wagon, driving off, leaving everything behind.

Still, he was left with a feeling of anxiety. He would feel a whole lot better once he heard her voice, once he could explain to her what had happened, that he was fine. But he wasn't fine. The man she knew—David Webb—had already been subsumed again by Bourne. Marie hated and feared Jason Bourne. And why shouldn't she? It was possible that one day Bourne would be all that was left of the personality in David Webb's body. And whose doing would that be? Alexander Conklin's.

It seemed astonishing and altogether improbable to him that he could both love and loathe this man. How mysterious the human mind that it could simultaneously contain such extreme contradictory emotions, that it could rationalize away those evil qualities it knew were there in order to feel affection for someone. But, Bourne knew, the need to love and be loved was a human imperative.

He continued this train of thought as he followed the stream, which, for all its bright sparkle, was exceptionally clear. Small fish darted this way and that, terrified by his advance. Once or twice he glimpsed a trout in a silvery flash, bony mouth slightly open as if seeking something. He had come to a bend in which a large willow, its roots greedy for moisture, overhung the streambed. Alert to any noise, any sign that his pursuers were drawing near, Bourne detected nothing but the rushing of the stream itself.

The attack came from above. He heard nothing, but he felt the shift in the light, then a weight pressing down on him in the instant before he was driven into the water. He felt the crushing pressure of the body on his midsection and lungs. As he struggled to breathe, his attacker slammed his head on the slick rocks of the streambed. A fist drove into his kidney and all the breath went out of him.

Instead of tensing against the attack, Bourne willed his body to go completely limp. At the same time, instead of striking out, he drew his elbows into his side and, at the moment when his body was at its most slack, he reared up onto them, twisting his torso. As he hurled himself around, he struck out and up with the edge of his hand. He gasped air into his lungs as the weight came off. Water streamed across his face, blurring his vision, so that he could see only the outline of his assailant. He struck out at him but connected with nothing but air.

His assailant vanished as quickly as he had appeared.

Khan, gasping and retching as he scrambled down the streambed, tried to force air past the spasming muscles and bruised cartilage of his throat. Stunned and enraged, he gained the underbrush and was soon lost within the tangle of the forest. Trying to force himself to breathe normally, he gently massaged the tender area Webb had struck. That had not been a lucky blow but a calculated, expert counterattack. Khan was confused, a tinge of fear creeping through him. Webb was a dangerous man—far more than any academic had any right to be. He had been shot at before; he could trace a bullet's trajectory, could track through wilderness, fight hand-to-hand. And at the first sign of trouble he had come to Alexander Conklin. Who was this man? Khan asked himself. One thing was certain, he would not underestimate Webb again. He would track him, regain the psychological advantage. Before the inevitable end, he wanted Webb to be afraid of him.

Martin Lindros, Deputy Director of the CIA, arrived at the Manassas estate of the late Alexander Conklin at precisely six minutes past six. He was met by the ranking Virginia State Police detective, a harried, balding man named Harris who was trying to mediate the territorial dispute that had sprung up between the state police, the county sheriff's office and the FBI, all of whom had begun vying for jurisdiction as soon as the identities of the deceased had been discovered. When Lindros emerged from his car, he counted a dozen vehicles, three times that number of people. What was needed was a sense of order and purpose.

As he shook hands with Harris, he looked him straight in the eye and said, "Detective Harris, the FBI is out. You and I will be working this double homicide ourselves."

"Yessir," Harris said crisply. He was tall and, perhaps in compensation, had developed a slight stoop, which along with his large watery eyes and lugubrious face made him seem as if he had run out of energy long ago. "Thanks. I've got some—"

"Don't thank me, Detective, I guarantee you this is going to be one bitch of a case." He dispatched his assistant to deal with the FBI and the sheriff's personnel. "Any sign of David Webb?" He'd gotten word from the FBI when he'd been patched through to them that Webb's car had been found parked in Conklin's driveway. Not Webb, really. Jason Bourne. Which was why the Director of Central Intelligence had dispatched him to take over the investigation personally.

"Not yet," Harris said. "But we have the dogs out."

"Good. Have you established a cordon perimeter?"

"I tried to send my men out, but then the FBI . . ." Harris shook his head "I told them time was of the essence."

Lindros glanced at his watch. "Half-mile perimeter. Use some of your men to work another cordon at a radius of a quarter-mile. They might pick up something useful. Call in more personnel if you have to."

While Harris was talking on his walkie-talkie, Lindros eyed him appraisingly. "What's your first name?" he asked when the detective was through giving orders.

The detective gave him an abashed look. "Harry."

"Harry Harris. You're kidding, right?"

"No, sir. I'm afraid not."

"What were your parents thinking?"

"I don't think they were, sir."

"Okay, Harry. Let's take a look at what we have here." Lindros was in his late thirties, a smart sandy-haired Ivy Leaguer who had been recruited to the Agency out of Georgetown. Lindros' father had been a strong-willed man who spoke his mind and had his own way of doing things. He instilled this quirky independence in young Martin, along with the sense of duty to his country, and Lindros believed it was these qualities that had caught the attention of the DCI.

Harris brought him into the study but not before Lindros had marked the two old-fashioned glasses on the cocktail table in the media room. "Anyone touch these, Harry?"

"Not to my knowledge, sir."

"Call me Martin. We're going to get to know each other fast." He looked up and smiled, to further put the other at ease. The manner in which he had thrown around the Agency's weight was deliberate. In cutting out the other law enforcement agencies, he had drawn Harris into his orbit. He had a feeling he was going to need a compliant detective. "Have your forensics people dust both glasses for prints, will you?"

"Right away."

"And now let's have a word with the coroner."

High atop the road that snaked along the ridge bordering the estate, a heavyset man stood peering at Bourne through a pair of powerful night-vision glasses. He had a wide melon face distinctly Slavic in character. The fingertips of his left hand were yellow; he smoked constantly, compulsively. Behind him, his large black SUV was parked in a scenic turnout. To anyone passing, he would look like a tourist. Tracking backward, he found Khan creeping through the woods on Bourne's trail. Keeping one eye on Khan's progress, he flipped open his tri-band cell phone, punched in an overseas number.

Stepan Spalko answered at once.

"The trap has been sprung," the heavyset Slav said. "The target is on the run. So far he has eluded both the police and Khan."

"Goddammit!" Spalko said. "What is Khan up to?"

"Do you want me to find out?" the man asked in his cold, casual manner.

"Keep as far away from him as possible. In fact," Spalko said, "get out of there now."

Staggering to the stream bank, Bourne sat down, slicked his hair back from his face. His body ached and his lungs felt as if they were on fire. Explosions went off behind his eyes, returning him to the jungles of Tam Quan, the missions David Webb had undertaken at Alex Conklin's behest, missions sanctioned by Saigon Command yet disavowed by them, insane missions so difficult, so deadly that no American military personnel could ever be associated with them.

Bathed in the failing light of a spring evening, Bourne knew that he had been thrust into the same kind of situation now. He was in a red zone—an area controlled by the enemy. The trouble was, he had no idea who the enemy was or what he intended. Was Bourne even now being herded as he apparently had been when he had been fired upon at Georgetown University, or had his enemy moved on to a new phase of his plan?

Far off, he heard the baying of dogs, and then, startlingly close at hand, the crisp, clear sound of a twig snapping. Had it been made by an animal or the enemy? His immediate objective had been altered. He still had to avoid the net of the police cordon but now, at the same time, he had to find a way to turn the tables on his attacker. The trouble was he had to find his assailant before he attacked Bourne again. If it was the same person as before, then he was not only a crack shot but also an expert at jungle warfare. In a way, knowing this much about his adversary heartened Bourne. He was getting to know his opponent. Now to avoid being killed before he could get to know him well enough to surprise him . . .

The sun had slipped below the horizon, leaving the sky the color of a banked fire. A cool wind caused Bourne to shiver in his wet clothes. He rose and began to move, both to get the stiffness out of his muscles and to warm himself. The forest was cloaked in indigo, and yet he felt as exposed as if he were in a treeless expanse beneath a cloudless sky.

He knew what he would do if he were in Tam Quan: He'd find shelter, a place to regroup and consider options. But finding shelter in a red zone was tricky; he might be putting his head in a trap. He moved through the forest slowly and deliberately, his eyes scanning tree trunk after tree trunk until he found what he was looking for. Virginia creeper. It was too early in the year for flowers, but the shiny five-lobed leaves were unmistakable. Using the switchblade, he carefully peeled off long lengths of the sturdy vine.

Moments after he was finished, his ears pricked up. Following a faint sound, he soon came to a small clearing. There. He saw a deer, a mid-sized buck. Its head was up, its black nostrils scenting the air. Had it smelled him? No. It was trying to find—

The deer took off, and Bourne with him. He ran lightly and silently through the forest paralleling the deer's path. Once, the wind shifted and he had to alter his course in order to remain downwind of the animal. They had covered perhaps a quarter of a mile when the deer slowed. The ground had risen, become harder, more compact. They were quite some distance from the stream and on the extreme edge of the estate. The deer leaped easily over the stone wall marking the northwestern corner of the property. Bourne clambered over the wall in time to see that the deer had led him to a salt lick. Salt licks meant rocks and rocks meant caves. He recalled Conklin telling him that the northwestern edge of the property abutted a series of caves honeycombed with chimneys, natural vertical holes the Indians had once used to vent their cooking fires. Such a cave was just what he was hoping for—a haven to temporarily hide in that, by virtue of its two egresses, would not become a trap.

Now I have him, Khan thought. Webb had made a huge mistake—he'd entered the wrong cave, one of the few without a second exit. Khan crept out from his hiding place, crossing the small clearing in silence and in stealth, entering the black mouth of the cave.

Creeping forward, he could sense Webb in the darkness up ahead. Khan knew by the smell that this one was shallow. It did not have the damp, sharp scent of built-up organic matter of a cave that went deep into the bedrock.

Up ahead, Webb had switched on the flashlight. In a moment he would see that there was no chimney, no other way out. The time to attack was now! Khan launched himself at his adversary, struck him flush in the face.

Bourne went down, the flashlight hitting the rock, the light bouncing crazily. At the same time, he could feel the rush of air as the balled fist flew toward him. He allowed it to strike him and, as the arm was extended to the fullest, chopped down hard on the exposed and vulnerable biceps.

Lunging forward, he jammed his shoulder into the sternum of the other body. A knee came up, connected with the inside of Bourne's thigh, and a line of nerve pain flashed through him. He seized a handful of clothes, jerked the body against the rock face. The body bounced back, rammed into him, bowling him off his feet. They rolled together, grappling at each other. He could hear the other's breathing, an incongruously intimate sound, like listening to a child's breath beside you.

Locked in an elemental struggle, Bourne was close enough to smell a complex mélange rising off the other like steam from a sunlit swamp that made the jungle of Tam Quan rear up once more in his mind. In that instant, he felt a bar against his throat. He was being hauled backward.

"I won't kill you," a voice said in his ear. "At least not yet."

He jabbed backward with an elbow, was rewarded with a knee to his already aching kidney. He doubled over but was hauled painfully erect by the bar against his windpipe.

"I could kill you now, but I won't," the voice said. "Not until there is enough light so that I can look into your eyes while you die."

"Did you have to kill two innocent decent men just to get to me?" Bourne said.

"What are you talking about?"

"The two people you shot to death back at the house."

"I didn't kill them; I never kill innocents." There was a chuckle. "On the other hand, I don't know that I could call anyone associated with Alexander Conklin an innocent."

"But you herded me here," Bourne said. "You shot at me so I'd run to Conklin, so you could—"

"You're talking nonsense," the voice said. "I merely followed you here."

"Then how did you know where to send the cops?" Bourne said.

"Why would I even call them?" the voice whispered harshly.

Startling though this information was, Bourne was only half-listening. He had relaxed a little during this conversation, leaning backward. This left the smallest bit of slack between the bar and his windpipe. Bourne now turned on the balls of his feet, dropping one shoulder as he did so, so that the other was obliged to focus his attention on keeping the bar in place. In that instant, Bourne used the heel of his hand to deliver a quick strike just below the ear. The body fell hard; the bar rang hollowly as it struck the rock floor.

Bourne took several deep breaths to clear his head, but he was still woozy from loss of oxygen. He took up the flashlight, illuminated the spot where the body had fallen, but it wasn't there. A sound, barely a whisper, came to him and he raised the beam. A figure sprang into the light against the mouth of the cave. As the light struck him, he turned, and Bourne got a glimpse of his face before he vanished into the trees.

Bourne ran after him. In a moment he heard the distinct snap and whoosh! He heard movement up ahead, and he pushed through the undergrowth to where he had set his trap. He had woven the Virginia creeper into a net and tied it to a green sapling he had bent almost double. It had caught his assailant. The hunter had become the prey. Bourne pushed forward to the base of the trees, prepared himself to face his attacker and cut the creeper netting down. But the net was empty.

Empty! He gathered it up, saw the rent his quarry had cut into its upper section. He had been quick, clever and prepared; he would be even more difficult to take by surprise again.

Bourne looked up, playing the cone of the flashlight beam in an arc across the maze of tree limbs. Despite himself, he experienced a fleeting twinge of admiration for his expert and resourceful adversary. Snapping off the flashlight, he was plunged into night. A whippoorwill cried out and then, in the lengthening silence, an owl's hoot echoed mournfully through the pine-clad hills.

He leaned his head back and took a deep breath. Against the screen of his mind's eye the flat planes, the dark eyes of the face was limned, and in a moment he was certain that it matched up with one of the students he had seen on his way to the university classroom the sniper had used.

At last, his enemy had a face as well as a voice.

"I could kill you now, but I won't. Not until there is enough light so that I can look into your eyes while you die."

CHAPTER THREE

Humanistas, Ltd., an international human-rights organization known the world over for its worldwide humanitarian and relief work, was headquartered on the deep green western slope of Gellért Hill in Budapest. From this magnificent vantage point, Stepan Spalko, peering through the huge angled plate-glass windows, imagined the Danube and the entire city genuflecting at his feet.

He had come around from behind his huge desk to sit on an upholstered chair facing the very dark-skinned Kenyan president. Flanking the door were the Kenyan's bodyguards, hands tucked at the smalls of their backs, the blank look endemic to all such government personnel etched on their faces. Above them, molded in bas-relief on the wall, was the green cross held in the palm of a hand that was Humanistas' well-marketed logo. The president's name was Jomo and he was a Kikuyu, the largest ethnic tribe of Kenya, and a direct descendant of Jomo Kenyatta, the Republic's first president. Like his famous forebear, he was a *Mzee*, Swahili for a respected elder. Between them was an ornate silver service dating back to the 1700s. Fine black tea had been poured, biscuits and exquisitely turned-out small sandwiches artfully arranged on a chased oval tray. The two men were talking in low, even tones.

"One doesn't know where to begin to thank you for the generosity you and your organization have shown us," Jomo said. He was sitting up very straight, his ramrod back pulled a little away from the comfort of the chair's plush back. Time and circumstance had combined to rob his face of much of the vitality it had held in his youth. There was, beneath the high gloss of his skin, a grayish pallor. His features had been compressed, ossified into stone by hardship and perseverance in the face of overwhelming odds. In short, he had the aspect of a warrior too long at siege. His legs were together, bent at the knee at a precise ninety-degree angle. He held in his lap a long, polished box of deep-grained bubinga wood. Almost shyly, he presented the box to Spalko. "With the heartfelt blessings of the Kenyan people, sir."

"Thank you, Mr. President. You are too kind," Spalko said graciously.

"The kindness is surely yours, sir." Jomo watched with keen interest as Spalko opened the box. Inside was a flat-bladed knife and a stone, more or less oval in shape, with a flattish bottom and top.

"My God, this isn't a *githathi* stone, is it?"

"It is, indeed, sir," Jomo said with obvious delight. "It is from my birth village, from the *kiama* to which I still belong."

Spalko knew Jomo was referring to the council of elders. The *githathi* was of great value to tribal members. When a dispute arose within the council that could not otherwise be settled, an oath was taken on this stone. Spalko gripped the knife's handle, which was carved from carnelian. It, too, had a ritualistic purpose. In cases of life or death disputes, the blade of this knife was first heated, then laid onto the tongues of the disputants. The extent of the tongues' subsequent blistering determined their guilt or innocence.

"I wonder, though, Mr. President," Spalko said with the hint of an impish tone, "whether the *githathi* comes from your *kiama* or your *njama*?"

Jomo laughed, a rumble deep in his throat that made his small ears quiver. It was so rare he had cause to laugh these days. He could not remember the last time. "So you have heard of our secret councils, have you, sir? I would say your knowledge of our customs and lore is formidable, indeed."

"The history of Kenya is long and bloody, Mr. President. I am a firm believer that it is in history we learn all our most important lessons."

Jomo nodded. "I concur, sir. And I feel compelled to reiterate that I cannot imagine what state the Republic would be in without your doctors and their vaccines."

"There is no vaccine against AIDS." Spalko's voice was gentle but firm. "Modern medicine can curtail the suffering and deaths from the disease with drug cocktails, but as for its spread, only the stringent application of contraceptives or abstinence will be effective."

"Of course, of course." Jomo wiped his lips fastidiously. He detested coming hat in hand to this man who had already so generously extended his help to all Kenyans, but what choice did he have? The AIDS epidemic was decimating the Republic. His people were suffering, dying. "What we need, sir, is more of the drugs. You have done much to alleviate the level of suffering in my country. But there are thousands yet to receive your help."

"Mr. President." Spalko leaned forward, and with him, Jomo as well. His head was now in the sunlight streaming in through the high windows, lending him an almost preternatural glow. The light also threw into prominence the shiny poreless skin on the left side of his face. This accentuation of his disfigurement served to provide a slight shock to Jomo, jolting him out of his predetermined pattern. "Humanistas, Ltd. is prepared to return to Kenya with twice the number of doctors, double the amount of drugs. But you—the government—must do your part."

It was at this point that Jomo realized that Spalko was asking of him something quite apart from promoting safe-sex lectures and distributing condoms. Abruptly, he turned, dismissing his two bodyguards from the room. When the door had closed behind them, he said, "An unfortunate necessity in these dangerous times, sir, but even so one sometimes wearies of never being alone."

Spalko smiled. His knowledge of Kenyan history and tribal customs made it impossible for him to take the president lightly, as others might. Jomo's need might be great, but one never wanted to take advantage of him. The Kikuyu were prideful people, an attribute made all the more important since it was more or less the only thing of value they possessed.

Spalko leaned over, opened a humidor, offered a Cuban Cohiba to Jomo, took one himself. They rose, lighting their cigars, walked across the carpet to stand at the window, looking out at the tranquil Danube sparkling in the sunlight.

"A most beautiful setting," Spalko said conversationally.

"Indeed," Jomo affirmed.

"And so serene." Spalko let go a blue cloud of aromatic smoke. "Difficult to come to terms with the amount of suffering in other parts of the world." He turned then to Jomo. "Mr. President, I would consider it a great personal favor if you would grant me seven days' unlimited access to Kenyan airspace."

"Unlimited?"

"Coming and going, landings and such. No customs, immigration, inspections, nothing to slow us down."

Jomo made a show of considering. He puffed some on his Cohiba, but

Spalko could tell that he was not enjoying himself. "I can grant you only three," Jomo said at length. "Longer than that will cause tongues to wag."

"That will have to do, Mr. President." Three days was all Spalko had wanted. He could have insisted on the seven days, but that would have stripped Jomo of his pride. A stupid and possibly costly mistake, considering what was to happen. In any event, he was in the business of promoting goodwill, not resentment. He held out his hand and Jomo slipped his dry, heavily calloused hand into his. Spalko liked that hand; it was a hand of a manual laborer, someone who was not afraid to get dirty.

After Jomo and his entourage had left, it was time to give an orientation tour to Ethan Hearn, the new employee. Spalko could have delegated the orientation to any one of a number of assistants, but he prided himself on personally making sure all his new employees were settled. Hearn was a bright young spark who had previously worked at the Eurocenter Bio-I Clinic on the other side of the city. He was a highly successful fund-raiser and was well connected among the rich and elite of Europe. Spalko found him to be articulate, personable and empathetic—in short, a born humanitarian, just the sort he needed to maintain the stellar reputation of Humanistas, Ltd. Besides which, he genuinely liked Hearn. He reminded him of himself when he was young, before the incident that had burned off half the skin of his face

He took Hearn through the seven floors of offices, comprising laboratories, departments devoted to compiling the statistics the development people used in fund-raising, the lifeblood of organizations such as Humanistas, Ltd., as well as accounting, procurement, human resources, travel, the maintenance of the company's fleets of private jets, transport planes, ships and helicopters. The last stop was the development department, where Hearn's new office awaited him. At the moment, the office stood empty save for a desk, swivel chair, computer and phone console.

"The rest of your furniture," Spalko told him, "will be arriving in a few days."

"No problem, sir. A computer and phones are all I really need."

"A warning," Spalko added. "We keep long hours here, and there will be times you'll be expected to work through the night. But we're not inhuman. The sofa we provide folds out into a bed."

Hearn smiled. "Not to worry, Mr. Spalko. I'm quite used to those hours."

"Call me Stepan." Spalko gripped the younger man's hand. "Everyone else does."

The Director of Central Intelligence was soldering the arm on a painted tin soldier—a British redcoat from the Revolutionary War—when the call came. At first he considered ignoring it, perversely letting the phone ring even though he knew who would be on the other end of the line. Perhaps, he thought, this was because he did not want to hear what the Deputy Director would have to say. Lindros believed the DCI had dispatched him to the crime scene because of the importance of the dead men to the Agency. This was true, as far as it went. The real reason, however, was that the DCI couldn't bear to go himself. The thought of seeing Alex Conklin's dead face was too much for him.

He was sitting on a stool in his basement workshop, a tiny, enclosed, perfectly ordered environment of stacked drawers, aligned cubbyholes, a world unto itself, a place his wife—and his children when they had lived at home—were forbidden to enter.

His wife, Madeleine, poked her head through the open door to the cellar. "Kurt, the phone," she said needlessly.

He took an arm out of the wooden bin of soldier parts, studied it. He was a large-headed man, but a mane of white hair combed back from his wide, domed forehead lent him the aspect of a wiseman, if not a prophet. His cool blue eyes were still as calculating as ever, but the lines at the corners of his mouth had deepened, pulling them down into something of a perpetual pout.

"Kurt, do you hear me?"

"I am not deaf." The fingers at the end of the arm were slightly cupped as if the hand was preparing to reach out for something unnameable and unknown.

"Well, are you going to answer it?" Madeleine called down.

"Whether I answer it or not is none of your goddamn business!" he shouted with vehemence. "Will you go to bed now." A moment later he heard the satisfying whisper of the basement door closing. Why couldn't she leave him alone at a time like this? he fumed. Thirty years married, you'd think she'd know better.

He returned to his work, fitting the arm with the cupped hand to the shoulder of the torso, red to red, deciding on the final position. This was how the DCI dealt with situations over which he had no control. He played god with his miniature soldiers, buying them, cutting them to pieces, then, later, reconstructing them, molding them into the positions that suited him. Here, in the world he himself had created, he controlled everyone and everything.

The phone continued to ring in its mechanical, monotonous fashion and the DCI gritted his teeth, as if the sound was abrasive. What marvelous deeds had been accomplished in the days when he and Alex had been young! The mission inside Russia when they had almost landed in the Lubyanka, running the Berlin Wall, extracting secrets from the Staasi, vetting the defector from the KGB in the Vienna safe house, discovering that he was a double. The killing of Bernd, their longtime contact, the compassion with which they had told his wife that they would take care of Bernd's son Dieter, take him back to America, put him through college. They had done precisely that and had been rewarded for their generosity. Dieter had never returned to his mother. Instead, he had joined the Agency, had for many years been the director of the Science & Technology Directorate until the fatal motorcycle accident.

Where had that life gone? Laid to rest in Bernd's grave, and Dieter's— now Alex's. How had it been reduced so quickly to flashpoints in his memory? Time and responsibilities had crippled him, no question. He was an old man now, in some respects with more power, yes, but the daring deeds of yesterday, the elan with which he and Alex had bestrode the secret world, changing the fate of nations, had burned to ash, never to return.

The DCI's fist hammered the tin soldier into a cripple. Then and only then did he pick up the phone.

"Yes, Martin."

There was a weariness in his voice Lindros picked up on immediately. "Are you all right, sir?"

"No, I fucking well am not all right!" This was what the DCI had wanted. Another opportunity to vent his anger and frustration. "How could I be all right given the circumstances?"

"I'm sorry, sir."

"No, you're not," the DCI said waspishly. "You couldn't be. You have no idea." He stared at the soldier he had crushed, his mind hounded by past glories. "What is it you want?"

"You asked for an update, sir."

"Did I?" The DCI rested his head in his hand. "Yes, I suppose I did. What have you found?"

"The third car in Conklin's driveway belongs to David Webb."

The DCI's keen ear responded to a tone in Lindros' voice. "But?"

"But there's no sign of Webb."

"Of course there isn't."

"He was definitely there, though. We gave the dogs a sniff at the interior of his car. They found his scent on the property and followed it into the woods but lost it at a stream."

The DCI closed his eyes. Alexander Conklin and Morris Panov shot to death, Jason Bourne MIA and on the loose five days before the terrorism summit, the most important international meeting of the century. He shuddered. He abhorred loose ends, but not nearly as much as Roberta Alonzo-Ortiz, the National Security Advisor, and these days she was running the show. "Ballistics? Forensics?"

"Tomorrow morning," Lindros said. "That was as much as I could push them."

"As far as the FBI and other law-enforcement agencies—"

"I've already neutralized them. We have a clear field."

The DCI sighed. He appreciated the DDCI's initiative, but he despised being interrupted. "Get back to work," he said gruffly, and cradled the receiver.

For a long time afterward, he stared into the wooden bin, listening to the house breathing. It sounded like an old man. Boards creaked, familiar as an old friend's voice. Madeleine must be making herself a cup of hot chocolate, her traditional sleep aid. He heard the neighbor's corgi bark, and for some reason he could not fathom, it seemed a mournful sound, full of sorrow and failed hope. At length, he reached into the bin, picked out a torso in Civil War gray, a new tin soldier to create.

CHAPTER FOUR

"Must've been some accident, by the look of you," Jack Kerry said.

"Not really, just a flat," Bourne replied easily. "But I didn't have a spare, and then I tripped on something—a tree root, I think. I took quite a tumble into the stream." He made a deprecating gesture. "I'm not exactly well coordinated."

"Join the crew," Kerry said. He was a large, rawboned man with a double chin and too much fat around his middle. He had picked Bourne up a mile back. "One time my wife asked me to run the dishwasher, I filled it up with Tide. Jesus, you should've seen the mess!" He laughed good-naturedly.

The night was pitch-dark, no moon or stars. A soft drizzle had begun and Kerry put on the windshield wipers. Bourne shivered a little in his damp clothes. He knew he had to focus, but every time he closed his eyes he saw images of Alex and Mo; he saw blood seeping, bits of skull and brain. His fingers curled, hands tightening into fists.

"So what is it you do, Mr. Little?"

Bourne had given his name as Dan Little when Kerry introduced himself. Kerry, it appeared, was an old-style gentleman who put great store in the niceties of convention.

"I'm an accountant."

"I design nuclear waste facilities, myself. Travel far and wide, yessir." Kerry gave him a sideways glance, light spinning off his glasses. "Hell, you don't look like an accountant, you don't mind me saying."

Bourne forced himself to laugh. "Everyone says that. I played football in college."

"Haven't let yourself go to seed like many ex-athletes," Kerry observed. He patted his rotund abdomen. "Not like me. Except I never was an athlete. I tried once. Never knew which way to run. Got screamed at by the coach. And then I got tackled good." He shook his head. "That was enough for me. I'm a lover, not a fighter." He glanced at Bourne again. "You got a family, Mr. Little?"

Bourne hesitated a moment. "A wife and two children."

"Happy, are ya?"

A wedge of black trees hurried by, a telephone pole leaning into the wind, a shack abandoned, draped with thorny creeper, returned to the wild. Bourne closed his eyes. "Very happy."

Kerry manhandled the car around a sweeping curve. One thing you could say about him—he was an excellent driver. "Me, I'm divorced. That was a bad one. My wife left me with my three-year-old in tow. That was ten years ago." He frowned. "Or is it eleven? Anyway, I haven't seen or heard from either her or the boy since."

Bourne's eyes snapped open. "You haven't been in touch with your son?"

"It's not that I haven't tried." There was a querulous note to Kerry's voice as he turned defensive. "For a while, I called every week, sent him letters, money, you know, for things he might like, a bike and such. Never heard a word back."

"Why didn't you go to see him?"

Kerry shrugged. "I finally got the message—he didn't want to see me."

"That was your wife's message," Bourne said. "Your son's only a child. He doesn't know what he wants. How can he? He hardly knows you."

Kerry grunted. "Easy for you to say, Mr. Little. You've got a warm hearth, a happy family to go home to every night."

"It's precisely because I have children that I know how precious they are," Bourne said. "If it was my son, I'd fight tooth and nail to know him and to get him back into my life."

They were coming to a more populated area now, and Bourne saw a motel, a strip of closed stores. In the distance, he could see a red flash, then another. There was a roadblock up ahead and, by the look of it, a major one. He counted eight cars in all, in two ranks of four each, turned at forty-five degrees to the highway in order to afford their occupants the greatest protection while allowing the cars to quickly close ranks if need be. Bourne knew he couldn't allow himself to get anywhere near the roadblock, not, at least, sitting in plain view. He would have to find some other way to get through it.

All at once, the neon sign of an all-night convenience store loomed out of the darkness.

"I think this is as far as I'll go."

"You sure, Mr. Little? It's still pretty desolate out here."

"Don't worry about me. I'll just have my wife come and pick me up. We don't live far from here."

"Then I should take you all the way home."

"I'll be fine here. Really."

Kerry pulled over and slowed to a stop just past the convenience store. Bourne got out.

"Thanks for the lift."

"Any time." Kerry smiled. "And, Mr. Little, thanks for the advice. I'll think on what you said."

Bourne watched Kerry drive off, then he turned and walked into the convenience store. The ultra-bright fluorescent lights made his eyes burn. The attendant, a pimply-faced young man with long hair and bloodshot eyes, was smoking a cigarette and reading a paperback book. He looked up briefly as Bourne entered, nodded disinterestedly and went back to his reading. Somewhere a radio was on; someone was singing "Yesterday's Gone," in a world-weary, melancholy voice. She might have been singing it for Bourne.

One look at the shelves reminded him that he hadn't eaten since lunch. He grabbed a plastic jar of peanut butter, a box of crackers, some beef jerky, orange juice and water. Protein and vitamins were what he needed. He also purchased a T-shirt, a long-sleeved striped shirt, razor and shaving cream, other items he knew from long experience he would need.

Bourne approached the counter, and the attendant put down the dog-eared book he had been reading. *Dhalgren* by Samuel R. Delany. Bourne remembered reading it just after he returned from Nam, a book as hallucinatory as the war. Fragments of his life came hurtling back—the blood, the death, the rage, the reckless killing, all to blot out the excruciating, never-ending pain of what had happened in the river just outside his house in Phnom Penh. *"You've got a warm hearth, a happy family to go home to every night,"* Kerry had said. If only he knew.

"Anything else?" the pimply-faced young man said.

Bourne blinked, returning to the present. "Do you have an electrical charger for a cell phone?"

"Sorry, bud, all out."

Bourne paid for his purchases in cash, took possession of the brown paper bag and left. Ten minutes later he walked onto the motel grounds. There were few cars. A tractor-trailer was parked at one end of the motel, a refrigerated truck, by the look of the compressor squatting on its top. Inside the office a spindly man with the gray face of an undertaker shuffled out from behind a desk in the rear, where he'd been watching an ancient portable black-and-white TV. Bourne checked in using another assumed name, paying for the room in cash. He was left with precisely sixty-seven dollars.

"Goddamn strange night," the spindly man rasped.

"How so?"

The spindly man's eyes lit up. "Don't tell me ya didn't hear about the murders?"

Bourne shook his head.

"Not twenty miles away." The spindly man leaned over the counter. His breath smelled unpleasantly from coffee and bile. "Two men—*government people*—nobody sayin' nothin' else about 'em, an' y'know what *that* means around here: hush-hush, deep-throat, cloak-an'-dagger, who the *hell* knows what they was up to? You turn on CNN when you get to the room, we got cable an' everything." He handed Bourne the key. "Putcha in a room at the other end from Guy—he's the trucker, might have seen his semi when you came in. Guy makes a reg'lar run from Florida to D.C.; he'll be leavin' at five, don't wantcha disturbed, now do we?"

The room was a drab brown, timeworn. Even the smell of an industrial-strength cleaner could not entirely blot out the odor of decay. Bourne turned on the TV, switching channels. He took out the peanut butter and crackers, began to eat.

"There is no doubt that this bold, visionary initiative of the president's has a chance to build bridges toward a more peaceful future," the CNN newsreader was saying. Behind her, a graphic banner in screaming red across the top of the screen proclaimed THE TERRORISM SUMMIT with all the subtlety of a London tabloid. "The summit includes, besides the president himself, the president of Russia and the leaders of the major Arab nations. Over the course of the coming week, we'll be checking in with Wolf Blitzer with the president's party and Christiane Amanpour with the Russian and Arab leaders for in-depth commentaries. Clearly, the summit has the makings of the news story of the year. Now, for an up-to-the-minute report from Reykjavík, Iceland . . ."

The scene switched to the front of the Oskjuhlid Hotel, where the terrorism summit would take place in five days' time. An overearnest CNN reporter began to conduct an interview with the head of American security, Jamie Hull. Bourne stared at Hull's square-jawed face, his short brush-cut hair, ginger-colored mustache, cold blue eyes, and an alarm went off in his head. Hull was Agency, high up in its Counterterrorist Center. He and Conklin had butted heads more than once. Hull was a clever political animal; he had his nose up the ass of everyone who counted. But he went by the book even when situations dictated he take a more flexible approach. Conklin must have been apoplectic at his being named head of the American security at the summit.

While Bourne was considering this, a news update took over the crawl on the screen. It concerned the deaths of Alexander Conklin and Dr. Morris Panov, both, according to the crawl, high-level government officials. All at once, the scene shifted and a banner reading BREAKING NEWS flashed on, followed by another, MANASSAS MURDERS, which was superimposed above a government photo of David Webb that took up almost the entire screen. The newsreader began her update on the brutal murders of Alex Conklin and Dr. Morris Panov. "Each was shot once in the head," the newsreader said with all the grim delight of her ilk, "indicating the work of a professional killer. The government's prime suspect is this man, David Webb. Webb may be using an alias, Jason Bourne. According to highly placed government sources, Webb, or Bourne, is delusional and is considered dangerous. If you see this man, do not approach. Call the number listed on your screen. . . ."

Bourne switched off the sound. Christ, the shit had really hit the fan now. No wonder that roadblock up ahead had looked so well organized— it was Agency, not the local cops.

He had better get to work. Brushing crumbs off his lap, he pulled out Conklin's cell phone. It was time to find out who Alex had been talking to when he had been shot. He accessed the auto-redial key, listened to the ring on the other end. A prerecorded message came on. This wasn't a personal number; it was a business. Lincoln Fine Tailors. The thought that Conklin was talking to his tailor when he was shot to death was depressing, indeed. It was no way for a master spy to go out.

He accessed the last incoming call, which was from the previous evening. It was from the DCI. *Dead end,* Bourne thought. He rose. As he padded to the bathroom, he stripped off his clothes. For a long time he stood under the hot shower spray, his mind deliberately blank as he sluiced the dirt and sweat off his skin. It was good to feel warm again and clean. Now if only he had a fresh set of clothes. All at once his head came up. He wiped water out of his eyes, his heart beating fast, his mind fully engaged again. Conklin's clothes were made by Old World Tailors off M Street; Alex had been going there for years. He even had dinner with the owner, a Russian immigrant, once or twice a year.

In something of a frenzy Bourne dried himself off, took up Conklin's phone again and dialed information. After he had gotten Lincoln Fine Tailors' address in Alexandria, he sat on the bed, staring at nothing. He was wondering just what it was Lincoln Fine Tailors did besides cut fabric and sew hems.

Hasan Arsenov appreciated Budapest in ways Khalid Murat could never have. He said as much to Zina Hasiyev as they passed through Immigration.

"Poor Murat," she said. "A brave soul, a courageous fighter for independence, but his thinking was strictly nineteenth century." Zina, Arsenov's trusted lieutenant as well as his lover, was small, wiry, as athletic as Arsenov himself. Her hair was long, black as night, swirling around her head like a corona. Her wide mouth and dark, lustrous eyes also contributed to her wild, gypsylike appearance, but her mind could be as detached and calculating as a litigator's, and she was stone-cold fearless.

Arsenov grunted in pain as he ducked into the back of the waiting limousine. The assassin's shot had been perfect, striking muscle only, the bullet exiting his thigh as cleanly as it had entered. The wound hurt like hell, but the pain was worth it, Arsenov thought as he settled in beside his lieutenant. No suspicion had fallen on him; even Zina had no idea he had colluded in Murat's assassination. But what choice had he had? Murat had been growing increasingly nervous regarding the consequences of the Shaykh's plan. He hadn't had Arsenov's vision, his monumental sense of social justice. He would have been content merely to win back Chechnya from the Russians, while the rest of the world turned its back in scorn.

Whereas, when the Shaykh had unfurled his bold and daring stratagem, it was, for Arsenov, the moment of revelation. He could vividly see the future the Shaykh was holding out to them like a ripe fruit. Gripped by the flash of supernal illumination, he had looked at Khalid Murat for confirmation, had seen instead the bitter truth. Khalid could not see past the borders of his homeland, could not understand that regaining the homeland was, in a way, secondary. Arsenov realized that the Chechens needed to gain power not only to throw off the yoke of the Russian infidel but to establish their place in the Islamic world, to gain the respect of the other Muslim nations. The Chechens were Sunnis who had embraced the teachings of the Sufi mystics, personified by the *zikr*, the remembrance of God, the common ritual involving chanted prayer and rhythmic dance that achieved a shared trancelike state during which the eye of God appeared to the assembled. Sunni, being as monolithic as other religions, abhorred, feared and therefore reviled those who deviated even slightly from its strict central doctrine. Mysticism, divine or otherwise, was anathema. *Nineteenth-century thinking, in every sense of the phrase,* Arsenov thought bitterly.

Since the day of the assassination, the long-dreamed-of moment when he had become the new leader of the Chechen freedom fighters, Arsenov had lived in a feverish almost-hallucinatory state. He slept heavily but not restfully, for his slumber was filled with nightmares in which he was trying to find something or someone through mazes of rubble and was defeated. As a consequence, he was edgy and short with his subordinates; he tolerated no excuses whatsoever. Only Zina had the power to calm him; her alchemical touch allowed him to return from the strange limbo into which he had somehow receded.

The twinge of his wound brought him back to the present. He stared out the window at the ancient streets, watched with an envy that bordered on agony as people went about their business without hindrance, without the slightest trace of fear. He hated them, each and every one who in the course of their free and easy lives gave not one thought to the desperate struggle he and his people had been engaged in since the 1700s.

"What is it, my love?" A frown of concern crossed Zina's face.

"My legs ache. I grow weary of sitting, that's all."

"I know you. The tragedy of Murat's murder hasn't left you, despite our vengeance. Thirty-five Russian soldiers went to their graves in retaliation for the murder of Khalid Murat."

"Not just Murat," Arsenov said. "Our men. We lost seventeen men to Russian treachery."

"You've rooted out the traitor, shot him yourself in front of the sublieutenants."

"To show them what awaits all traitors to the cause. The judgment was swift, the punishment hard. This is our fate, Zina. There aren't enough tears to shed for our people. Look at us. Lost and dispersed, hiding in the Caucasus, more than one hundred fifty thousand Chechens living as refugees."

Zina did not stop Hasan as he enumerated once again this agonizing history because these stories needed to be repeated as often as possible. They were the history books of the Chechens.

Arsenov's fists went white, his nails drawing crescents of blood from beneath the skin of his palms. "Ah, to have a weapon more deadly than an AK-47, more powerful than a packet of C4!"

"Soon, soon, my love," Zina crooned softly in her deep, musical voice. "The Shaykh has proved to be our greatest friend. Look how much aid his organization has provided our people in just the last year; look how much coverage his press people have gotten us in international magazines and newspapers."

"And still the Russian yoke is around our necks," Arsenov growled. "Still we die by the hundreds."

"The Shaykh has promised us a weapon that will change all that."

"He's promised us the world." Arsenov wiped grit out of his eye. "The time for promises is over. Let us now see the proof of his covenant."

The limousine the Shaykh had sent for the Chechens turned off the motorway at Kalmankrt Boulevard, which took them over the Arpad Bridge, the Danube with its heavy barges and brightly painted pleasure craft a dazzle below them. Zina glanced down. To one side were the breathtaking domed and needle-spired Gothic stone edifices of the Houses of Parliament; on the other was thickly forested Margaret Island, within which was the luxe Danubius Grand Hotel, where crisp white sheets and a thick down comforter were awaiting them. Zina, hard as armor plate during the day, reveled in her nights in Budapest, never more so than in the luxury of the huge hotel bed. She saw in this feast of pleasure no betrayal of her ascetic existence but rather a brief respite from hardship and degradation, a reward like a wafer of Belgian chocolate slipped beneath the tongue, there in secret to melt in a cloud of ecstasy.

The limo nosed into the car park in the basement level of the Humanistas, Ltd. building. As they got out of the car, Zina took the large rectangular package from the driver. Uniformed guards checked the pair's passports against photos in the data bank of their computer terminal, gave them laminated ID tags and ushered them into a rather grand bronze-and-glass elevator.

Spalko received them in his office. By this time the sun was high in the sky, beating the river to a sheet of molten brass. He embraced them both, asked after the comfort of their flight, the ease of their trip in from Ferihegy Airport and the status of Arsenov's bullet wound. When the amenities had been dispensed with, they went into an adjacent room, paneled in honey-toned pecan wood, where a table had been set with crisp white linen and sparkling dinnerware. Spalko had had a meal prepared, Western food. Steak, lobster, three different vegetables—all the Chechens' favorites. And not a potato anywhere in evidence. Potatoes were often all Arsenov and Zina had to eat for days on end. Zina put the package on an empty chair, and they sat at the table.

"Shaykh," Arsenov said, "as always, we're overwhelmed by the largesse of your hospitality."

Spalko inclined his head. He was pleased with the name he had given himself in their world, which meant the Saint, friend of God. It struck the right note of reverence and awe, an exalted shepherd to his flock.

He rose now and opened a bottle of powerful Polish vodka, which he poured into three glasses. He lifted his and they followed suit. "In memory of Khalid Murat, a great leader, a powerful warrior, a grim adversary," he intoned solemnly in the Chechen fashion. "May Allah grant him the glory he has earned in blood and courage. May the tales of his prowess as a leader and as a man be told and retold among all the faithful." They downed the fiery liquor in one quick gulp.

Arsenov stood, refilled the glasses. He raised his glass, and the others followed suit. "To the Shaykh, friend of the Chechens, who will lead us to our rightful place in the new order of the world." They drank down the vodka.

Zina made to rise, doubtless to make her own toast, but Arsenov stayed her with a hand on her arm. The restraining gesture did not fail to catch Spalko's attention. What interested him most was Zina's response. He could see past her veiled expression to her seething core. There were many injustices in the world, he knew, on every scale imaginable. It seemed to him peculiar and not a little perverse that human beings could be outraged by injustice on a grand scale, all the while missing the small wrongs that were daily visited on individuals. Zina fought side by side with the men; why, then, should she not have an opportunity to raise her voice in a toast of her own choosing? Rage seethed within her; Spalko liked that—he knew how to use another person's anger.

"My compatriots, my friends." His eyes were sparking with conviction. "To the meeting of sorrowful past, desperate present and glorious future. We stand on the brink of tomorrow!"

They began to eat, speaking of general and inconsequential matters just as if they were at a rather informal dinner party. And yet an air of anticipation, of incipient change, had crept into the room. They kept their eyes on their plates or on one another, as if now so close to it, they were reluctant to look at the gathering storm that was pressing in upon them. At length, they were finished.

"It's time," the Shaykh said. Arsenov and Zina rose to stand before him.

Arsenov bowed his head. "One who dies for the love of the material world dies a hypocrite. One who dies for the love of the hereafter dies an ascetic. But one who dies for the love of the Truth dies a Sufi."

He turned to Zina, who opened the package they had brought with them from Grozny. Inside were three cloaks. She handed one to Arsenov, who put it on. She donned hers. The third Arsenov held in his hands as he faced the Shaykh.

"The *kherqeh* is the garment of honor of the dervish," Arsenov intoned. "It symbolizes the divine nature and attributes."

Zina said, "The cloak is sewn with the needle of devotion and the thread of the selfless remembrance of God."

The Shaykh bowed his head and said, "*La illaha ill Allah.*" There is no God but God, who is One.

Arsenov and Zina repeated, "*La illaha ill Allah.*" Then the Chechen rebel leader placed the *kherqeh* around the Shaykh's shoulders. "It is enough for most men to have lived according to the Shariah, the law of Islam, in surrender to the divine will, to die in grace and to enter into Paradise," he said. "But there are those of us who yearn for the divine here and now and whose love for God compels us to seek the path of inwardness. We are Sufi."

Spalko felt the weight of the dervish cloak and said, "O thou soul which are at peace, return unto thy Lord, with gladness that is thine in Him and His in thee. Enter thou among My slaves. Enter thou My Paradise."

Arsenov, moved by this quotation from the Qur'an, took Zina's hand, and together they knelt before the Shaykh. In a call-and-response three centuries old, they recited a solemn oath of obedience. Spalko produced a knife, handed it to them. Both in turn cut themselves and, in a stemmed glass, offered up to him their blood. In this manner, they became *murids*, disciples of the Shaykh, bound to him in both word and deed.

Then, even though it was painful for Arsenov with his wounded thigh, they sat cross-legged, facing one another, and in the manner of the Naqshibandi Sufis, they performed the *zikr*, the ecstatic union with God. They placed their right hands on their left thighs, left hands atop right wrists. Arsenov began to move his head and neck to the right in the arc of a semicircle, and Zina and Spalko followed in perfect time to Arsenov's soft, almost sensual chanting: "Save me, my Lord, from the evil eye of envy and jealousy, which falleth upon Thy bountiful Gifts." They made the same movement to the left. "Save me, my Lord, from falling into the hands of the playful children of earth, lest they might use me in their games; they might play with me and then break me in the end, as children destroy their toys." Back and forth, back and forth. "Save me, my Lord, from all manner of injury that cometh from the bitterness of my adversaries and from the ignorance of my loving friends."

The chanted prayers and the movement became one, merging into an ecstatic whole in the presence of God. . . .

Much later, Spalko led them down a back corridor to a small stainless-steel elevator, which took them down below the basement into the very bedrock in which the building was set.

They entered a vaulted, high-ceilinged room, crisscrossed by iron struts. The low hiss of the climate control was the only sound they heard. A number of crates had been stacked along one wall. It was to these that Spalko led them. He handed a crowbar to Arsenov, watched with a good measure of satisfaction as the terrorist leader cracked open the nearest crate, stared down at the gleaming sets of AK-47 assault rifles. Zina took one up, inspected it with care and precision. She nodded to Arsenov, who opened another crate, which held a dozen shoulder-held rocket-launchers.

"This is the most advanced ordnance in the Russian arsenal," Spalko said.

"But what price?" Arsenov said.

Spalko spread his hands. "What price would be appropriate if this weaponry helped you gain your freedom?"

"How do you put a price on freedom?" Arsenov said with a frown.

"The answer is you cannot. Hasan, freedom has no known price tag. It is bought with the blood and the indomitable hearts of people like yourselves." He moved his eyes to Zina's face. "These are yours—all of them—to use as you see fit to secure your borders, make those around you take notice." At last, Zina looked up at him, through long lashes. Their eyes locked, sparked, though their expressions remained impassive.

As if responding to Spalko's scrutiny, Zina said, "Even this weaponry won't gain us entry to the Reykjavík Summit."

Spalko nodded, the corners of his mouth turning up slightly. "True enough. The international security is far too comprehensive. An armed assault would result in nothing but our own deaths. However, I have a plan that will not only gain us access to the Oskjuhlid Hotel but will allow us to kill every person inside without exposing ourselves. Within hours of the event, everything you have dreamed of for centuries will be yours."

"Khalid Murat was *afraid* of the future, *afraid* of what we, as Chechens, can accomplish." The fever of righteousness colored Arsenov's face. "We have been too long ignored by the world. Russia beats us into the ground while their comrades in arms, the Americans, stand by and do nothing to save us. Billions of American dollars flow into the Middle East but to Chechnya not a ruble!"

Spalko had assumed the self-satisfied air of a professor who sees his prize pupil perform well. His eyes glittered balefully. "That will all change. Five days from now all the world will be at your feet. Power will be yours, as well as the respect of those who have spit on you, abandoned you. Russia, the Islamic world and all of the West, *especially* the United States!"

"We're speaking here of changing the entire world order, Zina," Arsenov fairly shouted.

"But *how*?" Zina asked. "How is this *possible*?"

"Meet me in Nairobi in three days' time," Spalko replied, "and you'll see for yourself."

The water, dark, deep, alive with an unnameable horror, closes over his head. He is sinking. No matter how hard he struggles, how desperately he strikes out for the surface, he feels himself spiraling down, as if weighted with lead. Then he looks down, sees a thick rope, slimy with weed, tied around his left ankle. He cannot see what is at the end of the rope because it disappears into the blackness below him. But whatever it is must be heavy, must be dragging him down, because the rope is taut. Desperately, he reaches down, his bloated fingers scrabbling to free himself, and the Buddha drifts free, spinning slowly, falling away from him into the unfathomable darkness. . . .

Khan awoke with a start, as always, racked by a horrible sense of loss. He lay amid the humid tangle of sheets. For a time, the recurring nightmare still pulsed evilly in his mind. Reaching down, he touched his left ankle as if to reassure himself that the rope was not tied to him. Then, gingerly, almost reverently, he moved his fingers up the taut, slick muscles of his abdomen and chest until he touched the small carved stone Buddha that hung around his neck by a thin gold chain. He never took it off, even when he slept. Of course it was there. It was always there. It was a talisman, even though he had tried to convince himself that he didn't believe in talismans.

With a small sound of disgust, he rose, then padded into the bathroom, splashed cold water over his head. He turned on the light, blinking for a moment. Thrusting his head close to the mirror, he inspected his reflection, looking at himself as if for the first time. He grunted, relieved himself, then, turning on a table lamp, sat on the edge of the bed, read again the sparse dossier Spalko had given him. Nothing in it gave the slightest hint that David Webb possessed the abilities Khan had seen. He touched the black-and-blue mark on his throat, thought of the net Webb had fashioned out of vines and cleverly set. He tore up the single sheet of the dossier. It was useless, less than useless, since it had led him to underestimate his target. And there were other implications, just as immediate. Spalko had given him information that was either incomplete or incorrect.

He suspected that Spalko knew precisely who and what David Webb was. Khan needed to know if Spalko had set some gambit in motion that involved Webb. He had his own plans for David Webb and he was quite determined that no one—not even Stepan Spalko—got in the way.

With a sigh, he turned off the light and lay back down, but his mind was unprepared for sleep. He found his entire body abuzz with speculation. Up until making the deal for his last assignment with Spalko, he had had no idea David Webb even existed, much less was still alive. He doubted he would have taken the assignment had not Spalko dangled Webb in front of his face. He must have known that Khan would find the prospect of finding Webb irresistible. For some time now, working for Spalko had made Khan uncomfortable. Increasingly, Spalko seemed to believe that he owned Khan, and Spalko, Khan was sure, was a megalomaniac.

In the jungles of Cambodia, where he had been forced to make his way as a child and teenager, he had had more than a little experience with megalomaniacs. The hot, humid weather, the constant chaos of war, the uncertainty of daily life all combined to drive people to the edge of madness. In that malevolent environment, the weak died, the strong survived; everyone was in some elemental fashion changed.

As he lay in bed, Khan fingered the scars on his body. It was a form of ritual, a superstition, perhaps, a method of keeping him safe from harm— not from the violence one adult perpetrates on another, but from the creeping, nameless terror a child feels in the dead of night. Children, waking from such nightmares, run to their parents, crawl into the warmth and comfort of their bed and are soon fast asleep. But Khan had no parents, no one to comfort him. On the contrary, he had been constantly obliged to free himself from the clutches of addle-brained adults who thought of him only as a source of money or sex. Slavery was what he had known for many years, from both the Caucasians and the Asians he had had the misfortune to stumble across. He belonged to neither world and they knew it. He was a half-breed and, as such, reviled, cursed at, beaten, abused, laid low in every manner a human being can be degraded.

And still he had persevered. His goal, from day to day, had devolved simply to surviving. But he had learned from bitter experience that escape was not enough, that those who had enslaved him would come after him, punish him severely. Twice, he had almost died. That was when he understood that more was required of him if he was to survive. He would have to kill or, eventually, he would be killed.

It was just before five when the Agency assault team stole into the motel from their position at the highway roadblock. They had been alerted to the presence of Jason Bourne by the night manager, who had awakened from a Xanax-induced doze to see Bourne's face staring at him from the TV screen. He had pinched himself to make sure he wasn't dreaming, had taken a shot of cheap rye, and made his call.

The team leader had called for the motel's security lights to be switched off so the team could make their approach in darkness. As they began to move into position, however, the refrigerated truck at the opposite end of the motel started up and switched on its headlights, catching some of the team in its powerful beams. The team leader waved frantically to the hapless driver, then ran to his side of the truck, told him to haul ass out of there. The driver, goggle-eyed at the sight of the team, did as he was requested, turning out his lights until he was clear of the parking lot and rolling down the highway.

The team leader signed to his men and they headed directly toward Bourne's room. At his silent command two broke off, headed around the back. The leader gave them twenty seconds to position themselves before he gave the order for them to don gas masks. Two of his men knelt, fired canisters of tear gas through the front window of the room. The leader's extended arm came down and his men rushed the room, slamming open the door. Gas whooshed out as they scuttled in, machine guns at the ready. The TV was on, the sound muted. CNN was showing the face of their quarry. The remains of a hasty meal were strewn on the stained, worn carpet and the bed was stripped. The room was abandoned.

Inside the refrigerated truck hastening away from the motel, Bourne, wrapped in the bedding, lay amid wooden cases containing plastic baskets of strawberries stacked up almost to the ceiling. He had managed to get himself into a position above floor level, the crates on either side holding him in place. When he had entered the rear of the truck, he had locked the door behind him. All such refrigeration trucks had a safety mechanism that could open and lock the rear door from the inside to ensure no one inadvertently got trapped. Switching on his flashlight for a moment, he had made out the center aisle, wide enough for a man to pass through. On the upper right-hand wall was the exhaust grille for the refrigeration compressor.

All at once, he tensed. The truck was slowing now as it approached the roadblock, then it stopped completely. The flashpoint of extreme danger had arrived.

There was utter silence for perhaps five minutes, then, abruptly, the harsh sound of the rear door being opened. Voices came to him. "You pick up any hitchhikers?" a cop said.

"Uh-uh," Guy, the truck driver, answered.

"Here, look at this photo. Seen this fella on the side of the road maybe?"

"No, sir. Never seen the man. What'd he do?"

"What you got in there?" Another cop's voice.

"Fresh strawberries," Guy said. "Listen, Officers, have a heart. It ain't good for them to have the door open like this. What rots comes outta my pay."

Someone grunted. A powerful flashlight beam played along the center aisle, swept across the floor just beneath the spot where Bourne lay suspended amid the strawberries.

"Okay," the first cop said, "close it up, buddy."

The flashlight beam snapped off and the door slammed shut.

Bourne waited until the truck was in gear, rolling at speed down the highway to D.C., before extricating himself. His mind was buzzing. The cops must have shown Guy the same photo of David Webb that was being broadcast on CNN.

Within a half hour, the smooth highway driving had given way to the constant stop and start of urban streets with traffic lights. It was time to exit. Bourne went to the door, pushed on the safety lever. It wouldn't move. He tried again, this time with more force. Cursing under his breath, he snapped on the flashlight he'd taken from Conklin's house. In the bright circle of the beam, he saw that the mechanism had jammed. He was locked in.

CHAPTER FIVE

The Director of Central Intelligence was in a dawn conference with Roberta Alonzo-Ortiz, the National Security Advisor. They met in the president's Situation Room, a circular space in the bowels of the White House. Many floors above them were the wood-paneled, beautifully dentiled rooms most people associated with this storied, historical building, but down here the full muscle and might of the Pentagon oligarchs held sway. Like the great temples of the ancient civilizations, the Sit Room had been built to last for centuries. Carved out of the old subbasement, its proportions were intimidating, as befitted such a monument to invincibility.

Alonzo-Ortiz, the DCI and their respective staffs—as well as select members of the Secret Service—were going over, for the hundredth time, the security plans for the terrorism summit in Reykjavík. Detailed schematics for the Oskjuhlid Hotel were up on a projection screen, along with notes on security issues regarding entrances, exits, elevators, roof, windows and the like. A direct video hook-up to the hotel had been established, so that Jamie Hull, the DCI's emissary-in-place, could participate in the briefing.

"No margin for error will be tolerated," Alonzo-Ortiz said. She was a formidable-looking woman with jet-black hair and bright, keen eyes. "Every aspect of this summit must go off like clockwork," she continued. "Any breach of security no matter how minuscule will have disastrous effects. It would destroy what coin the president has spent eighteen months building up with the principal Islamic states. I don't have to tell any of you that beneath the facade of cooperation lurks an innate distrust of Western values, the Judeo-Christian ethic and all that stands for. Any hint that the president has deceived them will have the most dire and immediate consequences." She looked slowly around the table. It was one of her special gifts that when addressing a group she made each and every member believe that she was speaking only to him. "Make no mistake, gentlemen. We are talking about nothing less than a global war here, a massed *jihad* such as we have never before seen and, quite possibly, cannot imagine."

She was about to turn the briefing over to Jamie Hull when a young, slim man entered the room, went silently over to the DCI, handed him a sealed envelope.

"My apologies, Dr. Alonzo-Ortiz," he said as he slit open the envelope. He read the contents impassively, though his heart rate had doubled. The National Security Advisor did not like her briefings interrupted. Aware that she was glaring at him, he pushed back his chair and rose.

Alonzo-Ortiz directed at him a smile so compressed her lips fairly disappeared. "I trust you have sufficient cause to leave us so abruptly."

"I do, indeed, Dr. Alonzo-Ortiz." The DCI, though an old hand and, therefore, a wielder of his own power, knew better than to butt heads with the one person the president relied on most. He remained on his best behavior even though he deeply resented Roberta Alonzo-Ortiz both because she had usurped his traditional role with the president and because she was a woman. For these reasons, he employed what little power was at his command—the withholding of what she wanted most to know: the nature of the emergency dire enough to take him away.

The National Security Advisor's smile tightened further. "In that event, I would appreciate a full briefing of the crisis, whatever it may be, as soon as is practicable."

"Absolutely," the DCI said, beating a hasty retreat. As the thick door to the Sit Room swung shut behind him, he added, dryly, "Your Highness," eliciting a gust of laughter from the field agent his office had employed as a messenger.

It took the DCI less than fifteen minutes to return to HQ where a meeting of Agency directorate heads was awaiting his arrival. The subject: the murders of Alexander Conklin and Dr. Morris Panov. The prime suspect: Jason Bourne. These were whey-faced men in impeccably tailored conservative suits, rep ties, polished brogues. Not for them striped shirts, colored collars, the passing fads of fashion. Used to striding the corridors of power inside the Beltway, they were as immutable as their clothes. They were conservative thinkers from conservative colleges, scions from the correct families who, early on, had been directed by their fathers to the offices, and thence the confidences, of the right people—leaders with vision and energy who knew how to get the job done. The nexus in which they now sat was a tightly held secret world, but the tentacles that fanned out from it stretched far and wide.

As soon as the DCI entered the conference room, the lights were dimmed. On a screen appeared the forensic photos of the bodies *in situ*.

"For the love of God, take those down!" the DCI shouted. "They're an obscenity. We shouldn't be viewing these men like that."

Martin Lindros, the DDCI, pressed a button and the screen went blank. "To bring everyone up to date, yesterday we confirmed that it was David Webb's car in Conklin's driveway." He paused as the Old Man cleared his throat.

"Let's call a spade a spade." The DCI leaned forward, fists upon the gleaming table. "The world at large may know this . . . this man as David Webb but here he is known as Jason Bourne. We will use that name."

"Yessir," Lindros said, determined not to run afoul of the DCI's exceedingly black mood. He barely needed to consult his notes, so fresh and vivid in his mind were the findings. "W—Bourne was last seen on the Georgetown campus approximately an hour before the murders. A witness observed him hurrying toward his car. We can assume he drove directly to Alex Conklin's house. Bourne was definitely in the house at or around the time of the murders. His fingerprints are on a glass of half-finished Scotch found in the media room."

"What about the gun?" the DCI asked. "Is it the murder weapon?"

Lindros nodded. "Absolutely confirmed by ballistics."

"And it's Bourne's, you're certain, Martin?"

Lindros consulted a photocopied sheet, spun it across the table to the DCI. "Registration confirms that the murder weapon belongs to David Webb. *Our* David Webb."

"Sonuvabitch!" The DCI's hands were trembling. "Are the bastard's fingerprints on it?"

"The gun was wiped clean," Lindros said, consulting another sheet. "No fingerprints at all."

"The mark of a professional." The DCI looked abruptly weary. It wasn't easy to lose an old friend.

"Yessir. Absolutely."

"And Bourne?" the DCI growled. It appeared painful for him even to utter the name.

"Early this morning we received a tip that Bourne was holed up in a Virginia motel near one of the roadblocks," Lindros said. "The area was immediately cordoned off, an assault team sent into the motel. If Bourne was in fact there, he'd already fled, slipped through the cordon. He's vanished into thin air."

"Goddammit!" Color had risen to the DCI's cheeks.

Lindros' assistant came silently in, handed him a sheet of paper. He scanned it for a moment, then looked up. "Earlier, I sent a team to Webb's home, in the event he turned up there or contacted his wife. The team found the house locked up and empty. There's no sign of Bourne's wife or two children. Subsequent investigation revealed that she appeared at their school and pulled them out of class with no explanation."

"That seals it!" The DCI seemed almost apoplectic. "In every area he's a step ahead of us because he had these murders planned out beforehand!" During the short, swift drive to Langley, he'd allowed his emotions to get the better of him. Between Alex's murder and Alonzo-Ortiz's maneuvering, he had entered the Agency briefing in a rage. Now, presented with the forensic evidence, he was more than ready to convict.

"It's clear that Jason Bourne has gone rogue." The Old Man, still standing, fairly shook now. "Alexander Conklin was an old and trusted friend. I cannot remember or list the number of times he put his reputation—his very *life*—on the line for this organization, for his country. He was a true patriot in every sense of the word, a man of whom we were all justly proud."

Lindros, for his own part, was considering the number of times he could remember and list when the Old Man had ranted at Conklin's cowboy tactics, his rogue missions, his secret agendas. It was all well and good to eulogize the dead, but, he thought, in this business it was downright foolish to ignore the dangerous tendencies of agents past and present. That, of course, included Jason Bourne. He was a sort of sleeper agent, the worst kind really—one not fully under his own control. In the past, he had been activated by circumstance, not by his own choosing. Lindros knew very little about Jason Bourne, an oversight he was determined to rectify the moment this briefing was adjourned.

"If Alexander Conklin had one weakness, one blind spot, it was Jason Bourne," the DCI went on. "Years before he met and married his current wife, Marie, he lost the whole of his first family—his Thai wife and two kids—in an attack in Phnom Penh. The man was half-mad with grief and remorse when Alex picked him up off the street in Saigon and trained him. Years later, even after Alex enlisted the aid of Morris Panov, there were problems controlling the asset—despite Dr. Panov's regular reports to the contrary. Somehow, he too fell under the influence of Jason Bourne.

"I warned Alex over and over, I begged him to bring Bourne in to be evaluated by our team of forensic psychiatrists, but he refused. Alex, God rest his soul, could be a stubborn man; he believed in Bourne."

The DCI's face was slick with sweat, his eyes wide as he glanced around the room. "And what is the result of that belief? Both men have been gunned down like dogs by the very asset they sought to control. The simple truth is that Bourne is uncontrollable. And he is deadly, a poisonous viper." The DCI slammed his fist down on the conference table. "I will not have these heinous, cold-blooded murders go unpunished. I'm authorizing a world-wide sanction drawn up, ordering Jason Bourne's immediate termination."

Bourne shivered, by now chilled through and through. He glanced up, played his beam over the refrigeration vent. Heading back down the center aisle, he clambered up the right-hand stack of crates, crawled his way across the top of the stacks until he came to the grate. Flipping open the switchblade, he used the spine of the blade to unscrew the grille. The soft light of dawn flowed into the interior. There appeared to be just enough room for him to squeeze through. He hoped.

He rolled his shoulders in toward his chest, squeezing himself into the aperture, and began to wriggle from side to side. All went well for the first several inches or so, and then his forward progress abruptly stopped. He tried to move but couldn't. He was stuck. He exhaled all the air out of his lungs, allowed his upper body to go slack. He pushed with his feet and legs. A crate slid and tumbled, but he had inched forward. He lowered his legs until his feet found purchase on the crates below. Locking the heels of his shoes against the upper bar, he pushed again and again he moved. By slowly and carefully repeating this maneuver he was at last able to get his head and shoulders through. He blinked up into the candy pink sky, where fluffy clouds rose up, shifting shapes as he rolled by beneath them. Reaching up, he grabbed the corner of the roof, levered himself all the way out of the semi and onto its roof.

At the next stoplight he jumped down, tucking his lead shoulder in, rolling to cushion his fall. He rose, gained the sidewalk, dusted himself off. The street was deserted. He offered the unsuspecting Guy a brief salute as the semi drove off in a blue haze of diesel fumes.

He was on the outskirts of D.C., in the poor northeast district. Light was coming into the sky, the long shadows of dawn retreating before the sun. The hum of traffic could be heard in the distance, as well as the wail of a police siren. He breathed deeply. Beneath the urban stink, there was for him something fresh in the air, the exhilaration of freedom after the long night's struggle to remain hidden, to remain free.

He walked until he saw the fluttering of faded red, white and blue pennants. The used-car lot was shut down for the night. He walked onto the deserted lot, chose a car at random and switched its plates with the car next to it. He jimmied the lock, opened the driver's side door and hotwired the ignition. A moment later, he was driving out of the lot and down the street.

He parked in front of a diner whose chrome-plated facade was a relic of the fifties. A gigantic cup of coffee sat atop the roof, its neon lights long ago burned out. Inside, it was steamy. The smell of coffee grounds and hot oil was ingrained into every surface. To his left was a long Formica counter and a row of vinyl-topped chromium stools; to his right, against the bank of sun-streaked windows, were a line of booths, each one with one of those individual jukeboxes that held the cards of all the songs that could be played for a quarter.

Bourne's white skin was silently remarked upon by the dark faces that turned as the door shut behind him with a little tinkle of a bell. No one returned his smile. Some appeared indifferent to him, but others of a different nature seemed to interpret his presence as an evil omen of things to come.

Aware of the hostile glares, he slid into a lumpy booth. A waitress with a frizz of orange hair and a face like Eartha Kitt dropped a fly-blown menu in front of him, filled his cup with steaming coffee. Bright, overly made-up eyes in a care-worn face regarded him for a time with curiosity and something more—compassion, perhaps. "Don't you mind the stares, sugah," she breathed. "They're scared of you."

He ate an indifferent breakfast: eggs, bacon and home fries, washed down with the astringent coffee. But he needed the protein and the caffeine laid to rest his exhaustion, at least temporarily.

The waitress refilled his cup and he sipped, marking time until Lincoln Fine Tailors opened. But he was not idle. He dug out the notepad he had picked off the table in Alex's media room, once again looked at the imprint left on the top sheet. NX 20. It had the ring of something experimental, something ominous, but really it could be anything, including a new-model computer.

Glancing up, he observed the denizens of the neighborhood drifting in and out, discussing Welfare checks, drug scores, police beatings, the sudden deaths of family members, the illness of friends in jail. This was their life, more alien to him than life in Asia or Micronesia. The atmosphere inside the diner was darkened by their rage and sorrow.

Once, a police cruiser slid slowly by like a shark skirting a reef. All motion in the diner ceased, as if this significant moment was a frame in a photographer's lens. He turned his head away and looked at the waitress. She was watching the taillights of the cruiser disappear down the block. An audible sigh of relief swept the diner. Bourne experienced his own sense of relief. It seemed that, after all, he was in the company of fellow travelers in shadow.

His thoughts turned to the man who was stalking him. His face had an Asian cast, and yet not wholly so. Was there something familiar about it— the bold line of the nose, which was not Asian at all, or the shape of the full lips, which was very much so? Was he someone from Bourne's past, from Vietnam? But, no, that was impossible. Judging by his appearance, he was in his late twenties at most, meaning he couldn't have been more than five or six when Bourne had been there. Who was he, then, and what did he want? The questions continued to haunt Bourne. Abruptly, he set down his half-empty cup. The coffee was beginning to burn a hole in his stomach.

Not long after, he returned to the stolen car, switched on the radio, spun the dial until he came to a news announcer talking about the terrorism summit, followed by a brief rundown first of the national news, then the local items. First on the list were the murders of Alex Conklin and Mo Panov but, strangely, no new information was forthcoming.

"More news upcoming," the announcer said, "but first this important message. . . ."

". . . *this important message.*" At that moment, the office in Paris with its view down the Champs-Elysées to the Arc de Triomphe came roaring back to him, the memory sweeping away the diner and those who surrounded him. There was a chocolate-colored chair at his side from which he had just risen. In his right hand a glass of cut-crystal half full of the amber liquid. A voice, deep and rich, full of melody, was speaking, something about the time it would take to get everything Bourne needed. "Not to worry, my friend," the voice said, the English blurred by the heavy cast of its French accent, "I'm meant to give you this important message."

In the theater of his mind, he turned, straining to see the face of the man who had spoken, but all he saw was a blank wall. The memory had evaporated like the scent of the Scotch, leaving Bourne back, staring bleakly out the grimy windows of the broken-down diner.

A spasm of fury drove Khan to pick up his cell phone and call Spalko. It took some time, and a bit of doing on his part, but at length he was put through.

"To what do I owe this honor, Khan?" Spalko said in his ear. Listening hard, Khan heard the slight slur in his voice and determined that he had been drinking. His knowledge of the habits of his sometime employer went deeper than Spalko himself might have realized, if he'd wanted to consider it at all. He knew, for instance, that Spalko liked drink, cigarettes and women, though not necessarily in that order. His capacity for all three was immense. He thought now that if Spalko was even half as drunk as he suspected, he would have an advantage. Where Spalko was concerned, that was rare.

"The dossier you gave me appears incorrect, or at the very least incomplete."

"And what leads you to that sorry conclusion?" The voice had instantaneously hardened, like water into ice. Too late Khan knew the language he had used had been too aggressive. Spalko might be a great thinker—a visionary even, as he doubtless considered himself—but in the bedrock of his being he operated on instinct. So he had risen from his semi-stupor to fight aggression with more of the same. He was possessed of a furious temper quite at odds with his carefully cultivated public image. But then so much of him thrived beneath the saccharine surface of his day-to-day life.

"Webb's behavior has been curious," Khan said softly.

"Oh? In what way?" Spalko's voice had returned to its slurring, lazy diction.

"He hasn't been acting like a college professor."

"I'm wondering why it matters. Haven't you killed him?"

"Not yet." Khan, sitting in his parked car, watched through the window glass as a bus pulled into a stop across the street. The door opened with a sigh and people emerged: an old man, two teenage boys, a mother and her toddler son.

"Well, that's a change of plan, isn't it?"

"You knew I meant to toy with him first."

"Certainly, but the question is for how long?"

There was a verbal chess match of sorts in progress, as delicate as it was fevered, and Khan could only guess at its nature. What was it about Webb? Why had Spalko decided to use him as a pawn for the double murder of the government men, Conklin and Panov? Why, for that matter, had Spalko ordered them killed? Khan had no doubt this is what had happened.

"Until I'm ready. Until he understands who's coming for him."

Khan's eyes followed the mother as she put her child down on the sidewalk. The boy tottered a little as he walked and she laughed. His head tilted as he looked up at her and he laughed, too, mimicking her pleasure. She took his small hand in hers.

"You're not having second thoughts, are you?"

Khan thought he detected a slight tautness, a tremor of intent, and all at once he wondered whether Spalko was drunk at all. Khan considered asking him why it mattered to him whether or not he killed David Webb but, after some consideration, rejected the idea, fearing it might reveal his own concerns. "No, no second thoughts," Khan said.

"Because we're the same under the skin, you and I. Our nostrils dilate at the scent of death."

Lost in thought and unsure how to respond, Khan closed his cell phone. He put his hand up to the window, watched between his fingers as the woman walked her son down the street. She took tiny steps, trying as best she could to match her gait to his wobbly one.

Spalko was lying to him, Khan knew that much. Just as he had been lying to Spalko. For a moment, his eyes lost their focus and he was back in the jungles of Cambodia. He had been with the Vietnamese gunrunner for over a year, tied up in a shack like a mad dog, half-starved and beaten. The third time he had attempted to escape he had learned his lesson, beating the unconscious gunrunner's head to a pulp with the spade-shaped head of a shovel he used to dig latrine pits. He had spent ten days living off what he could before he had been taken in by an American missionary by the name of Richard Wick. He had been given food, clothing, a hot bath and a clean bed. In exchange, he responded to the missionary's English lessons. As soon as he was able to read, he was given a Bible, which he was required to memorize. In this way, he began to understand that in Wick's view he was on the road to not salvation but to civilization. Once or twice, he tried to explain to Wick the nature of Buddhism, but he was very young and the concepts he'd been taught at an early age didn't seem so well formed when they emerged from his mouth. Not that Wick would've been interested in any case. He held no truck with any religion that didn't believe in God, didn't believe in Jesus the Savior.

Khan's eyes snapped back into focus. The mother was leading her toddler past the chrome facade of the diner with the huge coffee cup on its roof. Just beyond and across the street, Khan could see the man he knew as David Webb through the reflection-streaked glass of a car window. He had to give Webb credit; he had led Khan on a tortured path from the edge of the Conklin estate. Khan had seen the figure on the ridge road, observing them. By the time he had scrambled up there after escaping from Webb's clever trap, he had been too late to accost the man, but with his IR field glasses, he had been able to follow Webb's progress onto the highway. He had been ready to follow when Webb had been picked up. He watched Webb now, knowing what Spalko already knew: that Webb was a very dangerous man. A man like that surely had no concern about being the only Caucasian in the diner. He looked lonely, although Khan could not be sure, loneliness being entirely alien to him.

His gaze turned again to the mother and child. Their laughter drifted back to him, insubstantial as a dream.

———

Bourne arrived at Lincoln Fine Tailors in Alexandria at five minutes past nine. The shop looked like all the other independently owned businesses in Old Town; that is to say, it had a vaguely Colonial facade. He crossed the red-brick sidewalk, pushed open the door, and went inside. The public area of the shop was divided in half by a waist-high barrier made up of a counter on the left and cutting tables on the right. The sewing machines were midway back behind the counter, manned by three Latinas who did not even glance up when he entered. A thin man in shirtsleeves and open striped vest stood behind the counter frowning down at something. He had a high, domed forehead, a fringe of light brown hair, a face with sagging cheeks and muddy eyes. His glasses were pushed up onto the crown of his scalp. He had a habit of pinching his hawklike nose. He paid no attention to the door opening but looked up as Bourne approached the counter.

"Yes?" he said with an expectant air. "How can I help you?"

"You're Leonard Fine? I saw your name on the window outside."

"That's me," Fine said.

"Alex sent me."

The tailor blinked. "Who?"

"Alex Conklin," Bourne repeated. "My name is Jason Bourne." He looked around. No one was paying them the slightest attention. The sound of the sewing machines made the air sparkle and hum.

Very deliberately, Fine pulled his glasses down onto the narrow bridge of his nose. He peered at Bourne with a decided intensity.

"I'm a friend of his," Bourne said, feeling the need to prompt the fellow.

"There are no articles of clothing here for a Mr. Conklin."

"I don't think he left any," Bourne said.

Fine pinched his nose, as if he were in pain. "A friend, you say?"

"For many years."

Without another word, Fine reached over, opened a door in the counter for Bourne to step through. "Perhaps we should discuss this in my office." He led Bourne through a door, down a dusty corridor reeking of sizing and spray starch.

The office wasn't much, a small cubicle with scuffed and pitted linoleum on the floor, bare pipes running from floor to ceiling, a battered green metal desk with a swivel chair, two stacks of cheap metal filing cabinets, piles of cardboard boxes. The smell of mold and mildew rose like steam from the contents of the office. Behind the chair was a small square window, so grimed it was impossible to see the alley beyond.

Fine went behind the desk, pulled out a drawer. "Drink?"

"It's a little early," Bourne said, "don't you think?"

"Yeah," Fine muttered. "Now that you mention it." He removed a gun from a drawer and aimed it at Bourne's stomach. "The bullet won't kill you right away, but while you're bleeding to death, you'll wish it had."

"There's no reason to get excited," Bourne said easily.

"But there's *every* reason." the tailor said. His eyes were set close together, making him appear somewhat cross-eyed. "Conklin's dead and I heard you did it."

"I didn't," Bourne said.

"That's what you all say. Deny, deny, deny. It's the government's way, isn't it?" A crafty smile crossed the other's face. "Sit down, Mr. Webb—or Bourne—whatever you're calling yourself today."

Bourne looked up. "You're Agency."

"Not at all. I'm an independent operator. Unless Alex told them, I doubt if anyone inside the Agency knows I even exist." The tailor's smile grew wider. "That's why Alex came to me in the first place."

Bourne nodded. "I'd like to know about that."

"Oh, I have no doubt." Fine reached for the phone on his desk. "On the other hand, when your own people get hold of you, you'll be too busy answering their questions to care about anything else."

"Don't do that," Bourne said sharply.

Fine halted with the receiver in midair. "Give me a reason."

"I didn't kill Alex. I'm trying to find out who did."

"But you did kill him. According to the bulletin I read, you were at his house at the time he was shot to death. Did you see anyone else there?"

"No, but Alex and Mo Panov were dead when I arrived."

"Bullshit. Why did you kill him, I wonder." Fine's eyes narrowed. "I imagine it was because of Dr. Schiffer."

"I never heard of Dr. Schiffer."

The tailor emitted a harsh laugh. "More bullshit. And I suppose you never heard of DARPA."

"Of course I have," Bourne said. "It stands for Defense Advanced Research Projects Agency. Is that where Dr. Schiffer works?"

With a sound of disgust, Fine said, "I've had enough of this." When he momentarily took his eyes off Bourne to dial a number, Bourne lunged at him.

The DCI was in his capacious corner office, on the phone with Jamie Hull. Brilliant sunlight spilled in the window, firing the jewel tones of the carpet. Not that the magnificent play of colors had any effect on the DCI. He was still in one of his black moods. Bleakly, he looked at the photos of himself with presidents in the Oval Office, foreign leaders in Paris, Bonn and Dakar, entertainers in L.A. and Vegas, evangelical preachers in Atlanta and Salt Lake City, even, absurdly, the Dalai Lama in his perpetual smile and saffron robes, on a visit to New York City. These pictures not only failed to rouse him from his gloom but made him feel the years of his life, as if they were layers of chain-mail weighing him down.

"It's a fucking nightmare, sir," Hull was saying from far-off Reykjavík. "First off, setting up security in conjunction with the Russians and Arabs is like chasing your tail. I mean, half the time I don't know what the hell they're saying and the other half I don't trust the interpreters—ours or theirs—are telling me exactly what they're saying."

"You should have taken foreign language courses in grad school, Jamie. Just get on with it. I'll send you other interpreters, if you like."

"Really? And where would be we getting them? We've excised all the Arabists, haven't we?"

The DCI sighed. That was a problem, of course. Almost all the Arab-speaking intelligence officers they'd had on their payroll had been deemed sympathetic to the Islamic cause, always shouting down the hawks, trying to explain how peace-loving most Islamics really were. Tell that to the Israelis. "We've got a whole crop of new ones due here day after tomorrow from the Center for the Study of Intelligence. I'll have a couple sourced out to you ASAP."

"That's not all, sir."

The DCI scowled, vexed that he heard no hint of gratitude in the other's voice. "What now?" he snapped. What if he removed all the photos? he wondered. Would that improve the lugubrious atmosphere in here?

"Not to complain, sir, but I'm trying my damnedest to establish proper security measures in a foreign country with no particular allegiance to the

United States. We don't give them aid, so they aren't beholden to us. I invoke the president's name and what do I get? Blank stares. That makes my job triply difficult. I'm a member of the most powerful nation on the planet. I know more about security than everyone in Iceland put together. Where's the respect I'm supposed to—"

The intercom buzzed, and with a certain amount of satisfaction, the Old Man put Hull on hold. "What is it?" he barked into the intercom.

"Sorry to bother you, sir," the duty officer said, "but a call's just come in on Mr. Conklin's emergency line."

"What? Alex is dead. Are you sure?"

"Absolutely, sir. That line has not been reassigned yet."

"All right. Continue."

"I heard the sound of a brief scuffle and someone said a name—Bourne, I think."

The DCI sat ramrod straight, his black mood dissolving as quickly as it had come on. "Bourne. That's the name you heard, son?"

"It sure sounded like it. And the same voice said something like 'kill you.'"

"Where did the call come from?" the Old Man demanded.

"It was cut off, but I did a reverse trace. The number belongs to a shop in Alexandria. Lincoln Fine Tailors."

"Good man!" The DCI was standing now. The hand that held the phone was trembling slightly. "Dispatch two teams of agents immediately. Tell them Bourne has surfaced! Tell them to terminate him on sight."

Bourne, having wrested the gun away from Leonard Fine without a shot being fired, now shoved him so hard against the smudgy wall that a calendar was dislodged from its nail, fell to the floor. The phone was in Bourne's hand; he had just severed the connection. He listened for any commotion out front, any hint that the women had heard the sounds of the brief but violent struggle.

"They're on their way," Fine said. "It's over for you."

"I don't think so." Bourne was thinking furiously. "The call went to the main switchboard. No one would know what to do with it."

Fine shook his head, a smirk on his face. "The call bypassed the normal

Agency switchboard; it rang directly through to the DCI's duty officer. Conklin insisted I memorize the number, to be used only in event of an emergency."

Bourne shook Fine until his teeth rattled. "You idiot! What have you done?"

"Paid my final debt to Alex Conklin."

"But I told you. I didn't kill him." And then something occurred to Bourne, one last desperate try to win Fine over to his side, to get him to open up about what Conklin had been up to, a clue to why he might have been killed. "I'll prove to you Alex sent me."

"More bullshit," Fine said. "It's too late—"

"I know about NX 20."

Fine stood immobile. There was a slackness to his face; his eyes were open wide in shock. "No," he said. "No, no, no!"

"He told me," Bourne said. "Alex told me. That's why he sent me, you see."

"Alex could never have been coerced to tell about NX 20. Never!" The shock was fading from Fine's face, to be replaced by a slow dawning of the grievous error he had made.

Bourne nodded. "I'm a friend. Alex and I go all the way back to Vietnam. This is what I have been trying to tell you."

"God in heaven, I was on the phone with him when . . . when it happened." Fine put a hand to his forehead. "I heard the shot!"

Bourne grabbed the tailor by his vest. "Leonard, get hold of yourself. We don't have time for a replay."

Fine stared into Bourne's face. He had responded, as people most often do, to his given name. "Yes." He nodded, licked his lips. He was a man coming out of a dream. "Yes, I understand."

"The Agency will be here within minutes. I need to be gone by then."

"Yes, yes. Of course." Fine shook his head in sorrow. "Now let go of me. Please." Freed from Bourne's grip, he knelt beneath the back window, pulled out the radiator grille, behind which was a modern safe built into the plaster and lathe wall. He spun the dial, unlocked it, swung the heavy door open, pulled out a small manila envelope. Closing the safe, he replaced the grille and rose, handing the envelope to Bourne.

"This arrived for Alex late the other night. He called me yesterday morning to check on it. He said he was coming to pick it up."

"Who sent it?"

At that moment, they heard voices raised in sharp command emanating from the shop out front.

"They're here," Bourne said.

"Oh God!" Fine's features were pinched, bloodless.

"You must have another way out."

The tailor nodded. He gave Bourne quick instructions. "Go on now," he said urgently. "I'll keep them occupied."

"Wipe your face," Bourne said, and when Fine took the sheen of sweat off his face, he nodded.

While the tailor hurried into the shop to confront the agents, Bourne ran silently down the filthy corridor. He hoped Fine would be able to hold up under their questioning; otherwise he'd be finished. The bathroom was larger than he would have expected. To the left was an old porcelain sink beneath which were a stack of old paint cans, the tops rusted shut. A toilet was set against the rear wall, a shower to the left. Following Fine's instructions, he stepped into the shower, located the panel in the tile wall, opened it. He stepped through, replacing the tile panel.

Raising his hand, he pulled the old-fashioned light cord. He found himself in a narrow passage that looked to be in the adjacent building. The place stank; black plastic garbage bags had been stuffed between the rough wooden studs, possibly in lieu of insulation. Here and there, rats had scratched their way through the plastic, had gorged themselves on the rotting contents, left the rest spilling out onto the floor.

By the meager illumination provided by the bare bulb he saw a painted metal door that opened out onto the alley behind the stores. As he made his way toward it, the door burst open and two Agency suits sprinted through, guns drawn, their eyes intent on him.

CHAPTER SIX

The first two shots flew over Bourne's head as he ducked into a crouch. Coming out of it, he kicked hard at a plastic bag of garbage, sending it flying toward the two agents. It struck one and came apart at the seam. Refuse flew everywhere, sending the agents backward, coughing, their eyes streaming, arms over their faces.

Bourne struck upward, shattering the light bulb, plunging the narrow space into darkness. He turned and, flicking on his flashlight, saw the blank wall at the other end of the passageway. But there was a doorway to the outside, how . . . ?

Then he saw it and immediately extinguished the narrow beam of light. He could hear the agents shouting to each other, regaining their equilibrium. He went quickly to the far end of the passageway and knelt, feeling for the metal ring he had seen in a dull glint lying flush with the floor. He hooked his forefinger through it, pulled up, and the trap door to the cellar opened. A waft of stale, damp air came to him.

Without a moment's hesitation, he levered himself through the opening. His shoes struck the rung of a ladder and he went down, closing the trap door behind him. He smelled the roach spray first, then, switching on his flashlight, saw the gritty cement floor littered with their withered bodies like leaves on the ground. Rooting around in the splay of boxes, cartons and crates, he found a crowbar. Racing up the ladder, he slid the thick metal bar through the grips on the hatch. It was not a good fit; the crowbar remained loose, but it was the best he could hope for. All he needed, he thought, as he crunched across the roach-littered concrete floor, was enough time to get to the sidewalk delivery access common in all commercial buildings.

Above his head, he could hear the hammering as the two agents tried to open the hatch. It would not take long, he knew, for the crowbar to slip free under such vibration. But he had found the double metal panels to the street, had climbed the short flight of concrete steps that led upward. Behind him, the hatch burst open. He switched off his flashlight as the agents dropped to the basement floor.

Bourne was trapped now, and he knew it. Any attempt to lift the metal panels would bring in enough daylight for them to shoot him before he was halfway to the sidewalk. He turned, crept down the stairs. He could hear them moving around, looking for the light switch. They were speaking to each other in brief, staccato undertones, marking them as seasoned professionals. He crept along the jumbled piles of supplies. He, too, was looking for something specific.

When the lights snapped on, the two agents were spread apart, one on either side of the basement.

"What a shithole," one of them said.

"Never mind that," the other cautioned. "Where the fuck's Bourne?"

With their bland, impassive faces there was not much to distinguish them. They wore Agency-issue suits and Agency-issue expressions with equal assurance. But Bourne had had much experience with the people the Agency swept into its nets. He knew how they thought and, therefore, how they would act. Though not physically together, they moved in concert. They would not give much thought to where he might hide. Rather they had mathematically divided the basement into quadrants they would search as methodically as machines. He could not now avoid them, but he could surprise them.

Once he appeared, they would move very fast. He was counting on this and so positioned himself accordingly. He had wedged himself into a crate, his eyes smarting from the fumes of the caustic industrial cleansers with which he shared the cramped space. His hand scrabbled around in the darkness. Feeling something curved against the back of his hand, he picked it up. It was a can, heavy enough for his purpose.

He could hear his heart beating, a rat scratching at the wall against which the crate rested; all else was silent as the agents continued their painstakingly thorough search. Bourne waited, patient, coiled. His lookout, the rat, had ceased its scratching. At least one of the agents was near.

It was deathly quiet now. Then, all at once, the quick catch of a breath came to him, the rustle of fabric nearly directly above his head, and he uncoiled, popping the lid off. The agent, gun in hand, reared back. His partner, across the basement, whirled. With his left hand, Bourne grabbed a handful of the nearest agent's shirt, jerked him forward. Instinctively, the agent pulled back, resisting, and Bourne lunged forward, using the agent's own momentum to slam his spine and head against the brick wall. He could hear the rat squeak even as the agent's eyes rolled up and he slid down, unconscious.

The second agent had taken two steps toward Bourne, thought better of engaging him hand-to-hand and aimed the Glock at his chest. Bourne threw the can into the agent's face. As he recoiled, Bourne closed the gap between them, drove the edge of his hand into the side of the agent's neck, felling him.

An instant later, Bourne was up the concrete stairs, opening the metal panels into fresh air and blue sky. Dropping the panels back into place, he calmly walked down the sidewalk until he reached Rosemont Avenue. There, he lost himself in the crowd.

A half-mile away, after assuring himself that he had not been followed, Bourne went into a restaurant. As he was seated at a table, he scanned every face in the room, searching for anomalies—feigned nonchalance, covert scrutiny. He ordered a BLT and a cup of coffee, then got up and headed toward the rear of the restaurant. Determining the men's room was empty, he locked himself in a cubicle, sat down on the toilet and opened the envelope meant for Conklin that Fine had given him.

Inside, he found a first-class airline ticket in Conklin's name to Budapest, Hungary, and a room key for the Danubius Grand Hotel. He sat looking at the items for a moment, wondering why Conklin had been on his way to Budapest and whether the trip had anything to do with his murder.

He took out Alex's cell phone, dialed a local number. Now that he had a direction, he felt better. Deron picked up after the third ring.

"Peace, Love and Understanding."

Bourne laughed. "It's Jason." He never knew how Deron was going to answer the phone. Deron was quite literally an artist at his trade. It just happened that his trade was forgery. He made his living painting copies of Old Master oils that hung on mansion walls. They were so exacting, so expert that every so often one was sold at auction or ended up in a museum collection. On the side, just for the fun of it, he forged other things.

"I've been following the news on you and it has a distinctly ominous tone," Deron said, in his slight British accent.

"Tell me something I don't know." At the sound of the men's room door opening, Bourne paused. He stood up, put his shoes on either side of the toilet, peered over the top of the stall. A man with gray hair, a beard and a slight limp had bellied up to the urinal. He wore a dark suede bomber jacket, black slacks, nothing special. And yet, all at once Bourne felt trapped. He had to curb his desire to get out immediately.

"Damn, is the man on your ass?" It was always interesting to hear argot coming out of that cultured mouth.

"He was, up until I lost him.." Bourne left the bathroom and went back into the restaurant, scanning every table as he went. By this time his sandwich had come, but his coffee was cold. He flagged down the waitress, asked for it to be replaced. When she had walked away, he said softly into the phone, "Listen, Deron, I need the usual—passport and contact lenses in my prescription, and I need them yesterday."

"Nationality?"

"Let's keep it American."

"I get the idea. The man won't expect that."

"Something like that. I want the name on the passport to be Alexander Conklin."

Deron gave a low whistle. "It's your call, Jason. Give me two hours."

"Do I have a choice?"

Deron's odd little giggle exploded down the line. "You can go away hungry. I have all your photos. Which one d'you want?"

When Bourne told him, he said, "Are you sure? You've got your hair shaved down to the nub. Doesn't look like you at all now."

"It will when I get through with my makeover," Bourne replied. "I've been put on the Agency hit list."

"Number one with a bullet, I shouldn't think. Where should we meet?"

Bourne told him.

"Good enough. Yo, listen, Jason." Deron's tone was abruptly more somber. "That must have been tough. I mean, you saw them, didn't you?"

Bourne stared at his plate. Why had he ordered this sandwich? The tomato had a raw and bloody look. "I saw them, yes." What if he could somehow roll back time, make Alex and Mo reappear? That would be quite a trick. But the past stayed the past, receding further from memory with every day.

"It's not like *Butch Cassidy*."

Bourne did not say a word.

Deron sighed. "I knew Alex and Mo, too."

"Of course you did. I introduced you," Bourne said, as he closed the phone.

He sat at the table for a while, thinking. Something was bothering him. An alarm bell had gone off in his head as he had exited the men's room, but he had been distracted by his conversation with Deron and so he had not taken full note of it. What was it? Slowly, carefully, he scanned the room again. Then he had it. He did not see the man with the beard and slight limp. Perhaps he had finished his meal and had been on his way out. On the other hand, his presence in the men's room had made Bourne distinctly uneasy. There was something about him. . . .

He threw some money onto the table and went to the front of the restaurant. The two windows that looked out onto the street were separated by a wide mahogany pillar. Bourne stood behind it, using it as a screen while he checked the street. Pedestrians were first—anyone walking at an unnaturally slow pace, anyone loitering, reading a newspaper, standing too long in front of the shop window directly across the street, possibly scanning it for the reflection of the restaurant's entrance. He saw nothing suspicious. He marked three people sitting inside parked cars—one woman, two men. He could not see their faces. And then, of course, there were the cars parked on the restaurant side of the street.

Without a second thought, he went out onto the street. It was late morning and the crowd was denser now. That suited his current needs. He spent the next twenty minutes surveilling his immediate environment, checking doorways, storefronts, passing pedestrians and vehicles, windows and rooftops. When he'd satisfied himself that the field contained no Agency suits, he crossed the street, went into a liquor store. He asked for a bottle of the Speyside sherry-cask single-malt that had been Conklin's drink. While the proprietor went to fetch it, he looked out the window. No one in any of the cars parked on the restaurant side of the street. As he watched, one of the men he had noted got out of his car, went into a pharmacy. He had neither a beard nor a limp.

He had nearly two hours before he had to meet Deron, and he wanted to use the time productively. The memory of the Paris office, the voice, the half-remembered face that had been pushed aside by the exigencies of current circumstance, had now returned. According to Mo Panov's methodology, he needed to inhale the Scotch again in order to pull out more of the memory. In this way, he hoped to try to find out who the man in Paris was and why the particular memory of him had surfaced now. Had it been simply the scent of the single-malt, or was it something in his current predicament that had provoked it?

Bourne paid for the Scotch with a credit card, feeling he was safe enough using it in a liquor store. A moment later, he exited the store with his package. He passed the car with the woman inside. A small child was sitting next to her in the passenger's seat. Since the Agency would never allow a child to be used on an active field surveillance, that left the second man as a possibility. Bourne turned, walking away from the car in which the man sat. He did not look behind him, did not try to use any covert methods of spying or the standard procedures for shaking a tail. He did keep track of all the cars immediately in front and behind him, however.

Within ten minutes, he had reached a park. He sat down on a wrought-iron bench, watched the pigeons rise and fall, wheeling against the blue sky overhead. The other benches were perhaps half-full. An old man came into the park; he held a brown bag as crumpled as his face from which he extracted handfuls of bread crumbs. The pigeons, it seemed, had been expecting him, for they swooped down, swirling around him, cooing and clucking in delight as they gorged themselves.

Bourne opened the bottle of single-malt, sniffed its elegant and complex aroma. Immediately, Alex's face flashed before him, and the slow creep of blood over the floor. Gently, almost reverently, he set this image aside. He took a small sip of the Scotch, holding it on his palate, allowing the fumes to rise up into his nose, to bring him back to the shard of memory he was finding so elusive. In his mind's eye, he saw again the view out onto the Champs-Elysées. He was holding the cut-crystal glass in his hand, and as he took another sip of the Scotch, he willed himself to bring the glass to his lips. He heard the strong, operatic voice, willed himself to turn back into the Paris office where he had been standing an unknown time ago.

Now, for the first time, he could see the plush appointments of the room, the painting by Raoul Dufy of an elegant horse and rider in the Bois de Boulogne, the dark green walls with their deep luster, the high cream ceiling etched in the clear, piercing light of Paris. *Go on,* he urged himself. *Go on.* . . . A patterned carpet, two high-backed upholstered chairs, a heavy polished walnut desk in the Regency style of Louis XIV, behind which stood, smiling, a tall, handsome man with worldly eyes, a long Gallic nose and prematurely white hair. Jacques Robbinet, French Minister of Culture.

That was it! How Bourne knew him, why they had become friends and, in a sense, compatriots, was still a mystery, but at least now he knew that he had an ally he could contact and count on. Elated, Bourne put the Scotch bottle underneath the bench, a gift for the first vagrant who noticed it. He looked around without seeming to. The old man had gone and so had most of the pigeons; just a few of the largest ones, chests puffed out to protect their territory, were strutting around, scrounging the last of the crumbs. A young couple were kissing on a nearby bench; three kids with a boombox passed through, made lewd noises at the snuggled couple. His senses were on high alert—something was wrong, out of place, but he could not figure out what it was.

He was keenly aware that the deadline to meet Deron was fast approaching, but instinct warned him not to move until he had identified the anomaly. He looked again at all the people in the park. No bearded man, certainly none with a limp. And yet . . . Diagonally across from him was a man sitting forward, elbows on knees, hands together. He was watching a young boy whose father had just handed him an ice cream cone. What interested Bourne was that he was dressed in a dark suede bomber jacket and black slacks. His hair was black, not gray, he had no beard, and by the normal way his legs were bent, Bourne was certain that he didn't have a limp.

Bourne, himself a chameleon, an expert in disguise, knew that one of the best methods of keeping hidden was to change your gait, especially if one was trying to hide from a professional. An amateur might notice superficial aspects such as hair color and clothes, but to a trained agent the way you moved and walked was as individual as a fingerprint. He tried to bring up the image of the man in the restaurant men's room. Had he been wearing a wig and fake beard? Bourne couldn't be sure. What he was certain of, though, was that the man had been wearing a dark suede bomber jacket and black slacks. From this position he couldn't see the man's face, but it was clear that he was far younger than the man in the men's room had appeared.

There was something else about him, but what was it? He studied the side of the man's face for several moments before he had it. A flash image of the man who'd jumped him in the woods of Conklin's estate came to him. It was the shape of the ear, the deep brownish color, the configuration of the whorls.

Good God, the thought, abruptly disoriented, this was the man who'd shot at him, who'd almost succeeded in killing him in the Manassas cave! How had he trailed Bourne all the way from there when Bourne had given the slip to every Agency and state trooper in the area? He felt a momentary chill run through him. What kind of man could do that?

He knew there was only one way to find out. Experience told him that when you are up against a formidable foe the only way to get a true measure of him is to do the last thing he would expect. Still, for a moment, he hesitated. He'd never been up against an antagonist like this. He understood that he had crossed over into unknown territory.

Knowing this, he rose and slowly and deliberately crossed the park and sat down beside the man, whose face he now saw had a distinctly Asian cast to it. To his credit, the man did not start or give any overt indication of surprise. He continued to watch the little boy. As the ice cream started to melt, his father showed him how to turn the cone to lick up the drippings.

"Who are you?" Bourne said. "Why do you want to kill me?"

The man beside him looked straight ahead, gave no sign at all that he had heard what Bourne had said. "Such a beatific scene of domestic bliss." There was an acid edge to his voice. "I wonder if the child knows that at a moment's notice his father could abandon him."

Bourne had an odd reaction to hearing the other's voice in this setting. It was as if he had moved out of the shadows to fully inhabit the world of those around them.

"No matter how much you want to kill me," Bourne said, "you can't touch me here in this public place."

"The boy is, what, six, I would say. Far too young to understand the nature of life, far too young to fathom why his father would leave."

Bourne shook his head. The conversation was not proceeding as he had intended. "What makes you think that? Why would the father abandon his son?"

"An interesting question from a man with two children. Jamie and Alison, isn't it?"

Bourne started as if the other had plunged a knife into his side. Fear and anger swirled inside him but it was the anger that he allowed to rise to the surface. "I won't even ask how you know so much about me, but I will tell you this, in threatening my family you've made a fatal mistake."

"Oh, there's no need to think that. I have no designs on your children," Khan said evenly. "I was merely wondering how Jamie will feel when you never come back."

"I'll never abandon my son. I'll do whatever it takes to come safely back to him."

"It seems odd to me that you're so passionate about your current family when you failed Dao, Joshua and Alyssa."

Now the fear was gaining ground inside Bourne. His heart was pounding painfully, and there was a sharp pain in his chest. "What are you talking about? Where did you get the idea that I failed them?"

"You abandoned them to their fate, didn't you?"

Bourne felt as if he was losing his grip on reality. "How dare you! They died! They were pulled away from me, and I've never forgotten them!"

The hint of a smile curled the edges of the other's lips, as if he had scored a victory in dragging Bourne across the invisible barrier. "Not even when you married Marie? Not even when Jamie and Alison where born?" His tone was tightly wound now, as if he was struggling to keep something deep inside him held in check. "You tried to replicate Joshua and Alyssa. You even used the same first letters in their names."

Bourne felt as if he'd been beaten senseless. There was an inchoate roaring in his ears. "Who are you?" he repeated in a strangled voice.

"I'm known as Khan. But who are *you*, David Webb? A professor of linguistics might possibly be at home in the wilderness, but he surely doesn't know hand-to-hand combat; he doesn't know how to fashion a Viet Cong cage-net; he doesn't know how to hijack a car. Above all, he doesn't know how to successfully conceal himself from the CIA."

"It seems, then, that we're a mystery to one another."

That same maddening enigmatic smile played around Khan's mouth. Bourne felt a prickling of the short hairs at the nape of his neck, the sense that something in his shattered memory was trying to surface.

"Keep telling yourself that. The fact is, I *could* kill you now, even in this public place," Khan said with a great deal of venom. The smile had vanished as quickly as a cloud changes its shape, and there was a small tremor in the smooth bronze column of his neck, as if some fury, long held in check, had briefly escaped to the surface. "I *should* kill you now. But such extreme action would expose me to the pair of CIA agents who have entered the park from the north entrance."

Without moving his head, Bourne directed his gaze in the indicated direction. Khan was quite right. Two Agency suits were scanning the faces of those in the immediate vicinity.

"I believe that it's time we left." Khan rose, looked down at Bourne for a moment. "This is a simple situation. Either come with me or be taken."

Bourne got up and, walking side by side with Khan, went out of the park. Khan was between Bourne and the agents, and he took a route that would keep him in that position. Again, Bourne was impressed with the young man's expertise as well as his thinking in extreme situations.

"Why are you doing this?" Bourne asked. He had not been immune to the other's significant flare of temper, an incandescence as enigmatic to Bourne as it was alarming. Khan didn't answer.

They entered the stream of pedestrians and were soon lost within the flow. Khan had witnessed the four agents heading into Lincoln Fine Tailors, and he had quickly memorized their faces. It hadn't been difficult; in the jungle where he had raised himself, the instant identification of an individual often meant the difference between life and death. In any event, unlike Webb, he knew where all four were and he was on the lookout for the other two now, because at this crucial juncture when he was leading his target to a place of his choosing, he did not want any intrusion.

Sure enough, up ahead in the crowd, he spotted them. They were in standard formation, one on either side of the street, heading directly toward them. He turned to Webb to alert him, only to find that he was alone in the throng. Webb had vanished into thin air.

CHAPTER SEVEN

Deep within the bowels of Humanistas, Ltd. was a sophisticated listening station that monitored the clandestine signals traffic from all the various major intelligence networks. No human ear heard the raw data because no human ear would be able to make sense of it. Since the signals were encrypted, the intercepted traffic was run through a series of sophisticated software programs made up of heuristic algorithms—that is to say, they had the ability to learn. There was a program for each intelligence network because each agency had selected a different encryption algorithm.

Humanistas' battery of programmers were more successful at breaking some codes than others, but the bottom line was that Spalko more or less knew what was going on all over the world. The American CIA code was one of the ones that had been broken, so within hours of the DCI ordering the termination of Jason Bourne, Stepan Spalko was reading about it.

"Excellent," he said. "Now everything is going according to plan." He set down the decryption, then pulled up a map of Nairobi on a monitor screen. He kept moving around the city until he found the area on the outskirts where President Jomo wanted the Humanistas medical team sent in to minister to the quarantined known AIDS patients.

At that moment his cell phone rang. He listened to the voice on the other end of the line. He checked his watch, said, finally, "There should be enough time. You've done well." Then he took the elevator upstairs to Ethan Hearn's office. On the way up, he made a single call, achieving in minutes what many others in Budapest had tried in vain for weeks to get— an orchestra seat for that night's opera.

Humanistas, Ltd.'s newest young development officer was hard at work on his computer, but he stood up as soon as Spalko walked in. He looked as clean and neat as Spalko imagined he had when he had walked in to work this morning.

"No need to be formal around here, Ethan," Spalko said with an easy smile. "This isn't the army, you know."

"Yes, sir. Thank you." Hearn stretched his back. "I've been at it since seven this morning."

"How goes the fund-raising?"

"I have two dinners and a lunch with solid prospects set up for early next week. I've e-mailed you a copy of the pitch letters I want to give to them."

"Good, good." Spalko glanced around the room as if to make certain no one else was in hearing distance. "Tell me, do you own a tux?"

"Absolutely, sir. I couldn't do my job otherwise."

"Excellent. Go home and change into it."

"Sir?" The young man's brows had knitted together in surprise.

"You're going to the opera."

"Tonight? At such short notice? How did you manage to get tickets?"

Spalko laughed. "You know, I like you, Ethan. I'm willing to bet you're the last honest man on earth."

"Sir, I have no doubt that would be you."

Spalko laughed again at the bewildered expression that had come over the young man. "That was a joke, Ethan. Now, come on. There's no time to lose."

"But my work." Hearn gestured at the computer screen.

"In a way, tonight *will* be work. There'll be a man at the opera I want to recruit as a benefactor." Spalko's demeanor was so relaxed, so nonchalant that Hearn never suspected a thing. "This man—his name is László Molnar—"

"I've never heard of him."

"You wouldn't." Spalko's voice lowered, became conspiratorial. "Though he is quite wealthy, he is paranoid about anyone knowing. He's not on any donor list, that I can assure you, and if you make any allusion to his wealth, you might as well forget ever talking to him again."

"I understand completely, sir," Hearn said.

"He is a connoisseur of sorts, though nowadays it seems to me the word has lost much of its meaning."

"Yes, sir." Hearn nodded. "I think I know what you mean."

Spalko was quite certain the young man had no idea what he meant, and a vague undertone of regret crept into his thoughts. He had once been as naive as Hearn, a hundred years ago, or so it now seemed. "In any event, Molnar loves opera. He has had a subscription for years."

"I know exactly how to proceed with difficult prospects like László Molnar." Hearn deftly pulled on his suit jacket. "You can count on me."

Spalko grinned. "Somehow I knew I could. Now, once you've hooked him, I want you to take him to Underground. Do you know the bar, Ethan?"

"Of course, sir. But it will be quite late. After midnight, surely."

Spalko put his forefinger beside his nose. "Another secret. Molnar is something of a night owl. He'll resist, however. It seems he enjoys being persuaded. You must persevere, Ethan, do you understand?"

"Perfectly."

Spalko handed him a slip of paper with Molnar's seat number. "Then go on. Have a good time." He gave him a small shove. "And good luck."

The imposing Romanesque facade of Magyar Állami Operaház, the Hungarian State Opera House, was ablaze with light. Inside, the magnificent, ornate gilt-and-red interior, three stories high, glittered with what seemed like ten thousand spearpoints of light from the elaborate cut-crystal chandelier that descended from the muraled domed ceiling like a giant bell.

Tonight, the company was presenting Zoltán Kodály's *Háry János*, a traditional favorite that had been in its repertory since 1926. Ethan Hearn hurried into the vast marble lobby, echoing with the voices of Budapest society assembled for the evening's festivities. His tuxedo was of a fine worsted fabric and was well cut, but it was hardly a name brand. In his line of work, what he wore and how he wore it was extremely important. He tended toward elegant, muted clothes, never anything flashy or too expensive. Humility was the name of the game when one was asking for donations.

He did not want to be late, but he slowed himself down, reluctant to miss a moment of that peculiar electric time just before the curtain rose that made his heart thump.

Having assiduously boned up on the hobbies of Hungarian society, he fancied himself something of an opera buff. He liked *Háry János* both because of its music, which was derived from Hungarian folk music, and because of the tall tale the veteran soldier János spins of his rescue of the emperor's daughter, his promotion to general, his virtual single-handed defeat of Napoleon and his eventual winning of the heart of the emperor's daughter. It was a sweet fable, drenched in the bloody history of Hungary.

In the end, it was fortuitous that he had arrived late, because by consulting the slip of paper Spalko had given him, he was able to identify László Molnar, who, along with most others, was already seated. From what Hearn could determine at first sight, he was a middle-aged man of medium height, heavy around the gut, and, with a slicked-back mass of black hair, a head not unlike a mushroom. A forest of bristles sprouted from his ears and the backs of his blunt-fingered hands. He was ignoring the woman on his left, who, in any case, was speaking, rather too loudly, to her companion. The seat to Molnar's right was vacant. It appeared that he had come to the opera on his own. All the better, Hearn thought, as he took his seat near the rear of the orchestra. A moment later the lights dimmed, the orchestra struck up the prelude and the curtain slid smoothly up.

Later, during the intermission, Hearn took a cup of hot chocolate and mingled with the soigné crowd. This was how humans had evolved. As opposed to the animal world, the female was definitely the more colorful of the species. The women were sheathed in long dresses of shantung silk, Venetian moiré, Moroccan satin that just months ago had been displayed on the couturier runways of Paris, Milan and New York. The men, clad in designer tuxedos, appeared content to circle their mates, who gaggled in clusters, fetching them champagne or hot chocolate when needed but, for the most part, looking thoroughly bored.

Hearn had enjoyed the first half of the opera and was looking forward to the conclusion. He had not, however, forgotten his assignment. In fact, during the performance he had spent some time coming up with an approach. He never liked to lock himself into a plan; rather he used his first visual assessment of the prospect to figure out an approach. To the discerning eye, so much could be determined by visual cues. Did the prospect care about his appearance? Did he like food, or was he indifferent to it? Did he drink or smoke? Was he cultured or uncouth? All these factors and many more went into the mix.

So it was that by the time Hearn made his approach, he was confident he could strike up a conversation with László Molnar.

"Pardon me," Hearn said in his most deprecating tone of voice. "I'm a lover of opera. I was wondering if you were, too."

Molnar had turned. He wore an Armani tuxedo that emphasized his broad shoulders while cleverly hiding the bulk of his gut. His ears were very large and, this close up, even hairier than they had seemed at first glance. "I am a student of the opera," he said slowly and, to Hearn's attuned senses, warily. Hearn smiled his most charming smile and engaged Molnar's dark eyes with his own. "To be frank," Molnar continued, apparently mollified, "I'm consumed by it."

This fit in perfectly with what Spalko had told him, Hearn thought. "I have a subscription," he said in his effortless fashion. "I've had one for some years, and I couldn't help noticing that you have one also." He laughed softly. "I don't get to meet too many people with a love of opera. My wife prefers jazz."

"Mine loved the opera."

"You're divorced?"

"A widower."

"Oh, I'm so sorry."

"It happened some time ago," Molnar said, warming a little now that he'd given up this intimate bit of knowledge. "I miss her so terribly that I've never sold her seat."

Hearn held out a hand. "Ethan Hearn."

After the slightest hesitation, László Molnar gripped it with his hairy-backed paw. "László Molnar. I'm pleased to make your acquaintance."

Hearn gave a courtly little bow. "Would you care to join me in a hot chocolate, Mr. Molnar?"

This offer appeared to please the other, and he nodded. "I'd be delighted." As they walked together through the milling crowd, they exchanged lists of their favorite operas and opera composers. Since Hearn had asked Molnar to go first, he made certain they had many in common. Molnar was again pleased. As Spalko had noted, there was something open and honest about Hearn that even the most jaundiced eye could not help but appreciate. He possessed the knack of being natural even in the most artificial situations. It was this sincerity of spirit that caught Molnar, dissolving his defenses.

"Are you enjoying the performance?" he inquired as they sipped their hot chocolate.

"Very much," Hearn said. "But *Háry János* is so full of emotion I confess I'd enjoy it all the more if I could see the expressions on the principals' faces. Sad to say, when I bought the subscription I couldn't afford anything closer, and now it's quite impossible to obtain a better seat."

For a moment, Molnar said nothing, and Hearn feared that he was going to let the opening pass. Then he said, as if he had just thought of it, "Would you care to sit in my wife's seat?"

"Once more," Hasan Arsenov said. "We need to go over again the sequence of events that will gain us our freedom."

"But I know them as well as I know your face," Zina protested.

"Well enough to negotiate the route to our final destination blindfolded?"

"Don't be ridiculous," Zina scoffed.

"In Icelandic, Zina. We speak now only in Icelandic."

In their hotel room, the schematics for the Oskjuhlid Hotel in Reykjavík were spread out across the large desk. In the inviting glow of lamplight, every layer of the hotel was laid bare, from the foundation, to the security, sewage and heating and air-conditioning systems, to the floor plans themselves. On each oversized bluesheet were neatly written a series of notes, directional arrows, markouts indicating the layers of security that had been added by each of the participating nations for the terrorism summit. Spalko's intel was impeccably detailed.

"From the time we breach the hotel's defenses," Arsenov said, "we'll have very little time to accomplish our goal. The worst part is we won't know *how* little time until we get there and make a dry run. That makes it even more imperative that there be no hesitation, no mistake—not one wrong turn!" In his ardor, his dark eyes were blazing. Taking up a sash of hers, he led her to one end of the room. He wrapped it around her head, tying it tightly enough so that he knew she couldn't see.

"We've just entered the hotel." He let go of her. "Now I want you to walk out the route for me. I'll be timing you. Now go!"

For two-thirds of the circuitous journey, she did well, but then, at the junction of what would be two branching corridors, she went left instead of right.

"You're finished," he said harshly as he whipped off the blindfold. "Even if you corrected your mistake, you wouldn't make the target on time. Security—be it American, Russian or Arab—would catch up to you and shoot you dead."

Zina was trembling, furious with herself and with him.

"I know that face, Zina. Put your anger away," Hasan said. "Emotion breaks concentration, and concentration is what you need now. When you can make the path blindfolded without making a mistake, we will be finished for this evening."

An hour later, her mission accomplished, Zina said, "Come to bed, my love."

Arsenov, dressed now only in a simple muslin robe, dyed black, belted at the waist, shook his head. He was standing by the huge window, looking out at the diamond night-sparkle of Budapest reflected in the dark water of the Danube.

Zina sprawled naked on the down comforter, laughed softly, deep in her throat. "Hasan, feel." She moved her palm, her long, splayed fingers over the sheets. "Pure Egyptian cotton, so luxurious."

He wheeled on her, a frown of disapproval darkening his face. "That's just it, Zina." He pointed to the half-empty bottle on the night table. "Napoleon brandy, soft sheets, a down comforter. These luxuries are not for us."

Zina's eyes opened wide, her heavy lips forming a moue. "And why not?"

"Has the lesson I've just taught you gone in one ear only to fly out the other? Because we are *warriors*, because we have renounced all worldly possessions."

"Have you renounced your weapons, Hasan?"

He shook his head, his eyes hard and cold. "Our weapons have a purpose."

"These soft things also have a purpose, Hasan. They make me happy."

He made a guttural sound in the back of his throat, curt and dismissive.

"I don't want to possess these things, Hasan," Zina said huskily, "just use them for a night or two." She held out a hand to him. "Can't you relax your iron-bound rules for even that short a time? We've both worked hard today; we deserve a little relaxation."

"Speak for yourself. I won't be seduced by luxuries," he said shortly. "It disgusts me that you have been."

"I don't believe I disgust you." She had seen something in his eyes, a sort of self-denial that she naturally enough misinterpreted as the rock of his strict ascetic nature.

"All right, then," she said. "I'll break the brandy bottle, sow the bed with glass, if only you'll come join me."

"I've told you," he warned darkly. "Do not joke of these matters, Zina."

She sat up, on her knees moved toward him, her breasts, sheened in golden lamplight, swaying provocatively. "I'm perfectly serious. If it's your wish to lie in a bed of pain while we make love, who am I to argue?"

He stood looking at her for a long time. It did not occur to him that she might be mocking him still. "Don't you understand." He took a step toward her. "Our path is set. We are bound to the *Tariqat*, the spiritual path to Allah."

"Don't distract me, Hasan. I'm still thinking of weapons." She grabbed a handful of muslin and pulled him toward her. Her other hand reached out, gently caressed the fabric of the bandage that wrapped the area of his thigh where he'd been shot. Then it moved higher.

Their lovemaking was as fierce as any hand-to-hand combat. It arose as much out of wanting to hurt the other as it did from physical need. In their jackhammer thrashing, moaning and release, it was doubtful that love played any role. For his part, Arsenov longed to be ground into the bed of glass shards that Zina had joked about, so that when her nails gripped him, he resisted her, obliging her to hold on tighter, to score his skin. He was rough enough to bait her, so that she bared her teeth, used them on the powerful muscles of his shoulders, his chest, his arms. It was only with the rising tide of pain threatening to overpower the pleasure that the strange hallucinatory sensation in which he was lost receded somewhat.

Punishment was required for what he had done to Khalid Murat, his compatriot, his friend. Never mind that he had done what was needed in order for his people to survive and flourish. How many times had he told himself that Khalid Murat had been sacrificed on the altar of Chechnya's future? And yet, like a sinner, an outcast, he was hounded by doubt and fear, in need of cruel punishment. Though truly, he thought now in the little death that comes in sexual release, was it not always thus with prophets?

Was not this torture further proof that the road he had embarked upon was the righteous one?

Beside him, Zina lay in his arms. She might have been miles away, though in a manner of speaking her mind was also filled with thoughts of prophets. Or, more accurately, one prophet. This latter-day prophet had dominated her mind ever since she had drawn Hasan to the bed. She hated that Hasan could not let himself take pleasure in the luxuries around him, and so, when he grasped her, it was not him she was thinking of, when he entered her, in her mind it was not him at all, but Stepan Spalko to whom she crooned. And when, nearing her end, she bit her lip it was not out of passion, as Hasan believed, but out of a fear that she would shout Spalko's name. She so much wanted to, if only to hurt Hasan in a manner that would cut him to the quick, for she had no doubt of his love for her. This love she found dumb and unknowing, an infantile thing like a baby reaching for its mother's breast. What he craved from her was warmth and shelter, the quick thrust back into the womb. It was a love that made her skin crawl.

But what *she* craved . . .

Her thoughts froze in their tracks as he moved against her, sighing. She had supposed that he was asleep, but he was not, or else something had roused him. Now, attendant on his desires, she had no time for her own thoughts. She smelled his manly scent, rising like a pre-dawn mist, and his breathing quickened just a little.

"I was thinking," he whispered, "about what it means to be a prophet, whether one day I will be called that among our people."

Zina said nothing, knowing that he wished her to be silent now, to listen only, as he reassured himself of his chosen path. This was Arsenov's weakness, the one unknown to anyone else, the one he showed only to her. She wondered if Khalid Murat had been clever enough to have suspected this weakness. She was almost certain Stepan Spalko was.

"The Qur'an tells us that each of our prophets is the incarnation of a divine attribute," Arsenov said. "Moses is the manifestation of the transcendent aspect of reality, because of his ability to speak with God without an intermediary. In the Qur'an, the Lord said to Moses, 'Fear not, you are transcendent.' Jesus is the manifestation of prophethood. As an infant, he cried, 'God gave me the book and placed me as a prophet.'

"But Mohammad is the spiritual incarnation and manifestation of all of God's names. Mohammad himself said, 'What God first created was my light. I was a prophet while Adam was still between water and earth.'"

Zina waited the space of several heartbeats to be certain that he had finished pontificating. Then, with a hand placed on his slowly rising and falling chest, she asked as she knew he wanted her to ask, "And what is *your* divine attribute, my prophet?"

Arsenov turned his head on the pillow so that he could see her fully. The lamplight behind her cast most of her face in shadow, just a fiery line along her cheek and jawbone was limned in a long painterly stroke, and he was caught out in a thought he most often kept hidden, even from himself. He did not know what he would do without her strength and vitality. For him, her womb represented immortality, the sacred place from which his sons would issue, his line continuing through all eternity. But he knew this dream could not happen without Spalko's help. "Ah, Zina, if you only knew what the Shaykh will do for us, what he will help us become."

She rested her cheek against her folded arm. "Tell me."

But he shook his head, a small smile playing at the corners of his mouth. "That would be a mistake."

"Why?"

"Because you must see for yourself without any foreknowledge the devastation caused by the weapon."

Now, peering into Arsenov's eyes, she experienced a chill deep in the core of her, where she rarely dared to look. Possibly she felt an intimation of the terrible power that would be unleashed in Nairobi in three days' time. But with the clairvoyance sometimes granted lovers, she understood that what interested Hasan most was the fear this form of death—whatever it would turn out to be—would engender. It was fear he meant to wield, that was clear enough. Fear to use as a righteous sword to regain all that had been lost to the Chechens over centuries of abuse, displacement and bloodshed.

From an early age, Zina had been on intimate terms with fear. Her father, weak and dying of the disease of despair that ran like a plague through Chechnya, who had once provided for his family as all Chechen men must but could not now even show his face on the street for fear of being picked up by the Russians. Her mother, once a beautiful young woman, in her last years a sunken-chested crone with thinning hair, bad eyesight and faulty memory.

After she came home from the long day's scavenging, she was obliged to walk three kilometers to the nearest public water pump, stand in the queue for an hour or two, only to walk back, lug the full bucket up the five flights to their filthy room.

That water! Sometimes, even now, Zina would awake, gagging, with its foul turpentine taste in her mouth.

One night her mother sat down and did not get up. She was twenty-eight but looked more than twice that age. From the constantly burning oil fires, her lungs were full of tar. When Zina's younger brother had complained of thirst, the old woman had looked at Zina and said, "I can't get up. Even for our water. I can't go on. . . ."

Zina rolled and, twisting her torso, turned off the lamp. The moon, previously unseen, filled the casement of the window. At the point where her upper torso dipped down to her narrow waist, a small pool of its cool light fell upon the bed, illuminating the tip of her breast, below which, under the deep curve, lay Hasan's hand. Outside that pool there was only darkness.

For a long time she lay with her eyes open, listening to Hasan's regular breathing, waiting for sleep to claim her. Who knew the meaning of fear better than Chechens? she wondered. In Hasan's face was written the lamentable history of their people. Never mind death, never mind ruin, there was only one outcome that he could see: vindication for Chechnya. And with a heart made heavy by despair, Zina knew that the attention of the world needed to be snapped into focus. These days, there was only one way to do that. She knew Hasan was right: Death had to come in a manner heretofore unthinkable, but what price they might all pay she could not begin to imagine.

CHAPTER EIGHT

Jacques Robbinet liked to spend mornings with his wife, drinking café au lait, reading the papers and talking with her about the economy, their children and the state of their friends' lives. They never spoke about his work.

He made it a strict rule never to come into the office before noon. Once there, he spent an hour or so scanning documents, interdepartmental memos and the like, writing e-mail responses when necessary. His phone was answered by his assistant, who logged calls and brought him messages deemed urgent by her. In this, as in all things she did for Robbinet, she was exemplary. She had been trained by him and her instincts were unerring.

Best of all, she was utterly discreet. This meant that Robbinet could tell her where he was lunching each day with his mistress—be it a quiet bistro or the mistress's apartment in the fourth arrondissement. This was crucial, since Robbinet took long lunches, even by French standards. He rarely returned to the office before four, but he was often at his desk until well past midnight, in signals with his counterparts in America. Robbinet's official title might be Minister of Culture, but in fact he was a spy at such a high level that he reported directly to the French president.

On this particular evening, however, he was out to dinner, the afternoon having proved so tiresomely hectic he'd had to postpone his daily tryst until late in the evening. There was a flap that concerned him greatly. A worldwide sanction had been routed to him by his American friends, and as he read it, his blood had run cold, for the target for termination was Jason Bourne.

Some years ago Robbinet had met Bourne at, of all places, a spa. Robbinet had booked a weekend at the spa just outside Paris so that he could be with his then-mistress, a tiny thing with enormous appetites. She had been a ballet dancer; Robbinet still recalled with great fondness the marvelous suppleness of her body. In any event, they had met in the steam room and they had gotten to talking. Eventually, in a most unsettling manner, he was to discover that Bourne had been there looking for a certain double agent. Having ferreted her out, he had killed her while Robbinet was getting a treatment—green mud, if memory served. Good thing, too, since the double agent was posing as Robbinet's therapist in order to assassinate him. Is there any place where one is more vulnerable than on a therapist's table? Robbinet wondered. What could he do after that, except take Bourne out to a lavish dinner. That night, over foie gras, veal kidneys in mustard-spiked *jus* and *tarte Tatin*, all washed down with three magnificent bottles of the finest ruby Bordeaux, having uncovered each other's secrets, they became fast friends.

It was through Bourne that Robbinet had met Alexander Conklin and had become Conklin's conduit to the operations of the Quai d'Orsay and Interpol.

In the end, Robbinet's trust in his assistant was Jason Bourne's good fortune, for it was over café and thoroughly decadent *millefeuille* at Chez Georges with Delphine that he received the call from her. He loved the restaurant for both its food and its location. Because it was across the street from the Bourse—the French equivalent of the New York Stock Exchange— it was frequented by brokers and businessmen, people far more discreet than the gossiping politicians with whom Robbinet was, from time to time, obliged to rub elbows.

"There's someone on the line," his assistant said in his ear. Thankfully, she monitored his after-hours calls from home. "He says it's urgent he speak with you."

Robbinet smiled at Delphine. His mistress was an elegant, mature beauty whose looks were diametrically opposed to those of his wife of thirty years. They had been having a most delightful conversation about Aristide Maillot, whose voluptuous nudes graced the Tuilleries, and Jules Massenet, whose opera *Manon* they both thought overrated. Really, he could not understand the American male obsession with girls scarcely out of their teens. The thought of taking as a mistress someone his daughter's age seemed frightful to him, not to mention pointless. What on earth would there be to talk about over café and *millefeuille*? "Has he given you his name?" he said into the phone.

"Yes. Jason Bourne."

Robbinet's pulse started to pound. "Put him through," he said immediately. Then, because it was inexcusable to speak on the phone for any length of time in front of one's mistress, he excused himself, went outside into the fine mist of the Parisian evening and waited for the sound of his old friend's voice.

"My dear Jason. How long has it been?"

Bourne's spirits rose the moment he heard Jacques Robbinet's voice booming through his cell phone. At last the voice of someone inside who wasn't—he hoped!—trying to kill him. He was barreling down the Capital Beltway in another car he had stolen on his way to meet Deron.

"To tell you the truth, I don't know."

"It's been years, can you believe it?" Robbinet said. "But, really, I must tell you that I've kept track of you through Alex."

Bourne, who'd felt some initial trepidation, now began to relax. "Jacques, you've heard about Alex."

"Yes, *mon ami*. The American DCI has sent out a worldwide sanction on you. But I don't believe a word of it. You couldn't possibly have murdered Alex. Do you know who did?"

"I'm trying to find out. All I know for certain at the moment is that someone named Khan may be involved."

The silence at the other end of the line went on so long that Bourne was forced to say, "Jacques? Are you there?"

"Yes, *mon ami*. You startled me, that's all." Robbinet took a deep breath. "This Khan, he is known to us. He's a professional assassin of the first rank. We ourselves know that he's been responsible for over a dozen high-level hits worldwide."

"Whom does he target?"

"Mainly politicians—the president of Mali, for instance—but also from time to time prominent business leaders. As far as we've been able to determine, he's neither political nor an ideologue. He takes the commissions strictly for money. He believes in nothing but that."

"The most dangerous kind of assassin."

"Of that there can be no doubt, *mon ami*," Robbinet said. "Do you suspect him of murdering Alex?"

"It's possible," Bourne said. "I encountered him at Alex's estate just after

I found the bodies. It might have been he who called the police because they showed up while I was still in the house."

"A classic setup," Robbinet concurred.

Bourne was silent for a moment, his mind filled with Khan, who could have shot him dead on campus or, later, from his vantage point in the willow. The fact that he didn't told Bourne a great deal. This apparently wasn't a normal commission for Khan; his stalking was personal, a vendetta of some sort that must have had its origins in the jungles of Southeast Asia. The most logical assumption was the Bourne had killed Khan's father. Now the son was out for revenge. Why else would he be obsessed with Bourne's family? Why else would he ask about Bourne abandoning Jamie? This theory fit the circumstances perfectly.

"What else can you tell me about Khan?" Bourne said now.

"Very little," Robbinet replied, "other than his age, which is twenty-seven."

"He looks younger than that," Bourne mused. "Also, he's part Asian."

"Rumor is he's half-Cambodian, but you know how reliable rumors can be."

"And the other half?"

"Your guess is as good as mine. He's a loner, no known vices, residence unknown. He burst on the scene six years ago, killing the prime minister of Sierra Leone. Before that, it's as if he didn't exist."

Bourne checked his rear-view mirror. "So he made his first official kill when he was twenty-one."

"Some coming-out party, eh?" Robbinet said dryly. "Listen, Jason, about this man Khan, I can't overemphasize how dangerous he is. If he's involved in any way, you must use extreme caution."

"You sound frightened, Jacques."

"I am, *mon ami*. Where Khan is concerned, there's no shame in it. You should be, too. A healthy dose of fear makes one cautious, and believe me, now is a time for caution."

"I'll keep that in mind," Bourne said. He maneuvered through traffic, looking for the right exit. "Alex was working on something, and I think he was killed because of it. You don't know anything about what he was involved with, do you?"

"I saw Alex here in Paris perhaps six months ago. We had dinner. My impression was that he was terribly preoccupied. But you know Alex, al-

ways secretive as the tomb." Robbinet sighed. "His death is a terrible loss
for all of us."

Bourne turned off the Beltway at the Route 123 exit, drove to Tysons
Corner. "Does 'NX 20' mean anything to you?"

"That's all you have? NX 20?"

He drove to the Tysons Corner center parking terrace C. "More or less.
Look up a name: Dr. Felix Schiffer." He spelled it out. "He works for
DARPA."

"Ah, now you have given me something useful. Let me see what I can do."

Bourne gave him his cell phone number as he exited the car. "Listen,
Jacques, I'm on my way to Budapest but I'm just about out of cash."

"No problem," Robbinet said. "Shall we use our same arrangement?"

Bourne had no idea what that was. He had no choice but to agree.

"*Bon*. How much?"

He went up the escalator, past Aviary Court. "A hundred thousand
should do it. I'll be staying at the Danubius Grand Hotel under Alex's
name. Mark the packet 'Hold for Arrival.'"

"*Mais oui*, Jason. It will be done just as you wish. Is there any other assistance I can provide?"

"Not at the moment." Bourne saw Deron up ahead, standing outside a
store called Dry Ice. "Thanks for everything, Jacques."

"Remember caution, *mon ami*," Robbinet said before signing off. "With
Khan in the field, anything can happen."

Deron had spotted Bourne and began walking at a slower pace so Bourne
could catch up to him. He was a slight man with skin the color of cocoa, a
chiseled, high-cheekboned face and eyes that flashed his keen intelligence.
With his lightweight coat, smartly tailored suit and gleaming leather attaché case, he looked every inch the businessman. He smiled as they
walked side by side through the mall.

"It's good to see you, Jason."

"Too bad the circumstances are so dire."

Deron laughed. "Hell, when disaster strikes is the *only* time I see you!"

While they spoke, Bourne was gauging sight lines, assessing escape
routes, checking faces.

Deron unlocked his briefcase, handed Bourne a slim packet. "Passport and contacts."

"Thanks." Bourne put the packet away. "I'll get payment to you within the week."

"Whenever." Deron waved a long-fingered artist's hand. "Your credit is good with me." He handed Bourne another item. "Dire situations require extreme measures."

Bourne held the gun in his hand. "What is this made of? It's so light."

"Ceramic and plastic. Something I've been working on for a couple of months now," Deron said with no little pride. "Not useful for distance but spot-on at close range."

"Plus, it won't be picked up at the airport," Bourne said.

Deron nodded. "Ammo, as well." He handed Bourne a small cardboard box. "Plastic-tipped ceramic, makes up for the small caliber. Another plus, look here, see these vents on the barrel—they dissipate the noise of percussion. The firing makes almost no sound."

Bourne frowned. "Doesn't that cut down on the stopping power?"

Deron laughed. "Old school ballistics, m'man. Believe me, you take someone down with this, they stay down."

"Deron, you're a man of unusual talents."

"Hey, I gotta be me." The forger sighed deeply. "Copying the Old Masters has its charm, I suppose. You cannot believe how much I've learned studying their techniques. On the other hand, the world you opened up to me—a world no one else here in this entire mall but us knows exists—now that is what I call excitement." A wind had come up, a damp harbinger of change, and he raised the collar of his coat against it. "I admit I once harbored a secret desire to market some of my more unusual products to people like you." He shook his head. "But no more. What I do now on the side, I do for fun."

Bourne saw a man in a trench coat stop in front of a store window to light up a cigarette. He was still standing there, seemingly gazing at the shoes on display. The trouble was, they were women's shoes. Bourne gave a hand signal and they both turned to their left, walking away from the shoe store. In a moment Bourne used the available reflective surfaces to glance behind them. The man in the trench coat was nowhere to be seen.

Bourne hefted the gun, which seemed light as air. "How much?" he said.

Deron shrugged. "It's a prototype. Let's say this, you name the price based on its use to you. I trust you'll be fair."

When Ethan Hearn had first come to Budapest, it had taken him some time to get used to the fact that Hungarians were as literal as they were deliberate. Accordingly, the bar Underground was situated in Pest at 30 Teréz Körúta, in a cellar beneath a cinema. Being below a movie theater also adhered to the Hungarian idiosyncrasy, for Underground was an homage to the well-known Hungarian film by Emir Kusticura of the same name. As far as Hearn was concerned, the bar was postmodern in the ugliest sense of the word. Steel beams were visible across the ceiling, interspersed with a line of gigantic factory fans that blew the smoke-thickened air down around the drinking and dancing denizens. But what Hearn liked least about Underground was the music—a loud and cacophonous mixture of aggrieved garage rock and sweaty funk.

Oddly, László Molnar did not seem to mind. In fact, he appeared to want to stay out among the hip-swaying crowd, as if reluctant to return home. There was something brittle about his manner, Hearn thought, in his quick abrasive laugh, the way his eyes roamed the room, never alighting on anything or anyone for long, as if he carried a dark and corrosive secret close under his skin. Hearn's occupation caused him to run up against a great deal of money. He wondered, not for the first time, whether so much wealth could have a ruinous effect on the human psyche. Perhaps this was the reason he had never aspired to riches.

Molnar insisted on ordering for both of them, a nastily sweet cocktail called a Causeway Spray that involved whiskey, ginger ale, Triple Sec and lemon. They found a table in a corner where Hearn could barely see the small menu and continued their discussion of opera, which, given the venue, seemed absurd.

It was after his second drink that Hearn spotted Spalko, standing in the haze at the rear of the club. His boss caught his eye, and Hearn excused himself. Two men were loitering near Spalko. They did not look as if they belonged at Underground, but then, Hearn told himself, neither did he or

László Molnar. Spalko led him down a dim corridor lit with pin lights like stars. He opened a narrow door into what Hearn imagined was the manager's office. No one was inside.

"Good evening, Ethan." Spalko smiled as he closed the door behind them. "It appears you have lived up to your billing. Well done!"

"Thank you, sir."

"And now," Spalko said with great bonhomie, "it is time for me to take over."

Hearn could hear the bone-jarring thump of the electronic bass through the walls. "Don't you think I ought to stay around long enough to introduce you?"

"Not necessary, I assure you. Time for you to get some rest." He looked at his watch. "In fact, given the late hour, why don't you take tomorrow off."

Hearn bridled. "Sir, I couldn't—"

Spalko laughed. "You can, Ethan, and you will."

"But you told me in no uncertain terms—"

"Ethan, I have the power to make policy and I have the power to make exceptions to it. When your sleeper-sofa arrives, you can do what you want, but tomorrow you have off."

"Yes, sir." The young man ducked his head, grinning sheepishly. He hadn't had a day off in three years. A morning in bed with nothing to do but read the paper, spread orange marmalade on his toast, sounded like heaven to him. "Thank you. I am most grateful."

"Go on, then. By the time you're back in the office, I'll have read and made suggestions on your pitch letter." He guided Hearn out of the overheated office. When he saw the young man mount the steps to the front door, he nodded to the two men flanking him and they set off through the frenetic hubbub of the bar.

László Molnar had begun peering through the fog of smoke and colored lights for his new friend. When Hearn had gotten up, he had been engrossed in the gyrating backside of a young girl in a short skirt, but he'd finally noticed that Hearn had been gone longer than expected. Molnar was taken aback when instead of Hearn the two men sat down on either side of him.

"What is this?" he said, his voice cracking in fright. "What do you want?"

The men said nothing. The one on his right clamped him with a fearsome strength that made him wince. He was too much in shock to cry out, but even if he had had the presence of mind to do so, the incessant clangor of the club would have drowned him out. As it was, he sat petrified as the man on his left jabbed his thigh with a syringe. It was over so quickly, done so discreetly under the table that no one could possibly notice.

It took but thirty seconds for the drug Molnar had been injected with to take effect. His eyes rolled up in their sockets and his body went limp. The two men were prepared for this, and they held him up as they rose, maneuvering him to a standing position.

"Can't hold his liquor," one of the men said to a nearby patron. He laughed. "What can you do with people like that?" The patron shrugged and, grinning, returned to his dancing. No one else gave them a second look as they took László Molnar out of Underground.

Spalko was waiting for them in a long, sleek BMW. They bundled the unconscious Molnar into the trunk of the car, then scrambled into the front, one behind the wheel, the other in the front passenger's seat.

The night was bright and clear. A full moon rode low in the sky. It seemed to Spalko that all he need do was reach out a finger and he could flick it like a marble across the black velvet table of the sky. "How did it go?" he asked.

"Sweet as honey," the driver replied as he fired the ignition.

Bourne got out of Tysons Corner as quickly as he could. Though he had deemed it a secure place for his rendezvous with Deron, security for him was now a relative word. He drove to the Wal-Mart on New York Avenue. It was in the belly of the city, a busy enough area for him to feel that he would have some anonymity.

He pulled into the lot between 12th and 13th Streets across the avenue and parked. The sky had begun to fill up with clouds; it was ominously dark on the southern horizon. Inside, he picked out clothes, toiletry items, a battery charger for the cell phone, along with a number of other items. Then he searched for a backpack in which he could easily stow everything. Waiting on the checkout line, shuffling along with everyone else, he felt his anxiety mounting. He seemed to look at no one, but in reality he was keeping his eye out for any untoward attention directed his way.

Too many thoughts crowded his mind. He was a fugitive from the Agency with what amounted to a price on his head. He was being stalked by a strangely arresting young man of extraordinary talents who just happened to be one of the most accomplished international assassins in the world. He had lost his two best friends, one of whom appeared to be involved in what was clearly an exceedingly dangerous extracurricular activity.

Thus preoccupied, he missed the chief security guard walking behind him. Early this morning a government agent had briefed him on the fugitive, handing him the same photo he'd seen last night on TV, asking him to keep an eagle eye out for the perp. The agent had explained that his visit was part of the dragnet, him and other CIA agents going around to all the major stores, movie theaters and the like, making sure the security people knew that finding this Jason Bourne should be their number-one priority. The guard felt a combination of pride and fear as he turned right around, went into his office cubicle and dialed the number the agent had given him.

Moments after the guard hung up the phone, Bourne was in the men's room. Using the electric clipper he had bought, he shaved off almost all his hair. Then he changed clothes, pulling on jeans, a red-and-white checked cowboy shirt with pearl-tone buttons and a pair of Nike running shoes. At the mirror in front of the line of sinks, he pulled out the small pots he had purchased at the makeup counter. He applied the contents of these judiciously, deepening the skin tone of his face. Another product thickened his brows, making them more prominent. The contact lenses Deron had provided turned his gray eyes a dull brown. Occasionally, he was obliged to pause as someone entered or washed up, but mainly the men's room was deserted.

When he was finished, he stared at himself in the mirror. Not quite satisfied, he gave himself a mole, prominently displayed high up on one cheek. Now the transformation was complete. Donning his backpack, he went out, through the store, heading toward the glass-encased front entrance.

Martin Lindros was in Alexandria, picking up the pieces of the botched termination at Lincoln Fine Tailors when he had gotten the call from the chief security officer at the Wal-Mart on New York Avenue. This morning he had decided that he and Detective Harry Harris would split up, canvassing the area with their respective squads. Lindros knew that Harris was a couple of miles closer than he was because the state policeman had checked in not ten minutes ago. He was in a diabolical quandary. He knew he was going to catch six kinds of hell from the DCI because of the Fine fiasco. If the Old Man found out that he had allowed a state police detective to arrive at Jason Bourne's last-known location before him, he'd never hear the end of it. It was a bad situation, he thought as he gunned his car. But the overriding priority was to get Bourne. All at once he made his decision. *To hell with interdepartmental secrets and jealousies*, he thought. He toggled his phone on, got Harris on the line, gave him the Wal-Mart address.

"Harry, listen carefully, you are to make a silent approach. Your job is to secure the area. You are to make sure Webb does not escape, nothing more. Under no circumstances are you to show yourself or try to apprehend him. Is that clear? I'm only minutes behind you."

I'm not as stupid as I look, Harry Harris thought as he coordinated the three patrol cars he had under his command. *And I'm certainly not as stupid as Lindros thinks I am*. He'd had more than adequate experience with federal types and he had yet to like what he had seen. The feds had ingrained in them this superior attitude, as if the other police forces were clueless, had to be led around like children. This attitude was like a bone stuck in Harris' craw. Lindros interrupted him when he had tried to tell him of his own theories, so why should he bother to share them now? Lindros saw him as nothing more than a pack mule, someone so grateful to be chosen to work with the CIA that he would follow orders unfailingly and unquestioningly. It was clear to Harris now that he was totally out of the loop. Lindros had deliberately failed to inform him of the Alexandria sighting. Harris had only learned about it by accident. As he turned into the Wal-Mart parking lot, he decided to take full control of the situation while he still had the chance. His mind made up, he grabbed his two-way radio, began barking orders to his men.

Bourne was near the entrance to the Wal-Mart when three Virginia State Police cars came barreling down New York Avenue, sirens blaring. He shrank back into shadows. There could be no doubt, they were heading directly for the Wal-Mart. He'd been made, but how? No time to worry about that now. He had to work out an escape plan.

The patrol cars screeched to a halt, blocking traffic, causing immediate irate shouts from motorists. Bourne could think of only one reason why they were out of their jurisdiction. They had been recruited by the Agency. The D.C. Metro Police would be livid.

He pulled out Alex's cell phone, dialed the police emergency line.

"This is Detective Morran of the Virginia State Police," he said. "I want to speak to a district commander pronto."

"This is Third District Commander Burton Philips," a steely voice said in his ear.

"Listen, Philips, you boys were told in no uncertain terms to keep your noses out of our business. Now I find your cruisers showing up at the Wal-Mart on New York Avenue and I—"

"You're in the heart of the district, Morran. What the hell are you doing poaching on my jurisdiction?"

"That's my business," Bourne said in his nastiest voice. "Just get on the horn and pull your goddamned boys out of my hair."

"Morran, I don't know where you get your shit attitude, but it won't play with me. I swear I'll be there in three minutes to tear your balls off myself!"

By this time the street was swarming with cops. Instead of retreating back to the store, Bourne, keeping his left knee rigid, limped calmly out along with perhaps a dozen other shoppers. Half of the contingent of cops, led by a tall stoop-shouldered detective with a haggard face, quickly scanned the faces of the dozen, Bourne included, as they rushed inside the store. The remaining cops fanned out in the parking lot. Some were securing New York Avenue between 12th and 13th Streets, others were busy ensuring that newly arriving patrons remained in their cars; still others were on their walkie-talkies, coordinating traffic.

Instead of heading for his car, Bourne turned to his right, went around the corner toward the loading dock at the rear of the building where the deliveries came in. Up ahead, he could see three or four semis parked, in the process of being unloaded. Diagonally across the street was Franklin Park. He set off in that direction.

Someone shouted at him. He kept on walking as if he hadn't heard.

Sirens screamed and he glanced his watch. Commander Burton Philips was right on time. He was halfway down the side of the building when the shouts came again, more commanding. Then there was a welter of harsh voices, raised in heated expletive-laden argument.

He turned, saw the stoop-shouldered detective, his service revolver out. Behind the detective came running the tall, imposing figure of Commander Philips, silver hair shining, his heavy-jowled face in high color from exertion and rage. In the fashion of dignitaries the world over, he was flanked by a pair of heavyweights armed with scowls as big as their shoulders. They had their right hands on their sidearms, apparently ready to blast to smithereens anyone foolish enough to intervene in their commander's wishes.

"You in charge of these Virginia troopers?" Philips called.

"State police," the stoop-shouldered detective said. "And, yeah, I'm in charge." He frowned as he saw the D.C. Metro uniforms. "What in hell are you doing here? You'll muck up my operation."

"*Your* operation!" Commander Philips was apoplectic. "Get the hell out of my swamp, you fucking hick bastard!"

The detective's narrow face went white. "Who are you calling a fucking hick bastard?"

Bourne left them to it. The park was out now; having come under the detective's scrutiny, he needed a more immediate means of escape. Slipping to the end of the building, he went down the row of semis until he found one that had already been unloaded. He climbed into the cab. The key was in the ignition and he turned it over. With a basso profundo rumble, the truck started up.

"Hey, where ya think you're goin', dude?"

The driver yanked open the door. He was a huge man with a neck like a tree stump and arms to match. As he swung up, he grabbed a sawed-off shotgun from a hidden berth above his head. Bourne slammed a balled fist into the bridge of his nose. Blood flew, the driver's eyes went out of focus and he lost his grip on the shotgun.

"Sorry, dude," Bourne said as he delivered a blow designed to render even a man of the trucker's oxlike size unconscious. Hauling him into the passenger's seat by the back of his studded belt, Bourne slammed the door closed and put the semi in gear.

At that moment, he became aware of a new presence on the scene. A youngish man had come between the two law-enforcement antagonists, pushing them roughly apart. Bourne recognized him: Martin Lindros, the Agency's DDCI. So the Old Man had put Lindros in domestic charge of the sanction. That was bad news. Through Alex, Bourne knew that Lindros was exceptionally bright; he would not be so easy to outfox, as evidenced by the tightly designed net in Old Town.

All this was technically moot now because Lindros had spotted the semi moving out of the parking lot and was trying to wave it down.

"No one leaves the area!" he shouted.

Bourne ignored him, depressed the accelerator. He knew he couldn't afford to have a face to face with Lindros; with his field expertise the man might see through his disguise.

Lindros drew his gun. Bourne could see him running toward the galvanized steel gates through which Bourne would have to pass, waving and shouting as he went.

Up ahead, responding to his screamed orders, two Virginia state cops stationed there hastily shut the gates, while an Agency vehicle plowed its way past the blockade of New York Avenue, on an intercept course with the semi.

Bourne jammed his foot down on the gas pedal, and like a wounded behemoth, the semi lurched forward. At the last moment, the cops leaped out of the way as he barreled through the gates, ripping them off their hinges so that they spun high in the air, crashed down on either side of him. He downshifted, turning hard to the right, heading up the street at an ever-increasing speed.

Glancing in the driver's oversized side mirror, he could see the Agency car slowing down. The passenger's door popped open and Lindros leaped in, slamming the door shut after him. The car took off like a rocket, gaining on the semi with little difficulty. Bourne knew that he could not outrun the Agency car with this lumbering beast, but its size, a drawback as far as speed was concerned, could be an asset in other ways.

He allowed the car to tailgate him. Without warning, it accelerated faster, coming up on his side of the cab. He saw Martin Lindros, his lips compressed in a line of concentration, holding his gun in one hand, his arm locked, steadying it with the other. Unlike actors in action films, he knew how to fire a gun from a speeding vehicle.

Just as he was about to pull the trigger, Bourne swerved the semi to the left. The Agency vehicle slammed into its side; Lindros put his gun up as the driver fought to keep the car away from the line of parked cars on the other side.

The moment the driver was able to swerve back into the street, Lindros began firing at the semi's cab. His angle was not good and he was being jolted incessantly, but the fusillade was enough to make Bourne turn the cab to the right. One bullet had smashed his side window and two others had penetrated the backseat, lodging in the trucker's side.

"Goddammit, Lindros," Bourne said. Dire as his circumstances were, he did not want this innocent man's blood on his hands. He was already heading west; George Washington University Hospital was on 23rd Street, not that far away. He made a right, then a left onto K Street, thundering along, sounding his air horn as he went through traffic lights. A motorist on 18th, possibly half-asleep at the wheel, missed the warning, slammed head-on into the right rear of the semi. Bourne slewed dangerously, fought the truck back to center, kept going. Lindros' car was still behind him, stuck there because K Street, a divided thoroughfare with a planted median, was too narrow for the driver to creep up his side.

By the time he crossed 20th Street, he could see the underpass that would take him beneath Washington Circle. The hospital was a block away from there. Glancing behind him, he saw that the Agency car was no longer behind him. He had been planning to take 22nd Street down to the hospital, but just as he was about the make the left, he saw the Agency car come speeding toward him on 22nd. Lindros leaned out the window and began to fire in his methodical manner.

Bourne tramped on the gas and the truck leaped forward. He was now committed to going through the underpass, coming around to the hospital on the far side. But as he approached the underpass, he realized something was wrong. The tunnel beneath Washington Circle was completely dark; no daylight at all showed at the far end. That could mean only one thing: a roadblock had been set up, a fortress of vehicles set across both lanes of K Street.

He entered the underpass at speed, downshifting, stamping down hard on the air brakes only when he was engulfed in darkness. At the same time, he kept the heel of his hand on the air horn. The screaming noise ricocheted off the stone and concrete until it became deafening, concealing the shriek of the tires as Bourne turned the wheel hard to the left, rolling the cab of the truck over the divider so that the vehicle was turned at right angles to the road. He was out of the cab in an instant, sprinting the north wall behind the protection of the last car to come barreling through in the other direction. It had stopped for a moment as the driver rubbernecked the accident, then as more police arrived it had taken off. The semi was between him and his pursuers, stretched from wall to wall across both lanes of K Street. He scrabbled around for the steel maintenance ladder bolted to the tunnel wall, leaped up it and began to climb just as floodlights were switched on. He turned his head away, closed his eyes and kept climbing.

A few moments later he saw the lights illuminating the truck and the roadbed beneath it. Bourne, almost to the curved top of the underpass, could make out Martin Lindros. He spoke into a walkie-talkie, and floodlights came on from the opposite direction. They had the semi in a pincer grip. Agents were running toward the truck from both ends of K Street, guns at the ready.

"Sir, there's someone in the truck's cab." The agent moved closer. "He's been shot; he's bleeding pretty bad."

Lindros was running, his face bursting into the floodlit field, lined with tension. "Is it Bourne?"

High above them, Bourne had gained the maintenance hatch. He slid back the bolt, opened it, found himself amidst the decorative trees that lined Washington Circle. All around him, traffic raced, a relentless procession of blurred motion that never ceased. In the tunnel below him, the wounded trucker was being taken to the nearby hospital. Now it was time for Bourne to save himself.

CHAPTER NINE

Khan had accumulated too much respect for David Webb's skill for vanishing to have wasted time trying to find him in the swirling mass of people in Old Town. Instead, he had concentrated on the Agency men, shadowing them back to Lincoln Fine Tailors, where they met with Martin Lindros for the sorry debriefing following the botched termination. He observed them talking to the tailor. In accordance with standard intimidation practices, they had taken him out of his own environment—in this case, his shop—stuffing him into the backseat of one of their cars, where he had been detained without explanation, squeezed between two stone-faced agents. From what he had gathered from the conversation he overheard between Lindros and the agents, they had gotten nothing of substance from the tailor. He claimed the agents had arrived at his shop with such speed that Webb had had no time to tell him why he had come. As a consequence, the agents recommended cutting him loose. Lindros had agreed, but after the tailor had returned to his shop, Lindros had posted two new agents in an unmarked car across the street just in case Webb tried to contact him a second time.

Now, twenty minutes after Lindros had left them, the agents were bored. They'd eaten their donuts and drunk their Cokes and were sitting in their car grumbling about being stuck here on surveillance duty when their brethren were off running down the notorious agent, David Webb.

"Not David Webb," the heavier of the two agents said. "The DCI has decreed that we call him by his operational name, Jason Bourne."

Khan, who was still close enough to hear every word, went rigid. He had, of course, heard of Jason Bourne. For many years, Bourne had had the reputation of being the most accomplished international killer-for-hire on the planet. Khan, knowing his field the way he did, had discounted half the stories as fabrications, the other half as exaggeration. It was simply not possible for one man to have had the daring, the expertise, the sheer animal cunning attributed to Jason Bourne. In fact, a part of him disbelieved in Bourne's existence altogether.

And yet, here were these CIA agents speaking about David Webb as Jason Bourne! Khan felt as if his brain was about to explode. He was shaken to his very foundation. David Webb wasn't simply a college professor of linguistics as Spalko's dossier had claimed, he was one of the field's great assassins. He was the man who Khan had been playing cat-and-mouse with since yesterday. So many things came together for him, not the least of which was how Bourne had made him in the park. Changing his face and hair and even his gait had always been enough to fool people in the past. But now he was dealing with Jason Bourne, an agent whose skills and expertise at, among other things, disguise were legendary and quite possibly the equal of his own. Bourne wasn't going to be gulled by the normal tricks of the trade, clever though they might be. Khan understood that he was going to have to raise the level of his game if he was going to win.

Fleetingly, he wondered if Webb's real identity was another fact Stepan Spalko had known when he had handed Khan the expurgated file. Considering it further, Khan believed that he had to have known. It was the only explanation for why Spalko had arranged to pin the murders of Conklin and Panov on Bourne. It was a classic disinformation technique. As long as the Agency believed that Bourne was responsible, they had no reason to look elsewhere for the real murderer—and surely they would have no chance to uncover the truth about why the two men were killed. Spalko was clearly trying to use Khan as a pawn in some larger game, the way he was using Bourne. Khan had to find out what Spalko was up to—he would not be anyone's pawn.

To unearth the truth behind the murders, Khan knew he had to get to the tailor. Never mind what he had told the Agency. Having followed Webb—it was still difficult for Khan to think of him as Jason Bourne—he knew the tailor Fine had had plenty of time to cough up what information he possessed. Once during his observation of the scene, the tailor Fine had turned his head, staring out the car window, and Khan had taken the opportunity to look into his eyes. He knew him, then, for a proud and obstinate man. Khan's Buddhist nature caused him to look upon pride as an undesirable trait, but in this situation he could see that it had served Fine well because the harder the Agency pushed him, the deeper he had dug in his heels. The Agency would get nothing out of him, but Khan knew how to neutralize pride as well as obstinacy.

Taking off his suede jacket, he ripped part of the lining enough so that the agents on stake-out would see him as nothing more than another Lincoln Fine Tailors customer.

Crossing the street, he entered the shop, the musical bell tinkling behind him. One of the Latina women looked up from reading the newspaper comics pages, her lunch, a Tupperware container of beans and rice, half-eaten in front of her. She came over, asked if she could help him. She was voluptuously built, with a firm, wide brow and large chocolate eyes. He told her that as the ripped jacket was a favorite of his, he'd come to see Mr. Fine himself. The woman nodded. She disappeared into the back and, a moment later, came out and sat down at her position without saying another word to Khan.

Several minutes passed before Leonard Fine appeared. He looked much the worse for his long and thoroughly unpleasant morning. Truth to tell, such close and intimate proximity to the Agency as he had endured seemed to have drained him of vitality.

"How can I help you, sir? Maria tells me you have a jacket in need of restoration."

Khan spread the suede jacket out on the counter inside out.

Fine touched it with the same delicacy with which a doctor palpates an ill patient. "Oh, it's just the lining. Lucky for you. Suede is almost impossible to repair."

"Never mind that," Khan said in a low whisper. "I am here on orders from Jason Bourne. I'm his representative."

Fine did an admirable job of keeping his face closed. "I've no idea what you're talking about."

"He thanks you for your part in his successful escape from the Agency," Khan went on as if Fine hadn't spoken. "And he wants you to know that even now two agents are spying on you."

Fine winced slightly. "I expected as much. Where are they?" His knobby fingers were kneading the jacket anxiously.

"Just across the street," Khan said. "In the white Ford Taurus."

Fine was canny enough not to look. "Maria," he said just loud enough for the Latina to hear, "is there a white Ford Taurus parked across the street?"

Maria turned her head. "Yes, Mr. Fine."

"Can you see if anyone's in it?"

"Two men," Maria said. "Tall, crew-cut. Very Dick Tracy, like the ones who were in here earlier."

Fine swore under his breath. His eyes rose to meet Khan's. "Tell, Mr. Bourne . . . tell him that Leonard Fine says, 'May God go with him.'"

Khan's expression was impassive. He found thoroughly distasteful the American habit of invoking God in almost any instance one cared to name. "I need some information."

"Of course." Fine nodded gratefully. "Whatever you want."

Martin Lindros finally understood the meaning of the phrase 'So angry he could spit blood.' How was he ever going to face the Old Man, knowing that Jason Bourne had evaded him, not once but twice.

"What the hell d'you think you were doing disobeying my direct orders?" he screamed at the top of his lungs. Noises were echoing in the tunnel underneath Washington Circle as DOT personnel were trying to extricate the semi from the position in which Bourne had lodged it.

"Hey, listen, it was me who spotted the subject leaving the Wal-Mart."

"And subsequently let him get away!"

"That was you, Lindros. I had an irate district commander chewing up my ass!"

"And that's another thing!" Lindros yelled. "What the fuck was he doing there?"

"You tell me, wise guy, you're the one who fucked things up in Alexandria. If you'd bothered to clue me in, I could've helped you canvass Old Town. I know it like I know my own face. But no, you're the fed, you know better, you're the one running the show."

"Damn right, I am! I've already directed my people to call all personnel stationed at the airports, train terminals, bus stations, rental car agencies to be on the lookout for Bourne."

"Don't be absurd, even if you hadn't tied my hands behind my back, I lack the authority to make those kinds of calls. But I do have my men scouring the area and let's not forget that it was my detailed last best description of Bourne you disseminated to all the transportation egress points."

Even though Harris was right, Lindros continued to fume. "I demand to know why the hell you dragged the D.C. Metro Police into it? If you needed more backup, you should've come to me."

"Why the fuck should I come to you, Lindros? Can you give me a reason? Are you my asshole buddy or something? Are we collaborating, anything along that line? Fuck no." Harris had a disgusted look on his lugubrious face. "And for the record, I didn't send for the D.C. I told you, he was on my ass from the second he showed up, frothing at the mouth about my poaching on his jurisdiction."

Lindros barely heard him. The ambulance, its light flashing, its siren screaming, was taking off, ferrying the truck driver he had inadvertently shot to George Washington University Hospital. It had taken them nearly forty-five minutes to secure the area, mark it off as a crime scene and extricate him from the cab. Would he live or die? Lindros didn't want to think about that now. It would be easy to say that his injury was Bourne's fault— he knew the Old Man would see it that way. But the DCI had a crust formed of two parts pragmatism and one part bitterness that Lindros knew he could never match, and thank God for that. Whatever the trucker's fate now, he knew he was responsible, and this knowledge served as the perfect fuel for his antagonism. He may not have had the DCI's cynical crust, but he was not in the market of beating himself up for actions long past remedy. Instead, he spewed the poisonous feeling outward.

"Forty-five minutes!" Harris grunted as an ambulance cut its way through the backed-up traffic. "Christ, that poor bastard could've died ten times over!"

"Civil servants!"

"You're a civil servant, Harry, if memory serves," Lindros said nastily.

"And you aren't?"

The venom rose up in Lindros. "Listen, you over-the-hill fuck, I am made of different cloth than the rest of you. My training—"

"All your training didn't help you to catch Bourne, Lindros! You had two chances and you blew them both!"

"And what did *you* do to help?"

Khan watched Lindros and Harris going at it. In his DOT overalls, he looked like everyone else on the scene. No one questioned his comings or goings. He had been passing close by the rear of the semi, ostensibly examining the damage done by the car that had rammed into it when he had noticed in the shadows the iron ladder that rose along the side of the tunnel. He looked up, craning his neck. He wondered where it led. Had Bourne wondered the same thing, or had he already known? Now, glancing around to make sure no one was looking in his direction, he quickly climbed the ladder, out of the range of the police spotlights, where no one could see him. He found the hatch and was not surprised to discover the slide bolt newly opened. He pushed the hatch open, went up.

From the vantage point of Washington Circle, he turned slowly in a clockwise direction, scanning all things near and far. A gathering wind whipped about his face. The sky had darkened further, looking bruised by the hammerblows of thunder, muffled by distance, that rolled now and again through the canyons and wide European-style avenues of the city. To the west was Rock Creek Parkway, Whitehurst Freeway and Georgetown. To the north rose the modern towers of Hotel Row—the ANA, Grand, Park Hyatt, and Marriott, and Rock Creek beyond. To the west was K Street, running past McPherson Square and Franklin Park. To the south was Foggy Bottom, sprawling George Washington University, the massive monolith of the State Department. Farther out, where the Potomac River bent to the east, widening out to form the placid bywaters of the Tidal Basin, he saw a silver mote, a plane hanging almost motionless, shining like a mirror, caught high up above the thickening clouds by a last bolt of sunlight before it began its descent into Washington National Airport.

Khan's nostrils dilated as if he had caught a scent of his quarry. The airport was where Bourne was going. He was certain of it because, had he been in Bourne's shoes, that was where he would be right now.

The terrible portent of David Webb and Jason Bourne being one and the same man had been marinating in his mind ever since he had heard Lindros and his CIA brethren discussing it. The very idea that he and Bourne were in the same profession felt like an outrage to him, a violation of everything he had painstakingly built for himself. It had been he—and only he—who had drawn himself out of the mire of the jungles. That he had survived those hateful early years was a miracle in itself. But at least those early days had been his and his alone. Now to find himself sharing the stage he had committed himself to conquering with, of all people, David Webb seemed like a cruel jest as well as an intolerable injustice. It was a wrong that must be rectified, the sooner the better. Now he could not wait to confront Bourne, to tell him the truth, to see in his eyes how that revelation would destroy him from the inside out as Khan bled him of life.

CHAPTER TEN

Bourne stood in the glass and chrome shadows of the International Departures building. Washington National Airport was a madhouse, thronged with businessmen with laptops and carry-ons, families with multiple suitcases; children with Mickey Mouse, Power Ranger and Teddy bear backpacks; the elderly in wheelchairs; a group of proselytizing Mormons on their way to the Third World; lovers hand in hand, tickets to paradise. But despite the crowds, there was an emptiness about airports. As a result, Bourne saw nothing but empty stares, the inward look that was the human being's instinctual defense against fearful boredom.

It was an irony not lost on him that in airports, where waiting was an institution, time seemed to stand still. Not for him. Now, every minute counted, bringing him closer to termination by the very people he used to work for.

In the fifteen minutes he had been here he had seen a dozen suspicious plainclothesmen. Some were prowling the departure lounges, smoking, drinking from big paper cups, as if they could blend in with the civilians. But most were at or near the airline check-in counters, eyeballing the passengers as they queued up to have their bags checked and receive their boarding passes. Bourne saw almost immediately that it was going to be impossible for him to get on a commercial flight. What other choices were there for him? He had to get to Budapest as quickly as possible.

He was wearing tan slacks, a cheap rain shell over a black turtleneck pullover, a pair of Sperry Top-Sider shoes in lieu of the sneakers, which he had dropped in the trash bin, along with a bundle of the other clothes he had on when he walked out of Wal-Mart. Since he had been spotted there, it was vital that he change his profile as quickly as possible. But now that he had assessed the situation at the terminal, he was not at all happy with what he had chosen.

Avoiding the roaming agents, he went outside into a night fizzing with a

fine rain, picked up a shuttle bus that would take him to the Cargo Air Terminal. He sat right behind the driver, striking up a conversation with him.
His name was Ralph. Bourne had introduced himself as Joe. They shook
hands briefly as the shuttle braked at a pedestrian crosswalk.

"Hey, I'm supposed to meet my cousin at OnTime Cargo," Bourne said,
"but stupid me, I lost the directions he gave me."

"What's he do?" Ralph said, pulling ahead into the fast lane.

"He's a pilot." Bourne shifted closer. "He was desperate to fly with
American or Delta, but you know how it goes."

Ralph nodded his head in sympathy. "The rich get richer and the poor
get shafted." He had a button nose, a mop of unruly hair and dark circles
under his eyes. "Tell me about it."

"Anyway, can you direct me?"

"I'll do better than that," Ralph said with a glance at Bourne in his long
mirror. "My shift's over when I get to the cargo terminal. I'll take you there
myself."

Khan stood in the rain, the crystal lights of the airport all around him, and
thought matters through. Bourne would have smelled the Agency suits
even before he spotted them. Khan had counted more than fifty, which
meant perhaps three times that many sniffing their way throughout other
sections of the airport. Bourne would know that he could never get
through them onto an overseas flight no matter how he changed his clothing. They had made him at the Wal-Mart, they knew what he looked like
now, he'd heard as much in the underpass.

He could feel Bourne close by. Having sat next to him on the park
bench, having sensed the weight of him, the spread of his bones, the
stretch of his muscles, the play of light over the features of his face. He
knew he was here. It was Bourne's face that he had clandestinely studied in
their brief moments together. He had been keenly aware of needing to
memorize every contour, how each expression changed those contours.
What had Khan been searching for in Bourne's expression when he had
noted the other's intense interest? Confirmation? Validation? Even he did
not know. He only knew that the image of Bourne's face had become part
of his consciousness. For better or for worse, Bourne had a hold on him.

They were bound together on the wheel of their own desires until the on-set of death.

Khan looked around him once more. Bourne needed to get out of the city and possibly country. But the Agency would be adding on personnel, expanding its search even as it sought to tighten its noose. If it was Khan, he'd want to get out of the country as quickly as possible, so he headed to-ward the International Arrivals building. Inside he stood in front of a huge color-coded map of the airport, traced out the most efficient route to the cargo terminal. With the commercial flights already under such tight secu-rity, if Bourne was going to leave from this airport, his best chance would be aboard a cargo plane. Time was a critical factor now for Bourne. It wouldn't be long before the Agency realized that Bourne wasn't going to try to board a regular flight and began to monitor the cargo shippers.

Khan went back out into the rain. Once he determined which flights were departing in the next hour or so, all that remained would be to keep an eye out for Bourne and, should he have guessed correctly, deal with him. He had no more illusions about the difficulty of his task. Much to his shock and chagrin, Bourne had proved to be a clever, determined and resourceful antagonist. He had hurt Khan, had trapped him, slipped away from his grasp more than once. Khan knew that if he was to succeed this time, he would need a way to surprise Bourne, knowing that Bourne would be on the lookout for him. In his mind, the jungle called to him, repeating its message of death and destruction. The end of his long journey was in sight. He would outwit Jason Bourne this one last time.

Bourne was the only passenger by the time they reached their destination. It was raining harder, an early dusk settling in on the afternoon. The sky was indistinct, a blank slate on which any future could now be written.

"OnTime's at Cargo Five, along with FedEx, Lufthansa and Customs." Ralph pulled the bus over and turned off the ignition. They got out, half-ran across the tarmac to one in a line of huge flat-roofed ugly buildings. "Right in here."

They went inside and Ralph shook rain off himself. He was a pear-shaped man, with oddly delicate hands and feet. He pointed now to their left. "You see where U.S. Customs is? Down the building, two stations past is where you'll find your cousin."

"Thanks a lot," Bourne said.

Ralph grinned and shrugged. "Don't mention it, Joe." He held out his hand. "Glad to help."

As the driver ambled away, hands in his pockets, Bourne headed down toward OnTime's offices. But he had no intention of going there—not yet, anyway. He turned, following Ralph to a door that had affixed to it a sign reading NO ADMITTANCE—AUTHORIZED PERSONNEL ONLY. He took out a credit card as he watched Ralph feed his laminated ID card into a metal slot. The door swung open and, as Ralph disappeared inside, Bourne silently darted forward, inserted the credit card. The door shut, just as it should have, but Bourne's maneuver had prevented the lock from engaging. He counted silently to thirty in order to make certain that Ralph was no longer near the door. Then he opened it, pocketing his credit card as he went through.

He found himself in the maintenance locker room. The walls were of white tile; a rubber webbing had been laid on top of the concrete floor to keep the men's bare feet dry as they padded to and from the showers. Eight ranks of standard metal lockers were arrayed in front of him, most with simple combination locks on them. Off to his right was an opening to the showers and sinks. In a smaller space just beyond were the urinals and toilets.

Bourne cautiously peered around the corner, saw Ralph padding toward one of the showers. Closer to hand, another maintenance man was lathering up, his back to both Bourne and Ralph. Bourne looked around, immediately saw Ralph's locker. The door was slightly ajar, the combination lock hanging unhinged on the door handle itself. Of course. In a secure place like this what was there to fear in leaving your locker open for the few minutes it took to shower? Bourne opened the door wider, saw Ralph's ID tag lying atop an undershirt on a metal shelf. He took it. Nearby was the other maintenance man's locker, similarly open. He exchanged the locks, securing Ralph's locker. That should keep the driver from discovering that his ID tag had been stolen for as long as Bourne hoped he'd need.

He grabbed a pair of maintenance overalls from the open cart meant for laundering, making sure the size was more or less right, then quickly changed. Then, with Ralph's ID tag around his neck, he went out, walked quickly down to U.S. Customs, where he obtained the current flight schedule. There was nothing to Budapest, but Rush Service Flight 113 to Paris was leaving from Cargo Four in eighteen minutes. Nothing else was scheduled within the next ninety minutes, but Paris was fine; it was a major hub for intra-European travel. Once there, he would have no trouble getting to Budapest.

Bourne hurried back out to the slick tarmac. The rain was now coming down in sheets, but there was no lightning, and the thunder he had heard earlier was nowhere in evidence. That was good, as he had no desire to see Flight 113 delayed for any reason. He picked up his pace, hurrying to the next building, home to Cargo Three and Four.

He was drenched by the time he arrived inside the terminal. He looked to left and right, hurried toward the Rush Service area. There were few people about, which was not good. It was always easier to blend in with a crowd than with a sparse few. He found the door marked for authorized personnel, slid his ID card into the slot. He heard the gratifying click of the lock opening; he pushed on the door and went through. As he wended his way through the cinder-block corridors, the rooms stacked high with packing crates, the smells of resinous wood, sawdust and cardboard became overpowering. There was about the place an air of impermanence, a sense of constant motion, of lives ruled by schedules and weather, the anxiety of mechanical and human error. There was nothing to sit on, no place to rest.

He kept his eyes straight ahead, walking with the air of authority that no one would question. He soon came to another door, this one steel-clad. Through its small window, he could see planes arrayed on the tarmac, loading and unloading. It did not take him long to spot the Rush Service jet, its cargo bay door open. A fuel line ran from the plane to a tanker truck. A man in a rain slicker, its hood up over his head, was monitoring the gas flow. The pilot and co-pilot were in the cockpit going through their pre-flight instrument check.

Just as he was about to slide Ralph's ID card into the slot, Alex's cell phone rang. It was Robbinet.

"Jacques, it looks as if I'm about to head your way. Can you meet me at the airport in, say, seven hours or so?"

"*Mais oui, mon ami.* Call me when you land." He gave Bourne his cell phone number. "I am delighted that I will be seeing you so soon."

Bourne knew what Robbinet was saying. He was pleased that Bourne was able to slip through from the Agency's noose. *Not yet*, Bourne thought. *Not quite yet.* But his escape was only moments away. In the meantime . . .

"Jacques, what have you discovered? Have you found out what NX 20 is?"

"I am afraid not. No record of any such project exists."

Bourne's heart sank. "What about Dr. Schiffer?"

"Ah, there I had a bit more luck," Robbinet said. "A Dr. Felix Schiffer works for DARPA—or at least he did."

A cold hand had wrapped around Bourne's gut. "What do you mean?"

Bourne could hear a rustling of paper, could imagine his friend reading through the intel he had managed to procure from his sources in Washington. "Dr. Schiffer is no longer on DARPA's 'active' roster. He left there thirteen months ago."

"What happened to him?"

"I've no idea."

"He simply dropped out of sight?" Bourne asked incredulously.

"In this day and age, as unlikely as it seems, that's just what happened."

Bourne closed his eyes for an instant. "No, no. He's around somewhere—he has to be."

"Then what—?"

"He's been 'disappeared'—by professionals."

With Felix Schiffer vanished, it was more imperative than ever that he get to Budapest with all due haste. His only lead was the hotel key from the Danubius Grand Hotel. He glanced at his watch. He was cutting it close. He had to go. Now. "Jacques, thanks for sticking your neck out."

"I'm sorry I couldn't be of more help." Robbinet hesitated. "Jason . . ."

"Yes?"

"*Bon chance.*"

Bourne pocketed the cell phone, opened the stainless-steel-clad door, headed out into the heavy weather. The sky was low and dark, sheets of rain slanting down, a shimmering silver curtain in the airport's brilliant lights, running in glittering streamers over the depressions in the tarmac. He walked slightly bent over into the wind, walking purposefully, as he had before, a man who knew his job, wanted to get it done quickly and efficiently. Rounding the nose of the jet, he could see the cargo bay door ahead of him. The man fueling the jet had finished and had removed the nozzle from the tank.

Out of the corner of his eye, Bourne saw movement off to his left. One of Cargo Four's doors had burst open and several airport security guards spilled out, weapons drawn. Ralph must have gotten his locker open; Bourne had run out of time. He kept moving at the same deliberate pace. He was almost at the cargo bay door when the fueler said, "Hey, buddy, got the time? My watch stopped."

Bourne turned. At the same moment he recognized the Asian features of the face inside the hood; Khan shot a burst of aviation fuel into his face. Bourne's hands came up and he choked, completely blinded.

Khan rushed him, pushing him back against the slick metal skin of the fuselage. He delivered two vicious blows, one to Bourne's solar plexus, one to the side of his head. As Bourne's knees collapsed, Khan shoved him into the cargo hold.

Turning, Khan saw a cargo handler heading toward him. He lifted an arm. "It's okay, I'll lock up," he said. Luck was with him, as the rain made it difficult for anyone to see his face or his uniform. The cargo handler, grateful to get out of the rain and wind, returned a salute of thanks. Khan slammed the cargo door shut, locked it. Then he sprinted to the fuel truck, drove it far enough away from the plane so that it would not look suspicious.

The security police that Bourne had spotted before were making their way down the row of jets. They signaled to the pilot. Khan put the jet between himself and the oncoming police. He reached up, unlocked the cargo bay door, swung himself inside. Bourne was on his hands and knees, his head hanging down. Khan, surprised at his recuperative powers, kicked him hard in the ribs. With a grunt, Bourne fell over on his side, his arms wrapped around his waist.

Khan took out a length of cord. He pressed Bourne face-first onto the cargo bay deck, took his arms behind his back and wrapped the wire around his crossed wrists. Over the sound of the rain, he could hear the security police shouting to the pilot and co-pilot for their IDs. Leaving Bourne incapacitated, Khan walked over and quietly pulled the bay door closed.

For a few minutes Khan sat cross-legged in the darkness of the cargo bay. The pinging of the rain on the skin of the fuselage set up an arrhythmic percussion that reminded him of the drums in the jungle. He had been quite ill when he had heard those drums. To his fever-stricken mind, they had sounded like the roaring of aircraft engines, the frantic beating of the air about the outflow vents just before it begins a steep dive. The sound had frightened him because of the memories it brought up, memories he had fought long and hard to keep at the very bottom of his consciousness. Because of the fever, all his senses were heightened to an almost painful pitch. He was aware that the jungle had come alive, that shapes were coming warily toward him in an ominous wedgelike formation. His one conscious action was to bury the small carved stone Buddha he wore around his neck under leaves in a shallow hurriedly dug grave beneath where he lay. He could hear voices, and after a while he became aware that the shapes were asking him questions. He squinted through the fever-sweat to make them out in the emerald twilight, but one of them covered his eyes with a blindfold. Not that it was needed. When they lifted him off the bed of leaves and detritus he had made for himself, he passed out. Waking two days later, he found himself inside a Khmer Rouge encampment. As soon as he was deemed fit by a cadaverous man with sunken cheeks and one watery eye, the interrogation began.

They had thrown him into a pit with writhing creatures which to this day he could not identify. He was cast into a darkness more complete, more profound than any he had ever known before. And it was this darkness, enveloping, constricting, pressing against his temples like a weight growing in baleful proportion to the hours that passed, that terrified him the most.

A darkness not unlike this one, in the belly of Rush Service Flight 113.

. . . *Then Jonah prayed unto the Lord his God out of the fish's belly. And said, I cried by reason of mine affliction unto the Lord, and he heard me; out of the belly of hell cried I, and thou heardest my voice. For thou hadst cast me into the deep, in the midst of the seas; and the floods compassed me about: all thy billows and thy waves passed over me . . .*

He still remembered that section from the frayed and stained copy of the Bible the missionary had made him memorize. Horrible! Horrible! Because Khan, in the midst of the hostile and murderous Khmer Rouge, had been cast quite literally into the belly of hell, and he had prayed—or what passed for prayer in his still unformed mind—for deliverance. This was before the Bible had been pushed on him, before he had understood the teachings of the Buddha, for he had descended into formless chaos at a very early age. The Lord had heard Jonah cry out from the belly of the whale, but no one had heard Khan. He had been utterly alone in the darkness and then, when they felt that they had softened him up sufficiently, they pulled him out and slowly, expertly, with a cold passion it would take him years to acquire began to bleed him.

Khan snapped on the flashlight he carried with him, sat immobile, staring at Bourne. Unfolding his legs, he kicked out violently, the sole of his shoe catching Bourne on the shoulder so that he rolled over on his side facing Khan. Bourne groaned, and his eyes fluttered open. He gasped, took another shuddering breath, inhaling the fumes from the aviation fuel, and convulsed, vomiting in the space between where he lay in burning pain and misery and where Khan sat serene as Buddha himself.

"I've been down to the bottoms of the mountains; the earth with her bars was about me forever; yet have I brought up my life from the darkness," Khan said, paraphrasing Jonah. He continued to stare fixedly into Bourne's reddened swollen face. "You look like shit."

Bourne struggled to rise onto one elbow. Khan calmly kicked it out from under him. Again Bourne tried to sit up and again Khan thwarted him. The third time, however, Khan did not make a move and Bourne sat up, facing him.

The faint and maddeningly enigmatic smile played across Khan's lips, but there was a sudden spark of flames in his eyes.

"Hello, Father," he said. "It's been such a long time I was beginning to think we'd never have this moment."

Bourne shook his head slightly. "What the hell are you talking about?"

"I'm your son."

"My son is ten years old."

Khan's eyes were glittery. "Not that one. I'm the one you left behind in Phnom Penh."

All at once, Bourne felt violated. A red rage rose up inside him. "How dare you? I don't know who you are, but my son Joshua is dead." The effort cost him, for he had inhaled more of the fumes, and he bent over suddenly, retching again, but there was nothing left inside him to vomit up.

"I'm not dead." Khan's voice was almost tender as he leaned forward, pulled Bourne back up to face him. In so doing, the small carved stone

Buddha fell away from his hairless chest, swinging a little with his efforts to keep Bourne upright. "As you can see."

"No, Joshua *is* dead! I put the coffin in the ground myself, along with Dao and Alyssa! They were wrapped in American flags."

"Lies, lies and more lies!" Khan held the carved stone Buddha in the palm of his hand, held it toward Bourne. "Look at this, and remember, Bourne."

Reality seemed to slip away from Bourne. He heard his rapid pulse thundering in his inner ears, a tidal wave that threatened to pick him up and carry him off. It couldn't be! It couldn't! "Where—where did you get that?"

"You know what this is, don't you?" The Buddha disappeared behind the curl of his fingers. "Have you finally recognized your long-lost son Joshua?"

"You're not Joshua!" Bourne was enraged now, his face dark, his lips pulled back from his teeth in an animal snarl. "Which Southeast Asia diplomat did you kill to get it?" He laughed grimly. "Yes, I know more about you than you think."

"Then you're sadly mistaken. This is mine, Bourne. Do you understand?" He opened his hand, revealed the Buddha again, the stone dark with the imprint of his sweat. "The Buddha is mine!"

"Liar!" Bourne leaped at him, his arms coming around from behind his back. He had flexed his muscles—the cords expanding as Khan had wound the wire around him—then using the slack had worked his way out of the bonds while Khan had been gloating.

Khan was caught out, unprepared for his headlong bull-rush. He tumbled backward, Bourne on top of him. The flashlight struck the deck, rolling back and forth, its potent beam flashing on them, then off, illuminating an expression here, a bulging muscle there. In this eerily striped and stippled darkness and light, so like the dense jungle they had left behind, they fought like beasts, breathing in each other's enmity, struggling for supremacy.

Bourne, his teeth gritted, struck Khan again and again in a maddened attack. Khan managed to gain a grip on Bourne's thigh, pressed in on the nerve bundle there. Bourne lurched, his temporarily paralyzed leg buckling beneath him. Khan struck him hard on the point of the chin, and Bourne staggered further, shaking his head. He grabbed hold of his switchblade just as Khan delivered another massive blow. Bourne dropped the knife and Khan picked it up, flipped open the blade.

He stood over Bourne now, pulled him up by the front of his shirt. A brief tremor passed through him, as a current sizzles through a wire when the switch is thrown. "I'm your son. Khan is a name I took, just as David Webb took the name Jason Bourne."

"No!" Bourne fairly shouted this over the rising noise and vibration of the engines. "My son died with the rest of my family in Phnom Penh!"

"I *am* Joshua Webb," Khan said. "You abandoned me. You left me to the jungle, to my death."

The point of the knife hovered over Bourne's throat. "How many times I almost died. I would have, I'm sure of it, if I didn't have your memory to hold on to."

"How dare you use his name! Joshua is dead!" Bourne's face was livid, his teeth bared in animal rage. His vision was clouded with blood-lust.

"Maybe he is." The knife-blade lay against Bourne's skin. A millimeter more and it would draw blood. "I'm Khan now. Joshua—the Joshua you knew—is dead. I've come back for revenge, to deliver your punishment for abandoning me. I could've killed you so many times in the last few days, but I stayed my hand because before I killed you I wanted you to know what you had done to me." Khan's lips opened and a bubble of spittle grew at the corner of his mouth. "Why did you abandon me? How could you have run away!"

The plane gave a terrific lurch as it began to taxi out onto the runway. The blade sprayed blood as it sliced into Bourne's skin, then it was lifted away as Khan lost his balance. Bourne took the advantage, drove his balled fist into Khan's side. Khan swept his foot back, hooking it behind Bourne's ankle, and Bourne went down. The plane slowed, turning onto the head of the runway.

"I didn't run away!" Bourne shouted. "Joshua was taken from me!"

Khan pounced on him, the knife flashing down. Bourne twisted and the blade drove past his right ear. He was aware of the ceramic gun secreted at his right hip, but try as he might he wouldn't be able to get to it without leaving himself open to a fatal attack. They struggled, their muscles bulging, their faces engorged with effort and rage. Their breath sawed from between half-open mouths, their eyes and minds searching for the most minute opening as they attacked and defended, counterattacked only to be rebuffed. They were well matched, if not in age, then in speed, strength, skill and cunning. It was as if they knew each other's minds, as if they could anticipate each other's moves a split second beforehand, thus neutralizing whatever advantage had been sought. They did not fight with dispassion and, therefore, they did not fight at peak level. All their emotion had been flushed out of the depths, lay stranded and squirming in the conscious mind, like an oil slick clouding water.

The plane lurched, the fuselage trembling as the plane began its race down the runway. Bourne slipped and Khan used his free hand as a cudgel to draw Bourne's attention away from the knife. Bourne countered, striking the inside of Khan's left wrist. But now the blade-point flashed in on him. He stepped back and to the side, inadvertently unlatching the bay door. The rising motion of the plane caused the unlocked door to swing open.

As the runway blurred by below, Bourne splayed himself out like a starfish to keep himself inside the plane, gripping the doorframe tightly with both hands. Grinning maniacally, Khan leaned in toward Bourne, the knife-blade describing a wicked shallow arc that would cut across the entire width of Bourne's abdomen.

Khan lunged just as the plane was about to lift off the runway. At the last possible instant, Bourne let go with his right hand. His body, driven out and back by gravity, swung so violently away that his shoulder was nearly dislocated. Where his body had been was now a gaping space through which Khan fell, tumbling to the tarmac below. Bourne had one final glimpse of him, nothing more than a gray ball against the black of the runway.

Then the plane was airborne and Bourne was swinging up, farther from the open doorway. He struggled; rain whipped against him like chain-mail. The wind threatened to take his breath away, but it scrubbed the last of the jet fuel from his face, the rain rinsing his stinging red-rimmed eyes, flushing the poison from his skin and tissue. The plane banked to the right and Khan's flashlight rolled across the cargo bay deck, tumbled out after him. Bourne knew that if he did not get himself inside within seconds, he would be lost. The terrible strain on his arm was far too intense for him to hold on much beyond that.

Swinging his leg around, he managed to hook the back of his left ankle into the doorway. Then, with a mighty effort, he heaved himself forward, the back of his knee clamped against the raised frame, giving himself both purchase and leverage enough to turn so that he was facing the fuselage. He got his right hand on the lip of the seal and in this fashion was able to work his way into the interior. His last act was to slam the door shut.

Bourne, bruised, bleeding and in a great deal of pain, collapsed into an exhausted heap. In the frightful, turbulent darkness of the shuddering interior, he saw again the small carved stone Buddha that he and his first wife had given Joshua for his fourth birthday. Dao had wanted the spirit of Buddha to be with their son from the earliest age. Joshua, who had died along with Dao and his little sister when the enemy plane had strafed the river they had been playing in.

Joshua was dead. Dao, Alyssa, Joshua—they were all dead, their bodies ripped asunder by the hail of bullets from the dive-bombing plane. His son could not be alive, he *could not*. To think otherwise would be to invite insanity. Then who was Khan really, and why was he playing this hideously cruel game?

Bourne had no answers. The plane dipped and rose, the pitch of the engines changing as it reached cruising altitude. It grew frigid, his breath clouding as it left his nose and mouth. He wrapped his arms around himself, rocking. It was not possible. It was not!

He gave an inarticulate animal cry, and all at once he was undone by pain and utter despair. His head sank, and he wept bitter tears of rage, disbelief and grief.

PART TWO

CHAPTER ELEVEN

In the full belly of Flight 113, Jason Bourne was asleep, but in his unconscious mind his life—a far-off life he had buried long ago—was once again unspooling. His dreams were filled to overflowing with images, feelings, sights and sounds he had spent the intervening years pushing down as far from his conscious thoughts as they would go.

What had happened that hot summer's day in Phnom Penh? No one knew. At least, no one who was still alive. This much was fact: While he sat bored and restless in his air-cooled office at the American Foreign Services complex, attending a meeting, his wife Dao had taken their two children swimming in the wide, muddy river just outside their house. From out of nowhere, an enemy plane had banked, dropping from the sky. It strafed the river where David Webb's family swam and splashed and played.

How many times had he envisioned the terrible sight? Had Dao seen the plane first? But it had come upon them so swiftly, swooping down in a silent glide. If so, she must have gathered their children to her, pushing them beneath the water, covering them with her own body in a vain attempt to save them even while their screams echoed in her ears, their blood flecked her face, even while she felt the pain of her own impending death. This, in any event, was what he believed, what he dreamed, what had driven him to the edge of madness. For the screams he imagined Dao had heard just before the end were the same screams he heard night after night, starting awake, his heart racing, his blood pounding. Those dreams had forced him to abandon his house, all that he had held dear, for the sight of each familiar object had been like a stab in his guts. He had fled Phnom Penh for Saigon, where Alexander Conklin had taken charge of him.

If only he could have left his nightmares behind in Phnom Penh. In the dripping jungles of Vietnam, they came back to him again and again, as if they were wounds he needed to inflict on himself. Because this truth, above all others, remained: He could not forgive himself for not being there, for not protecting his wife and children.

He cried out now in his tortured dreams thirty thousand feet over the stormy Atlantic. Of what use is a husband and a father, he asked himself as he had a thousand times before, if he failed to protect his family?

The DCI was woken out of a sound sleep at five in the morning by a priority call from the National Security Advisor, summoning him to her office in one hour. Just when did this bitch-woman sleep? he wondered as he put down the phone. He sat on the edge of his bed, facing away from Madeleine. *Nothing disturbed* her *sleep*, he thought sourly. Long ago she had taught herself to sleep through the phone ringing at all hours of the night and morning.

"Wake up!" he said, shaking Madeleine awake. "There's a flap on and I need coffee."

Without a note of complaint, she rose, slipped on her robe and slippers and went down the hall to the kitchen.

Rubbing his face, the DCI padded into the bathroom, closed the door. Sitting on the toilet, he called the DDCI. Why the hell should Lindros be sleeping when his superior was not? To his consternation, however, Martin Lindros was wide awake.

"I've been spending all night in the Four-Zero archives." Lindros was referring to the maximum-security files on CIA personnel. "I think I know all there is to know about both Alex Conklin and Jason Bourne."

"Great. Find me Bourne then."

"Sir, knowing what I know about the two of them, how closely they worked together, how many times they went out on a limb for each other, saved each other's lives, I find it highly improbable that Bourne would murder Alex Conklin."

"Alonzo-Ortiz wants to see me," the DCI said irritably. "After that fiasco at Washington Circle, d'you think I should tell her what you've just told me?"

"Well, no, but—"

"You're goddamned right, sonny boy. I've got to give her facts, facts that add up to *good* news."

Lindros cleared his throat. "At the moment, I don't have any. Bourne has vanished."

"Vanished? Jesus Christ, Martin, what the hell kind of intelligence operation are you running?"

"The man's a magician."

"He's flesh and blood, just like the rest of us," the DCI thundered. "How the hell did he slip through your fingers yet again? I thought you had all the bases covered!"

"We did. He simply—"

"Vanished, I know. This is what you have for me? Alonzo-Ortiz will have my fucking head on a platter, but not before I have yours!"

The DCI cut the connection, flung the phone through the open doorway onto the bed. By the time he had showered, dressed and taken a sip of coffee from the mug Madeleine obediently held out, his car was waiting for him.

Through the pane of bullet-proof glass, he drank in the facade of his house, dark-red brick with pale stone quoins at the corners, working shutters at every window. It had once belonged to a Russian tenor, Maxim something-or-other, but the DCI liked it because it had about it a certain mathematical elegance, an aristocratic air that could no longer be found in buildings of a younger vintage. Best of all was its sense of Old World privacy, owing to a cobbled courtyard screened by leafy poplars and a hand-worked iron fence.

He sat back in the plush seat of the Lincoln Town Car, watching morosely as Washington slept on around him. *Christ, at this hour only the fucking robins are up*, he thought. *Aren't I due the privilege of seniority? After all these years of service, don't I deserve to sleep past five o'clock?*

They sped across the Arlington Memorial Bridge, the Potomac gunmetal gray, looking flat and hard as an airport runway. On the other side, looming over the more or less Doric temple of the Lincoln Memorial, was the Washington Monument, dark and forbidding as the spears the Spartans once used to drive through the hearts of their enemies.

Each time the water closes over him, he hears a musical sound, as of the bells the monks are sounding, echoing from ridge to ridge in the forested mountains; the monks he hunted when he was with the Khmer Rouge. And the smell of, what is it? cinnamon. The water, swirling with a malevolent current, is alive with sounds and scents from he knows not where. It seeks to drag him down, and once again he's sinking. No matter how hard he struggles, how desperately he strikes out for the surface, he feels himself spiraling down, as if weighted with lead. His hands are scrabbling at the thick rope tied around his left ankle, but it's so slick it keeps sliding through his fingers. What is at the end of the rope? He peers down into the shadowy depths through which he's sinking. It seems imperative to him that he know what is dragging him to his death, as if that knowledge might save him from a horror for which he has no name. He's falling, falling, tumbling into darkness, unable to understand the nature of his desperate predicament. Below him, at the end of the taut rope, he sees a shape—the thing that will cause his death. Emotion sticks in his throat like a mouthful of nettles, and as he tries to define the shape, the musical sound comes to him again, clearer this time, not bells, something else, something at once intimate and barely remembered. At last, he identifies the thing that's causing him to drown: It's a human body. All at once, he begins to weep. . . .

Khan awoke with a start, a whimper caught in his throat. He bit down hard on his lip, looked around the darkened cabin of the plane. Outside, all was black as pitch. He had fallen asleep even though he'd promised himself he wouldn't, knowing that if he did he would be trapped in his recurring nightmare. He rose, went to the lavatory, where he used the paper towels to wipe the sweat off his face and arms. He felt more tired than when the flight had taken off. While he was staring at himself in the mirror, the pilot announced their airtime to Orly Airport: four hours, fifty minutes. An eternity for Khan.

There was a line of people waiting as he exited. He made his way back to his seat. Jason Bourne had a specific destination in mind; he knew that from the information the tailor, Fine, had provided: Bourne was now in possession of a packet meant for Alex Conklin. Was it possible, he wondered, that Bourne would now take on Conklin's identity? It would be something Khan would consider if he were in Bourne's shoes.

Khan stared out the window at the black sky. Bourne was somewhere in the sprawling metropolis ahead of him, this much was known, but he had no doubt that Paris was just a way station. Bourne's final destination was yet to be learned.

———

The National Security Advisor's assistant cleared her throat discreetly and the DCI glanced at his watch. Roberta Alonzo-Ortiz, the bitch-woman, had kept him waiting almost forty minutes. Inside the Beltway, playing games of power was standard operating procedure, but Jesus Christ, she was a *woman*. And weren't they both on the National Security Council? But she was the president's direct appointee; she had his ear like no one else. Where the hell was Brent Scowcroft when you needed him? Pasting a smile on his face, he turned away from the window out which he had been gazing while his mind had been engaged.

"She's ready to see you now," the assistant cooed sweetly. "Her call with the president just ended."

The bitch-woman doesn't miss a trick, the DCI thought. *How she loves to rub my nose in her power-stink.*

The National Security Advisor was entrenched behind her desk, a huge antique affair she'd had trucked in at her own expense. The DCI thought it absurd, especially since there was nothing on her desk except the brass pen-set the president had given her upon her acceptance of the appointment. He didn't trust people with tidy desks. Behind her, on elaborate gold standards, were the American flag and the flag with the seal of the President of the United States. Between them was a view of Lafayette Park. Two high-backed upholstered chairs sat facing her. The DCI looked at them somewhat longingly.

Roberta Alonzo-Ortiz looked bright and chipper in a dark-blue knit suit and white silk blouse. In her ears were gold-backed enamel earrings of the American flag.

"I just got off the phone with the president," she said without preamble, not even a "Good morning" or "Have a seat."

"So your assistant told me."

Alonzo-Ortiz glared at him, a momentary reminder that she hated being interrupted. "The conversation concerned you."

Despite his best intentions, the DCI felt his body flush. "Perhaps I should have been here then."

"That would not have been inappropriate." The National Security Advisor went on before he could respond to her verbal slap in the face. "The terrorism summit will take place in five days. Every element is in place, which is why it pains me to have to reiterate that we are walking on eggshells here. Nothing can disturb the summit, *especially* not a CIA assassin gone crimi-

nally insane. The president is anticipating that the summit will be an unqualified success. He expects to make it the cornerstone of his drive for reelection. Even more, it will be his legacy." She put her hands flat on the
highly polished surface of her desk. "Let me be perfectly clear—I have
made the summit my number-one priority. Its success will ensure that this
presidency is lauded and revered for generations to come."

The DCI had been standing throughout this discourse, not having been
invited to sit down. The verbal dressing-down was especially humiliating,
given its subtext. He did not care for threats, particularly veiled ones. He
felt as if he was being given detention in elementary school.

"I had to brief him about the Washington Circle debacle." She said it as if
the DCI had made her deliver a shovelful of shit to the Oval Office. "There
are consequences to failure; there always are. You need to put a stake
through the heart of this one so it can be buried as soon as possible. Do
you understand me?"

"Perfectly."

"Because it won't go away on its own," the National Security Advisor said.

A vein had started to pulse in the DCI's temple. He felt the urge to throw
something at her. "I said I understood perfectly."

Roberta Alonzo-Ortiz scrutinized him for a moment, as if she was deciding whether he was worthy of being believed. At length, she said,
"Where's Jason Bourne?"

"He's fled the country." The DCI's fists were clenched and white. It was
beyond him to tell the bitch-woman that Bourne had simply vanished. As
it was, he could scarcely get the words out. But the moment he saw the look
on her face, he realized his error.

"Fled the country?" Alonzo-Ortiz rose. "Where has he gone?"

The DCI remained silent.

"I see. If Bourne gets anywhere near Reykjavík . . ."

"Why would he do that?"

"I don't know. He's insane, remember? He's gone rogue. He must know
that sabotaging the summit security would embarrass us like nothing else."
Her fury was palpable, and for the first time the DCI was truly afraid of her.

"I want Bourne dead," she said in a voice of steel.

"As much as I do." The DCI was fuming. "He's already killed twice, and
one of the victims was an old friend."

The National Security Advisor came around from behind her desk. "The president wants Bourne dead. An agent gone rogue—and let's be honest here, Jason Bourne is a worst-case scenario—is a wild card we can't afford. Do I make myself clear?"

The DCI nodded. "Believe me when I tell you that Bourne is as good as dead, *vanished* as if he had never existed at all."

"From your mouth to God's ear. The president's eye is on you," Roberta Alonzo-Ortiz said, ending the interview as abruptly and unpleasantly as she had begun it.

Jason Bourne arrived in Paris on a wet, overcast morning. Paris, city of light, was not at its best in the rain. The mansard-roofed buildings looked gray and wan, and the usually gay and lively outdoor cafés that lined the city's boulevards were quite deserted. Life went on in its muted fashion, but the city was not the same as when it sparkled and shone in sunlight, when good conversation and laughter could be heard on almost every corner.

Exhausted both physically and emotionally, Bourne had spent most of the flight on his side, curled in a ball, asleep. His slumber, though now and again interrupted by dark and disturbing dreams, had the benefit of providing a well-needed respite from the pain that had wracked him in the first hour after the plane had taken off. He awoke, chilled and stiff, thinking of the small carved stone Buddha that had hung around Khan's neck. The image seemed to mock him, to be grinning, a mystery yet to be solved. He knew there must be many such carvings—in the shop where he and Dao had chosen the one they would give Joshua there were more than a dozen! He also knew that many Asian Buddhists wore such charms, for both protection and good luck.

In his mind's eye, he saw again Khan's knowing expression, so alight with anticipation and hatred when he had said, *"You know what this is, don't you?"* And then, uttered with such vehemence: *"This is mine, Bourne. Do you understand? The Buddha is mine!"* Khan was not Joshua Webb, Bourne told himself. Khan was clever but cruel—an assassin who had killed many times. He could not be Bourne's son.

Despite a bout of heavy crosswinds as they had left the coastline of the United States behind, Rush Service Flight 113 landed at Charles de Gaulle

International Airport more or less on time. Bourne felt the urge to remove himself from the cargo hold while it was still on the runway, but he restrained himself.

Another plane was preparing to land. If he got off now, he would be out in the open, exposed in an area where even airport personnel should not be. And so he waited patiently while the plane taxied onward.

As it slowed, he knew that now was the time to act. While the plane was still moving, the jet engines running, none of the ground crew would approach the plane. He opened the door, jumped out onto the tarmac just as a fuel truck was passing by. He caught a ride on the back of it. Hanging there, he experienced a violent wave of nausea as the fumes triggered the memory of Khan's surprise attack. He leaped off the truck as quickly as was practical, making his way into the terminal building.

Inside, he collided with a baggage handler, apologized profusely in French, with a hand to his head complaining of a migraine. Around the corner of the corridor, he used the ID tag he had swiped from the handler to go through the two sets of doors, out into the terminal proper, which, much to his consternation, was nothing more than a converted hangar. There were precious few people about, but at least he had successfully bypassed Customs and Immigration.

At the first opportunity, he dropped the ID tag into the nearest waste bin. He did not want to be caught wearing it when the handler reported it missing. Standing beneath a large clock, he adjusted his watch. It was just after six in the morning, Paris time. He called Robbinet, described where he was.

The minister seemed puzzled. "Did you come in on a charter flight, Jason?"

"No, cargo plane."

"*Bon*, that explains why you are in old Terminal Three. You must have been diverted from Orly," Robbinet said. "Stay right where you are, *mon ami*. I will collect you shortly." He chuckled. "In the meantime, welcome to Paris. Confusion and ill-fortune to your pursuers."

Bourne went to wash up. Staring at himself in the men's room mirror, he saw a haggard face, haunted eyes and a bloody throat, someone he barely recognized. Cupping his hands, he threw water over his face and head, sluicing away the sweat, grime and whatever was left of the makeup he had applied earlier. With a damp paper towel, he cleaned the darkened horizontal wound across his throat. He knew he would need to get some antibiotic cream on it as soon as possible.

His stomach was in a knot, and though he didn't feel hungry, he knew he needed to eat. Every once in a while the taste of the jet fuel came back to him and he gagged, eyes tearing with the effort. To get his mind off the sick sensation, he performed five minutes of stretching, five more of calisthenics, ridding his muscles of their cramped and aching condition. He ignored the pain the exercises cost him, concentrating instead on breathing deeply and evenly.

By the time he walked back into the terminal, Jacques Robbinet was waiting for him. He was a tall, extraordinarily fit man, neatly dressed in a dark pinstripe suit, gleaming brogues and a stylish tweed topcoat. He was a bit older and a bit grayer, but otherwise he was the figure out of Bourne's fragmented memory.

He spotted Bourne immediately and a grin broke out on his face, but he made no move toward his old friend. Instead, he used hand signals to indicate that Bourne should walk down the terminal to Bourne's right. Bourne immediately saw why. Several members of the Police Nationale had entered the hangar, were questioning airport personnel, doubtless on the lookout for the suspect who had stolen the baggage handler's ID. Bourne walked at a natural pace. He was almost at the doors when he saw two more Police Nationale, machine pistols slung across their chests, carefully watching everyone who went in and out of the terminal.

Robbinet had seen them as well. Putting a frown on his face, he hurried past Bourne, pushing through the doors and engaging the policemen's attention. As soon as he introduced himself, they told him that they were on the lookout for a suspect—an assumed terrorist—who had stolen a baggage handler's ID tag. They showed him a faxed copy of Bourne's photo.

No, the minister had not seen this man. Robbinet's face assumed an expression of fear. Perhaps—was such a thing possible?—the terrorist was after him, he said. Would they be so kind as to escort him to his car?

As soon as the three men had moved off, Bourne went quickly through the door, out into the gray mist. He saw the policemen accompanying Robbinet to his Peugeot and he walked in the opposite direction. As the minister got into his car, he gave Bourne a furtive glance. He thanked the policemen, who walked back to their post outside the terminal doors.

Robbinet drove off, made a U-turn, coming back to exit the airport. Out of sight of the policemen, he slowed the car, rolled down the off-side window.

"That was close, *mon ami*."

When Bourne made a move to get in, Robbinet shook his head. "With the airport on high alert, there is certain to be more Police Nationale about." He reached down, popped the trunk. "Not the most comfortable of places." He looked apologetic. "But for now surely the safest."

Without another word, Bourne crawled into the trunk, shutting himself in, and Robbinet took off. It was well the minister had thought ahead; there were two roadblocks to negotiate before they could exit the airport, the first manned by Police Nationale, the second by members of the Quai d'Orsay, the French equivalent of the CIA. With Robbinet's credentials, he got through both without incident, but he was repeatedly shown Bourne's photo, asked if he had seen the fugitive.

Ten minutes after he had turned onto the A1, Robbinet pulled over into a breakdown area, popped the trunk. Bourne got out, slid into the passenger's seat, and Robbinet accelerated onto the motorway, heading north.

"That's him!" The baggage handler pointed to the grainy photo of Jason Bourne. "That's the man who stole my ID."

"You're certain, monsieur? Please look again, more closely this time." Inspector Alain Savoy centered the photo in front of the potential witness. They were in a concrete room inside Terminal Three of Charles de Gaulle Airport, where Savoy had decided to set up temporary headquarters. It was a mean place, smelling strongly of mildew and disinfectant. He was always in such places, it seemed to him. There was nothing permanent in his life.

"Yes, yes," the baggage handler said. "He bumped into me, said he had a migraine. Ten minutes later, when I went to go through a secure door, I discovered the tag was gone. He took it."

"We know he did," Inspector Savoy said. "Your presence was electronically reported in two places while your ID tag was missing. Here." He handed over the tag. He was a short man and sensitive about it. His face looked as rumpled as his longish dark hair. His lips seemed permanently pursed, as if even in repose he was assessing innocence or guilt. "We found it in a trash bin."

"Thank you, Inspector."

"You'll be fined, you know. One day's pay."

"That's an outrage," the baggage handler said. "I'll report this to the union. There may be a demonstration."

Inspector Savoy sighed. He was used to these threats. Among the union workers, there were always demonstrations. "Is there anything more you can tell me about the incident?" When the man shook his head, the inspector dismissed him. He stared down at the faxed sheet. Besides Jason Bourne's photo, it contained an American contact. Pulling out a tri-band cell phone, he punched in the number.

"Martin Lindros, Deputy Director of Central Intelligence."

"Monsieur Lindros, this is Inspector Alain Savoy of the Quai d'Orsay. We have found your fugitive."

"What?"

A slow smile crept over Savoy's unshaven face. The Quai d'Orsay was always sucking at the CIA teat. There was a great deal of pleasure, not to mention national pride, in having the situation reversed. "That's right. Jason Bourne arrived at Charles de Gaulle Airport around six this morning, Paris time." Savoy's heart gladdened at the swift intake of breath at the other end of the line.

"Do you have him?" Lindros asked. "Is Bourne in custody?"

"Sadly, no."

"What do you mean? Where is he?"

"This is a mystery." There ensued a silence so long and deep that Savoy was obliged at length to say, "Monsieur Lindros, are you still on the line?"

"Yes, Inspector. I'm just going through my notes." Another silence, briefer this time. "Alex Conklin had a clandestine contact high up in your government, a man named Jacques Robbinet—do you know him?"

"*Certainement*, Monsieur Robbinet is the Minister of Culture. Surely you don't expect me to believe that a man of his stature is in league with this madman?"

"Of course not," Lindros said. "But Bourne has already murdered Monsieur Conklin. If he's in Paris now, it stands to reason that he may be after Monsieur Robbinet."

"One moment, hold the line, if you please." Inspector Savoy was certain that he'd heard or read M. Robbinet's name somewhere today. He gestured to a subordinate, who handed him a sheaf of files. Savoy leafed rapidly through the interviews made this morning at Charles de Gaulle by all the various police and security services. Sure enough, there was Robbinet's name. Hurriedly, he got back on the line. "Monsieur Lindros, it happens that Monsieur Robbinet was here today."

"At the airport?"

"Yes, and not only that. He was interviewed at the same terminal as the one Bourne was in. In fact, he seemed alarmed when he was told the name of the fugitive. He asked the Police Nationale to accompany him back to his automobile."

"This proves my theory." Lindros' voice was slightly breathless with a combination of excitement and alarm. "Inspector, you've got to find Robbinet, and fast."

"There's no problem," Inspector Savoy said. "I'll simply call the minister's office."

"That's precisely what you *won't* do," Lindros said. "I want to keep this operation absolutely secure."

"But surely Bourne can't—"

"Inspector, in the brief course of this investigation I've learned never to utter the phrase 'Bourne can't' because I know that he *can*. He's an exceedingly clever and dangerous assassin. Anyone who goes near him is in danger of their life, get me?"

"Pardon, monsieur?"

Lindros tried to slow down his speech. "However you choose to find Robbinet, you'll do it through back channels only. If you surprise the minister, chances are you'll be surprising Bourne as well."

"*D'accord.*" Savoy stood up and looked for his trench coat.

"Listen closely, Inspector. I'm very much afraid Monsieur Robbinet's life is in imminent danger," Lindros said. "Everything now depends on you."

Concrete high-rises, office buildings, gleaming factories flashed by, squat and blocky by American standards, made even more ugly by the gloomy overcast. Soon enough, Robbinet turned off, driving west on the CD47 into the oncoming downpour.

"Where are we going, Jacques?" Bourne asked. "I need to get to Budapest as quickly as possible."

"*D'accord,*" Robbinet said. He'd been periodically glancing in his rearview mirror, checking for Police Nationale vehicles. The Quai d'Orsay was another matter; their operatives used unmarked cars, switching make and models among their divisions every few months. "I had booked you on an outboard flight that left five minutes ago, but while you were in the air the game board has changed. The Agency is howling for your blood—and that howl is being heard in all corners of the world where they have leverage, including mine."

"But there must be a way—"

"Of course there's a way, *mon ami.*" Robbinet smiled. "There's always a way—a certain someone named Jason Bourne taught me that." He turned north again, onto the N17. "While you rested in the boot of my car, I was far from idle. There's a military transport leaving from Orly at sixteen hundred hours."

"That's not until four this afternoon," Bourne said. "What about driving to Budapest?"

"Such a plan is unsafe, too many Police Nationale. And your maddened American friends have pricked the Quai d'Orsay into action." The Frenchman shrugged. "It's all arranged. I've all your credentials with me. Under military cover you'll be secure from scrutiny, and in any event it's best to let the incident at Terminal Three die down, *non*?" He swung past some slow-moving traffic. "Until then, you'll need a place to go to ground."

Bourne turned his head away, stared out at the dreary industrial landscape. The impact of what had happened during his last encounter with Khan had hit him with the impact of a train derailing. He couldn't help exploring the fierce ache inside himself, much as one keeps pressing a sore tooth, if only to determine just how deep the pain went. The fiercely analytical portion of his mind had already determined that Khan hadn't really said anything that indicated he possessed intimate knowledge of David or Joshua Webb. He had made intimations, innuendoes, yes, but what did they amount to?

Bourne, aware that Robbinet was scrutinizing him, turned further toward the window.

Robbinet, misconstruing the reason for Bourne's brooding silence, said, "*Mon ami,* you will be in Budapest by eighteen hundred hours, have no fear."

"*Merci*, Jacques." Bourne momentarily freed himself from his melancholy thoughts. "Thanks for all your kindness and help. What now?"

"*Alors*, we are going to Goussainville. Not the most scenic town in France, but there's someone there who I suspect will interest you."

Robbinet said nothing more for the remainder of the trip. He was right about Goussainville. It was one of those French villages that, because of its proximity to the airport, had been transformed into a modern industrial town. The depressing rows of high-rises, glass-fronted offices and giant retailers not unlike Wal-Mart were only slightly alleviated by the roundabouts and curbsides planted with row upon row of colorful flowers.

Bourne noticed the radio unit mounted below the dashboard, presumably used by Jacques' driver. As Robbinet pulled into a gas station, he asked his friend for the frequencies used by the Police Nationale and the Quai d'Orsay. While Robbinet pumped gas into the car, Bourne monitored both frequencies but heard nothing about the incident at the airport, nothing of interest about him. Bourne watched the cars coming and going in and out of the gas station. A woman got out of her car, asked Robbinet his opinion about her front driver's side tire. She was worried it needed air. A vehicle with two young men pulled in. They both got out. One man lounged against the fender of the car while the driver went into the station. The lounging man eyed Jacques' Peugeot, then gazed appreciatively at the woman as she walked back to her car.

"Anything on the air?" Robbinet inquired as he slid in beside Bourne.

"Not a thing."

"That at least is good news," Robbinet said as they drove off.

They went down more ugly streets, and Bourne used the mirrors to check that the car with the two young men wasn't tailing them.

"Goussainville had an ancient and royal beginning," Robbinet said. "Once upon a time it belonged to Clotaire, wife of Clovis, the king of France early in the sixth century. While we Franks were still considered barbarians, he converted to Catholicism, making us acceptable to the Romans. The emperor made him a consul. Barbarians no longer, we became true champions of the Faith."

"You'd never know this place was once a medieval city."

The minister pulled up to a series of concrete apartment buildings. "In France," he said, "history is often hidden in the most unexpected places."

Bourne looked around. "This isn't where your current mistress lives, is it?" he said. "Because the last time you introduced me to your mistress I had to pretend she was my girlfriend when your wife walked into the café where we were having drinks."

"I recall you having quite a good time that afternoon." Robbinet shook his head. "But no, with her Dior this and her Yves Saint Laurent that I'm certain Delphine would rather slit her wrists than live in Goussainville."

"Then what are we doing here?"

The minister sat staring out at the rain for some time. "Filthy weather," he said at last.

"Jacques . . . ?"

Robbinet looked around. "Ah, yes, forgive me, *mon ami*. My mind wanders. *Alors*, I am taking you to meet Mylene Dutronc." He cocked his head. "Have you heard her name?" When Bourne shook his head, Robbinet continued. "I thought not. Well, now that he's dead, I suppose I can say it. Mlle. Dutronc was Alex Conklin's lover."

At once, Bourne said, "Let me guess: light eyes, long wavy hair and a smile with something of the ironic about it."

"He *did* tell you about her!"

"No, I saw a photo. It's pretty much all he had of a personal nature in his bedroom." He waited a moment. "Does she know?"

"I phoned her as soon as I found out."

Bourne wondered why Robbinet hadn't told her in person. It would have been the decent thing to do.

"Enough talk." Robbinet grabbed an overnight bag from the footwell of the backseat. "We'll go see Mylene now."

Exiting the Peugeot, they went through the rain, along a little flower-flanked walk, and mounted a short flight of poured-concrete stairs. Robbinet pressed the button for 4A and a moment later the buzzer sounded.

The apartment building was as plain and unlovely on the inside as it was on the outside. They walked up the five flights of stairs to the fourth floor and went along a hallway, past rows of identical doors on either side. At the sound of their approach, the door opened. Just inside stood Mylene Dutronc.

She was perhaps a decade older than the image in the photo—in fact, she must have been sixty by now, Bourne thought, though she appeared at least ten years younger—but her light eyes had the same sparkle and her smile had the same enigmatic twist to it. She wore jeans and a man-tailored shirt, an outfit that made her appear feminine because it showed off her full figure. She was in low heels and her hair, a natural-looking ash-blond, was tied back from her face.

"*Bonjour*, Jacques." She lifted her face for Robbinet to kiss on both cheeks, but she was already looking at his companion.

Bourne could see details that the snapshot hadn't revealed. The color of her eyes, the sculpted flare of her nostrils, the whiteness of her even teeth. Her face was both powerful and compassionate.

"And you must be Jason Bourne." Her gray eyes appraised him coolly.

"I'm sorry about Alex," Bourne said.

"You're kind. It's been a shock to all of us who knew him." She stepped back. "Please come in."

As she shut the door behind her, Bourne took in the room. Mlle. Dutronc lived in the middle of a blocky urban landscape, but her apartment was altogether different. Unlike many people her age, she had not continued to surround herself with furniture decades old, relics of the past. Instead, her furnishings were both stylishly modern and comfortable. A scattering of chairs, a matching pair of sofas facing each other on either side of a brick fireplace, patterned curtains. It was a place you would not easily want to leave, Bourne decided.

"I understand you've had a long flight," she said to Bourne. "You must be starving." She made no mention of his disheveled appearance, for which he was grateful. She seated him in the dining room, served him food and drink from a typical European kitchen, small and dark. When she was finished, she sat down opposite him, put her clasped hands on the table.

Bourne could see now that she had been crying.

"Did he die instantly?" Mlle. Dutronc asked. "You see, I've been wondering whether he suffered."

"No," Bourne said truthfully. "I very much doubt he did."

"That's something, at least." A look of profound relief came over her face. Mlle. Dutronc sat back and, with this movement, Bourne became aware that she had been holding her body tensely. "Thank you, Jason." She looked up, her expressive gray eyes locked on his, and he could see all the emotion in her face. "May I call you Jason?"

"Of course," he said.

"You knew Alex well, didn't you?"

"As well as one could ever know Alex Conklin."

For just an instant, her gaze flicked in Robbinet's direction, but it was enough.

"I have some calls to make." The minister had already pulled out his cell phone. "You won't mind if I leave you two for a little while."

She looked bleakly after Robbinet as he headed for the living room. Then she turned back to Bourne. "Jason, what you told me just now was said as a true friend. Even if Alex had never spoken to me about you, I would say the same thing."

"Alex talked to you about me?" Bourne shook his head. "Alex never told civilians about his work."

There was that smile again; this time the irony in it was quite apparent. "But I'm not, as you say, a civilian." There was a pack of cigarettes in her hand. "Do you mind if I smoke?"

"Not at all."

"Many Americans do. It's something of an obsession with you, isn't it?"

She had not been seeking an answer and Bourne did not give her one. He watched as she lit up, drew the smoke deep into her lungs, let it out slowly, luxuriously. "No, I'm definitely not a civilian." The smoke swirled around her. "I'm Quai d'Orsay."

Bourne sat very still. Beneath the table, his hand grasped the butt of the ceramic pistol Deron had given him.

As if reading his mind, Mlle. Dutronc shook her head. "Calm yourself, Jason. Jacques hasn't led you into a trap. You're among friends here."

"I don't understand," he said thickly. "If you're Quai d'Orsay, Alex would've been doubly sure not to involve you in anything he was working on, so as not to compromise your loyalties."

"True enough. And this was how it remained for many years." Mlle. Dutronc took in more smoke, let it drift out of her flared nostrils. She had a habit of raising her head slightly as she exhaled. It made her look like Marlene Dietrich. "Then, very recently, something happened. I don't know what, he wouldn't tell me, though I begged him to."

She regarded him through the smoke haze for some moments. Any member of an intelligence organization had to maintain a stone facade that revealed nothing of their inner thoughts or feelings. But through her eyes he could see her mind working, and he knew that she had let her guard down.

"Tell me, Jason, as a long-time friend of Alex's, do you ever remember him being frightened?"

"No," Bourne said. "Alex was utterly fearless."

"Well, that day he *was* frightened. That's why I begged him to tell me what it was, so I could help, or at least convince him to move himself out of harm's way."

Bourne leaned forward, his body now as tense as Mlle. Dutronc's had been before. "When was this?"

"Two weeks ago."

"Did he tell you anything at all?"

"There was a name he mentioned, Felix Schiffer."

Bourne's pulse began to race. "Dr. Schiffer worked for DARPA."

She frowned. "Alex told me that he worked for the Tactical Non-Lethal Weapons Directorate."

"That's an Agency adjunct," Bourne said, half to himself. Now the pieces were starting to fall together. Could Alex have convinced Felix Schiffer to leave DARPA for the Directorate? Surely, it would not have been difficult for Conklin to make Schiffer "disappear." But why would he want to? If he was merely poaching on DOD territory, he could've handled the resulting flak. There had to be another reason Alex needed to get Felix Schiffer to ground.

He looked at Mylene. "Was Dr. Schiffer the reason Alex was frightened?"

"He wouldn't say, Jason. But how could it be otherwise? That day, Alex made and received many calls in a very short period of time. He was terribly tense and I knew he was at the crisis point of a hot field operation. I heard Dr. Schiffer's name mentioned several times. I suspect that he was the subject of the operation."

Inspector Savoy sat in his Citroën, listening to the scraping sound of his windshield wipers. He hated the rain. It had been raining the day his wife had left him, the day his daughter had gone off to school in America, never to return. His wife was living in Boston now, married to a straight-laced investment banker. She had three children, a house, property, all that she could wish for, while here he was sitting in this shitty town—what was its name? ah, yes, Goussainville—biting his nails down to the quick. And, to top it off, it was raining again.

But today was different because he was closing in on the CIA's most wanted target. Once he got Jason Bourne, his career would skyrocket. Perhaps he'd come to the attention of the president himself. He glanced over at the car across the street—Minister Jacques Robbinet's Peugeot.

From the Quai d'Orsay files, he had retrieved the make, model and license plate of the minister's car. His fellow officers had informed him that upon exiting the airport checkpoint the minister had headed north onto the A1. After having ascertained from headquarters who had been assigned to the northerly section of the dragnet, he had methodically called each car—mindful of Lindros' warning, keeping away from radio transmission, whose frequency wasn't secure. None of his contacts had seen the minister's car, and he was working himself up into a fit of despair when he had gotten to Justine Bérard, who told him that, yes, she had seen Robbinet's car—had spoken to him briefly—at a gas station. She remembered because the minister seemed tense, nervous, even a bit rude.

"Did his behavior strike you as odd?"

"Yes, it did. Though I didn't make much of it at the time," Bérard had said. "Though now, of course, my thinking has changed."

"Was the minister alone?" Inspector Savoy asked.

"I'm not certain. It was raining hard and the window was up," Bérard said. "To be candid, my attention was on Monsieur Robbinet."

"Yes, a handsome specimen," Savoy said, more dryly than he had intended. Bérard had been a great help. She had seen the direction in which the minister's car had gone, and by the time he had arrived in Goussainville, she had found it sitting outside a block of concrete apartment buildings.

Mlle. Dutronc's eyes strayed to Bourne's throat and she stubbed out her cigarette. "Your wound has begun bleeding again. Come. We must take care of it."

She led him into her bathroom, tiled in sea-green and cream. A small window overlooking the street let in the dismal light of day. She sat him down and began to wash the wound with soap and water.

"The bleeding has subsided," she said as she applied antibiotic to the reddened flesh across his throat. "This wound wasn't accidental. You were in a fight."

"It was difficult getting out of the States."

"You're as tight-lipped as Alex." She stood a little back, as if she needed to get him in better focus. "You are sad, Jason. So very sad."

"Mlle. Dutronc—"

"You must call me Mylene. I insist." She had fashioned an expert bandage from sterile gauze and surgical tape and now applied it to his wound. "And you must change the dressing at least every three days, yes?"

"Yes." He responded to her smile. "*Merci*, Mylene."

She put a hand gently against his cheek. "So very sad. I know how close you and Alex were. He thought of you as a son."

"He said that?"

"He didn't have to; he had a special look on his face when he spoke about you." She examined the dressing one last time. "So I know I'm not the only one hurting."

Bourne felt the urge, then, to tell her everything, that it wasn't just the deaths of Alex and Mo affecting him, but the encounter with Khan. In the end, however, he remained silent. She had her own grief to bear.

Instead, he said, "What's the deal with you and Jacques? You act as if you hate each other."

Mylene looked away for a moment, toward the small window with its pebbled glass, running now with rain. "It was brave of him to bring you here. It must have cost him much to ask for my help." She turned back, her gray eyes brimming. Alex's death had brought so much emotion to the surface, and at once he intuited that her own past was being churned up by the restless ocean of present events. "So much sorrow in this world, Jason." A single tear rolled from her eye, lay quivering on her cheek, before sliding down. "Before Alex, you see, there was Jacques."

"You were his mistress?"

She shook her head. "Jacques was not yet married. We were both very young. We made love like crazy, and because we were both young—and foolish—I became pregnant."

"You have a child?"

Mylene wiped her eyes. "*Non*, I wouldn't have it. I didn't love Jacques. It took what happened to make me see that. Jacques *did* love me, and he—well, he's so very Catholic."

She laughed, a little sadly, and Bourne recalled the story Jacques had told him of Goussainville's history and how the barbarian Franks had been won over by the church. King Clovis' conversion to Catholicism had been a shrewd decision, but it had been more a matter of survival and politics than of faith.

"Jacques has never forgiven me." There was no self-pity in her, making her confession all the more affecting.

He leaned in and tenderly kissed her on both cheeks, and with a small sob she drew him briefly to her.

She left him to shower, and when he was finished, he found a French military uniform piled neatly on the toilet seat. As he dressed, he peered out the window. A linden's branches swung back and forth in the wind. Below him, a handsome woman in her early forties got out of her car, walked down the street to a Citroën in which a man of indeterminate age sat behind the wheel, gnawing obsessively at his fingernails. Opening the passenger's-side door, she slid in.

There was nothing particularly unusual about the scene, except for the fact that Bourne had seen the same woman at the gas station. She had spoken to Jacques about the air pressure in her tire.

Quai d'Orsay!

Quickly, he went back into the living room, where Jacques was still on the phone. The moment the minister saw Bourne's expression, he got off his call.

"What is it, *mon ami*?"

"We've been made," Bourne said.

"What? How is that possible?"

"I don't know, but there are two Quai d'Orsay agents across the street in a black Citroën."

Mylene walked in from the kitchen. "Two more are watching the street behind. But don't worry, they cannot even know which building you're in."

At that moment, the doorbell rang. Bourne drew his gun but Mylene's eyes flashed their warning. She jerked her head and Bourne and Robbinet moved out of sight. She opened the door, saw a very rumpled inspector in front of her.

"Alain, *bonjour*," she said.

"I'm sorry to intrude on your vacation," Inspector Savoy said, a sheepish grin on his face, "but I was sitting outside and all of a sudden I remembered that you lived here."

"Would you like to come in, have a cup of coffee?"

"Thank you, no. I can't spare the time."

Greatly relieved, Mylene said, "And what were you doing sitting outside my house?"

"We're looking for Jacques Robbinet."

Her eyes opened wide. "The Minister of Culture? But why would he be in, of all places, Goussainville?"

"Your guess is as good as mine," Inspector Savoy said. "Nevertheless, his car is parked across the street."

"The inspector is too clever for us, Mylene." Jacques Robbinet strode into the living room buttoning his white shirt. "He has found out about us."

With her back turned to Savoy, Mylene shot Robbinet a look. He returned it, smiling easily.

His lips brushed hers, as he came up beside her.

By this time Inspector Savoy's cheeks had grown warm. "Minister Robbinet, I had no idea . . . that is, there was no intention to intrude—"

Robbinet raised a hand. "Apology accepted, but why are you looking for me?"

With an overt show of relief, Savoy handed over the grainy photo of Jason Bourne. "We're searching for this man, Minister. A known CIA assassin who's turned rogue. We have reason to believe that he means to kill you."

"But that's terrible, Alain!"

To Bourne, observing this charade from the shadows, Mylene looked shocked indeed.

"I don't know this man," Robbinet said, "nor why he would want to take my life. But then who can fathom the minds of assassins, eh?" He shrugged, turned as Mylene handed him his jacket and raincoat. "But by all means, I'll return to Paris as quickly as possible."

"With us as an escort," Savoy said firmly. "You'll ride with me and my associate will drive your official car." He held out his hand. "If you would be so kind."

"As you wish." Robbinet delivered the key to his Peugeot. "I'm in your hands, Inspector."

Then, he turned, took Mylene in his arms. Savoy discreetly withdrew, saying he would wait in the hallway for Robbinet.

"Take Jason down to the car park," Robbinet whispered in her ear. "Take my attaché case with you and give him the contents just before you leave him." He whispered the combination to her and she nodded.

She stared up at him, then she kissed him hard on the mouth and said, "Godspeed, Jacques."

For just an instant, his eyes opened wide in response. Then he was gone, and Mylene went quickly through the living room.

She called softly to Bourne, and he appeared. "We must make the most of the advantage Jacques has given you."

Bourne nodded. *"D'accord."*

Mylene grabbed Robbinet's attaché case. "Come now. We must hurry!"

She opened the front door, peered out to ensure that the way was clear, then led him down to the underground car park. She stopped just inside the metal-clad door. Peering through the wire-reinforced glass pane, she reported back to him. "The car park looks clear, but be vigilant, you never know."

She unlocked the attaché case, held out a packet. "Here is the money you requested, along with your identity card and your orders. You're Pierre Montefort, a courier due to hand over top-secret documents to the military attaché in Budapest not later than eighteen hundred hours, local time." She dropped a set of keys into Bourne's palm. "A military motorcycle is parked in the third rank, next-to-last space on the right."

For a moment, Bourne and Mylene stood looking at each other. He opened his mouth, but she spoke first, "Remember, Jason, life is too short for regrets."

Bourne left then, striding with ramrod-straight back through the door into a grim and gloomy place of naked concrete block and oil-stained macadam. He looked neither to the left nor right as he went down the car ranks. At the third one, he turned right. A moment later, he found the motorcycle, a silver Voxan VB-1, with a huge 996-cubic V2 engine. Bourne strapped his attaché case to the back, where it would be prominently displayed for the Quai d'Orsay to see. He found a helmet in the carry pack, stowed his hat. Climbing on, he walked the machine out of its parking spot, started the engine and wheeled out of the car park into the rain.

Justine Bérard had been thinking about her son, Yves, when she received the call from Inspector Savoy. These days it seemed as if the only way she could relate to Yves was through his video games. The first time she had beaten him in *Grand Theft Auto* by outmaneuvering his car with hers was the moment he had looked at her—and really seen her as a living, breathing human being, rather than the annoyance that cooked him food and washed his clothes. Ever since then, though, he'd been begging her to take him for a spin in her official car. So far, she had been successful in staving him off, but there was no doubt that he was wearing her down, not only because she was proud of her nerveless driving but because she desperately wanted Yves to be proud of her.

Following the call from Savoy, informing her that he had found Minister Robbinet and that they were escorting him back to Paris, she had immediately gotten things rolling, pulling the men off surveillance duty, directing them into standard VIP protection formation. Now she gestured to the Police Nationale standing by as Inspector Savoy escorted the Minister of Culture out the front door of the apartment building. At the same time, she checked the street for any sign of the insane assassin Jason Bourne.

Bérard was elated. It made no difference whether Inspector Savoy had found the minister in this maze of residences through cleverness or good fortune, she would benefit hugely, for it was she who had led Savoy here and it was she who would be in at the end when they brought Jacques Robbinet back to Paris safe and sound.

Savoy and Robbinet had crossed the street under the watchful eyes of the phalanx of policemen, machine pistols at the ready. She had Savoy's car door open, and as he passed her, he handed her the key to the minister's Peugeot.

As Robbinet ducked his head to get into the backseat of Savoy's car, Bérard heard the throaty roar of a powerful motorcycle engine. By the echo, it was coming from the car park below the building in which Savoy had found Minister Robbinet. She cocked her head, recognizing the roar of a Voxan VB-1. A military vehicle.

A moment later, she saw the courier accelerate out of the car park and she grabbed her cell phone. What was a military courier doing in Goussainville? Unconsciously, she was walking toward the minister's Peugeot. She barked out her Quai d'Orsay authorization code, asked to be patched through to Military Liaison. She had reached the Peugeot, unlocked it, slid behind the wheel. With the Code Rouge alert on, it did not take her long to receive the information she was seeking. There was currently no known military courier anywhere near Goussainville.

She started the car, jerked it into gear. Inspector Savoy's shout of query was drowned in the screech of the Peugeot's tires as she stood on the gas pedal, accelerating down the street in pursuit of the Voxan. She could only surmise that Bourne had been on to them, knew that he was trapped here unless he could make a quick escape.

The urgent CIA circular she had read had noted that he was able to change identity and appearance with astonishing rapidity. If he was the courier—and, really, when she thought about it, what other possibility was there?—then apprehending or killing him would provide her career an entirely new trajectory. She could imagine the minister himself—so grateful for saving his life—interceding on her behalf, even, possibly, offering her the position of chief of his security.

In the meantime, though, she would have to bring down this faux courier. Lucky for her, the minister's car was far from a standard Peugeot sedan. Already she could feel the souped-up engine responding to the pressure she was putting on it as she slewed hard left around a corner, shot through a traffic light, passed a lumbering truck on the wrong side. She ignored the indignant blare of its air horn. All of her being was concentrated on keeping the Voxan in sight.

At first Bourne couldn't believe that he'd been made so quickly, but as the Peugeot continued its dogged pursuit, he was forced to conclude that something had gone terribly wrong. He had seen the Quai d'Orsay taking Robbinet, knew one of their operatives was driving his car. His assumed identity wouldn't be enough to protect him now; he had to lose this tail permanently. He hunched over, weaving in and out of traffic, varying his speeds, the ways in which he overtook slower traffic. He took turns at dangerously acute angles, aware that at any instant he could go over and send the Voxan screaming onto its side. A glance in the side mirror confirmed that he was unable to shake the Peugeot. More ominously, it appeared to be gaining on him.

Though the Voxan wove in and out of traffic, though her car was less maneuverable, Bérard kept closing the distance between them. She had flipped the special lever installed in all ministerial cars that made the head- and taillights flash, and this signal caused the more alert motorists to give way. In her head scrolled the increasingly more intricate and hair-raising scenarios of *Grand Theft Auto*. The scrolling of the streets, the vehicles she needed to pass or get around were astonishingly similar. Once, in order not to lose the Voxan, she had to make a split-second decision, running up onto the sidewalk. Pedestrians scattered from her path.

All at once, she saw the entrance to the A1 and knew this was where Bourne must be headed. Her best chance of getting him was before he made it onto the motorway. Biting her lip in grim intent, she drew on every last bit of power the Peugeot's engine could give her, closing the gap even more. The Voxan was only two cars away from her. She pulled out to the right, overtook one car, waved the other one back, its driver cowed as much by her aggressive driving as by the Peugeot's flashing lights.

Bérard was not one to waste an opportunity. They were coming up on the entrance; it was now or never. She manhandled the Peugeot up onto the sidewalk, aiming to approach Bourne on the offside so that in order to keep her in sight he would have to take his eyes off the road. At the speed they were both going, she knew he couldn't afford to do that. She rolled down her window, floored the accelerator and the car leaped forward into the wind-driven rain.

"Pull over!" she cried. "I am Quai d'Orsay! Pull over or risk the consequences!"

The courier ignored her. Drawing her sidearm, she aimed it at his head. Her arm was straight, elbow locked. Tracking him with the gun's sight, she aimed at the leading edge of his silhouette. She squeezed the trigger.

But just as she did so, the Voxan swerved hard to their left, slipped in front of an oncoming car in the next lane, jumped the narrow concrete divider, shot through the oncoming traffic.

"My God!" Bérard breathed. "He's headed onto the off-ramp!"

Even as she slewed the Peugeot around, she saw the Voxan threading its way between the traffic exiting the A1. Tires screeched, horns blared, terrified drivers shook their fists and cursed. Bérard noted these reactions with only part of her mind. The other part was engaged in driving through the stalled traffic, up over the median, across the street and onto the off-ramp herself.

She made it as far as the top of the ramp before she ran into a virtual wall of vehicles. She raced out into the rain, saw the Voxan accelerating between lanes of the oncoming traffic. Bourne's driving was astounding, but how long could he continue such perilous acrobatics?

The Voxan disappeared behind the silver oval cylinder of a tanker truck. Bérard sucked in her breath as she saw the huge eighteen-wheeler come barreling along in the adjacent lane. She heard the harsh sound of air brakes, then the Voxan struck the semi's massive radiator grille head-on, instantly erupting in a howling ball of oily flame.

CHAPTER TWELVE

Jason Bourne saw what he liked to call the convergence of opportunity set up right in front of him. He was running between two lanes of oncoming traffic. To his right was a tanker truck; to his left, a bit farther ahead, was a massive eighteen-wheeler. The choice was instinctual, there was no time for second thoughts. He committed his mind and his body to the convergence.

He lifted his legs and, for an instant, he was balanced on the Voxan's seat with only his left hand for support. He aimed the Voxan at the eighteen-wheeler barreling toward him on the left, then let go of the handlebar. Reaching out with his right hand, his fingers grasped hold of a rung of the skeletal metal ladder that rose up the tanker truck's curved side and he was jerked off the bike. Then his grip slipped on the rain-slick metal, and he was on the verge of being swept away like a twig in the wind. Tears welled up in his eyes at the pain that ripped through the same shoulder he'd strained outside the cargo hold of the plane. Both hands on the rung, he tightened his grip. As he swung fully onto the ladder, pressing himself against the tanker, the Voxan slammed into the eighteen-wheeler's radiator.

The tanker truck shuddered, rocking on its shocks as it hurtled through the ball of flame. Then it was past, rolling its way south toward Orly Airport and Bourne's freedom.

There were many reasons for Martin Lindros' swift and unerring rise up the Agency's slippery slope to become DDCI at the age of thirty-eight. He was smart, he came from the right schools, and he had the ability to keep his head even in a crisis. Moreover, his near-eidetic memory gave him a singular edge in keeping the administrative side of the CIA running smoothly. All important assets, no doubt—mandatory, in fact, for any successful DDCI. However, the DCI had chosen Lindros for an even more crucial reason: He was fatherless.

The DCI had known Martin Lindros' father well. For three years they had served together in Russia and Eastern Europe—until the elder Lindros had been killed in a car bomb attack. Martin Lindros had been twenty at the time and the effect on him had been incalculable. It was at the elder Lindros' funeral, while watching the young man's pale and pinched face, that the DCI knew he wanted to draw Martin Lindros into the same web that had so fascinated his father.

Approaching him had been easy; he'd been in a vulnerable place. The DCI had been primed to act, because his unerring instinct had recognized Martin Lindros' desire for revenge. The DCI had seen that the young man went to Georgetown upon his graduation from Yale. This served two purposes: It physically brought Martin into his orbit, and it ensured he would take the requisite courses for the career path the DCI had chosen for him. The DCI himself had inducted the young man into the Agency, had overseen every phase of his training. And because he wanted to bind the young man to him for all time, he at last provided the revenge Martin so desperately sought— the name and address of the terrorist responsible for constructing the car bomb.

Martin Lindros had followed the DCI's instructions to the letter, show- ing a commendably steady hand when he had put a bullet between the terrorist's eyes. Had he actually been the one who had made the car bomb? Even the DCI couldn't be certain. But what difference did it make? He *was* a terrorist and in his day had made many car bombs. Now he was dead— one more terrorist disposed of—and Martin Lindros could sleep easy at night, knowing that he had avenged his father's murder.

"You see how Bourne fucked us," Lindros was saying now. "He was the one who called D.C. Metro as soon as he saw your cruisers. He knew you had no official jurisdiction in the district, unless you were working with the Agency."

"Sadly, you've got that fucking-A right." Detective Harris of the Virginia State Police nodded as he downed his sour mash whiskey. "But now that the Frogs have him in their sights, maybe they'll have better luck running him to ground than we did."

"They're Frogs," Lindros said morosely.

"Even so, they've gotta be able to do something right sometime, no?"

Lindros and Harris were sitting in the Froggy Bottom Lounge on Pennsylvania Avenue. At this hour, the bar was filled students from George Washington University. For more than an hour Lindros had been watching bare midriffs pierced by navel rings and pert buttocks almost tucked into short skirts nearly twenty years younger than he was. There came a time in a man's life, he thought, when he began looking in the rearview mirror and realizing that he was no longer young. None of these girls would give him a second look; they didn't even know he existed.

"Why is it," he said, "that a man can't stay young all his life?"

Harris laughed and called for more drinks.

"You think it's funny?"

They had passed beyond screaming at each other, beyond frosty silence, beyond snide and cutting remarks. In the end, they had said to hell with it and had decided to get drunk.

"Yeah, I think it's damn funny," Harris said, making room for the new drinks. "Here you are mooning over pussy, thinkin' life's passed you by. This isn't about pussy, Martin, though to tell you the truth, I never did pass up the opportunity to get laid."

"Okay, smart guy, what *is* it about?"

"We lost, that's all. We got into Jason Bourne's game and he beat us six ways from Sunday. Not that he didn't have good reason to."

Lindros sat up a little straighter, paid for the precipitate movement with a brief bout of vertigo. He put a hand to the side of his head. 'What the hell does that mean?"

Harris had a habit of swigging his whiskey around as if it was mouth-wash. His throat clicked when he swallowed. "I don't think Bourne murdered Conklin and Panov."

Lindros groaned. "Jesus, Harry, not that again."

"I'll say it till I'm blue in the face. What I want to know is why you don't wanna hear it."

Lindros picked up his head. "Okay, okay. Tell me why you think Bourne is innocent."

"What's the point?"

"I'm asking you, aren't I?"

Harris seemed to consider. He shrugged, pulled out his wallet, extracted a slip of paper, which he unfolded on the table. "Because of this parking ticket."

Lindros picked the slip up, read it. "This ticket is made out to a Dr. Felix Schiffer." He shook his head in confusion.

"Felix Schiffer's a scofflaw," Harris said. "I wouldn't've known anything about him, but we're cracking down on scofflaws this month and one of my men couldn't get to first base with tracking him down." He tapped the ticket. "It took some doing, but I found out why my guy couldn't find him. Turns out that all of Schiffer's mail is being sent to Alex Conklin."

Lindros shook his head. "So?"

"So when I tried to run a database check on this Dr. Felix Schiffer, I ran up against a wall."

Lindros felt his head starting to clear. "What kind of a wall?"

"One put up by the United States Government." Harris finished off his whiskey in a single toss, swish and swallow. "This Dr. Schiffer's been put on ice with a capital *I*. I don't know what the hell Conklin was into, but it was hidden so deep I'll bet even his own people didn't know nothin' about it." He shook his head. "He wasn't killed by a rogue agent, Martin; on that I'll stake my life."

As Stepan Spalko rode up the private elevator at Humanistas, Ltd., he was in as near to good spirits as he could get. Except for the unexpected development with Khan, everything was now back on track. The Chechens were his; they were intelligent, fearless and willing to die for their cause. As for Arsenov, he was, if nothing else, a dedicated and disciplined leader. This was why Spalko had chosen him to betray Khalid Murat. Murat had not quite trusted Spalko; he'd had a keen nose for duplicity. But now Murat was gone. Spalko had no doubt that the Chechens would perform as he envisioned. On the other front, the damnable Alexander Conklin was dead and the CIA was convinced Jason Bourne was his murderer, two birds with one stone. Still, there was the core issue of the weapon and of Felix Schiffer. He felt the intense pressure of what still needed to be done. He knew that he was running out of time; there was much yet to be accomplished.

He got off at a mid-level floor accessible only with a magnetic key he wore. Letting himself into his sun-splashed living quarters, he crossed to the bank of windows overlooking the Danube, the deep green of Margaret Island, the city beyond. He stood staring out at the Houses of Parliament, thinking of the time to come, when undreamed-of power would be his. Sunlight spun off the medieval facade, the flying buttresses, the domes and spires. Inside, men of power met daily, prattling inconsequentially. His chest filled with air. It was he, Spalko, who knew where the real power in this world resided. He held out his hand, clenched it into a fist. Soon they would all know—the American president in his White House, the Russian president in the Kremlin, the sheiks in their magnificent Arabian palaces. Soon they would all know the true meaning of fear.

Naked, he padded into the large, opulent bathroom whose tiles were the color of lapis lazuli. Beneath eight streaming jets, he took a shower, scrubbing himself until his skin turned red. Then he dried himself with a thick white oversized Turkish towel and changed into jeans and a denim shirt.

At a gleaming stainless-steel wet-bar, he drew a cup of freshly brewed coffee from the automatic maker. He added cream and sugar, a dollop of whipped cream from the half-fridge below. For several moments thereafter, he stood sipping the coffee, allowing his mind to go pleasurably out of focus, allowing the anticipation to build. There were so many wonderful things to look forward to today!

Setting down the coffee cup, he tied on a butcher's apron. He eschewed his loafers, polished to a wicked shine, for a pair of green rubber garden boots.

Sipping the delicious coffee, he crossed to a wood-paneled wall. There was a small table with one drawer, which he pulled open. Inside was a box of latex gloves. Humming to himself, he drew out a pair, snapped them on. Then he pressed a button and two of the wood panels slid aside. He stepped through into a decidedly odd room. The walls were of black concrete; the floor was composed of white tiles, lower in the center where a huge drain was set. A hose on a reel was attached to one wall. The ceiling was heavily baffled. The only furniture was a wooden table, scarred, stained dark in places with blood, and a dentist's chair with modifications made to Spalko's exacting specifications. Beside the chair was a three-tiered cart on which lay a gleaming array of metal implements barbed with ominous-looking ends—straight, hooked and corkscrewed.

In the chair, his wrists and ankles bound in steel cuffs, was László Molnar, as naked as the day he was born. Molnar's face and body were cut, bruised and swollen, his eyes sunk deep within black circles of agony and despair.

Spalko entered the room as briskly and professionally as any doctor.

"My dear László, I must say you're looking the worse for wear." He stood close enough to see Molnar's nostrils flare at the scent of the coffee. "It's to be expected, though, isn't it? You've had quite a difficult night. Nothing you could have expected when you set out for the opera, eh? But not to worry, the excitement isn't over yet." He put down the coffee cup at Molnar's elbow, took up one of the instruments. "This one, I think, yes."

"What . . . what are you going to do?" Molnar asked in a cracked voice, thin as parchment.

"Where is Dr. Schiffer?" Spalko asked in a conversational tone of voice.

Molnar's head jerked from side to side, his jaw clamped shut, as if to ensure that no words would pass his lips.

Spalko tested the needlepoint of the instrument. "I honestly don't know why you hesitate, László. I have the weapon, though Dr. Schiffer is missing—"

"Taken from under your nose," Molnar whispered.

Spalko, smiling, applied the instrument to his prisoner and in short order Molnar was sufficiently stimulated to scream.

Standing back for a moment, he brought the coffee cup to his lips, swallowed. "As you've no doubt realized by now, this room is soundproof. You can't be heard—no one is going to save you, least of all Vadas; he doesn't even know that you're missing."

Taking up another instrument, he spun it into Molnar. "So you see there is no hope," he said. "Unless you tell me what I want to know. As it happens, László, I'm your one and only friend now; I'm the one who can save you." He grasped Molnar under the chin and kissed his bloody forehead. "I'm the one who truly loves you."

Molnar closed his eyes and again shook his head.

Spalko looked directly into Molnar's eyes. "I don't want to hurt you, László. You know that, don't you?" His voice, unlike his actions, was gentle. "But your stubbornness troubles me." He continued his work on Molnar. "I am wondering whether you understand the true nature of the circumstances into which you've fallen. This pain you feel is Vadas' doing. It's Vadas who got you into these dire straits. Conklin, too, I shouldn't wonder, but Conklin is dead."

Molnar's mouth opened wide in a terrible scream. There were gaping black holes where his teeth had been slowly and agonizingly pulled.

"Let me assure you that I continue my work most reluctantly," Spalko said with great concentration. It was important at this stage for Molnar to understand, even through the pain being inflicted on him. "I'm only the instrument of your own stubbornness. Can't you see that it's Vadas who must pay for this?"

Spalko let up for a moment. Blood had splattered his gloves and he was breathing as hard as if he had just run up three flights of stairs. Interrogation for all its pleasures was not easy work. Molnar began to mewl.

"Why do you bother, László? You are praying to a god that doesn't exist and, therefore, can't protect you or help you. As the Russians say, 'Pray to God; row to shore.'" Spalko's smile was an intimation of a confidence shared between comrades. "And the Russians ought to know, eh? Their history is written in blood. First the tsars and then the apparatchiks, as if the Party was any better than a line of despots!

"I tell you, László, the Russians may have failed utterly at politics, but when it comes to religion, they have the right idea. Religion—all religion—is false. It's the grand delusion of the weak-willed, the fearful, the sheep of the world, who haven't the strength to lead but want only to be led. Never mind that it's inevitably to their own slaughter." Spalko shook his head sadly, sagely. "No, no, the only reality is power, László. Money and power. This is what matters, nothing else."

Molnar had relaxed somewhat during this discourse, which, in its conversational tone and illusion of camaraderie, had been meant to bind him to his interrogator. Now, however, his eyes opened wide in naked panic as Spalko began again. "Only you can help yourself, László. Tell me what I want to know. Tell me where Vadas has hidden Felix Schiffer."

"Stop!" Molnar gasped. "Please stop!"

"I can't stop, László. Surely by now you can understand that. You're in control of this situation now." As if to illustrate his point, Spalko applied the instrument. "Only you can make me stop!"

A look of confusion came over Molnar, and he gazed wildly around as if only now realizing what was happening to him. Studying him, Spalko understood. It often happened this way near the end of a successful interrogation. The subject did not come step by step to the altar of confession, but rather resisted as long as he was able. The mind could manage only so much. As some point, like a stretched rubber band, it reached its limit, and when it snapped back, a new reality—the reality artfully erected by the interrogator—was established.

"I don't—"

"Tell me," Spalko said in a velvet voice, his gloved hand stroking his victim's sweating brow. "Tell me and this will all be over, gone like awaking from a dream."

Molnar's eyes rolled upward. "Do you promise?" he asked like a small child.

"Trust me. László. I'm your friend. I want what you want, an end your suffering."

Molnar was crying now, big tears welling up in his eyes, turning cloudy and pink as they rolled down his cheeks. And then he began to sob as he had not done since he was a small child.

Spalko said nothing. He knew they were at the crucial stage. It was all or nothing now: Either Molnar would step off the precipice to which Spalko had carefully brought him, or he would force himself to drown in the pain.

Molnar's body shook in the storm of emotion the interrogation had unleashed. In time, he put his head back. His face was gray and terribly drawn; his eyes still with their glaze of tears seemed to have shrunk farther back in their sockets. There was no sign of the bright-cheeked, slightly drunk operaphile Spalko's men had drugged in Underground. He had been transformed. He was utterly spent.

"God forgive me," he whispered hoarsely. "Dr. Schiffer is in Crete." He babbled an address.

"There's a good boy," Spalko said softly. Now the final piece of the puzzle had fallen into place. Tonight, he and his "staff" would be on their way to retrieve Felix Schiffer and finish the process of extracting from him the information required to launch their assault on the Oskjuhlid Hotel.

Molnar made a small animal noise as Spalko dropped the instrument. His bloodshot eyes rolled in his head; he was on the verge of weeping again.

Slowly, tenderly, Spalko placed the coffee cup to the other's lips, watched with disinterest as he convulsively drank down the hot, sweet coffee. "At last, deliverance." Whether he was speaking to Molnar or to himself was an open question.

CHAPTER THIRTEEN

At night, Budapest's Parliament resembled a great Magyar shield against the invading hordes of yore. To the average tourist, awestruck at its size as well as its beauty, it appeared solid, timeless, inviolable. But to Jason Bourne, newly arrived from his harrowing passage out of Washington, D.C., and Paris, the Parliament seemed nothing more than a fantasy city straight out of a children's book, a confection of unearthly white stone and pale copper that could at any moment collapse beneath the fall of darkness.

He was in a bleak mood when the taxi dropped him at the glowing dome of the Mammut shopping mall, near Moszkva tér, where he intended to buy himself new clothes. He had entered the country as Pierre Montefort, French military courier, and had therefore been given only the most cursory inspection by Hungarian Immigration. But he needed to get rid of the uniform Jacques had provided for him before he showed up at the hotel as Alex Conklin.

He bought a pair of cords, a Sea Island cotton shirt and black turtleneck sweater, thin-soled black boots and a black leather bomber jacket. He moved through the stores, the crowds of shoppers, gradually absorbing their energy, for the first time in many days feeling part of the world at large. He realized this sudden lightening of mood was because his mind had resolved the enigma of Khan. Of course, he wasn't Joshua; he was a superb con artist. An entity unknown—either Khan or someone who had hired him—wanted to get to Bourne, shake him up so badly that he would lose his concentration and forget about the murders of Alex Conklin and Mo Panov. If they weren't able to kill him, then at least they would make him go off on a wild goose chase searching for his phantom son. How Khan or whoever had hired him knew about Joshua was another question he needed to answer. Still, now that he had reduced the shock to a rational problem, his supremely logical mind could parse the problem into its separate parts and this would lead him to devising a plan of attack.

Bourne needed information that only Khan could provide. He needed to turn the tables on Khan, to draw him into a trap. The first step was to ensure that Khan knew where he was. He had no doubt that Khan would be in Paris by now, having known the destination of the Rush Service flight. Khan might even have heard about Bourne's "death" on the Al. In fact, from what he knew of Khan, he was, like Bourne, an accomplished chameleon. If Bourne were in his place, the first place he'd look for information was the Quai d'Orsay.

Twenty minutes later Bourne strode out of the mall complex, got into a taxi that was letting off a passenger, and in no time he was in front of the imposing stone portico of the Danubius Grand Hotel on Margaret Island. A uniformed doorman escorted him inside.

Bourne, feeling as if he hadn't slept in a week, crossed the gleaming marble foyer. He introduced himself to the front desk clerk as Alexander Conklin.

"Ah, Mr. Conklin, you're expected. Please wait a moment, won't you?"

The man vanished into an inner office out of which, a moment later, emerged the hotel manager.

"Welcome, welcome! I'm Mr. Hazas and I'm at your disposal." This gentleman was short, squat and dark, with a pencil mustache and hair parted down the side. He extended a hand, which was warm and dry. "Mr. Conklin, such a pleasure." He gestured. "Would you be so good as to come with me, please?"

He led Bourne through into his office, whereupon he opened a safe, extracting a package roughly the size and shape of a shoebox, which he had Bourne sign for. On the wrapping was printed ALEXANDER CONKLIN. HOLD FOR PICK-UP. There were no stamps.

"The package was hand-delivered," the manager said in response to Bourne's query.

"By whom?" Bourne asked.

Mr. Hazas spread his hands. "I'm afraid I don't know."

Bourne felt a sudden flush of anger. "What do you mean, you don't know? Surely, the hotel must keep records of delivered packages."

"Oh, assuredly, Mr. Conklin. As in everything, we are meticulous in this area. However, in this particular case—and I cannot say how—there appears to be no record whatsoever." He smiled hopefully even as he shrugged helplessly.

After three days of constantly fighting for his life, of having to absorb shock after shock, he found he had no reservoir of patience left. Anger and frustration flared into blind rage. Kicking the door shut, he grabbed Hazas up by his heavily starched shirtfront, slammed him so hard against the wall, the hotel manager's eyes fairly bugged out of his head.

"Mr. Conklin," he stammered, "I don't—"

"I want answers!" Bourne shouted, "and I want them now!"

Mr. Hazas, clearly terrified, was fairly weeping. "But I have no answers." His blunt fingers fluttered. "There . . . there's the ledger! See for yourself!"

Bourne released the hotel manager, whose legs collapsed immediately, depositing him on the floor. Bourne ignored him, went to his desk, took up the ledger. He could see the entries laboriously written out in two distinct handwritings, one crimped, the other fussy—presumably the day and night managers. He was only mildly surprised to learn that he could read Hungarian. Turning the ledger a bit, he ran his eye up and down the columns, looking for any erasures, any hint that the ledger had been tampered with. He found nothing.

He whirled on Mr. Hazas, hauled him up from his curled position. "How do you account for this package not being logged in?"

"Mr. Conklin, I myself was here when it was delivered." The hotel manager's eyes showed their whites all around. His skin had gone pale; it crawled with sweat. "That is to say, I was on duty. I swear to you one moment it was there on the top of the check-in counter. It simply appeared. I didn't see the person who brought it and neither did anyone on my staff. It was noon, check-out time, a very busy period for us. It must have been left anonymously, deliberately—nothing else makes sense."

He was right, of course. In an instant, Bourne's intense rage drained away, leaving him wondering why he had so terrorized this perfectly harmless man. He let the hotel manager go.

"My apologies, Mr. Hazas. It's been a long day and I've had a number of difficult negotiations."

"Yes, sir." Mr. Hazas was doing his best to straighten his tie and jacket, all the while eyeing Bourne as if at any moment he might launch another attack.

"Of course, sir. The business world puts strains on all of us." He coughed, regaining a semblance of his composure. "May I suggest a spa treatment—there's nothing like a steam and massage to restore the inner balance."

"That's very kind of you," Bourne said. "Perhaps later."

"The spa closes at nine o'clock," Mr. Hazas said, relieved that he had gotten a sane response from this madman. "But it only takes a call from me to keep it open for you."

"Another time, thanks very much. Please have a toothbrush and paste sent up to the suite. I forget to bring some," Bourne said, opening the door and walking out.

The moment he was left alone, Hazas opened a drawer in his desk and, with a hand that trembled terribly, he took out a bottle of schnapps. Filling a shotglass, he spilled some onto his ledger. He didn't care; he swigged it down, felt the liquor burn its fiery path into his stomach. When he had calmed himself sufficiently, he picked up the phone, dialed a local number.

"He arrived not ten minutes ago," he said to the voice at the other end. There was no need to identify himself. "My impression? He's a madman. I'll tell you what I mean. He almost choked me to death when I wouldn't tell him who delivered the package."

The receiver slipped in the sweat of his palm and he switched hands. He poured himself another two fingers of schnapps.

"Of course I didn't tell him, and there's no record of the delivery anywhere. I saw to it myself. He searched carefully enough, I'll give him that." He listened for a moment. "He went up to his suite. Yes, I'm sure."

He put down the phone, then just as quickly dialed another number, delivered the same message, this time to a different and far more terrifying master. Finally, he slumped back in his chair and closed his eyes. *Thank God my part in this is over*, he thought.

Bourne took the elevator up to the top floor. The key opened one of the double doors of solid polished teak, and Bourne walked into a large one-bedroom suite furnished in sumptuous fabrics. Outside the window, the one-hundred-year-old parkland loomed dark and leafy. The island had been named after Margaret, the daughter of King Bela IV who lived in a Dominican convent here during the thirteenth century, the ruins of which were brightly lit on the east bank. He was already undressing as he went through the suite, dropping each article of clothing behind him as he made for the gleaming bathroom. He threw the package down on the bed unopened.

He spent ten blessed minutes naked under a spray of water as hot as he could tolerate, then he soaped up, scrubbing the accumulated grime and sweat off him. Gingerly, he tested his ribs, the muscles of his chest, seeking a final assessment of the damage Khan had inflicted on him. His right shoulder was very sore, and he spent another ten minutes carefully stretching and gently exercising it. He had nearly dislocated it when he had grabbed the tanker truck's rung, and it hurt like hell. He suspected that he had torn some ligaments, but there was nothing he could do about it except try not to overwork the area.

After standing under an icy spray for three minutes, he stepped out of the shower and toweled off. Wrapped in a luxurious bathrobe, he sat on the bed, unwrapped the package. Inside was a gun with extra ammunition. *Alex*, he asked, not for the first time, *what in the world were you involved in?*

For a long time, he sat staring at the weapon. There seemed something evil about it, a darkness seeping out of the barrel. And it was then that Bourne realized that the darkness was bubbling up from the depths of his own unconscious. All at once, he saw that his reality was not at all as he had imagined it at the Mammut mall. It wasn't neat and orderly, rational as a mathematical equation. The real world was chaotic; rationality was merely the system human beings tried to impose on random events in order the make them appear orderly. His explosion of rage was not at the hotel manager, he realized with something of a shock, but at Khan. Khan had shadowed him, bedeviled him, and in the end had tricked him. He wanted nothing less than to pummel that face into the ground, to expunge it from his memory.

The sight of the Buddha had caused the four-year-old Joshua to appear in his mind's eye. It was twilight in Saigon, the sky saffron and greenish-gold. Joshua was running out of the house by the river as David Webb drew up on his return from work. Webb took Joshua up in his arms, swung him around, kissed his cheeks, though the boy shied away. He never did like being kissed by his father.

Bourne now saw his son tucked into bed at night. The crickets and tree frogs were singing and lights from passing boats swept across the far wall of the room. Joshua was listening as Webb read him a story. On a Saturday morning Webb played catch with Joshua, using a baseball he had brought all the way from America. The light struck Joshua's innocent face, turning it incandescent.

Now Bourne blinked and despite himself he saw the small stone Buddha hanging around Khan's neck. He leaped up, and with a guttural cry of utter despair flung the lamp, blotter, writing pad, crystal ashtray off the table. Hands balled into fists, he struck himself repeatedly in the head. With a moan of despair, he fell to his knees, rocking himself. Only the phone ringing brought him around.

Viciously, he willed his head to clear. The phone kept on ringing and for a moment he had the urge to let it ring. Instead, he picked it up. "It's János Vadas," came a whispered, smoke-roughened voice. "Matthias Church. Midnight, not a moment later." The line clicked dead before Bourne could utter a word.

When Khan learned that Jason Bourne was dead, he felt as if he'd been turned inside out, as if all the nerves inside him had for one instant been exposed to the corrosive outside air. He touched the back of his hand to his forehead, certain that he was burning up from the inside out.

He was in Orly Airport, talking with the Quai d'Orsay. It had been ridiculously easy to get information from them. He was posing as a reporter from *Le Monde*, the French newspaper, whose credentials he had obtained— for an obscene price—from his Parisian contact. Not that it mattered to him; he had more money than he knew what to do with, but the time involved waiting had somehow put him on edge. As the minutes dragged into hours, as the afternoon turned into evening, he had realized that his vaunted patience had been shredded. The moment he had seen David Webb—Jason Bourne—time had been turned inside out, the past had become the present. His hands clenched into fists and a pulse beat strongly in his temple; how many times since sighting Bourne had he felt as if he was losing his mind? The absolute worst moment had been sitting on the bench in Old Town Alexandria, speaking to him as if there was nothing between them, as if the past had been rendered moot and meaningless, as if it had been part of someone else's life, someone Khan had only imagined. The un-reality of it—a moment he had dreamed of, prayed for for years—had evis-cerated him, leaving him feeling as if every nerve-ending had been rubbed raw, every emotion he had spent years trying to harness and suppress was now rebelling, rising to the surface, sickening him. And now came this news, like a hammerblow from heaven. He felt as if the void inside him he as-sumed would be filled had only become wider, deeper, threatening to swal-low him whole. He could not bear to be here a moment longer.

One moment he was talking, notepad in hand, with the Quai d'Orsay press liaison and the next moment he was hurtled back in time to the jun-gles of Vietnam, to the wood and bamboo house of Richard Wick, the mis-sionary, a tall, slender man with a somber demeanor who had taken him from out of the wild after he'd escaped from the Vietnamese gunrunner he'd killed. Nevertheless, he was quick to laughter and there was a softness to his brown eyes that spoke of a great sympathy. Wick might have been a tough taskmaster in converting the heathen Khan into a child of Christ, but in the more intimate time of dinner and its quiet aftermath, he was kind and gentle and, in the end, provoked Khan's trust.

So much so, that one evening Khan made up his mind to tell Wick about his past, to lay bare his soul in order that he be healed. Khan desperately wanted to be healed, to vomit up the abscess that had been churning its poison inside him as it grew ever larger. He wanted to confess his rage at his abandonment, he wanted to be rid of it, for he had lately come to un-derstand that he was being held prisoner by his extreme emotions.

He longed to confide in Wick, to describe to him the roil of emotion churning in his guts, but the opportunity never arose. Wick was extremely busy bringing the Word of God to "this forlorn Godless backwater." As such, he sponsored Bible study groups of which Khan was ordered to be a part. In fact, one of Wick's favorite pastimes involved calling on Khan to rise in front of this group and recite from memory sections of the Bible, like some form of idiot savant shown off for money at a carnival side show.

Khan hated it, felt humiliated by it. In fact, strange to say, the more proud of him Wick seemed the greater his humiliation. Until, one day, the missionary brought in another young boy. But because the boy was Cau-casian, the orphan of a missionary couple of Wick's acquaintance, Wick lavished the love and attention on him that Khan had craved and now saw that he'd never had and, worse, never would have. Still, his abominable recitations continued while the other boy sat and watched, silent, free of the humiliation that racked Khan.

He could never get over the fact of Wick using him, and it was only on the day he ran away that he understood the depths of Wick's betrayal of him. His benefactor, his protector, was not interested in *him*—in Khan—but rather in adding another convert, bringing another savage into the light of God's love.

At that moment, his cell phone rang, and he was dragged back into the awful present. He looked at his phone's screen to see who was calling, then, excusing himself, stepped away from the Quai d'Orsay officer into the swirling anonymity of the concourse proper.

"This is a surprise," he said into his phone.

"Where are you?" Stepan Spalko's voice sounded curt, as if he had too many things on his mind.

"Orly Airport. I've just learned from the Quai d'Orsay that David Webb is dead."

"Is that so?"

"It seems he rode a motorcycle into the grille of an oncoming truck." Khan paused for a moment, waiting for a reaction. "I must say you don't sound happy. Isn't that what you wanted?"

"It's premature to celebrate Webb's death, Khan," Spalko said dryly. "I've heard from my contact at the desk of the Danubius Grand Hotel here in Budapest that Alexander Conklin just checked in."

Khan was so shocked that he felt his knees begin to give out, and he walked to a wall, leaned against it. "Webb?"

"It isn't Alex Conklin's ghost!"

To his chagrin, he discovered that he'd broken out into a cold sweat. "But how can you be sure it's him?"

"I got a description from my contact. I've seen the composite drawing that's been circulated."

Khan gritted his teeth. He knew the conversation would likely lead to a bad end, and yet he saw himself moving inexorably forward. "You knew David Webb was Jason Bourne. Why didn't you tell me?"

"I don't see why I needed to," Spalko said blandly. "You asked about Webb and I delivered. I'm not in the habit of reading people's minds. But I applaud your initiative."

Khan was gripped by a spasm of hatred so strong he felt himself shiver. He kept his voice calm, however. "Now that Bourne's gotten all the way to Budapest, how long do you think it will take him to follow his leads back to you?"

"I've already taken steps to ensure that doesn't happen," Spalko said. "But it occurs to me that I wouldn't have needed to go through the trouble if you'd killed the sonuvabitch when you had the chance."

Khan, distrustful of a man who had lied to him, who had, furthermore, played him for a cat's-paw, felt another devastating stab of anger. Spalko wanted him to kill Bourne, but why? He was going to find that out before he completed his own act of vengeance. When he spoke next, he'd lost a modicum of his icy self-control so that his voice took on a decidedly sharp edge. "Oh, I'll kill Bourne," he said. "But it'll be on *my* terms, according to *my* timetable, not yours."

Humanistas, Ltd. owned three hangars at Ferihegy Airport. In one of them, a container truck was backed up to a small jet on whose curving silver fuselage was painted the Humanistas logo: the green cross held in the palm of a hand. Uniformed men were loading the last of the weapons crates on board while Hasan Arsenov checked the manifest. When he went to talk to one of the workers, Stepan Spalko turned to Zina and in a conversational voice said, "In just a few hours I'm leaving for Crete. I want you to come with me."

Zina's eyes opened wide in surprise. "Shaykh, I am scheduled to return with Hasan to Chechnya in order to make the last-minute preparations for our mission."

Spalko's eyes did not leave hers. "Arsenov doesn't need your help with the final touches. In fact, in my estimation he'll be better off without the . . . distraction of having you around."

Zina, trapped by his gaze, opened her lips.

"I want to make this absolutely clear, Zina." Spalko saw Arsenov coming back toward them. "I'm not giving you an order. The decision's entirely up to you."

Despite the urgency of the moment, he spoke slowly and distinctly, and the import of his words wasn't lost on her. He was offering her an opportunity—for what she had no idea—but it was clear that this was a defining moment in her life. Either choice she made, there was no going back; by the manner in which he'd spoken to her, he'd made that quite clear. The decision might be up to her, but she was certain that if she said no, it would be the end for her in one way or another. The fact was, she didn't want to say no.

"I've always wanted to see Crete," she whispered as Arsenov came up to them.

Spalko nodded to her. Then turned to the Chechen terrorist leader. "Everything accounted for?"

Arsenov looked up from his clipboard. "How could it be otherwise, Shaykh?" He checked his watch. "Zina and I will be taking off within the hour."

"Actually, Zina will be accompanying the arms," Spalko said easily. "The shipment is due to rendezvous with my fishing boat in the Faeroe Islands. I want one of you there to oversee the transfer and the last leg of the trip to Iceland. You're needed with your unit." He smiled. "I've no doubt that you can spare Zina for a few days' time."

Arsenov frowned, glanced at Zina, who smartly met his gaze with a neutral look, then nodded. "It will be as you wish, Shaykh, of course."

Zina found it interesting that the Shaykh had lied to Hasan about his plans for her. She found herself bound inside the little conspiracy he had woven, both excited and nervous with anticipation. She saw the look on Hasan's face and part of her felt a pang, but then she thought of the mystery awaiting her, and the honey of the Shaykh's voice, *"I'm leaving for Crete. I want you to come with me."*

Standing beside Zina, Spalko held out his arm and Arsenov gripped his forearm in the manner of warriors. *"La illaha ill Allah."*

"La illaha ill Allah," Arsenov replied, bowing his head.

"There's a limousine waiting outside to take you to the passenger terminal. Until Reykjavík, my friend." Spalko turned away, walked over to the pilot to speak with him a moment, leaving Zina to say her farewell to her current lover.

Khan felt ravaged by unfamiliar emotions. Forty minutes later, waiting for the flight to Budapest to board, he still had not gotten over the shock he'd received on learning that Jason Bourne was, in fact, alive. He sat, elbows on knees, face in his hands, trying—and failing miserably—to make sense of the world. To someone like him, whose past informed every moment of his present, it was impossible to find a pattern that could make things understandable. The past was a mystery—and his memory of it was a whore that did the bidding of his subconscious, distorting facts, telescoping events or omitting them altogether, all in the service of the sac of poison growing inside him.

But these emotions running rampant through him were even more devastating. He was enraged by the fact that he'd needed Stepan Spalko to tell him that Jason Bourne was still alive. Why hadn't his normally finely tuned instincts told him to check a little deeper? Would an agent of Bourne's skills run into the grille of an oncoming truck? And where was the body? Had there been a proper identification? He'd been told they were still sifting through the remains, that the explosion and subsequent fire had done so much damage that it would take hours more, if not days, to make sense of it all, and even then, there might not be enough found to give them a confirming ID. He should have been suspicious. It was a ploy he would use—in fact, he had employed a variant three years ago when he needed to make a very hot exit from the docks in Singapore.

But there was another question running over and over in his mind, and though he'd been trying to block it out, he couldn't. What had he felt at the precise moment of knowing that Jason Bourne was still alive? Elation? Fear? Rage? Despair? Or was it a melange of all of these—a sickening kaleidoscope that ran the gamut and back again?

He heard his flight being called, and in a something of a daze, he joined the line to board.

Spalko, walking past the entrance to the Eurocenter Bio-I Clinic at 75 Hattyu utca, was deep in thought. It appeared as if Khan was going to present a problem. Khan had his uses; he was better than anyone else at eliminating targets, there could be no debate on that score, but even that rare talent faded against the danger he felt Khan was becoming. This very question had been much on his mind ever since the first time Khan had failed to kill Jason Bourne. Something anomalous in the situation had stuck in his craw like a fish bone, and ever since, he'd been trying to cough it up or to swallow it. And yet, there it still sat, refusing to be dislodged. With this last conversation, he was acutely aware that he'd need to see to the final disposition of his former assassin-for-hire without delay. He couldn't afford anyone getting close to his forthcoming operation in Reykjavík. Bourne or Khan, it didn't matter now. In this regard, they were both equally dangerous.

He entered the café around the corner from the ugly modernist structure of the clinic. He smiled into the bland face of the man, tilted slightly up at him now.

"Sorry, Peter," he said as he slid into a chair at their table.

Dr. Peter Sido raised a hand equally. "It's of no moment, Stepan. I know how busy you are."

"Not too busy to find Dr. Schiffer."

"And thank God for that!" Sido ladled whipped cream into his coffee cup. He shook his head. "Honestly, Stepan, I don't know how I'd do without you and your contacts. When I discovered that Felix was missing, I was ready to lose my mind."

"Don't worry, Peter. Every day we're closer to finding him. Trust me."

"Oh, I do." Sido was in all ways physically unremarkable. He was of middle height and weight with eyes the color of mud, magnified behind steel-rimmed spectacles, and short brown hair that seemed to fall across his scalp with no design or attention from him. He wore a brown herringbone tweed suit, slightly shabby at the cuffs, white shirt and a brown-and-black tie that was at least a decade out of date. He might have been a salesman or an undertaker, but he was not, for his unremarkable exterior concealed a most remarkable mind.

"The question I have for you," Spalko said now, "is whether you have the product for me."

Sido was apparently expecting the question because he nodded immediately. "It's all synthesized and ready whenever you need it."

"Did you bring it?"

"Just the sample. The rest is safely locked away in the Bio-I Clinic's cold room. And don't worry about the sample; it's locked in a travel case I made myself. The product is extremely delicate. You see, up until the moment it's to be used, it must be kept at minus thirty-two degrees Celsius. The case I constructed has its own integrated cooling unit that will last for forty-eight hours." He reached beneath the table, brought up a small metal box more or less the size of two stacked paperback books. "Is that long enough?"

"Quite enough, thank you." Spalko took possession of the box. It was heavier than it looked, no doubt owing to the refrigeration unit "It's in the vial I specified?"

"Of course." Sido sighed. "I still don't fully understand why you need such a lethal pathogen."

Spalko studied him for a moment. He took out a cigarette and lit it. He knew that to come up with an explanation too quickly would spoil the effect, and with Dr. Peter Sido effect was everything. Though he was a genius at creating airborne pathogens, the good doctor's people skills left something to be desired. Not that he was much different from most scientists with their noses in their beakers, but in this case, Sido's naïveté suited Spalko's purposes perfectly. He wanted his friend back, nothing else much mattered, which was why he wouldn't listen too carefully to Spalko's explanation. It was his conscience that needed reassuring, nothing more.

Spalko spoke at last. "As I said, I was contacted by the joint American–British Anti-Terrorist Task Force."

"Will they be at the summit next week?"

"Of course," Spalko lied. There was no joint American–British Anti-Terrorist Task Force except for the one he had concocted. "In any case, they're on the verge of a breakthrough against the threat of bioterrorism, which, as you know better than most, includes lethal airborne pathogens as well as chemical substances. They need to test it, which is why they came to me, and why we've made this agreement. I find Dr. Schiffer for you and you provide the product the task force needs."

"Yes, I know all that. You explained . . ." Sido's voice trailed off. He played nervously with his spoon, drumming it up and down against his napkin until Spalko asked him to stop.

Sorry," he mumbled and pushed his spectacles back up the bridge of his nose. "But what I still don't understand is what they're going to do with the product. I mean, you mentioned a test of some sort."

Spalko leaned forward. Now was the crucial time; he had to sell Sido. He looked to his left and right. When he spoke, he lowered his voice considerably. "Listen very carefully. Peter. I've told you more than I perhaps should have. This is all most top-secret, d'you see?"

Sido, hunched forward in response, nodded his head.

"In fact, I'm afraid that I've violated the confidentiality agreement they made me sign just by telling you this much."

"Oh, dear." Sido's expression was mournful. "I've put you at risk."

"Please don't worry about that, Peter. I'll be fine," Spalko said. "Unless, of course, you tell someone."

"Oh, but I wouldn't. Never."

Spalko smiled. "I know you wouldn't, Peter. I trust you, you see."

"And I appreciate that, Stepan. You know I do."

Spalko had to bite his lip in order not to laugh. Instead, he dove deeper into this farce. "I don't know what the test is, Peter, because they haven't told me," he said so softly that the other was obliged to lean in so close their noses were almost touching. "And I wouldn't ask."

"Of course not."

"But I believe—and you must also—that these people are doing their utmost to keep us safe in an increasingly unsafe world." What it always boiled down to, Spalko thought, was a matter of trust. But for the patsy—in this case, Sido—to be taken in, he had to know that *you* had given *him* your trust. After that, you could fleece him of everything he owned and he'd never suspect it was you who'd done it to him. "I say, whatever they have to do, we must help them in any way we can. This is what I told them when they first approached me."

"It's what I would've told them, as well." Sido wiped the perspiration off his unremarkable upper lip. "Believe me, Stepan, if you can count on anything you can count on that."

The U.S. Naval Observatory at Massachusetts Avenue and 34th Street was the official source for all standard time in the United States. It was one of the few places in the country where the moon, the stars and the planets were kept under constant observation. The largest telescope on the property was more than one hundred years old and was still in use. Peering through it in 1877, Dr. Asaph Hall discovered the two moons of Mars. Nobody knows why he chose to call them Deimos (Anxiety) and Phobos (Fear), but the DCI knew that when his melancholia lay most deeply about him, he was drawn to the observatory. That was why he'd had an office set up for himself deep in the heart of the building, not far from Dr. Hall's telescope.

It was here that Martin Lindros found him on a closed-circuit teleconference linkup with Jamie Hull, head of the U.S. security detail in Reykjavík.

"Feyd al-Saoud I'm not concerned with," Hull was saying in his rather supercilious voice. "The Arabs don't know shit about modern-day security, so they're happy to take our lead." He shook his head. "It's the Russian, Boris Illyich Karpov, who's giving me a royal pain in the ass. He questions everything. If I say white, he says black. I think the fucker gets off on arguing."

"Are you saying you can't handle one goddamn Russian security analyst, Jamie?"

"Uh, what?" Hull's blue eyes looked startled and his ginger mustache jumped up and down. "No, sir. Not at all."

"Because I can have you replaced in a heartbeat." The DCI's voice projected a thorny note of cruelty.

"No, sir."

"And believe me, I will. I'm in no fucking mood for—"

"That won't be necessary. I'll get Karpov under control."

"See that you do." Lindros could hear the sudden weariness in the old warrior's voice, hoped Jamie couldn't detect it through the electronic connection. "We need a solid front before, during and after the president's visit. Is that clear?"

"Yessir."

"No sign of Jason Bourne, I suppose."

"None whatsoever, sir. Believe me, we've been extra vigilant."

Lindros, aware that the DCI had gotten all the information he required for the moment, cleared his throat.

"Jamie, my next appointment just showed," the DCI said without turning around. "I'll be in touch tomorrow." He toggled off the teleconferencer, sat with his hands steepled, staring at the a large color photograph of the planet Mars and its two uninhabitable moons.

Lindros shrugged off his raincoat, came and sat down beside his boss. The room the DCI had chosen was small, cramped and over-hot even in the depths of winter. A portrait of the president was on one wall. Opposite was a single window through which tall pines could be seen, black and white, all detail washed out of them by the brilliant security floodlights. "The news from Paris is good," he said. "Jason Bourne is dead."

The DCI picked up his head, a certain animation flooding features that had been slack moments ago. "They got him? How? I hope the bastard died in a world of pain."

"Chances are he did, sir. He died in a highway collision on the Al just northwest of Paris. The motorcycle he was driving rammed head-on into an eighteen-wheeler. A Quai d'Orsay officer was an eyewitness."

"My God," the DCI breathed. "Nothing left but an oil slick." His brows knitted together. "There can be no doubt?"

"Until we have a confirmed identification, there's always doubt," Lindros said. "We forwarded Bourne's dental records and a sample of his DNA, but the French authorities tell me there was a terrific explosion, and in the aftermath the fire burned so hotly that they fear even the bones might not have survived. In any case, it's going to take them a day or two to sift through the scene of the accident. They've assured me that they'll be in touch as soon as they have further information."

The DCI nodded.

"And Jacques Robbinet is unharmed," Lindros added.

"Who?"

"The French Minister of Culture, sir. He was a friend of Conklin's and a sometime asset. We were afraid he was Bourne's next target."

The two men sat very still. The DCI's eyes had turned inward. Perhaps he was thinking of Alex Conklin, perhaps he was contemplating the roles anxiety and fear played in modern life, wondering how Dr. Hall had been so prescient. He had gotten into clandestine work in the mistaken notion that it would help alleviate the anxiety and fear with which he had seemed to have been born. Instead, operating in the twilight had done just the opposite. And yet he had never contemplated leaving his profession. He could not imagine life without it; his very being was defined by who he was and what he had done in the sub-rosa world invisible to civilians.

"Sir, if I may say so, it's late."

The DCI sighed. "Tell me something I don't know, Martin."

"I think it's time you went home to Madeleine," Lindros said softly.

The DCI passed a hand across his face. All off a sudden he was very tired. "Maddy's at her sister's in Phoenix. The house is dark tonight."

"Go home anyway."

As Lindros rose, the DCI turned his head in his deputy's direction. "Martin, listen to me, you may think this Bourne business is over, but it isn't."

Lindros had taken up his raincoat; now he paused. "I don't understand, sir."

"Bourne may be dead, but in the last few hours of his life he managed to make monkeys of us."

"Sir—"

"Public spectacles. We can't have that. In this day and age, there's just too much damn scrutiny. And where there's scrutiny, there are hard questions asked, and these questions unless immediately put to rest inevitably lead to grave consequences." The DCI's eyes sparked. "We are lacking only one element to wrap up this sorry episode and consign it to the dustbin of history."

"What's that, sir?"

"We need a scapegoat, Martin, someone to whom the shit will stick completely, leaving us smelling like rosebuds in May." He looked hard at his DDCI. "Do you have someone like that, Martin?"

A cold ball of anxiety had formed in the pit of Lindros' stomach.

"Come, come, Martin," the DCI said with asperity, "do speak up."

Still, Lindros looked at him mutely. He seemed as if he could not get his jaws to work.

"Of course you do, Martin," the DCI snapped.

"You're loving this, aren't you?"

The DCI winced inside at the accusation. Not for the first time, he was grateful that his boys were safely away from this business where he would have had to hold them down. No one was going to surpass him; he'd make sure of that. "If you won't name him, I will. Detective Harris."

"We can't do that to him," Lindros said tightly. He could feel the anger fizzing in his head like a just-popped can of soda.

"We? Who said anything about we, Martin? This was your assignment. I made that clear from the get-go. Now it's entirely up to you to assign the blame."

"But Harris didn't do anything wrong."

The DCI arched an eyebrow. "I very much doubt that, but even if it's true, who cares?"

"I do, sir."

"Very well, Martin. Then I suppose you'll be taking the blame for the fiascos in Old Town and Washington Circle yourself."

Lindros' lips clamped shut. "This is my choice?"

"I don't see any others, do you? The bitch-woman intends to extract her pound of flesh from me one way or the other. If I have to sacrifice someone, I would damn well rather it be some aging detective in the Virginia State Police than my own DDCI. If you fell on your own sword, how do you suppose that would reflect on me, Martin?"

"Christ," Lindros said, in a seething rage, "how in the hell did you manage to survive this snakepit for so long?"

The DCI stood up, drew on his overcoat. "What makes you think I have?"

Bourne arrived at the Gothic stone edifice of Matthias Church at eleven-forty. He spent the following twenty minutes reconnoitering the area. The air was crisp and chill, the sky clear. But near the horizon a bank of thick clouds roiled and on the freshening wind the damp musk of rain came to him. Now and again a sound or a scent fired something in his damaged memory. He was certain that he had been here before, though when and on what mission he couldn't say. Once again, as he touched the void of loss and longing, he thought of Alex and Mo so strongly he might have been able to conjure them up this very moment.

With a grimace, he went on with his task, securing the area, making sure as best he could that the rendezvous site wasn't under enemy surveillance.

At the stroke of midnight, he approached the enormous southern facade of the church from which rose the eighty-meter Gothic stone tower, laden with gargoyles. A young woman was standing on the lowest step. She was tall, slim, strikingly beautiful. Her long red hair shone in the streetlights. Behind her, over the portal was a fourteenth-century relief of the Virgin Mary. The young woman asked him his name.

"Alex Conklin," he replied.

"Passport, please," she said as crisply as an Immigration official.

He handed it over, watched her as she examined it with her eyes and the pad of her thumb. She had interesting hands; they were slender, long-fingered, strong, blunt-nailed. A musician's hands. She could not be more than thirty-five.

"How do I know you're really Alexander Conklin?" she said.

"How does one know anything absolutely?" Bourne said. "Faith."

The woman snorted. "What's your first name?"

"It says right on the pass—"

She gave him a hard look. "I mean your *real* first name. The one you were born with."

"Alexsei," Bourne said, remembering that Conklin was a Russian emigré.

The young woman nodded. She had a well-sculpted face dominated by green Magyar eyes, large and hooded, and wide, generous lips. There was about her a certain sharp-edged primness, but at the same time a fin de siè- cle sensuality that in its sub-rosa nature hinted intriguingly of a more in- nocent century when what was kept unspoken was often more important than what was freely expressed. "Welcome to Budapest, Mr. Conklin. I'm Annaka Vadas." She lifted a shapely arm, gestured. "Please come with me."

She led him across the plaza fronting the church and around the corner. In the shadowed street, a small wooden door with ancient iron bands was barely visible. She took out a small flashlight, snapped it on. It produced a very powerful beam of light. Taking an old-fashioned key from her purse, she inserted it in the lock, turned it first one way, then the other. The door opened at her touch.

"My father is waiting for you inside," she said. They entered the vast inte- rior of the church. By the wavering beam of the flashlight, Bourne could see that the plastered walls were iced with colored ornamental design. The frescoes depicted the lives of Hungarian saints.

"In 1541 Buda fell to the invading Turks and for the next one hundred fifty years the church became the main mosque of the city," she said. Playing the flashlight over her subject. "In order to serve their needs, the Turks stripped the furnishings and whitewashed the magnificent frescoes. Now, however, everything has been restored to the way it was in the thirteenth century."

Bourne saw dim light up ahead. Annaka led him into the northern sec- tion, where there was a series of chapels. In the one nearest to the chancel the sarcophagi of tenth-century Hungarian king, Bélla III, and his wife, Anne of Châtillon, lay in ghostly precision. In the former crypt, beside a row of medieval carvings, stood a figure in the shadows.

János Vadas extended his hand. As Bourne moved to grasp it, three glowering men appeared from out of the shadows. Bourne, very quick, drew the gun. This only produced a smile from Vadas.

"Look at the firing pin, Mr. Bourne. Did you think I would provide you with a gun that worked?"

Bourne saw that Annaka had a gun trained on him.

"Alexsei Conklin was a long-time friend of mine, Mr. Bourne. And, in any case, your face is on the news." He had a hunter's calculating face, all dark and brooding brows, a square jaw and glittering eyes. In his youth he had had a distinct widow's peak, but now, in his mid-sixties, time had eroded his hairline, leaving a gleaming triangular promontory on his forehead. "It's believed you killed Alexsei and another man, a Dr. Panov, I believe. For Alexsei's death alone I would be justified in ordering you killed here and now."

"He was an old friend, more, even—a mentor."

Vadas looked sad, resigned. He sighed. "And you turned on him, I suppose, because you, like everyone else, want what is in Felix Schiffer's mind."

"I have no idea what you're talking about."

"No, of course you don't," Vadas said with a good degree of skepticism.

"How do you think I knew Alex's real name? Alexsei and Mo Panov were friends."

"Then killing them would have been an act of utter insanity."

"Exactly."

"It is Mr. Hazas' considered opinion that you're insane," Vadas said calmly. "You remember Mr. Hazas, the hotel manager you almost beat to a pulp. A madman, I believe he called you."

"So that's how you knew to call me," Bourne said. "I may have twisted his arm a little too hard, but I knew he was lying."

"He was lying for me," Vadas said with a touch of pride.

Under the watchful gaze of Annaka and the three men, Bourne went across to Vadas, held out the useless gun. The moment Vadas reached for it, Bourne spun him around. At the same instant he drew his ceramic gun, pressed it hard against Vadas' temple. "Did you really think I would use an unknown gun without pulling it apart and putting it back together again?"

Directing himself to Annaka, he said in a calm, matter-of-fact voice, "Unless you want your father's brains spattered all over five centuries of history, put down your gun. Don't look at him; do as I tell you!"

Annaka put down her gun.

"Kick it over here."

She did as he ordered.

None of the three men had made a move, and now they wouldn't. Bourne kept one eye on them just the same. He took the muzzle away from Vadas' temple, let him go.

"I could have shot you dead, if that had been my wish."

"And I would have killed you," Annaka said fiercely.

"I've no doubt you'd have tried," Bourne said. He put up the ceramic gun, showing her and Vadas' men that had he no intention of using it. "But these are hostile acts. We'd have to be enemies to make them." Picking up Annaka's gun, he handed it to her, grips first.

Without a word, she took it, aimed it at him.

"What have you turned your daughter into, Mr. Vadas? She would kill for you, yes, but it also seems as if she would kill too quickly and for no reason at all."

Vadas stepped between Annaka and Bourne, pushed her gun down with his hand. "I've enough enemies as it is, Annaka," he said softly.

Annaka put away her gun, but her flashing eyes still held a hostility Bourne noted.

Vadas turned to Bourne. "As I said, for you, killing Alexsei would have been an act of insanity, and yet you seem to be the very opposite of a madman."

"I was set up, made to be the patsy for the killings, so that the real killer would remain free."

"Interesting. Why?"

"I came here to find that out."

Vadas stared hard at Bourne. Then he looked around him, raised his arms. "I would have met Alexsei here, you know, had he lived. You see, this is a place of great significance. Here, at the dawn of the fourteenth century, once stood Buda's first parish church. The huge pipe organ you see up there on the balcony played at the two weddings of King Matthias. The last two kings of Hungary, Francis Joseph I and Charles IV, were crowned on this spot,. Yes, there's great history here, and Alexsei and I, we were going to change history."

"With the help of Dr. Felix Schiffer, wasn't it?" Bourne said.

Vadas had no time to answer. Just then, an echoing roar sounded and he was thrown backward, arms outstretched. Blood oozed from a bullethole in his forehead. Bourne grabbed Annaka, dived onto the stonework paving. Vadas' men turned and, fanning out, began to return fire as they headed for cover. One was shot almost immediately, and he skidded over the marble floor, dead before he collapsed. A second gained the edge of a bench and was desperately trying to get behind it when he, too, was felled by a bullet that entered his spine. He arched back, his weapon crashing to the floor.

Bourne looked from the third man taking cover to Vadas, who lay sprawled face-up in a widening pool of blood. He was unmoving, no respiration visible in his chest. More gunfire brought Bourne's attention back to Vadas' third man, who was now rising out of a crouch, squeezing off a series of shots, his trajectory upward toward the cathedral's great organ. His head flung backward and his arms opened wide as a speck of blood on his chest rapidly widened. He tried to clutch at the fatal wound, but his eyes were already rolling up in his head.

Bourne looked up into the gloom of the organ balcony, saw a darker shadow flitting, and he fired. Stone chips flew. Then he had grabbed Annaka's flashlight, playing the beam over the balcony as he ran toward the spiral stone staircase up to it. Annaka, at last released and able to make sense of the chaos, saw her father and screamed.

"Back!" Bourne shouted. "You're in danger!"

Ignoring him, Annaka rushed to her father's side.

Bourne covered her, sending more shots into the shadows of the balcony, but he was not surprised at the lack of return fire. The sniper had achieved his aim; in all liklihood he was already on the run.

With no more time to waste, Bourne leaped up the staircase up to the balcony. Seeing a spent shell casing, he kept on going. The balcony appeared deserted. Its floor was stone-flagged, and the wall behind the organ ornately carved wood paneling. Bourne ducked behind the organ, but the space was deserted. He checked the floor around the organ, then the wood wall. The spacing around one of the panels appeared slightly different from the others, one side several millimeters wider as if . . .

Bourne felt around with his fingertips, discovered that the panel was in fact a narrow doorway. He went through it, found himself confronting a steep spiral staircase. With his gun at the ready, he climbed up the treads, which ended at another door. When he pushed it open, he saw that it gave out onto the rooftop of the church. The moment he poked his head out, a shot was fired at him. He ducked back but not before seeing a figure making its way onto the roof tiles, which were pitched at an extreme angle. To make matters worse, it had begun to rain and the tiles were even more treacherous. The positive side to this was that the assassin was too engaged with keeping his balance to risk firing off another shot at Bourne.

Bourne saw immediately that his new boot soles would skid and he pulled them off, dropped them over the side of the parapet. He then went crab-wise across the roof. Thirty meters below him, a dizzying drop away, the square in which the church sat gleamed in the Old World streetlights. Using his fingers and toes to anchor him, he continued his pursuit of the sniper. In the back of his mind was the suspicion that the figure he was pursuing was Khan, but how could he have arrived in Budapest before Bourne and why would he shoot Vadas rather than Bourne?

Lifting his head, he could see the figure was making for the south spire. Bourne scrambled after him, determined not to let him get away. The tiles were old and crumbly. One tile split down the center as he grasped it, coming off in his hand, and for a moment, he flailed about, balancing precariously on the acute pitch. Then he regained his balance, threw the tile away. It shattered on the flat rooftop of the small chapel extension ten feet below him.

His mind was racing ahead. The moment of extreme peril for him was when the sniper reached the safe haven of the spire. If Bourne was still exposed on the roof, the sniper would have a clear shot at him. It was raining harder now, making touch and sight that much more difficult. The south spire was no more than a hazy outline some fifty feet away.

Bourne was three-quarters of the way to the spire when he heard something—the clang of metal against stone—and he threw himself prone onto the tiles. Water sluiced over him and as he felt the zing of the bullet whizz past his ear, the tiles near his right knee exploded and he lost his purchase. He slid down the precipitous slope, tumbling off the edge.

Instinctively, he had relaxed his body, and when his shoulder struck the roof of the chapel below, he rolled himself into a ball, using his own momentum to launch himself across the roof, dissipating the energy of the drop. He fetched up against a stained-glass window, which kept him out of the sniper's line of sight.

Looking up, he could see that he was not that far from the spire. A lesser tower was just in front of him, a narrow slit of a window presenting itself. It was medieval in nature and therefore had no pane of glass in it. He squeezed through, found his way up to the top, which gave out onto a narrow stone parapet that led directly to the south spire.

Bourne had no way of knowing whether he would become visible to the sniper as he crossed the parapet. He took a deep breath, bolted out of the doorway, sprinted along the narrow stone passageway. Ahead of him, he saw the movement of a shadow, and he dove into a ball as a shot rang out. He was up and running again all in one motion, and before the sniper could fire again he had left his feet, this time diving head-first through an open window of the spire.

More shots resounded, and shards of stone flew past him as he scrambled up the spiral staircase at the core of the spire. Above him, he heard the metallic click that told him his adversary had run out of ammo, and he leaped up the stairs three at a time, making the most of his temporary advantage. He heard another metallic sound, and an empty cartridge came bouncing down the stone stairs. Bounding ahead, he bent his back, keeping his profile low. No more shots ensued, increasing the probability that he was gaining on the sniper.

But probability was not good enough; he had to be certain. He aimed Annaka's flashlight up the spiral, flicked the beam on. At once he saw the trace of a shadow on the treads just above him, slipping away almost immediately, and he redoubled his efforts. He switched off the beam before the sniper could get a reading on his position.

They were near the top of the spire now, some eighty meters in the air. There was nowhere else for the sniper to go. He would have to kill Bourne to get himself out of the trap. This desperation would make him both more dangerous and more reckless. It was up to Bourne to use the latter possibility to his advantage.

Up ahead of him, he could see the spire's ending, a circular space surrounded by high arches that let in the rain and wind, and he checked his headlong ascent. He knew that if he continued, the chances were good that he would be met with a fusillade of bullets. And yet he could not stay here. He took his flashlight, set it on a step above him at an angle, then he lay down, and keeping his head down, he reached out, stretching as far as he could, and flicked on the beam.

The resulting hail of bullets was deafening. Even while the noise was still echoing up and down the length of the spire, Bourne had launched himself up the remaining stairs. He had gambled that the sniper's desperation would lead him to empty his entire cartridge at what he assumed was Bourne's final assault.

Out of the haze of stone dust, Bourne bull-rushed the sniper, driving him back across the stone floor, against one of the stone arches. The man slammed his combined fists down on Bourne's back, driving Bourne to his knees. His head went down, exposing his neck, too tempting a target to pass up. As the sniper drove a hand-strike at Bourne's neck, Bourne twisted, grasping the descending arm, using the sniper's own momentum against him, pulling the man off his feet. Bourne struck him in the kidney as he went down.

The sniper brought his ankles together around Bourne's, twisting, so that Bourne fell backward. Immediately, the man leaped at him. They grappled hand-to-hand, the light from the flashlight picked apart by the hail of dust. By its illumination, Bourne saw the sniper's long, hatchet face, blond hair, light eyes. Bourne was briefly taken aback. He realized that he'd expected the sniper to be Khan.

Bourne did not want to kill this man; he wanted to question him. He desperately wanted to know who he was, who had sent him and why Vadas had been marked for death. But the man fought with the strength and tenacity of the damned, and when he struck Bourne on the right shoulder, Bourne's arm went numb. The man was on him before he could shift his stance and protect himself. Three punches in succession sent him reeling through one of the arches until he was backed over the low stone railing. The man came after him, his empty gun reversed in his hand so that he could use the butt as a cudgel.

Shaking his head, Bourne tried to rid himself of the pain in his right side. The sniper was almost upon him, his right arm raised, the heavy butt of the gun gleaming in the lights of the square. There was a murderous look on his face, his lips pulled back in an animal snarl. He swung in a shallow, vicious arc; the butt came down, its clear intention to shatter Bourne's skull. At the last moment, Bourne slid aside just enough and the sniper's own momentum sent him hurtling over the rail.

Bourne reacted instantly, reached down and grabbed the man by his hand, but the rain made the flesh slippery as oil and the fingers slid through his grip. With a scream the man fell away, plummeting to the pavement far below.

CHAPTER FOURTEEN

With the fall of night, Khan arrived in Budapest. He took a taxi from the airport and checked into the Danubius Hotel as Heng Raffarin, the name he'd used as a *Le Monde* reporter in Paris. This was how he'd come through Immigration, but he was also carrying other documents, purchased like the other that identified him as a deputy inspector for Interpol.

"I've flown in from Paris to interview Mr. Conklin," he said in a harassed tone of voice. "All these delays! I'm frightfully late. Do you think you could inform Mr. Conklin that I've finally arrived? We're both on rather tight schedules."

As Khan had foreseen, the desk clerk automatically looked at the cubbyholes behind him, each with a room number printed in gold-leaf. "Mr. Conklin isn't in his suite at the moment. Would you care to leave a note?"

"I suppose I have no other choice. We'll get a fresh start in the morning." Khan pretended to write a note for "Mr. Conklin," sealed it, gave it to the clerk. Taking his key, he turned away, but out of the corner of his eye he watched as the clerk stuck the envelope in the cubbyhole marked PENT-HOUSE 3. Satisfied, he took the elevator up to his room, which was on the floor below the penthouse level.

He washed up, took some implements out of a small bag and went out of his room. He took the stairway up one flight to the penthouse level. He stood in the corridor a very long time, simply listening, accustoming himself to the small noises endemic to any building. He stood, still as stone, waiting for something—a sound, a vibration, a *feel*—that would tell him whether to go forward or to retreat.

In the end, nothing untoward presented itself, and so he moved cautiously forward, reconnoitering the entire corridor, assuring himself that it, at least, was secure. At length, he found himself in front of the polished teak double doors of Penthouse 3. Extracting a pick, he inserted it into the lock. A moment later, the door opened.

Again, he stood for some time in the open doorway, breathing in the suite. Instinct told him that the room was empty. Still, he was wary of a trap. Swaying slightly with the effects of sleeplessness and the rising tide of his emotions, he scanned the room. Besides the remnants of a package the approximate size of a shoebox, there was precious little in the suite to indicate that it was occupied. Judging by the look of the bed, it hadn't been slept in. Where was Bourne now? Khan wondered.

At length, he drew his wandering mind back into his body, crossed to the bathroom, turned on the light. He saw the plastic comb, the toothbrush, toothpaste, tiny bottle of mouthwash the hotel had provided along with soap, shampoo and hand cream. He unscrewed the toothpaste top, squeezed out a bit into the sink, washed it away. Then he pulled out a paper clip and a small silver box. Inside the box were two capsules with shells of quick-dissolving gelatin. One was white, the other black.

"One pill makes your heart beat, the other makes it slow, and the pills that Father gives you don't do anything at all," he sang to the tune of "White Rabbit" in a clear tenor as he extracted the white capsule from its bed.

He was about to place it into the open top of the toothpaste tube, tamp it down with the end of the paper clip, when something stopped him. He counted to ten, then replaced the cap, careful to put the tube back precisely as he had found it.

He stood, for a moment, bewildered, staring at the two capsules that he himself had prepared while waiting for his flight out of Paris. He had been clear, then, about what he'd wanted to do—the black capsule was filled with just enough krait venom to paralyze Bourne's body while still allowing his mind to remain conscious and alert. Bourne knew more about what Spalko was planning than Khan did; he had to, having followed his trail of leads all the way back to Spalko's home base. Khan wanted to know what Bourne knew before he killed him. This is what he told himself, at least.

But it was impossible to deny any longer that his mind, so long filled with fevered visions of revenge, had lately made room for other scenarios. No matter how much energy he expended on rejecting them, they persisted. In fact, he realized now, the more violently he dismissed them, the more stubbornly they refused to disappear.

Feeling like a fool, he was standing in the room of his nemesis, unable to follow through on the plan he had meticulously formulated. Instead, in the theater of his mind he was replaying the look on Bourne's face when he had seen the carved stone Buddha that hung by a gold chain around his neck. He clutched at the Buddha now, feeling as he always did a certain sense of solace and safety in its soft shape and singular weight. What was wrong with him?

With a small grunt of anger, he turned and stalked out of the suite. On his way down to his room, he pulled out his cell phone, punched in a local number. After two rings, a voice answered.

"Yes?" said Ethan Hearn.

"How's the job going?" Khan asked.

"Actually, I'm finding it enjoyable."

"Just as I predicted."

"Where are you?" Humanistas, Ltd.'s newest development officer asked.

"Budapest."

"That's a surprise," Hearn said. "I thought you had a commission in East Africa."

"I've declined it," Khan said. He had reached the lobby and now crossed it, heading to the front door. "In fact, for the time being I've taken myself off the market."

"Something pretty important must've brought you here."

"It's your boss, as a matter of fact. What have you been able to ferret out?"

"Nothing concrete, but he's up to something, I can tell, and it's very, very big."

"What makes you say that?" Khan asked.

"First, he entertains a pair of Chechens," Hearn said. "On the surface, there's nothing strange about that. We have an important initiative in Chechnya. And yet it *was* strange, very strange, because even though they were dressed as Westerners—the man was beardless, the woman without her head scarf—I recognized them, well, *him*, at least. Hasan Arsenov, leader of the Chechen rebels."

"Go on," Khan urged, thinking he was getting more than his money's worth from this mole.

"Then, two nights ago, he asked me to go to the opera," Hearn continued. "He said he wanted to snag a wealthy prospect by the name of László Molnar."

"What's so strange about that?" Khan said.

"Two things," Hearn replied. "First, Spalko took over midway through the evening. He pretty much ordered me to take the next day off. Second, Molnar's disappeared."

"Disappeared?"

"Vanished utterly, like he never existed," Hearn said. "Spalko thinks I'm too naive not to have checked up." He laughed softly.

"Don't get overconfident," Khan warned. "That's when you make a mistake. And, remember what I told you, don't underestimate Spalko. Once you do, you're as good as dead."

"I got it, Khan. Christ, I'm not stupid."

"You wouldn't be on my payroll if you were," Khan reminded him. "D'you have this László Molnar's home address?"

Ethan Hearn gave it to him.

"Now," Khan said, "all you have to do is keep your ears open and your head down. I want everything of his you can burrow into."

Jason Bourne watched Annaka Vadas as she exited the morgue, where, he suspected, she had been taken in the company of the police in order to identify her father and the three men who had been gunned down. As for the sniper, he had landed on his face, which ruled out identification by dental records. The police must be running his fingerprints through the EU database. From fragments of the conversation he had overheard at Matthias Church, the police were rightly curious as to why a professional assassin would want to kill János Vadas, but Annaka had no explanation and at length the police had given up and allowed her to go. They, of course, had no inkling of Bourne's involvement. He had stayed away from the investigation by necessity—he was, after all, an internationally wanted man—but he felt some trepidation. He had no idea whether he could trust Annaka. It hadn't been that long ago when she had been intent on putting a bullet through his brain. But he had hoped that his actions following her father's murder would convince her of his good intentions.

Apparently they had, because she had not told the police about him. Instead, he had found his boots in the chapel Annaka had shown him, lying between the crypts of King Bélla III and Anne of Châtillon. Bribing a taxi driver, he'd shadowed her to the police station, and then to the morgue.

Now he watched as the police touched their caps, said their goodnights. They had offered to drive her home, but she had refused. Instead, she pulled out her cell phone, in order to call a taxi, he surmised.

When he was certain that she was alone, he quit the shadows in which he had been hiding, walked quickly across the street toward her. She saw him, put her cell phone away. Her look of alarm brought him up short.

"You! How did you find me?" She looked around, rather wildly, he thought. "Have you been following me all this time?"

"I wanted to make sure you were okay."

"My father was shot to death in front of me," she said shortly. "Why would I be okay?"

He was conscious of the fact that they were standing beneath a streetlight. At night, he always thought in terms of targets and security; it was second nature—he couldn't help it. "The police here can be difficult."

"Really? And how would you know that?" Apparently, she wasn't interested in his answer, for she began to walk away from him, her heels click-clacking over the cobbles.

"Annaka, we need each other."

Her back was very straight, her head held high on her long neck. "What would make you say such an absurd thing?"

"Because it's true."

She turned on her heel, confronting him. "No, it's not true." Her eyes blazed. "It's because of you that my father's dead."

"Now who's being absurd?" He shook his head. "Your father was murdered because of whatever he and Alex Conklin were into. That's why Alex was murdered in his home, and that's why I'm here."

She snorted in derision. Bourne understood the source of her brittleness. She had been forced into a male-dominated arena, perhaps by her father, and was now more or less at war. At the very least, she was highly defended.

"Don't you want to know who killed your father?"

"Frankly, no." Her balled fist was on one hip. "I want to bury him and forget I ever heard of Alexsei Conklin and Dr. Felix Schiffer."

"You can't mean that!"

"Do you know me, Mr. Bourne? Do you know anything about me?" Her clear eyes observed him from her slightly cocked head. "I think not. You're

completely in the dark. That's why you came here, posing as Alexsei. A stupid ruse, transparent as plastic. And now that you've blundered your way
in, now that blood has been spilled, you think it's your due to find out what
my father and Alexsei were up to."

"Do you know me, Annaka?"

A sardonic smile split her face as she took a step closer to him. "Oh, yes,
Mr. Bourne, I know you well. I've seen your kind come and go, each one
thinking in the moments before he is gunned down that he's more clever
than the last one."

"So who am I?"

"You think I won't tell you? Mr. Bourne, I know exactly who you are.
You're a cat with a ball of string. Your only thought is to unravel that ball of
string no matter the cost. This is all a game to you—a mystery that must be
solved. Nothing else matters. You're defined by the very mystery you seek to
unravel. Without it, you wouldn't even exist."

"You're wrong."

"Oh, no, I'm not." The sardonic smile widened. "It's why you can't
fathom how I can walk away from this, why I don't want to work with you,
help you find out who killed my father. Why should I? Will knowing the
answer bring him back? He's dead, Mr. Bourne. He no longer thinks or
breathes. He's just a pile of refuse now, waiting for time to finish what it
started."

She turned and began to walk away again.

"Annaka—"

"Go away, Mr. Bourne. Whatever you have to say, I'm not interested."

He ran to catch up with her. "How can you say that? Six men have lost
their lives because of—"

She gave him a rueful look and he could tell that she was on the verge of
tears. "I begged my father not to get involved, but you know, old friends,
the lure of the clandestine, who knows what it was. I warned him that it
would all come to an evil end, but he just laughed—yes, laughed—and said
I was his daughter and couldn't possibly understand. Well, that put me in
my place, didn't it?"

"Annaka, I am being hunted for a double murder I didn't commit. My
two best friends were shot to death and I've been framed as the prime suspect. Can you understand—"

"Jesus, have you not heard a word I've said? Has it all gone in one ear and out the other?"

"I can't do this alone, Annaka. I need your help. I've nowhere else to turn. My life is quite literally in your hands. Tell me, please, about Dr. Felix Schiffer. Tell me what you know and I swear you'll never see me again."

She lived at 106–108 Fo utca in Víziváros, a narrow neighborhood of hills and steep stairs, rather than streets, wedged between the Castle District and the Danube. From her front bay windows you could see Bem tér. It was here, hours before the 1956 Uprising, that thousands congregated, waving Hungarian flags from which they had painstakingly and joyously cut the hammer and sickle, prior to marching on parliament.

The apartment was cramped and crowded, primarily because of the concert grand piano that took up fully half the space of the living room. Books, periodicals and journals on music history and theory, biographies of composers, conductors, musicians, crammed the floor-to-ceiling bookcase.

"Do you play?" Bourne asked.

"Yes," Annaka said simply.

He sat down on the piano bench, looked at the music chart splayed on the rack. A Chopin Nocturne, Opus 9, No. 1 in B-Flat Minor. *She would have to be quite accomplished to tackle that*, he thought.

From the bay window in the living room there was a view of the boulevard as well as the buildings on the other side. A few lights were on; the sound of fifties jazz—Thelonious Monk—drifted through the night. A dog barked and was still. From time to time, the rattle of traffic intruded.

After turning on the lamps, she went immediately into the kitchen, put on water for tea. From a buttercup-colored cupboard, she took out two sets of cups and saucers, and while the tea was brewing, she uncapped a bottle of schnapps, poured a generous dollop into each cup.

She opened the refrigerator. "Would you like something to eat? Cheese, a bit of sausage?" Speaking as if to an old friend.

"I'm not hungry."

"Neither am I." She sighed and shut the door. It was as if, having made the decision to bring him home, she had also decided to lose the attitude.

They made no more mention of János Vadas or Bourne's fruitless pursuit of the killer. That suited him.

She handed him the laced tea and they went into the living room, sat on a sofa old as a dowager.

"My father was working with a professional intermediary named László Molnar," she said without preamble. "He was the one who secreted your Dr. Schiffer."

"Secreted?" Bourne shook his head. "I don't understand."

"Dr. Schiffer had been kidnapped."

Bourne's tension level rose. "By whom?"

She shook her head. "My father knew, but I didn't." She frowned, concentrating. "That was why Alexsei first contacted him. He needed my father's help in rescuing Dr. Schiffer and spiriting him away to a secret location."

All at once, he heard Mylene Dutronc's voice in his head: *"That day, Alex made and received many calls in a very short period of time. He was terribly tense and I knew he was at the crisis point of a hot field operation. I heard Dr. Schiffer's name mentioned several times. I suspect that he was the subject of the operation."* This was the hot field operation.

"So your father was successful in getting Dr. Schiffer."

Annaka nodded. The lamplight burnished her hair to a deep copper sheen. Her eyes and half of her forehead were cast in its shadow. She sat with her knees together, slightly hunched over, her hands around the teacup as if she needed to absorb its warmth.

"As soon as my father had Dr. Schiffer, he handed him over to László Molnar. This was strictly for security purposes. Both he and Alexsei were terribly afraid of whoever it was who had kidnapped Dr. Schiffer."

This, too, jibed with what Mylene had told him, Bourne thought. *"That day he was frightened."*

He was thinking furiously. "Annaka, for all this to start making sense, you have to understand that your father's murder was a setup. That sniper was already at the church when we came in; he knew what your father was up to."

"What do you mean?"

"Your father was shot before he could tell me what I need to know. Someone doesn't want me to find Dr. Schiffer, and it seems increasingly clear that this is the same someone who kidnapped Schiffer, who your father and Alex were afraid of."

Annaka's eyes opened wide. "It is possible now that László Molnar is in danger."

"Would this mystery man know of your father's involvement with Molnar?"

"My father was extremely careful, very security conscious, so it seems unlikely." She looked at him, her eyes darkened with fright. "On the other hand, his defenses were penetrated at Matthias Church."

Bourne nodded his agreement. "Do you know where Molnar lives?"

Annaka drove them to Molnar's apartment, which was in the posh embassy district of Rózsadomb, or Rose Hill. Budapest showed itself in jumbled buildings of pale stone, elaborately iced like birthday cakes, carved into ornamental lintels and cornices, quaintly cobbled streets, wrought-iron balconies with flowerpots, coffeehouses illuminated by elaborate chandeliers whose lemon light revealed ruddy wood-paneled walls, brilliant splashes of glass, stained, etched into fin de siècle patterns. Like Paris, it was a city defined first and foremost by the sinuous river that clove it in two, then by the bridges that spanned it. Beyond that, it was a city of etched stone, Gothic spires, sweeping public staircases, lamplit ramparts, copper-encrusted domes, ivied walls, monumental statuary and glittering mosaics. And when it rained, umbrellas, thousands of umbrellas, unfurled like sails along the river.

All these things and more affected Bourne deeply. It was for him like arriving at a place and remembering it from a dream, with a dream's suprareal clarity that stemmed from its direct connection to the unconscious. And yet he could separate no specific remembrance from the tide of emotion that arose from his shattered memory.

"What is it?" Annaka said, as if sensing his unease.

"I've been here before," he said. "Remember how I said that the police could be difficult here?"

She nodded. "You're absolutely right about that. Are you telling me that you don't know how you know?"

He put his head back against the seat rest. "Years ago I suffered a terrible accident. It wasn't an accident, really. I was shot on a boat and fell overboard. I almost died of shock, blood loss and exposure. A doctor in Île de Port Noir in France excised the bullet, took care of me. I returned to perfect physical health, but my memory was affected. For some time I had amnesia, and then slowly, painfully, shards of my former life came back to me. The truth I have to live with is that my memory's never fully recovered and it likely never will."

Annaka drove on, but by the look on her face he could tell that she had been affected by his story.

"You can't imagine what it's like not to know who you are," he said. "Unless it's happened to you, there's no way to know or even to explain what it feels like."

"Unmoored."

He glanced at her. "Yes."

"The sea all around you with no sight of land, no sun or moon or stars to tell you which way you need to go to get back home."

"It's not unlike that." He was surprised. He wanted to ask her how she could know something like that, but they were pulling into the curb in front of a large, ornate stone building.

They got out and went into the vestibule. Annaka pressed a button and a low-watt bulb came on, its sickly illumination revealing the mosaic floor, the wall of bell pushes. László Molnar's bell remained unanswered.

"It could mean nothing," Annaka said. "More than likely Molnar is with Dr. Schiffer."

Bourne went to the front door, a wide, thick affair with an etched frosted-glass panel running upward from waist level. "We'll find out in a minute."

He bent over the lock and a moment later he had the door open. Annaka hit another button and a light came on for thirty seconds as she led the way up the wide curving staircase to Molnar's second-floor apartment.

Bourne had a bit more difficulty picking this lock, but in the end it gave way. Annaka was about to rush inside, but he held her back. He drew his ceramic gun, pushed the door slowly open. Lamps were lit, but it was very quiet. Moving from the living room into the bedroom to the bathroom, the kitchen, they found the apartment neat as a pin, no evidence of a struggle and no sign of Molnar.

"What bothers me," Bourne said as he put the gun away, "is the lights being on. He can't be off with Dr. Schiffer."

"Then he'll be back any time," Annaka said. "We should wait for him."

Bourne nodded. In the living room he picked up several framed photos off the bookshelves and desk. "Is this Molnar?" he asked Annaka as he pointed to a heavyset man with a thick mane of slicked-back black hair.

"That's him." She looked around. "My grandparents used to live in this building, and as a child, I used to play in the halls. The children who lived here knew all sorts of hiding places."

Bourne ran his fingers over the spines of old-fashioned 33⅓ rpm record sleeves stacked next to an expensive stereo with an elaborate turntable. "I see he's an opera buff as well as an audiophile."

Annaka peered in. "No CD player?"

"People like Molnar will tell you that the transfer to digital music takes all the warmth and subtlety out of a recording."

Bourne turned to the desk, on which sat a notebook computer. He saw that it was plugged in both to an electrical outlet and to a modem. The screen was black, but when he touched the chassis it was warm. He pressed the "Escape" key and the screen immediately sprang to life; the computer had been in "sleep" mode—it had never been turned off.

Coming up behind him, Annaka looked at the screen, read from it, "Anthrax, Argentinean hemorrhagic fever, cryptococcosis, pneumonic plague . . . God in heaven, why was Molnar on a Web site that describes the effects of lethal—what does it call them?—pathogens?"

"All I know is that Dr. Schiffer is the beginning and end to this enigma," Bourne said. "Alex Conklin approached Dr. Schiffer when he was in DARPA—that's the advanced weapons program run by the U.S. Department of Defense. Within a year, Dr. Schiffer had transferred to the CIA's Tactical Non-Lethal Weapons Directorate. Shortly after that, he vanished altogether. I have no idea what Schiffer was working on that interested Conklin so much that he would go to the trouble of pissing off the DOD and vanishing a prominent government scientist from the Agency's program."

"Maybe Dr. Schiffer is a bacteriologist or an epidemiologist." Annaka shivered. "The information on this Web site is terrifying."

She went into the kitchen to get a glass of water while Bourne navigated around the Web page to see if he could get any further clue as to why Molnar would be on this site. Finding nothing, he went to the top of the browser, where he accessed a drop-down menu next to the "Address" bar that showed the most recent sites Molnar had been on. He clicked on the last one Molnar had accessed. It turned out to be a real-time scientific forum. Navigating to the "Archives" section, he went back in time to see if he could find out when Molnar had used the forum and what he'd talked about. Approximately forty-eight hours ago, László1647M had logged onto the forum. Bourne, his heart beating fast, spent several minutes reading the dialogue he had had with another forum member.

"Annaka, look at this," he called. "It seems Dr. Schiffer is neither a bacteriologist nor an epidemiologist. He's an expert in bacteriological particulate behavior."

"Mr. Bourne, you'd better come here," Annaka replied. "Right now."

The tightness in her voice brought him into the kitchen at the run. She was standing in front of the sink as if held spellbound. A glass of water was suspended halfway to her lips. She seemed pale, and when she saw him, she licked her lips nervously.

"What is it?"

She pointed to a space between the counter and the refrigerator, where he saw neatly stacked seven or eight white-coated wire racks.

"What the hell are those?" he said.

"They're the refrigerator shelves," Annaka said. "Someone took them out." She turned to him. "Why would they do that?"

"Maybe Molnar's getting a new refrigerator."

"This one *is* new."

He checked behind the refrigerator. "It's plugged in and the compressor seems to be running normally. You didn't look inside?"

"No."

He grabbed hold of the handle, opened the door. Annaka gasped.

"Christ," he said.

A pair of death-clouded eyes stared sightlessly out at them. There in the depths of the shelfless refrigerator was the curled-up, blue-white body of László Molnar.

CHAPTER FIFTEEN

The seesaw wail of sirens brought them out of their shock. Racing to the front window, Bourne looked down onto Rose Hill, saw five or six white Opal Astras and Skoda Felicias drawing up, blue-and-white lights flashing. The officers inside tumbled out, making directly for Molnar's building. He had been set up again! The scene was so similar to what had happened at Conklin's house that he knew the same person must be behind both incidents. This was important because it told him two things: First, he and Annaka were being watched. By whom, Khan? He didn't think so. Khan's methodology was increasingly confrontational. Second, Khan may have been telling the truth when he claimed he wasn't responsible for the murders of Alex and Mo. Right now, Bourne couldn't think of a reason why he'd lie about that. That left the unknown person who'd called the police at Conklin's estate. Was the person he was working for based in Budapest? There was a convincing logic to it. Conklin was on his way to Budapest when he was murdered. Dr. Schiffer had been in Budapest, along with János Vadas and László Molnar. Every road led back to this city.

Even as his mind raced through these thoughts, he was yelling to Annaka to wipe off and put away the water glass, wipe down the kitchen faucet. He grabbed Molnar's laptop, wiped down the stereo and the knob on the front door, and they sprinted out of the apartment.

Already, they could hear the police pounding up the stairs. The elevator would be filled with police and so was out of the question.

"They've left us no choice," Bourne said as they mounted the stairs. "We have to go up."

"But why have they come now?" Annaka asked. "How could they have known we were here?"

"They couldn't," Bourne said, continuing to lead her upward, "unless we were under surveillance." He didn't like the position the police were putting them in. He recalled all too well the fate of the sniper at Matthias Church. When you went up, all too often you came down, hard.

They were a floor from the roof when Annaka tugged on his hand and whispered, "This way!"

She led him into the corridor. Behind them, the stairwell resounded with the noises any group of men would make, especially one on its way to apprehend a heinous murderer. Three-quarters of the way down the corridor was a door that looked like an emergency exit. Annaka pulled it open. They were in a short hallway, not more than ten feet long, at the end of which was another door, this one made of battered metal plates. Bourne went ahead of her.

He saw that the door was bolted at top and bottom. He slid the slides back, pulled it open. There was only a brick wall, cold as a grave.

"Would you look at that!" Detective Csilla said, ignoring the new recruit who had vomited all over his polished shoes. The academy certainly wasn't turning them out the way they used to, he mused as he studied the victim, curled stiff in his own refrigerator.

"No one in the apartment," one of his officers said.

"Dust it anyway," Detective Csilla said. He was a burly, blond-haired man with a broken nose and intelligent eyes. "I doubt the perpetrator was stupid enough to leave his prints, but you never know," he said now. Then he pointed. "Look at those burn marks, would you? And the puncture wounds seem to go very deep."

"Tortured," his sergeant, a slim-hipped young man, said, "by a professional."

"This one's more than a professional," Detective Csilla said, leaning in and sniffing as if the corpse were a side of meat he suspected of having begun to rot. "He enjoys his work."

"The phone tip said the murderer was here in the apartment."

Detective Csilla looked up. "If not the apartment, then surely the building." He backed away as the forensic team arrived with their kits and flash cameras. "Have the men fan out."

"Already done," his sergeant said in a subtle reminder to his boss that he didn't want to remain a sergeant forever.

"Enough time with the dead," Detective Csilla said. "Let's join them."

As they went down the hallway, the sergeant explained that the elevator had already been secured, as had the floors below. "The murderer has only one way to go."

"Get the sharpshooters onto the roof," Detective Scilla said.

"Already there," his sergeant replied. "I put them into the elevator when we entered the building."

Csilla nodded. "How many floors above us? Three?"

"Yessir."

Csilla mounted the stairs two at a time. "With the roof secured, we can afford to take our time."

It did not take them long to find the doorway to the short corridor.

"Where does this lead?" Csilla asked.

"I don't know, sir," his sergeant said, irked that he couldn't provide an answer.

As the two men approached the far end of the corridor, they saw the battered metal door. "That's this?" Csilla took a look at it. "Bolts at top and bottom." He leaned in, saw the gleam of metal. "They've been recently pulled." He drew his gun, pulled the door open onto the bricked-up wall.

"Looks like our murderer was as frustrated as we are."

Csilla was staring at the brickwork, trying to discern if any of it was new. Then he put a hand out, tested one brick after another. The sixth one he touched moved just slightly. Aware that his sergeant was about to exclaim, he clamped a hand across his mouth, gave him a warning look. Then he whispered in his ear, "Take three of the men and canvass the building next door."

At first, Bourne, his ears straining to catch the slightest sound in the pitch blackness, thought the noise was one of the rats with whom they were sharing this dank and uncomfortable space between the walls of Molnar's building and the adjacent one. Then it came again, and he knew it for what it was: the scrape of brick against mortar.

"They've found our hiding place," he whispered as he grabbed hold of Annaka. 'We've got to move."

The space they occupied was narrow, not more than two feet in width, but it seemed to rise indefinitely into the darkness above their heads. They stood on a floor of sorts, made up of metal pipes. It was not the most secure of floors and Bourne did not care to think about the open space below them into which they would plunge should one or more of the pipes give way.

"Do you know a way out of here?" Bourne whispered.

"I think so," she said.

She turned to their right, felt her way along the space with the palms of her hands on the wall of the adjacent building.

She tripped once, righted herself. "It's here somewhere," she muttered.

They continued onward, putting one foot in front of the other. Then, all at once, a pipe gave way beneath Bourne's weight and his left leg plunged downward. He canted wildly over, his shoulder striking the wall, and Molnar's laptop was thrown from his grip. He tried to catch it even as Annaka was reaching down to grab him, pull him up. Instead, he saw it strike a pipe on edge, then plunge through the gap the rotten pipe had made, lost forever.

"Are you okay?" Annaka said as he regained his feet.

"I'm fine," he said grimly, "but Molnar's laptop's gone."

A moment later he froze. Behind them, he could hear movement, slow and stealthy—someone else was breathing in the space—and he took out his flashlight, his thumb on the slide switch. He put his lips against Annaka's ear, "He's here with us. No more talking." He could sense her nod, even as he smelled the scent of her rising off her bare skin, citrus and musk.

Something clanked behind them as the policeman's shoe struck a protrusion of solder where two pipes joined. All of them stood very still. Bourne's heart beat fast. Then Annaka's hand found his, guided it along the wall where a line of grout was missing or had been deliberately gouged away.

But another problem presented itself. As soon as they pushed in the section of wall, the policeman behind them would see the pale patch of light, however feeble, coming in from the other side. He would see them, know where they were going. Bourne took a chance, put his lips against Annaka's ear and whispered, "You must tell me the moment before you push through the wall."

She squeezed his hand in response, kept hold of it. When he felt her squeeze it again, he aimed the flashlight directly behind them, snapped on the beam. The burst of glaring light temporarily blinded their pursuer, and

Bourne lent his energy to helping her push through the three-foot-by-three-foot section of the wall.

Annaka ducked through while Bourne kept the beam focused on their adversary, but he felt the pipes vibrate under the soles of his boots and an instant later he was struck a terrific blow.

Detective Csilla tried to fight off the light-dazzle. He had been caught totally unprepared, a fact that enraged him, as he prided himself on being prepared for every possibility. He shook his head, but it was no good—the beam of light had temporarily rendered him blind. If he maintained his ground until the light was turned off, he had no doubt the murderer would have already fled. So he used his own advantage of surprise and attacked even though he was blinded. With a grunt of effort, he rushed along the pipes, crashing into the perpetrator, his head down in a street fighter's crouch.

In such close quarters and in the dark, eyesight was of little value, and he proceeded to use his fists, the edges of his hands and the heels of his stout shoes precisely as he had been taught in the academy. He was a man who believed in discipline, in rigor and in the power of advantage. He knew the moment he launched himself that the murderer would never have suspected him of attacking blind, and so he rained down as many blows as he could on the other in as short a space of time as he could manage in order to make the most of the advantage of surprise.

But the man was strong and solidly built. Worse, he was an accomplished hand-to-hand fighter, and almost immediately Csilla knew that in a prolonged fight he would be defeated. He sought, therefore, to end the combat swiftly and surely. In doing so, he made the fatal error of exposing the side of his neck. He felt the surprise of the pressure but no pain. He was already unconscious as his legs buckled under him.

Bourne went through the hole in the wall, helped Annaka slide the square of bricks back into place.

"What happened to you?" she said a little breathlessly.

"A policeman was smarter than he ought to have been."

They were in another short brick-lined utility corridor. Through a door was the hallway of the building next door to Molnar's, warm light emanating from etched-glass sconces along the flowered-paper walls. Here and there were scattered dark wooden benches.

Annaka had already punched the button for the elevator, but when it rose to their level, Bourne could see through the cage two policemen with their guns drawn.

"Oh, hell!" he said, grabbing Annaka's hand and dragging her to the stairwell. But he heard the heavy tread of footsteps and knew that egress was denied them as well. Behind them, the two policemen had opened the elevator cab gates, were in the hallway, racing toward them. Bourne took her up one flight. In the hallway he quickly picked the lock of the first door they came to, closing the door before the police followed them up the stairs.

Inside, the apartment was dark and still. Whether anyone was home was impossible to say. Crossing to the side window, Bourne opened it, looked out at a stone ledge that overlooked a narrow alley housing a pair of huge green metal trash bins. Illumination came from a streetlamp on Endrodi Street. Three windows over, a fire escape led downward to the alley which, as far as Bourne could see, was deserted.

"Come on," he said, climbing out onto the ledge.

Annaka's eyes opened wide. "Are you crazy?"

"Do you want to get caught?" He looked at her levelly. "This is our only way out."

She swallowed uneasily. "I'm afraid of heights."

"We're not that far up." He held out a hand, waggled his fingers. "Come on, there's no time to lose."

Taking a deep breath, she climbed out and he closed the window behind her. She turned and, glancing down, would have fallen if Bourne hadn't grabbed her, pulled her back against the stone side of the building. "Jesus Christ, you said we weren't that far up!"

"For me, that's true."

She bit her lip. "I'll kill you for this."

"You've already tried." He squeezed her hand. "Just follow me and you'll be fine, I promise."

They moved to the end of the ledge. He didn't want to push her, but there was good cause for haste. With the police swarming all through the building, it was only a matter of time until they came around to this alley.

"You'll have to let go of my hand now," he said, and then, because he saw what she was about to do, he added sharply enough to arrest her, "Don't look down! If you feel yourself getting dizzy, look at the side of the building, concentrate on something small, the carving of the stonework, whatever. Keep your mind occupied with that and your fear will fade."

She nodded, let go of his hand, and he stepped out, bridging the gap between ledges. His right hand gripped the top of the ledge above the next window and he transferred his weight from his left side to his right side. Lifting his left leg off the ledge on which Annaka was still standing, he moved smoothly across to the next ledge. Then he turned and smiled, held his hand out to her.

"Now you."

"No." She shook her head violently from side to side. All the color had drained from her face. "I can't do it."

"Yes, you can." He waggled his fingers again. "Come on, Annaka, take the first step; after that, the rest is easy. You simply shift your weight from left to right."

She shook her head mutely.

He continued to smile, showing none of the rising anxiety he felt. Here on the side of the building, they were completely vulnerable. If the police should come into the alley now, they were dead. He had to get them to the fire escape and do it fast. "One leg, Annaka, reach out with your right leg."

"Christ!" She was at the end of the ledge, where he had been moments before. "What if I fall?"

"You won't fall."

"But what—"

"I'll catch you." His smile broadened. "It's time to move now."

She did as he bade, moving her right leg out and across. He showed her how to grasp the ledge above with her right hand. This she did without hestitation.

"Now shift your weight, left to right, and step across."

"I'm frozen."

She was about to look down and he knew it. "Close your eyes," he said. "Do you feel my hand on yours?" She nodded, as if terrified that the vibration of her voicebox would send her spinning down into the void below. "Shift your weight, Annaka. Just shift it left to right. Good, now lift your left leg and step—"

"No."

He put his hand around her waist. "All right, then, just lift your left leg." As soon as she did, he pulled her, quickly and rather violently, against him onto the next ledge. She fell against him, shivering with fear and the release of tension.

Only two more to go. He moved them to the far end of the ledge, repeated the process. The quicker they got this over with, the better for both of them. She managed the second and third crossings somewhat better, either by sheer nerve or by shutting down her mind completely, following his orders without thinking.

At last, they made it onto the fire escape and began their descent to the street. The lamplight from Endrodi Street spilled long shadows down the alley. Bourne longed to kill it with a shot from his gun, but he didn't dare. Instead, he hurried them onward.

They were one tier from the vertical extending ladder that would take them to within two feet of the cobbles of the alley when out of the corner of his eye Bourne saw the quality of the light change. Shadows moved in the alley from opposing directions; a pair of policemen had entered the alley from either side.

Csilla's sergeant had taken one of their officers out of the building the moment the perpetrator had been spotted. He already knew that he was clever enough to have found his way from building to building. Having successfully escaped from László Molnar's apartment, he didn't now consider that the criminal would allow himself to get trapped in the adjacent building's stairway. That meant he'd find a way out, and the sergeant wanted all bases covered. He had a man on the roof, one each at the front and service entrances. That left the alleyway on the side. He didn't see how the murderer would get to the alley, but he wasn't taking any chances.

Lucky for him, he saw the figure outlined against the fire escape as he turned the building corner and entered the alley. By the light of the street-lamp on Endrodi Street he saw his officer enter the alley from the opposite end. He signed upward to the man, indicating the figure on the fire escape. He had drawn his gun and was steadily advancing toward the vertical ladder that led down from the fire escape when the figure moved, seemed to pull apart as if dividing. The sergeant started in surprise. There were *two* figures on the fire escape!

He raised his gun and fired. Sparks flew off the metal, and he saw one of the figures launch itself into the air, rolling into a ball only to disappear between the two enormous Dumpsters. The officer broke into a run, but the sergeant held back. He saw his officer reach the corner of the Dumpster nearest him, go into a crouch as he approached the space between the two.

The sergeant looked up for the second figure. The feeble illumination made it difficult to pick out details, but he saw no one standing. The fire escape looked clear. Where could the seond one have gone?

He returned his attention to his officer, only to find that the man had vanished. He took several steps forward, called out his name. No response. He pulled out his walkie-talkie, was about to call for reinforcements when something dropped onto him. He stumbled, fell heavily, got up on one knee, shaking his head. Then something emerged from the space between the Dumpsters. By the time he realized that it wasn't his officer, he had been dealt a blow hard enough to cause him to lose consciousness.

"That was really stupid," Bourne said, stooping to help Annaka up off cobbles of the alley.

"You're welcome," she said, shaking off his hand, standing on her own power.

"I thought you were afraid of heights."

"I'm afraid of dying more," she shot back.

"Let's get out of here before more policemen show up," he said. "I think you ought to lead the way."

The streetlight was in Khan's eyes as Bourne and Annaka ran out of the alley. Although he couldn't see their faces, he recognized Bourne by his shape and his gait. As for his female companion, though his mind registered her in a peripheral way, he did not give her much attention. He, like Bourne, was far more interested in why the police had been drawn to László Molnar's apartment when Bourne had been there. Also, like Bourne, he was

struck by the similarity of this scenario to the one at Conklin's estate in
Manassas. It had Spalko's thumbprint all over it. The trouble was that unlike in Manassas when he had spotted Spalko's man, he had come across no
such person during his thorough recon of the four square blocks around
Molnar's apartment building. So who had called the police? Someone had
to have been on the scene to tip them off when Bourne and the woman had
entered the building.

He started up his rental car and was able to follow Bourne as he got into
a taxi. The female continued on. Khan, knowing Bourne, was prepared for
the backtracking, the reversal of direction, the changing taxis, and so was
able to keep Bourne in sight during the maneuvers meant to shake any
tails.

At last Bourne's taxi reached Fo utca. Four blocks north of the magnificent domes of the Kiraly Baths, Bourne stepped out of the taxi and went
into the building at 106–108.

Khan slowed his car, pulled it into the curb up the block and across the
street—he didn't want to pass by the entrance. He turned off the engine,
sank into darkness. Alex Conklin, Jason Bourne, László Molnar, Hasan Arsenov. He thought about Spalko and wondered how all these disparate
names were connected. There was a line of logic here, there always was, if
only he could see it.

In this manner, five or six minutes passed and then another taxi pulled
up in front of the entrance to 106–108. Khan watched a young female get
out. He strained to catch a glimpse of her face before she pushed through
the heavy front doors, but all he was able to determine was that she had red
hair. He waited, watching the facade of the building. No light had gone on
after Bourne had entered the lobby, which meant that he must be waiting
for the woman—that this was her apartment. Sure enough, within three
minutes, lights went on in the fourth—and top—floor bay window.

Now that he knew where they were, he commenced to sink into *zazen*,
but after an hour of fruitlessly trying to clear his mind, he gave up. In the
darkness, his hand closed around the small carved stone Buddha. Almost
immediately thereafter, he fell into a deep sleep, from which he dropped
like a stone into the nether world of his recurring nightmare.

The water is blue-black, swirling restlessly as if alive with malignant en-
ergy. He tries to strike out for the surface, stretching up so hard his bones crack

with the strain. Still, he continues to sink into the darkness, dragged down by the rope tied around his ankle. His lungs are beginning to burn. He longs to take a breath, but he knows that the moment he opens his mouth, the water will rush in and he'll drown.

He reaches down, trying to untie the rope, but his fingers fail to gain a grip on the slick surface. He feels, like an electric current running through him, the terror of whatever waits for him in the darkness. The terror presses in on him like a vise; he forces down an urge to gibber. In that moment he hears the sound rising from the depths—the clangor of bells, of massed monks chanting before they are slaughtered by the Khmer Rouge. Eventually, the sound resolves itself into the song of a single voice, a clear tenor, a repeated ululation not unlike a prayer.

And it is as he stares down into the darkness, as he begins to make out the shape tethered to the other rope, the thing that is dragging him inexorably to his doom, that he feels the song he is hearing must be coming from that figure. For he knows the figure twirling in the powerful current below him; it's as familiar to him as his own face, his own body. But now, with a shock that pierces him to the quick, he realizes that the sound isn't coming from the familiar form below him because it's dead, which is why its weight is dragging him down to his doom.

The sound is nearer to hand, and now he recognizes the ululation as that of a clear tenor—his own voice coming from deep inside himself. It touches every part of him at once.

"Lee-Lee! Lee-Lee!" he is calling just before he drowns. . . .

CHAPTER SIXTEEN

Spalko and Zina arrived in Crete before the sun, touching down in Kazantzakis Airport just outside Iráklion. They were accompanied by a surgeon and three men, whom Zina had taken the time to scrutinize during the flight. They were not particularly big men, if only to ensure that they wouldn't stand out in a crowd. Spalko's heightened sense of security dictated that when, as now, he was engaged not as Stepan Spalko, president of Humanistas, Ltd., but as the Shaykh, he maintain the lowest of profiles, not only for himself but for all of his personnel. It was in their motionlessness that Zina recognized their power, for they had absolute control over their bodies, and when they moved, they did so with the fluidity and surety of dancers or yoga masters. She could see the intent in their dark eyes, which came only after years of hard training. Even when they were smiling deferentially at her, she could sense the danger that lurked within them, coiled, waiting patiently for its moment of release.

Crete, the largest island in the Mediterranean, was the gateway between Europe and Africa. For centuries it had lain baking in the hot Mediterranean sun, its southern eye trained on Alexandria in Egypt and Banghazi in Libya. Inevitably, however, an island so blessed in location was also surrounded by predators. At the crossroads of cultures, its history was by necessity bloody. Like waves breaking on the shore, invaders from different lands washed up on Crete's coves and beaches, bringing with them their culture, language, architecture and religion.

Iráklion had been founded by the Saracens in A.D. 824. They had called it Chandax, a bastardization of the Arabic word *kandak*, owing to the moat they dug around it. The Saracens ruled for one hundred forty years, before the Byzantines wrested control away from them. But the pirates were so astoundingly successful that it had taken three hundred boats to carry away all of their amassed booty to Byzantium.

During the Venetian occupation, the city was known as Candia. Under the Venetians, it became the most important cultural center in the Eastern Mediterranean. All of that came to an end with the first Turkish invasion.

This polyglot history was everywhere one looked: in Iráklion's massive Venetian fortress that protected its beautiful harbor from invasion; the town hall, housed in the Venetian Loggia; the "Koubes," the Turkish fountain near the former church of the Savior, which the Turks converted into the Valide mosque.

But in the modern, bustling city itself, there remained nothing of Minoan culture, the first and, from an archaeological point of view, the most important Cretan civilization. To be sure, the remnants of the palace of Knossos could be seen outside the city proper, but it was for historians to note that the Saracens had chosen this spot to found Chandax because it had been the main port of the Minoans thousands of years earlier.

At heart, Crete remained an island shrouded in myth, and it was impossible to set foot on it without being reminded of the legend of its birth. Centuries before the Saracens, the Venetians or the Turks existed, Crete had come to prominence from out of the mists of legend. Minos, Crete's first king, was a demigod. His father, Zeus, taking the form of a bull, raped his mother, Europa, and so from the first, the bull became the signifier of the island.

Minos and his two brothers battled for the rule of Crete, but Minos prayed to Poseidon, promising eternal obeisance to the god of the sea if he would use his power to help Minos defeat his brothers. Poseidon heard the prayer and from the churning sea rose a snow-white bull. This animal was meant as a sacrifice for Minos to pledge his subservience to Poseidon, but the greedy king coveted the bull and kept it for himself. Enraged, Poseidon caused Minos' wife to fall in love with it. In secret, she engaged Daedalus, Minos' favorite architect, to build her a hollow cow out of wood in which she hid so that the bull would mate with her. The issue of that sexual congress was the Minotaur—a monstrous man with a bull's head and tail— whose savagery wreaked so much havoc on the island that Minos had Daedalus build an enormous labyrinth, so elaborate that the captured Minotaur could never escape from it.

This legend was much in Stepan Spalko's mind as he and his team drove up the city's steep streets, for he had an affinity for Greek myths—their emphasis on rape and incest, bloodletting and hubris. He saw aspects of himself in many of them, so it was not difficult for him to believe himself a demigod.

Like many Mediterranean island towns, Iráklion was built on the side of a mountain, its stone houses rising up the steep streets mercifully plied by taxis and buses. In fact, the entire spine of the island rose in a chain known as the White Mountains.

The address Spalko had obtained by interrogation from László Molnar was a house perhaps halfway up the city slope. It belonged to an architect by the name of Istos Daedalika, who, as it turned out, was as mythical as his ancient namesake. Spalko's team had determined that the house had been leased by a company associated with László Molnar. They arrived at the address just as the night sky was about to be split open like the hull of a nut, revealing the bloody Mediterranean sun.

After a brief reconnoiter, they all donned tiny headphones, connecting themselves electronically over a wireless network. They checked their weapons, high-powered composite crossbows, excellent for the silence they needed to keep. Spalko synchronized his watch with two of his men, then sent them around to the rear entrance while he and Zina approached the front entrance. The remaining member of the team was ordered to keep watch and warn them of any suspect activity on the street or, alternatively, the approach of the police.

The street was deserted and quiet; no one was stirring. There were no lights on in the house, but Spalko didn't expect there to be any. He glanced at his watch, counting into his microphone as the second hand swept toward sixty.

Inside the house, the mercenaries were astir. It was moving day, the last few hours before they would depart as the others had before them. They moved Dr. Schiffer to a different location on Crete every three days; they did it quickly and quietly, the destination being decided upon only at the last minute. Such security measures required that some of them stay behind to ensure every last vestige of their presence was either taken or destroyed.

At this moment, the mercenaries were dispersed throughout the house. One of them was in the kitchen making thick Turkish coffee, a second was in the bathroom, a third had turned on the satellite TV. He watched the screen disinterestedly for a moment, then went to the front window, pulled aside the curtain, peered out into the street. Everything appeared normal. He stretched like a cat, bending his body this way and that. Then, strapping on his shoulder holster, he went to perform his morning perimeter check.

He unlocked the front door, pulled it open and was promptly shot through the heart by Spalko. He pitched backward, his arms splayed, his eyes rolling upward in their sockets, and was dead before he struck the floor.

Spalko and Zina entered the vestibule at the same moment his men crashed through the back door. The mercenary in the kitchen dropped his coffee cup, drew his weapon and wounded one of Spalko's men before he, too, was shot dead.

Nodding to Zina, Spalko took the stairs three at a time.

Zina had reacted to the shots coming through the bathroom door by ordering one of Spalko's men out the back door. She ordered another of Spalko's team to break down the door. This he did quickly and efficiently. No gunfire greeted them as they burst into the bathroom. Instead, they saw the window out which the mercenary had crawled. Zina had anticipated this possibility, hence her sending a man out the back.

A moment later she heard the telltale *thwok!* of the bolt being loosed, followed by a heavy grunt.

Upstairs, Spalko went from room to room in a crouch. The first bedroom was empty and he moved to the second. As he passed the bed, he caught a movement in the wall mirror above the dresser to his left. Something moved under the bed. At once, he dropped to his knees, shot the bolt. It passed through the dust ruffle and the bed was lifted off its feet. A body thrashed and groaned.

On his knees, Spalko fitted another bolt in his crossbow, began to aim it when he was bowled over. Something hard hit his head, a bullet ricocheted and he felt a weight on him. At once he let go of the crossbow, drew out a hunting knife and stabbed upward into his attacker. When it was buried to the hilt, he turned it, gritting his teeth with the effort, and was rewarded with a heavy gout of blood.

With a grunt, he threw the mercenary off him, retrieved his knife, wiped the blade down on the dust ruffle. Then he shot the second bolt down through the bed. Mattress stuffing flew through the air and the thrashing came to an abrupt halt.

He came back downstairs, after having checked the remaining second-floor rooms, into a living room reeking of cordite. One of his men was entering the open back door with the last remaining mercenary, whom he had seriously wounded. The entire assault had lasted less than three minutes, which suited Spalko's design; the less attention they brought to the house, the better.

There was no trace of Dr. Felix Schiffer. And yet Spalko knew that László Molnar hadn't lied to him. These men were part of the mercenary contingent Molnar had hired when he and Conklin had engineered Schiffer's escape.

"What's the final disposition?" he asked his men.

"Marco is wounded. Nothing major, the bullet went in and out the flesh of his left arm," one of them said. "Two opposition dead, one seriously wounded."

Spalko nodded. "And two dead upstairs."

Flicking the snout of his machine pistol at the last remaining mercenary, the man added, "This one won't last long unless he gets treatment."

Spalko looked at Zina, nodded. She approached the wounded man and, kneeling, turned him over on his back. He groaned and blood leaked out of him.

"What's your name?" she said in Hungarian.

He looked at her, with eyes darkened by pain and knowledge of his own impending death.

She took out a small box of wooden matches. "What's your name?" she repeated, this time in Greek.

When there was no reply forthcoming, she said to Spalko's men, "Hold him still."

Two of them bent to comply. The mercenary struggled briefly, then was still. He stared up at her with equanimity; he was a professional soldier, after all.

She struck the match. A sharp smell of sulphur accompanied the flare of the flame. With her thumb and forefinger, she pried apart the lids of one eye, brought the flame down toward the exposed eyeball.

The mercenary's free eye blinked maniacally and his breathing became stertorous. The flame, reflected in the curve of his glistening orb, moved ever closer. He felt fear, Zina could see that, but beneath that there was a sense of disbelief. He simply did not believe that she would follow through with her implied threat. A pity, but it made no difference to her.

The mercenary screamed, his body arching up despite the men's efforts to hold him down. He writhed and howled even after the match, guttering, fell smoking onto his chest. His good eyeball rolled around in its socket as if trying to find a safe haven.

Zina calmly lit another match, and all at once the mercenary vomited. Zina wasn't deterred. It was vital now that he understand that there was only one response that would stop her. He wasn't stupid; he knew what it was. Also, no amount of money was worth this torture. Through the tearing of his good eye, she could see his capitulation. Still, she wouldn't let him up, not until he'd told her where they had taken Schiffer.

Behind her, observing the scene from start to finish, Stepan Spalko was impressed despite himself. He'd had no clear idea of how Zina would react when he gave her the assignment of interrogation. In a way, it was a test; but it was more—it was a way to get to know her in the intimate fashion he found so pleasurable.

Because he was a man who used words every day of his life in order to manipulate people and events, Spalko had an innate distrust of them. People lied, it was as simple as that. Some liked to lie for the effect it had; others lied without knowing it, in order to protect themselves from scrutiny; still others lied to themselves. It was only in action, in what people did, especially in extreme circumstances or under duress, that their true natures were revealed. There was no possibility of lying then; you could safely believe the evidence arrayed before you.

Now he knew a truth about Zina he hadn't before. He doubted whether Hasan Arsenov knew it, whether he'd even believe it if told. At her core Zina was hard as a rock; she was tougher than Arsenov himself. Watching her now extracting the information from the hapless mercenary, he knew that she could live without Arsenov, though Arsenov couldn't live without her.

Bourne awoke to the sound of practice arpeggios and the aromatic smell of coffee. For a moment he hung between sleep and consciousness. He was aware that he was lying on Annaka Vadas' sofa, that he had an eiderdown comforter over him and a goose feather pillow beneath his head. At once he rose fully out of sleep into Annaka's sun-drenched apartment. He turned, saw her sitting at the gleaming grand piano, a huge cup of coffee by her side.

"What time is it?"

She continued her chord runs without picking up her head. "After noon."

"Christ!"

"Yes, it was time for my practice, time you got up." She began to play a melody he couldn't place. "I actually thought you'd have gone back to your hotel by the time I awoke, but I came in here and there you were, sleeping like a child. So I went and made coffee. Would you like some?"

"Absolutely."

"You know where it is."

She picked up her head then, refused to turn away, watched him as he peeled off the eiderdown, drew on his cords and shirt. He padded into the bathroom, and when he was finished, he went into the kitchen. As he was pouring himself coffee, she said, "You have a nice body, scarred though it is."

He searched for cream; apparently she liked her coffee black. "The scars give me character."

"Even the one around your neck?"

Poking through the refrigerator, he didn't answer her but, rather, involuntarily put a hand to the wound, and in so doing felt again Mylene Dutronc's compassionate ministrations.

"That one's new," she said. "What happened?"

"I had an encounter with a very large, very angry creature."

She stirred, abruptly uneasy. "Who tried to strangle you?"

He had found the cream. He poured in a dollop, then two teaspoonfuls of sugar, took his first sip. Returning to the living room, he said, "Anger can do that to you, or didn't you know?"

"How would I? I'm not a part of your violent world."

He looked at her levelly. "You tried to shoot me, or have you forgotten?"

"I don't forget anything," she said shortly.

Something he'd said had chafed her, but he didn't know what it was. Part of her was frayed thin. Perhaps it was only the shock of her father's sudden and violent death.

In any case he decided to try another tack. "There's nothing edible in your refrigerator."

"I usually go out to eat. There's a sweet café five blocks away."

"Do you think we could go there?" he said. "I'm starving."

"As soon as I'm finished. Our late night delayed my day."

The piano bench scraped the floor as she settled herself more fully. Then the first bars of Chopin's Nocturne in B-Flat Minor drifted through the room, swirling like leaves falling on a golden autumn afternoon. He was surprised at how much pleasure the music gave him.

After some moments, he got up, went to the small escritoire and opened her computer.

"Please don't do that," Annaka said without taking her eyes from the music sheet. "It's distracting."

Bourne sat, trying to relax, while the gorgeous music swept through the apartment.

While the last of the Nocturne was still echoing, Annaka rose, went into the kitchen. He heard the water in the sink running while she waited for it to get cold. It seemed to run for a long time. She returned then, with a glass of water in one hand, which she drank down in a single long swallow. Bourne, watching her from his position at the escritoire, saw the curve of her pale neck, the curl of several stray strands, a fiery copper, at her hairline.

"You did very well last night," Bourne said.

"Thank you for talking me down from the ledge." Her eyes slid away, as if she didn't want any part of his compliment. "I was never so frightened in my life."

They were in the café, which was filled with cut-glass chandeliers, velvet-seat cushions and translucent wall sconces affixed to cherrywood walls. They sat across from each other at a window table, overlooking the outdoor portion of the café, which was deserted, it being still too chilly to sit in the pale morning sun.

"My concern now is that Molnar's apartment was under surveillance," Bourne said. "There's no other explanation for the police arriving at just that time."

"But why would anyone be watching the apartment?"

"To see if we showed up. Ever since I've arrived in Budapest, my inquiries have been frustrated."

Annaka glanced nervously out the window. "What about now? The thought of someone watching my apartment—watching *us*—gives me the creeps."

"No one followed us here from your apartment, I made sure of that." He paused while their food was served. When the waiter had departed, he resumed. "Remember the precautions I made us take last night after we escaped the police? We took separate taxis, changed twice, reversed direction."

She nodded. "I was too exhausted then to question your bizarre instructions."

"No one knows where we went or even that we're together now."

"Well, that's a relief." She released a long-held breath.

Khan had just one thought when he saw Bourne and the woman walk out of her building: Despite Spalko's cocky assurances that he was safe from Bourne's search, Bourne was continuing to circle closer. Somehow Bourne had found out about László Molnar, the man Spalko was interested in. Furthermore, he'd discovered where Molnar lived and, presumably, he'd been inside the apartment when the police showed up. Why was Molnar important to Bourne? Khan had to find out.

He watched from behind as Bourne and the woman walked off. Then he got out of his rental car, went into the entrance of 106–108 Fo utca. He picked the lock on the lobby door and entered the hallway inside. Taking the elevator up to the top floor, he found the staircase up to the roof. Unsurprisingly, the door was alarmed, but for him it was a simple matter to jump the circuit, bypassing the alarm system altogether. He went through the door, onto the roof, crossing immediately to the front of the building.

With his hands on the stone parapet, he leaned over, saw immediately the bay window on the fourth floor just below him. Climbing over the parapet, he eased himself down onto the ledge beneath the window. The first window he tried was locked, but the other wasn't. He opened the window, climbed through into the apartment.

He would dearly have liked to look around, but without knowing how soon they would return, he knew he couldn't risk it. This was a time for business, not indulgences. Looking around for a likely spot, he glanced up at the frosted-glass light fixture hanging from the center of the ceiling. It was as good as any, he quickly determined, and better than most.

Dragging over the piano bench, he positioned it beneath the fixture, then climbed on it. He took out the miniature electronic bug, dropped it over the rim of the frosted-glass bowl. Then he climbed down, put an electronic ear-bud into his ear and activated the bug.

He heard the small noises as he moved the piano bench back into place, heard his own footfalls across the polished wooden floor as he went over to the sofa, where a pillow and down comforter lay. He took up the pillow, sniffed its center. He smelled Bourne, but the scent stirred a previously undisturbed memory. As it began to rise upward in his mind, he dropped the pillow as if it had burst into flame. Quickly now, he exited the apartment as he had come, retracing his steps down to the lobby. But this time he went back through the building, going out the service entrance. One could never be too careful.

Annaka began work on her breakfast. Sunlight streamed in through the window, illuminating her extraordinary fingers. She ate like she played, handling the cutlery as if they were musical instruments.

"Where did you learn to play piano like that?" he said.

"Did you like it?"

"Yes, very much."

"Why?"

He cocked his head. "Why?"

She nodded. "Yes, why did you like it? What did you hear in it?"

Bourne thought a moment. "A kind of mournfulness, I suppose."

She put down her knife and fork and, with her hands free, began to sing a section of the Nocturne. "It's the unresolved dominant sevenths, you see. With them, Chopin expanded the accepted limits of dissonance and key." She resumed singing, the notes ringing out. "The result is expansive. And at the same time mournful, because of those unresolved dominant sevenths."

She paused, her beautiful pale hands hanging suspended over the table, the long fingers arched slightly as if still imbued with the energy of the composer.

"Anything else?"

He gave it some more thought, then shook his head.

She took up her knife and fork, went back to eating. "My mother taught me to play. It was her profession, teaching piano, and as soon as she felt that I was good enough, she taught me Chopin. He was her favorite, but his music is immensely difficult to play—not only technically but also getting the emotion right."

"Does your mother still play?"

Annaka shook her head. "Like Chopin, her health was frail. Tuberculosis. She died when I was eighteen."

"A bad age to lose a parent."

"It changed my life forever. I was grief-stricken, of course, but much to my astonishment and shame, beneath that I was angry at her,"

"Angry?"

She nodded. "I felt abandoned, unmoored, left at sea with no way to find my way back home."

All at once Bourne understood how she could empathize with the difficulty of his loss of memory.

She frowned. "But, really, what I regret most is how shabbily I treated her. When she first proposed I take up the piano, I rebelled."

"Of course you did," he said gently. "It was her suggestion. Moreover, it was her profession." He felt a small *frisson* in the pit of his stomach, as if she had just now played one of Chopin's famous dissonances. "When I talked to my son about baseball, he turned up his nose, wanted to play soccer instead." As he dredged up the memory of Joshua, Bourne's eyes turned inward. "All his friends played soccer, but there was something else. His mother was Thai; he was schooled in Buddhism at a very early age, as was her wish. His 'American-ness' wasn't of interest to him."

Finished, Annaka pushed her plate away.

"On the contrary, I think it was probable that his 'American-ness' was very much on his mind," she said. "How could it be otherwise? Don't you think he was reminded of it every day at school?"

Unbidden came an image of Joshua in bandages, one eye black-and-blue. When he had asked Dao about it, she had told him that the child had fallen at home, but the following day she had taken Joshua to school herself, had stayed there for several hours. He'd never questioned her; at the time he'd been far too busy at work even to think it through himself.

"It never occurred to me," he said now.

Annaka shrugged and, without perceptible irony, said, "Why should it? You're American. The world belongs to you."

Was that the source of her innate animosity? he wondered. Was it simply generic, the fear of the ugly American that had lately been resurrected?'

She asked the waiter for more coffee. "At least you're able to work things out with your son," she said. "With my mother . . ." She shrugged.

"My son's dead," Bourne said, "along with his sister and mother. They were killed in Phnom Penh many years ago."

"Oh." It appeared that he had finally punctured her cool, steely exterior. "I'm so sorry."

He turned his head away; any talk of Joshua felt like salt being rubbed into an open wound. "Surely you came to terms with your mother before she died."

"I wish I had." Annaka stared down at her coffee, a look of concentration on her face. "It wasn't until she introduced me to Chopin that I understood the full measure of the gift she had given me. How I loved to play the Nocturnes, even when I was far from accomplished!"

"You didn't tell her?"

"I was a teenager; we weren't exactly talking." Her eyes darkened in sorrow. "Now that she's gone, I wish I had."

"You had your father."

"Yes, of course," she said. "I had him."

CHAPTER SEVENTEEN

The tactical Non-Lethal Weapons Directorate was housed in a series of anonymous-looking red-brick buildings covered with climbing ivy that had once been a women's boarding school. The Agency had deemed it more secure to take over an existing site than to build one from scratch. That way they could gut the structures, creating from the inside the warren of labs, conference rooms and testing sites the directorate required, using their own highly skilled personnel rather than outside contractors.

Even though Lindros showed his ID he was taken inside an all-white windowless room where he was photographed, fingerprinted and his retinas scanned. He waited alone.

Finally, after fifteen minutes or so, a CIA suit entered, addressed Lindros, "Deputy Director Lindros, Director Driver will see you now."

Without a word. Lindros followed the suit out of the room. They spent another five minutes marching up and down featureless corridors with indirect lighting. For all he knew, he was being led around in a circle.

At length, the suit stopped at a door that, as far as Lindros could tell, was identical to all the others they had passed. As with the others, there was no marking, no identification of any sort anywhere on or near the door, save for two small bulbs. One glowed a deep red. The suit rapped his knuckles three times on the door. A moment later the red light went out and the other bulb glowed green. The suit opened the door, stepped back for him to go through.

On the other side of it, he found Director Randy Driver, a sandy-haired individual with a Marine high-and-tight haircut, a blade-straight nose and narrow blue eyes that gave him a perpetually suspicious look. He had wide shoulders and a muscular torso he liked to show off a bit too much. He sat in a high-tech mesh swivel chair behind a smoked glass and stainless-steel desk. In the center of each white metal wall hung a reproduction of a Mark Rothko painting, each looking like swaths of colored bandages applied to a raw wound.

"Deputy Director, an unexpected pleasure," Driver said with a tight smile that belied his words. "I confess I'm not accustomed to snap inspections. I would've preferred the courtesy of an appointment."

"Apologies," Lindros said, "but this isn't a snap inspection. I'm conducting a murder investigation."

"Alexander Conklin's murder, I presume."

"Indeed. I need to interview one of your people. A Dr. Felix Schiffer."

It was as if Lindros had dropped an immobility bomb. Driver sat unmoving behind his desk, the tight smile frozen on his face like a rictus. At last, Driver seemed to regain his composure. "What on earth for?"

"I just told you," Lindros said. "It's part of our ongoing investigation."

Driver spread his hands. "I can't see how."

"It's not required that you do," Lindros said shortly. Driver had made him sit and wait like a child at detention, now he was being given a verbal runaround. Lindros was rapidly losing patience with him. "All that's required is that you tell me where Dr. Schiffer is."

Driver's face closed down entirely. "The moment you crossed my threshold, you entered my territory." He stood. "While you were undergoing our identification procedures, I took the liberty of calling the DCI. His office has no idea why you might be here."

"Of course not," Lindros retorted, knowing he'd already lost the battle. "The DCI debriefs me at the end of the each day."

"I've no interest whatsoever in your operations, Deputy Director. The bottom line is that no one interviews any of my personnel without express written authorization from the DCI himself."

"The DCI has empowered me to take this investigation wherever I deem it necessary."

"I've only your word for that." Driver shrugged. "You can see my point of vi—"

"As a matter of fact, I can't," Lindros said. He knew that continuing on in this vein would get him nowhere. Worse, it wasn't politic, but Randy Driver had pissed him off and he couldn't help himself. "In my view, you're being obstinate and obstructionist."

Driver leaned forward, his knuckles cracking as he pushed them down against the desk top. "Your view is irrelevant. In the absence of official signed documents, I have nothing more to say to you. This interview is at an end."

The suit must have been listening in on the conversation because just then the door opened and he stood there, waiting to escort Lindros out.

It was while riding down a perp that Detective Harris got the brainstorm. He'd received the all-points radio call about the male Caucasian in a black late model Pontiac GTO, Virginia plates, who'd run a red light outside of Falls Church, heading south on Route 649. Harris, who had been inexplicably banished by Martin Lindros from the Conklin-Panov murders, was in Sleepy Hollow, following up on a convenience store robbery-murder when the call came in. Right on 649.

He spun his cruiser around in a ragged U-turn, then had headed off, lights going, siren blaring, heading north on 649. Almost immediately, he saw the black GTO and behind it a string of three Virginia state trooper cars.

He veered across the median in a blare of horns and screeching tires coming from the oncoming traffic and headed straight at the GTO. The driver saw him, changed lanes, and as Harris began to follow him through the jigsaw puzzle of stalled traffic, he veered off the road itself, zipping across the breakdown lane.

Harris, calculating vectors, nosed his cruiser on an intercept course, which forced the plunging GTO onto the apron of a gas station. If he didn't pull up, he'd crash right into the line of pumps.

As the GTO screamed to a halt, rocking on its oversized shocks, Harris scrambled out of his car, his service revolver drawn, headed straight at the driver.

"Get out of the car with your hands in the air!" Harris called.

"Officer—"

"Shut up and do as I say!" Harris said, advancing steadily, his eyes peeled for any sign of a weapon.

"Okay, okay!"

The driver got out of the car just as the other cruisers caught up. Harris could see that the perp was no more than twenty-two, thin as a rail. They found a pint of liquor in the car and, underneath the front seat, a gun.

"I've got a license for it!" the young man said. "Just look in the glove compartment!"

The gun was, indeed, licensed. The young man was a diamond courier.

Why he'd been drinking was another story, one Harris wasn't particularly interested in.

Back at the station, what had caught his attention was that the license didn't check out. He made a call to the store that had supposedly sold the young man the gun. He got a foreign-sounding voice that admitted selling the young man the gun, but something in that voice nagged at Harris. So he'd taken a ride over to the store, only to find that it didn't exist. Instead, he found a single Russian with a computer server. He arrested the Russian and impounded the server.

Now he returned to the station, accessed the gun-permit database for the last six months. He plugged in the name of the bogus gun store and discovered, to his shock, more than three hundred false sales that were used to generate legitimate permits. But there was an even bigger surprise waiting for him when he accessed the files on the server he'd confiscated. When he saw the entry, he grabbed his phone and dialed Lindros' cell.

"Hey, it's Harry."

"Oh, hello," Lindros said, as if his attention was elsewhere.

"What's the matter?" Harris asked. "You sound terrible."

"I'm stymied. Worse, I just got my teeth figuratively kicked in and now I'm wondering if I have enough ammunition to go to the Old Man with it."

"Listen, Martin, I know I'm officially off the case—"

"Jesus, Harry, I've been meaning to talk to you about that."

"Never mind now," Detective Harris interrupted. He launched into an abbreviated account of the driver of the GTO, his gun, and the scam being run on falsely registered guns. "You see how it works," he went on. "These guys can get guns for anyone they want."

"Yeah, so?" Lindros said without much enthusiasm.

"So they can also put anyone's name on the registration. Like David Webb's."

"That's a nice theory, but—"

"Martin, it isn't a theory!" Harris was fairly shouting into the receiver; everyone around him looked up from their work, surprised at the rising sound of his voice. "It's the real deal!"

"What?!"

"That's right. This same ring 'sold' a gun to one David Webb, only Webb never bought it, because the store on the permit doesn't exist."

"Okay, but how d'we know Webb didn't know about this ring and used them to get a gun illegally?"

"That's the beauty part," Harris said. "I have the electronic ledger from the ring. Every sale is meticulously recorded. Funds for the gun Webb supposedly bought were wired in from Budapest."

The monastery perched atop a mountain ridge. On the steep terraces far below, it grew oranges and olives, but up above, where the building seemed implanted like a molar in the bedrock itself, there grew only thistle and wild laudanum. *Kri-kri*, the ubiquitous Cretan mountain goat, were the only creatures able to sustain themselves at the level of the monastery.

The ancient stone construction had long been forgotten. Which of the marauding peoples from the island's storied history had built it was difficult for a lay person to say. It had, like Crete itself, passed through many hands, been mute witness to prayers and sacrifice and the spilling of blood. Even from a cursory glance, however, it was clear that it was very old.

From the dawn of time, the issue of security had been of paramount importance to warriors and monastics alike, hence the monastery's place atop the mountain. On one slope were the fragrant terraced groves; on the other was a gorge, not unlike the slash of a Saracen's cutlass, scored deep into the rock, opening up the mountain's flesh.

Having encountered professional resistance at the house in Iraklion, Spalko proceeded to plan this assault with a great deal of care. Making a run at the place in daylight was out of the question. No matter in which direction they might try it, they were certain to be mowed down long before they reached the monastery's thick and crenelated outer walls. Therefore, while his men took their wounded compatriot back to the jet to be tended to by the surgeon and to assemble the needed supplies, Spalko and Zina rented motorcycles so that they could reconnoiter the area surrounding the monastery.

At the edge of the gorge, they left their vehicles and hiked down. The sky was an absorbent blue, so brilliant that it seemed to imbue every other color with its aura. Birds circled and rose on the thermals, and when the breeze picked up, the delicious scent of orange blossoms perfumed the air. Ever since she boarded his personal jet, Zina had been patiently waiting to find out why Spalko wanted to get her alone.

"There's an underground entrance to the monastery," Spalko said, as they descended the rocky scree into the end of the gorge closest to the structure. The chestnut trees on the lip of the gorge had given way to tougher cypresses, whose twisted trunks extended from the earthen crannies between boulders. They used the flexible branches as impromptu handholds as they continued down the steep slope of the gorge.

Where the Shaykh got his information, Zina could only guess at. In any event, it was clear that he possessed a worldwide network of people with ready access to almost any information he could require.

They rested for a moment, leaning against an outcropping. The afternoon was getting on, and they ate olives, flatbread and a bit of octopus marinated in olive oil, vinegar and garlic.

"Tell me, Zina," Spalko said now, "do you think of Khalid Murat—do you miss him?"

"I miss him very much." Zina wiped her lips with the back of her hand, bit into a wedge of flatbread. "But Hasan is our leader now; all things must pass. What happened to him was tragic but not unexpected. We're all targets of the savage Russian regime; we all have to live with that knowledge."

"What if I were to tell you that the Russians had nothing to do with Khalid Murat's death?" Spalko said.

Zina stopped eating. "I don't understand. I know what happened. Everyone does."

"No," Spalko said softly, "all you know is what Hasan Arsenov has told you."

She stared at him, and in the dawning of comprehension her knees felt weak.

"How—" She was so full of emotion her voice failed her and she was obliged to clear her throat, start over again, aware that part of her didn't want to know the answer to the question she was about to ask. "How d'you know this?"

"I know," Spalko said levelly, "because Arsenov contracted with me to assassinate Khalid Murat."

"But *why*?"

Spalko's eyes bored into hers. "Oh, you know, Zina—you, of all people—you who's his lover, who knows him better than anyone—you know very well."

And, sadly, Zina did; Hasan had told her as much many times. Khalid Murat was part of the old order. He couldn't think past the borders of Chechnya; in Hasan's opinion, he was afraid to take on the world when he could not yet see a way for them to hold back the Russian infidels.

"Didn't you suspect?"

And the truly galling thing, she thought, was that she *hadn't* suspected, not for a moment. She had believed Hasan's story from first word to last. She wanted to lie to the Shaykh, to make herself look more clever in his eyes, but under the burden of his gaze, she knew he'd see right through her and know she was lying, and then, she suspected, he'd know she couldn't be trusted and he'd be finished with her.

And so, humiliated, she shook her head. "He had me fooled."

"You and everyone else," he said evenly. "Never mind." He smiled suddenly. "But now you know the truth; you see the power of having information others don't."

She stood for a moment, her buttocks against the sun-heated rock, rubbing her palms down her thighs. "What I don't understand," she said, "is why you've chosen to tell me."

Spalko heard the twin notes of fear and trepidation in her voice and decided that was as it should be. She knew she stood on the edge of a precipice. If he was any judge of character, she had suspected as much from the moment he had proposed she come with him to Crete, certainly from the instant she had colluded with him in his lie to Arsenov.

"Yes," he said, "you've been chosen."

"But for what?" She found that she was shaking.

He came and stood close to her. Blocking out the sunlight, he exchanged the sun's warmth for his own. She could smell him, as she had in the hangar, and the male musk of him made her wet.

"You've been chosen for great things." As he came ever closer, his voice dropped in volume even while it was increasing in intensity.

"Zina," he whispered, "Hasan Arsenov is weak. I knew it the moment he came to me with his scheme for assassination. Why should he need me? I asked myself. A strong warrior who believes his leader is no longer fit to lead will undertake to murder the man himself; he will not hire out the deed to others who, if they are clever and patient, will one day use his weakness against him."

Zina was trembling, both from his words and the force of his physical presence, which was making her feel as if her skin was prickling, her hair standing on end. Her mouth was dry, her throat full with longing.

"If Hasan Arsenov is weak, Zina, of what use is he to me?" Spalko put a hand on her breast and Zina's nostrils flared. "I'll tell you." She closed her eyes. "The mission we'll shortly embark on is fraught with danger every step of the way." He squeezed gently, pulling upward with agonizing slowness. "In the event something goes wrong, it's prudent to have a leader who can like a magnet attract the attention of the enemy, drawing them toward him even as the real work goes on unimpeded." He pressed his body against hers, felt her rising against him in a kind of spasm she was powerless to control. "Do you see what I mean?"

"Yes," she whispered.

"You're the strong one, Zina. If you had wanted to dethrone Khalid Murat, you'd never have come to me first. You'd have taken his life yourself and considered it a blessing you'd done for yourself and for your people." His other hand moved inward along her thigh. "Isn't that so?"

"Yes," she breathed. "But my people will never accept a female leader. It's inconceivable."

"To them but not to us." He drew one leg away. "Think, Zina. How will you make it happen?"

With the hot rush of hormones racing through her, it was hard to think clearly. Part of her realized that that was the point. It wasn't simply that he wanted to take her here in the cleft of the gorge, against the naked rocks, beneath the naked sky. As he had back in the architect's house, he was submitting her to another test. If she lost herself completely now, if she failed to put her mind in gear, if he could make her so beclouded with desire that she couldn't answer his question, then he would be done with her. He would find another candidate to serve his purpose.

Even as he opened her blouse, touched her burning skin, she forced herself to remember how it had been with Khalid Murat, how after his advisors had left their twice-weekly councils, he had listened to what she had to say and often acted on it. She'd never dared tell Hasan the role she'd played, for fear she would be abandoned to the brutality of his jealousy.

But now, splayed out on the rock beneath the Shaykh's advances, she extrapolated forward. Grabbing the back of the Shayhk's head, pulling it down to her neck, she whispered in his ear, "I'll find someone—someone physically intimidating, someone whose love for me will make him compliant—and I will command through him. It'll be his face the Chechen see, his voice they'll hear, but he'll be doing precisely what I tell him to do."

He'd pulled his upper torso away for a moment and she looked up into his eyes, saw them glittering as much with admiration as with lust, and with another tremor of exultation she knew that she had passed her second test. And then, opened and all at once impaled, she groaned in a long, drawn-out exclamation of their shared joy.

CHAPTER EIGHTEEN

The scent of coffee still infused the apartment. They had returned after their meal without dawdling in time-honored tradition over coffee and dessert. Bourne had too much on his mind. But the respite, however brief, had served to revive him, had allowed his subconscious to work on information he needed to process.

They entered the apartment very close together. Citrus and musk rose off her like mist off a river; he couldn't help inhaling it deep into his lungs. In order to distract himself, he grimly turned his mind to the business at hand.

"Did you notice the burns and lesions, the punctures and ligature marks on László Molnar's body?"

She shuddered. "Don't remind me."

"He'd been tortured over a period of many hours, perhaps as much as a couple of days."

She looked at him from beneath straight and serious brows.

"Which means," he said, "that he may have given away Dr. Schiffer's location."

"Or he may not have," she said, "which would also be a reason to kill him."

"I don't think we can afford to make that assumption."

"What d'you mean 'we'?"

"Yes, I know, as of now I'm on my own."

"Are you trying to make me feel guilty? You forget, I have no interest in finding Dr. Schiffer."

"Even if it meant a disaster for the world at large if he fell into the wrong hands?"

"What d'you mean?"

Khan, in his rental car downstairs, pressed the ear-bud. Their words were coming in clearly.

"Alex Conklin was a master technician—it was his speciality. From what I've learned, he was better at planning and executing complex missions than anyone I ever met. As I told you, he wanted Dr. Schiffer so badly that he poached him off a top-secret Department of Defense program, brought him over to the CIA and then promptly 'disappeared' him. That means whatever Schiffer was working on was so important that Alex felt the need to keep him out of harm's way. And as it turned out, he was right, because someone kidnapped Dr. Schiffer. The operation your father ran for him got him away, hidden somewhere only László Molnar knew about. Now your father's dead and so is Molnar. The difference is that Molnar was tortured before he was killed."

Khan sat up straighter, his heart beating fast. *Your father?* Could the woman Bourne was with, the one to whom he'd paid no attention—could she really be Annaka?

Annaka stood in a patch of sunlight coming in through her bay window. "What d'you think Dr. Schiffer was working on that interested all these people so much?"

"I thought you had no interest in Dr. Schiffer," Bourne said.

"Don't be snide. Just answer the question."

"Schiffer is the world's foremost expert in bacteriological particulate behavior. That's what I found out from the forum site Molnar had visited. I told you, but you were too busy finding poor Molnar's corpse."

"That sounds like gibberish to me."

"Remember the Web site Molnar had accessed?"

"Anthrax, Argentinean hemorrhagic fever . . ."

"Cryptococcosis, pneumonic plague. I think it's possible that the good doctor was working with these lethal biologicals or something similar, maybe something even worse."

Annaka stared at him for a moment, shook her head.

"I think what got Alex so excited—and frightened—was that Dr. Schiffer has invented a device that could be used as a biological weapon. If so, he holds one of the terrorists' holy grails."

"Oh, my God! But that's only a guess. How can you be sure you're right?"

"I've just got to keep digging." Bourne said. "Still so sanguine about Dr. Schiffer's whereabouts?"

"But I don't see how we can find him." She turned and went to the piano, as if it were a touchstone or a talisman to keep her safe from harm.

"We," Bourne said. "You said 'we.' "

"A slip of the tongue."

"A Freudian slip, it would seem."

"Stop it," she said crossly, "right now."

He had gotten enough of the measure of her to know that she meant what she said. He went and sat down behind the escritoire. He saw the LAN line that connected her laptop computer to the Internet.

"I've got an idea." he said. That was when he saw the scratches. The sunlight was hitting the highly polished surface of the piano bench in such a way that he could see several marks, freshly made. Someone had been in the apartment while they had been out. For what reason? He looked around for any signs of a disturbance.

"What is it?" Annaka asked. "What's the matter?"

"Nothing," he said. But the pillow wasn't in quite the same position in which he'd left it; it was now skewed a bit to the right.

She put her hand on her hip. "So what's your idea?"

"I need to get something first," he improvised, "from the hotel." He didn't want to alarm her, but he needed to find a way to do some clandestine recon work. It was possible—perhaps even likely—that whoever had been in the apartment was still nearby. After all, they'd been under surveillance at László Molnár's apartment. But how the hell had the watcher trailed them here? he asked himself. He'd been careful in every way that he could imagine. There was a ready answer, of course: Khan had found him.

Bourne grabbed his leather jacket and headed for the door. "I won't be long, I promise. In the meantime, if you want to be useful, you can go back on that Web site, see what more you can discover."

Jamie Hull, head of American security at the terrorism summit in Reykjavik, had a thing for Arabs. He didn't like them; he didn't trust them. They didn't even believe in God—at least, not the right one—let alone believe in Christ the Savior, he thought sourly as he strode down the hallway of the vast Oskjuhlid Hotel.

Another reason to dislike them: They had under their control three-quarters of the world's oil. But then, if not for that, no one would've paid them the slightest attention, and all things being equal, they would've wiped themselves out through their indecipherable webs of intertribal warfare. As it was, there were four different Arabic security teams, one for each country present, but Feyd al-Saoud coordinated their work.

As Arabs went, Feyd al-Saoud wasn't so bad. He was a Saudi—or was it Sunni? Hull shook his head. He didn't know. This was another reason he didn't like them; you never could tell who the hell they were or whose arm they'd cut off, given the chance. Feyd al-Saoud was even Western-schooled, somewhere in London, Oxford—or was it Cambridge? Hull asked himself. As if there was any difference! The point was you could speak to the man in plain English without him looking at you as if you'd just grown a second head.

Also, it seemed to Hull, he was a reasonable man, which meant that he knew his place. When it came to the president's needs and desires, he deferred to Hull on almost everything, which was more than you could say for that sonuva-socialist-bitch Boris Illyich Karpov. He regretted bitterly having complained about him to the Old Man and being barked at in return, but, really, Karpov was the most exasperating bastard Hull had ever had the misfortune to work with.

He entered the multitiered conference theater where the summit itself would take place. It was a perfect oval, with a wave-form ceiling made up of blue panels of acoustic baffling. Hidden behind these panels were the large air ducts that allowed in the air filtered by the forum's sophisticated HVAC system, completely separate from the hotel's massive network. For the rest, the walls were of polished teak, the seats blue-cushioned, the horizontal surfaces either bronze or smoked-glass.

Here, every day since he had arrived, he and his two counterparts met in the mornings to refine and argue about details of the elaborate security arrangements. In the afternoons they reconvened with their respective staffs to review the details and to brief their respective personnel on the latest procedures. Ever since they'd arrived, the entire hotel had been closed to the public so that the security teams could do their electronic sweeps and inspections and make the area absolutely secure.

As he walked into the brightly lit forum, he saw his counterparts: Feyd al-Saoud, slim and dark-eyed above his beak of a nose, with a bearing that was almost regal; Boris Illyich Karpov, head of the FSB's elite Alpha Unit, brawny and bull-like, with wide shoulders and narrow hips, a flat Tatar face that seemed brutal beneath heavy brows and thick black hair. Hull had never seen Karpov smile, and as for Feyd al-Saoud, he doubted he knew how.

"Good morning, fellow travelers," Boris Illyich Karpov said in his ponderous deadpan manner that put Hull in mind of a 1950's newscaster. "We have but three days until the summit commences and there is still much work to accomplish. Shall we begin?"

"By all means," Feyd al-Saoud said, taking his accustomed seat on the dais where just thirty-six hours from now the five heads of the leading Arab states would sit side by side with residents of the United States and Russia in order to hammer out the first concerted Arab-Western initiative to stop international terrorism in its tracks. "I've received instructions from my counterparts in the other attending Islamic nations and will be pleased to relay them to you."

"Demands, you mean," Karpov said belligerently. He'd never gotten over their decision to speak English at their briefings; he'd been outvoted two to one.

"Boris, why must you always put a negative spin on things?" Hull said.

Karpov bristled; Hull knew he disliked American informality. "Demands have a certain stench, Mr. Hull." He tapped the end of his ruddy nose. "I can smell them."

"I'm surprised you can smell anything, Boris, after years of drinking vodka."

"Drinking vodka makes us strong, makes us real men." Karpov turned his red lips into a bow of derision. "Not like you Americans."

"I should listen to you, Boris? You, a Russian? Your country's an abject failure. Communism proved so corrupt Russia imploded under its weight. And as for your people, they're spiritually bankrupt."

Karpov leaped up, his cheeks as red as his nose and lips. "I've had enough of your insults!"

"Too bad." Hull stood, kicking his chair over, forgetting completely the DCI's admonishment. "I'm only just warming up."

"Gentlemen, gentlemen!" Feyd al-Saoud interposed himself between the two antagonists. "Tell me, please, how these childish arguments are going to further the task we've all been sent here to accomplish." His voice was calm and even-toned as he looked from one to the other. "We each have our respective heads of state, whom we serve with unswerving loyalty. Isn't that true? Then we must serve them in the best way we can." He wouldn't let up until both had agreed.

Karpov sat back down, though with arms crossed over his chest. Hull righted his chair, dragged it back to the table and threw himself into it, a sour expression on his face.

Observing them, Feyd al-Saoud said, "We may not like one another, but we must learn to work together."

Dimly, Hull was aware that there was something else about Karpov besides his aggressive intransigence that got under his skin. It took him some moments to locate its origin, but at length he did. Something about Karpov—his smug self-satisfaction—reminded him of David Webb, or Jason Bourne, as all Agency personnel had been ordered to call him. It was Bourne who'd become Alex Conklin's fair-haired boy, despite all the politicking and subtle campaigning Hull had done on his own behalf before he'd given up and gone into the Counterterrorist Center. He'd made a success of his new post, no question, but he never forgot what Bourne had forced him to leave behind. Conklin had been a legend within the Agency. Working with him was all Hull had dreamed about ever since he'd joined the Agency twenty years ago. There are dreams one has as a child; these aren't difficult to let go of. But the dreams one had as an adult, well, that was another matter entirely. The bitterness of what might have been never went away, at least, not in Hull's experience.

He'd actually celebrated when the DCI had informed him that Bourne might be on his way to Reykjavik. The thought of Bourne having turned on his mentor and gone rogue was one that made his blood boil. If only Conklin had chosen him, Hull had thought, he'd be alive today. The thought that he might be the one to terminate Bourne in an Agency sanction was a dream come true. But then he'd got the news that Bourne was dead and his elation had turned to disappointment. He'd become increasingly testy with everyone, including the Secret Service operatives with whom it was vital he keep a close and open relationship. Now, in the absence of any kind of fulfillment, he leveled a murderous look at Karpov and received one in return.

———

Bourne didn't take the elevator down when he left Annaka's apartment. Instead, he went up the short flight of utility stairs that led to the roof. There, he confronted the alarm system and defeated it quickly and efficiently.

The sun had abandoned the afternoon to slate-gray clouds and a stiff quartering wind. As Bourne gazed south, he could see the four elaborate domes of the Kiraly Turkish Baths. He went to the parapet, leaned over in more or less the same spot that Khan had occupied no more than an hour before.

From this vantage point, he scanned the street, first for anyone standing in a shadowed doorway, then for any pedestrians walking too slowly or stopped altogether. He watched two young women strolling arm in arm, a mother pushing a pram, and an old man he scrutinized, recalling Khan's expert work as a chameleon.

Finding nothing suspicious, he turned his attention to the parked cars, looking for anything out of the ordinary. All rental cars in Hungary were obliged to have a sticker identifying themselves as such. In this residential neighborhood, a rental car was something he'd need to investigate.

He found one on a black Skoda up the block and across the street. He studied its position in detail. Anyone sitting behind the wheel would have an unobstructed view of the front entrance to 106–108 Fo utca. At the moment, however, there was no one behind the wheel or anywhere else inside the car.

He turned and strode back across the rooftop.

Khan, crouched on the stairwell in readiness, watched Bourne coming toward him. This was his chance, he knew. Bourne, his mind no doubt filled with matters of surveillance, was completely unsuspecting. As if in a dream—a dream he'd had in his mind for decades—he saw Bourne heading straight toward him, his eyes clouded with thought. Khan was filled with rage. This was the man who had sat next to him and not recognized him, who even when Khan had identified himself had rejected him for who he was. This only intensified Khan's belief that Bourne had never wanted him, that he was all too ready to run away and abandon him.

Therefore, when Khan rose, it was with righteous fury. As Bourne stepped into the shadow of the doorway, Khan slammed his forehead hard into the bridge of his nose. Blood flew and Bourne staggered backward. Khan, pressing his advantage, moved in, but Bourne kicked out.

"*Che-sah!*" Bourne exhaled.

Khan absorbed the kick by partially deflecting it, then clamped his left arm against the side of his body, trapping Bourne's ankle in between. Bourne surprised him, then. Instead of being thrown off balance, he rose up, pressing his back and buttocks against the steel door, kicked with his right foot, delivering a sickening blow to Khan's right shoulder, so that Khan was obliged to let go of Bourne's left ankle.

"*Mee-sah!*" Bourne cried softly.

He came at Khan, who shuddered as if in pain even as he delivered a straight-fingered blow to Bourne's sternum. At once he gripped Bourne's head on either side, cracked it against the roof door. Bourne's eyes went out of focus.

"What's Spalko up to?" Khan said harshly. "You know, don't you?"

Bourne's head was swimming with pain and shock. He tried to focus his eyes and clear his mind at the same time.

"Who's . . . Spalko?" His voice seemed watery, as if it was coming from a long way off.

"Of course you know."

Bourne shook his head, which produced a fusillade of daggers in his head all digging in at once. He squeezed his eyes shut.

"I thought . . . I thought you wanted to kill me."

"Listen to me!"

"Who are you?" Bourne whispered hoarsely. "How d'you know about my son? How d'you know about Joshua?"

"Listen to me!" Khan put his head close to Bourne's. "Stepan Spalko is the man who ordered Alex Conklin's death, the man who set you up—who set us both up. Why did he do that, Bourne? You know and I need to know!"

Bourne felt as if were in the grip of an ice floe, everything moving with infinite slowness. He couldn't think, couldn't seem to put two ideas together. Then he noticed something. The oddness of it cut through the strange inertia in which he was gripped. There was something in Khan's right ear. What was it? Under the guise of extreme pain, he moved his head slightly, saw that it was a miniature electronic receiver.

"Who are you?" he said. "Goddammit, who are you!"

There seemed to be two conversations going on simultaneously, as if the two men were in different worlds, living different lives. Their voices raised, their emotions flamed from embers, and the more they shouted, the further apart they seemed to get.

"I told you!" Khan's hands were covered with Bourne's blood, which had now begun to coagulate in his nostrils. "I'm your son!"

And with those words, the stasis was broken, their worlds collided once again. The rage that had swept Bourne up in its fist when the hotel manager had frustrated him thundered again in his ears. He screamed, driving Khan backward through the door, out onto the roof.

Ignoring the pain in his head, he hooked his ankle behind Khan, shoved him hard. But Khan grabbed hold of him as he went down, raising his legs as his back struck the roof tiles, lifting Bourne off his feet, and with a powerful kick sent him tumbling head over heels.

Bourne tucked his head under, landed on his shoulders and rolled, dissipating most of the impact. They both regained their feet at the same time, their arms outstretched, their fingers grasping for purchase. Bourne brought his arms down suddenly, striking them hard onto Khan's wrists, breaking his hold, spinning him sideways. Bourne butted him, using his forehead against the nerve bundle just below Khan's ear. Khan's left side went slack, and Bourne, using his advantage, drove his balled fist into Khan's face.

Khan staggered, his knees buckling slightly, but like a punch-drunk heavyweight, he refused to go down. Bourne, a maddened bull, struck him again and again, driving him back with every blow, nearer and nearer the parapet. But in his extreme rage he made a mistake, allowing Khan inside his guard. It surprised him when, instead of staggering back beneath the blow, Khan attacked, driving *forward* off his back foot and, midway through, transferring all his weight to his front foot. The resulting strike rattled Bourne's teeth even as it took him off his feet.

Bourne fell to his knees, and Khan struck him a tremendous blow above his ribs. He began to topple over but Khan grabbed him by the throat and began to squeeze.

"You'd better tell me now," he said thickly. "You'd better tell me everything you know."

Bourne, panting and in intense pain, said, "Go to hell!"

Khan struck his jaw with the edge of his hand.

"Why won't you listen?"

"Try a little more force," Bourne said.

"You're completely insane."

"That's your plan, isn't it?" Bourne shook his head doggedly. "This whole sick story about you being Joshua—"

"I *am* your son."

"Listen to yourself—you can't even say his name. You can drop the farce; it'll avail you nothing now. You're an international assassin named Khan. I won't lead you to this Spalko or whoever it is you're planning to get to. I won't be anyone's cat's-paw again."

"You don't know what you're doing. You don't know—" He broke off, shook his head violently, changed tacks. He cradled the small carved stone Buddha in his free palm. "Look at this, Bourne!" He spat out the words as if they were poisonous. "*Look* at it!"

"A talisman anyone in Southeast Asia could pick up—"

"Not *this* one. You gave this one to me—*yes*, you did." His eyes blazed, and his voice held a tremor that, to his shame, he couldn't control. "And then you abandoned me to die in the jungles of—"

A gunshot ricocheted off the roof tiles beside Khan's right leg and, releasing Bourne, he jumped back. A second shot nearly struck his shoulder as he scuttled behind the brick wall of the elevator vent.

Bourne turned his head, saw Annaka crouched at the top of the stairwell, her gun gripped tightly in both hands. Cautiously, she came forward. She risked a glance at Bourne.

"Are you all right?"

He nodded, but at the same time Khan, choosing wisely, leaped from his hiding place, bounded to the side of the rooftop, jumped onto the next building. Bourne noted that instead of firing wildly, Annaka put up her gun and turned to him.

"How can you be all right?" she asked. "There's blood all over you!"

"It's just from my nose." He felt lightheaded as he sat up. Reacting to her dubious expression, he was compelled to add, "Really, it looks like a lot of blood, but it's nothing."

She put a wad of tissues against his nose as he started to bleed again.

"Thank you."

She brushed away his words with those of her own. "You said you needed to get something back at your hotel. Why did you come up here?"

Slowly, he rose to his feet but not without her help. "Wait a minute." She glanced in the direction Khan had gone, then turned back to Bourne, a look of revelation on her face. "He's the one who's been watching us, isn't he? The one who called the police when we were at László Molnar's apartment."

"I don't know."

She shook her head. "I don't believe you. It's the only plausible explanation for why you lied to me. You didn't want to alarm me because you'd told me we were safe here. What changed?"

He hesitated for a moment, then realized that he had no choice but to tell her the truth. "When we came back from the café, there were new scratch marks on your piano bench."

"What?" Her eyes opened wide and she shook her head. "I don't understand."

Bourne thought of the electronic receiver in Khan's right ear. "Let's go back to the apartment and I'll show you."

He walked toward the open doorway, but she hesitated. "I don't know."

Turning back, he said wearily, "What don't you know?"

A hard look had come into her face, along with a kind of ruefulness. "You lied to me."

"I did it to protect you, Annaka."

Her eyes were large and glistening. "How can I trust you now?"

"Annaka—"

"Please tell me, because I really want to know." She stood her ground, and he knew that she wouldn't take even a step toward the staircase. "I need to have an answer I can cling to and believe."

"What d'you want me to say?"

She lifted her arms, let them fall to her side in gesture of exasperation. "Do you see what you're doing, turning everything I say back on itself?" She shook her head. "Where did you learn to make people feel like shit?"

"I wanted to keep you out of harm's way," he said. She had hurt him deeply and, despite his carefully neutral expression, he suspected she knew it. "I thought I was doing the right thing. I still think so, even if it meant keeping the truth from you, at least for a little while."

She looked at him for a long time. The gusting wind took her copper hair, floated it out like a bird's wing. Querulous voices drifted up from Fo utca, people wanting to know what those noises were, a car backfiring or something else? There were no answers, and now, save for the intermittent barking of a dog, the neighborhood was quiet.

"You thought you could handle the situation," Annaka said, "you thought you could handle *him*."

Bourne walked stiff-legged over to the front parapet, where he leaned out. Against all odds, the rental car was still there, empty. Maybe it wasn't Khan's, or maybe Khan hadn't fled the scene. With some difficulty, Bourne stood up straight. The pain was coming in waves, breaking harder on the shore of his consciousness as the endorphins released by the shock of the trauma began to dissipate. Every bone in his body seemed to ache, but none more than his jaw and his ribs.

At last, he found it in himself to answer her truthfully. "I suppose so, yes."

She lifted a hand, pulled her hair away from her cheek. "Who *is* he, Jason?"

It was the first time she had called him by his given name, but it scarcely registered on him. At the moment, he was trying—and failing—to give her an answer that would satisfy himself.

Khan, splayed on the stairs of the building onto whose roof he had leaped, stared unseeing at the featureless ceiling of the stairwell. He waited for Bourne to come get him. Or, he wondered with the wandering mind of those in shock, was he waiting for Annaka Vadas to level her gun at him and pull the trigger? He should be in his car now, driving away, and yet here he was, as inert as a fly caught in a spiderweb.

His buzzing mind was swept by shoulds. He should've killed Bourne when he first had him in his sights, but he had a plan then, one that made sense, one that he had meticulously outlined to himself, one that would bring him—so he believed then!—the maximum measure of revenge that was his due. He should've killed Bourne in the cargo hold of the plane bound for Paris. Surely he'd meant to, just as he'd meant to just now.

It would be easy to tell himself that he'd been interrupted by Annaka Vadas, but the blinding, incomprehensible truth was that he'd had his chance before she arrived on the scene and had *made a choice not to exact his revenge.*

Why? He was completely at a loss to say.

His mind, usually as calm as a lake, jumped around from memory to memory, as if it found the present unbearable. He recalled the room in which he was incarcerated during his years with the Vietnamese gunrunner, his brief moment of freedom before being saved by the missionary, Richard Wick. He remembered Wick's house, the sense of space and freedom that gradually eroded, the creeping horror of his time with the Khmer Rouge.

The worst part—the part he kept trying to forget—was that initially, he'd been attracted to the Khmer Rouge philosophy. Ironically enough, because it was founded by a group of young Cambodian radicals trained in Paris, its ethos was based on French nihilism. "The past is death! Destroy everything to create a new future!" This was the Khmer Rouge mantra, repeated over and over until it ground down all other thought or points of view.

It was hardly surprising that their worldview would initially draw Khan—himself an unwitting refugee, abandoned, marginalized—an outcast by circumstance rather than by design. For Khan the past *was* death— witness his recurring dream. But if he first learned to destroy from them, it was because they had destroyed him first.

Not content to believe his story of abandonment, they'd slowly drained the life, the energy from him as they bled him a little every day. They wanted, so his interlocutor said, to empty his mind of everything; they required a blank slate on which to write their radical version of the new future that awaited them all. They bled him, his smiling interlocutor said, for his own good, to rid him of the toxins of the past. Every day, his interlocutor read to him from their manifesto and then recited the names of those opposing the rebel regime who had been killed. Most, of course, were unknown to Khan, but a few—monks, mainly, as well as a smattering of boys his age—he had known, if only in passing. Some, like the boys, had taunted him, settling the mantle of outcast on his immature shoulders. After a time a new item was added to the agenda. Following the interlocutor's reading of a particular section of the manifesto, Khan was required to repeat it back. This he did, in an ever-increasingly forceful manner.

One day, after the requisite recitation and response, his interlocutor read off the names of those newly killed in furtherance of the revolution. At the end of the list was Richard Wick, the missionary who had taken him in, thinking he'd bring Khan to civilization and to God. What roil of emotion this news elicited within Khan was impossible to say, but the overriding feeling was one of dislocation. His last link to the world at large was now gone. He was completely and utterly alone. In the relative privacy of the latrine, he had wept without knowing why. If there was ever a man he hated, it was the one who'd used and emotionally abandoned him, and now, unaccountably, he was crying over his death.

Later that day his interlocutor led him from the concrete bunker in which he'd been housed ever since being taken prisoner. Even though the sky was low and it was raining heavily, he'd blinked in the light of day. Time had passed; the rainy season had begun.

Lying in the stairwell, it occurred to Khan now that while he was growing up, he'd never been in control of his own life. The truly curious and disturbing thing was that he still wasn't. He'd been under the impression that he was a free agent, having gone to great pains to set himself up in a business where he'd believed—naively, as it turned out—free agents thrived. He could see now that ever since he'd taken on his first commission from Spalko, the man had been manipulating him, and never more so than now.

If he was ever to break free of the chains that bound him, he'd have to do something about Stepan Spalko. He knew he'd been immoderate with him at the end of their last phone conversation, and now he regretted it. In that quick flash of anger, so uncharacteristic of him, he'd accomplished nothing save to put Spalko on his guard. But then, he realized, ever since Bourne had sat down beside him on the park bench in Old Town Alexandria, his usual icy reserve had been shattered, and now emotions he could neither name nor understand kept shooting up to the surface, roiling his consciousness, muddying his intent. He realized with a start that when it came to Jason Bourne, he no longer knew what he wanted.

He sat up, then looked around. He'd heard a sound; he was certain of it. He rose, put one hand on the bannister, his muscles tense, poised for flight. And there it was again. His head turned. What was that sound? Where had he heard it before?

His heart beat fast, his pulse in his throat as the sound rose through the stairwell, echoing in his mind, for he was calling again: *"Lee-Lee! Lee-Lee!"*

But Lee-Lee couldn't answer; Lee-Lee was dead.

CHAPTER NINETEEN

The underground entrance to the monastery lay hidden by shadow and time in the deepest cleft of the northernmost wall of the gorge. The lowering sun had revealed the cleft to be more of a defile, as it must have centuries ago to the monks who had chosen this location for their well-defended home. Perhaps they had been monk-warriors, for the extensive fortifications spoke of battles and bloodshed and the need to keep their home sacrosanct.

Silently the team moved into the defile, following the sun. There was no intimate talk between Spalko and Zina now, no hint whatsoever of what had transpired between them, even though it had been momentous. In a manner of speaking, it could be termed a form of benediction; in any case, it was a transference of allegiance and of power whose silence and secrecy only added to the ramifications of its effect. It was Spalko who once again had metaphorically thrown a pebble in a still pond, only to sit back and watch the effect as the resulting ripples spread outward, altering the basic nature of the pond and all who lived in it.

The sun-splashed rocks vanished behind them as they moved into shadow, and they clicked on their lights. Besides Spalko and Zina, there were two of them—the third having been taken back to the jet at Kazantzakis Airport, where the surgeon awaited. They wore lightweight nylon backpacks, filled with all manner of paraphernalia from canisters of tear gas to balls of twine and everything in between. Spalko didn't know what they'd be up against and he was taking no chances.

The men went first, semiautomatic guns on wide straps slung over their shoulders, held at the ready. The defile narrowed, forcing them to continue on in single-file. Soon, however, the sky vanished beneath a wall of rock and they found themselves in a cave. It was dank and musty, filled with the fetid odors of decay.

"It stinks like an open grave," one of the men said.

"Look!" the other cried. "Bones!"

They paused, their lights concentrated on a scattering of small mammal bones, but not a hundred meters on they came upon the thigh-bone of a much larger mammal.

Zina squatted to take up the bone in her hand.

"Don't!" the first man cautioned. "It's bad luck to handle human bones."

"What are you talking about? Archaeologists do it all the time." Zina laughed. "Besides, this might not be human at all." Nevertheless, she dropped it back into the dust of the cave floor.

Five minutes later they were clustered around what was unmistakably a human skull. Their lights gleamed off the brow ridge, threw the eye sockets into deepest shadow.

"What d'you think killed him?" Zina asked.

"Exposure, probably," Spalko said. "Or thirst."

"Poor beggar."

They kept going, deeper into the bedrock upon which the monastery was built. The farther they went, the more numerous the bones became. Now they were all human, and increasingly they were broken or fractured.

"I don't think these people were killed by either exposure or thirst," Zina said.

"What then?" one of the men asked, but no one had an answer.

Spalko ordered them curtly on. They had, by his calculation, just about reached the spot below the monastery's crenelated outer walls. Up ahead, their lights picked out an odd formation.

"The cave is split in two," one of the men said, shining his light on first the passageway to the left, then the one to his right.

"Caves don't bifurcate," Spalko said. He pushed his way ahead of them, stuck his head into the left-hand opening. "This one's a dead end." He ran his hand over the edges of the openings. "These are man-made," he said. "Many years ago, possibly when the monastery was first built." He stepped into the right-hand opening, his voice echoing strangely. "Yes, this one goes on, but there are twists and turns."

When he came back out, he had an odd expression on his face. "I don't think this is a passageway at all," he said. "No wonder Molnar chose this place to hide Dr. Schiffer. I believe we're headed into a labyrinth."

The two men exchanged glances.

"In that case," Zina said, "how will we ever find our way back?"

"There's no way of knowing what we'll find in there." Spalko took out a small rectangular object no larger than a deck of playing cards. He grinned as he showed her how it worked. "A global positioning system. I've just electronically marked our starting point." He nodded. "Let's go."

It didn't take them long, however, to discover the error of their ways, and not more than five minutes later, they had reconvened outside the labyrinth.

"What's the matter?" Zina asked.

Spalko was frowning. "The GPS didn't work in there."

She shook her head. "What d'you think is wrong?"

"Some mineral in the rock itself must be blocking the signal from the satellite," Spalko said. He couldn't afford to tell them that he had no idea why the GPS failed to work in the labyrinth. Instead, he opened his backpack, took out a ball of twine "We'll take a lesson from Theseus and unwind the twine as we go."

Zina eyed the ball uncertainly. "What if we run out of twine?"

"Theseus didn't," Spalko said. "And we're almost inside the monastery's walls, so let's hope we don't run out, either."

Dr. Felix Schiffer was bored. For days now he'd done nothing but follow orders as his cadre of protectors flew him under cover of night to Crete, then proceeded to periodically move him from one location to another. They never stayed in one place for more than three days. He'd liked the house in Iraklion, but that too had proved boring in the end. There was nothing for him to do. They refused to bring him a newspaper or allow him to listen to the radio. As for television, there was none available, but he had to assume they would have kept him away from it, too. Still, he thought glumly, it was a damn sight better than this moldering pile of stone, with only a cot for a bed and a fire for warmth. Heavy chests and sideboards were virtually the only furniture, though the men had brought folding chairs, cots and linens. There was no plumbing; they'd made a privy in the courtyard and its stench reached all the way into the interior of the monastery. It was gloomy and dank, even at noon, and God help them all when darkness fell. Not even a light to read by, if there'd been anything to read.

He longed for freedom. If he'd been a God-fearing man, he would have prayed for his deliverance. So many days since he'd seen László Molnar or spoken to Alex Conklin. When he asked his protectors about that, they invoked the word most sacred to them: security. Communication was simply not secure. They took pains to reassure him that he would soon be reunited with his friend and his benefactor. But when he asked when, all they did was shrug and go back to their endless card game. He could sense that they were bored as well, at least the ones not on guard duty.

There were seven of them. Originally, there were more, but the others had been left behind in Iraklion. But from what he'd been able to glean, they should have been here by now. Accordingly, there was no card game today—every member of the cadre was on patrol. There was a distinct air of tension that set his teeth on edge.

Schiffer was a rather tall man, with piercing blue eyes and a strong-bridged nose below a mass of salt-and-pepper hair. There was a time before he'd been recruited into DARPA and had been more visible when he'd been taken for Burt Bacharach. Not being good with people, he'd never known how to respond. He'd merely mumble something unintelligible and turn away, but his obvious embarrassment only reinforced the misapprehension.

He got up, walked idly across the room to the window, but he was intercepted by one of the cadre and was turned away.

"Security," the mercenary said, his tension on his breath if not in his eyes.

"Security! Security! I'm sick to death of that word!" Schiffer exclaimed.

Nevertheless, he was herded back to the chair on which he was meant to sit. It was away from all doors and windows. He shivered in the dampness.

"I miss my lab; I miss my work!" Schiffer looked into the dark eyes of the mercenary. "I feel like I'm in prison, can you understand that?"

The cadre's leader, Sean Keegan, sensing his charge's unrest, strode swiftly over. "Please take your seat, Doctor."

"But I—"

"It's for your own good," Keegan said. He was one of those black Irishmen, dark of hair and eye, with a rough-hewn face brimming with grim determination, and a street-brawler's lumpy physique. "We've been hired to keep you safe and we take that responsibility seriously."

Obediently, Schiffer sat. "Would *someone* please tell me what's going on?"

Keegan stared down at him for some time. Then, making up his mind, he squatted next to the chair. In a low voice, he said, "I've avoided keeping you informed, but I suppose it might be best for you to know now."

"What?" Schiffer's face was pinched and pained. "What's happened?"

"Alex Conklin's dead."

"Oh, God, no." Schiffer wiped his suddenly sweating face with his hand.

"And as for László Molnar, we haven't heard from him in two days."

"Christ almighty!"

"Calm yourself, Doctor. It's entirely possible Molnar's been out of touch for security reasons." Keegan's eyes met his. "On the other hand, the personnel we left at the house in Iraklion have failed to show."

"I gathered as much," Schiffer said. "Do you think something . . . untoward has happened to them?"

"I can't afford not to."

Schiffer's face shone; he couldn't stop himself from sweating in fear. "Then it's possible Spalko's found out where I am; it's possible that he's here on Crete."

Keegan's face was set in stone. "That's the premise we're going by."

Schiffer's terror made him aggressive. "Well," he demanded, "what're you doing about it?"

"We have men with machine pistols manning the ramparts, but I very much doubt Spalko's foolish enough to try a ground assault across a treeless terrain." Keegan shook his head. "No, if he's here, if he's coming for you, Doctor, he'll have no choice." He stood, slung his machine-pistol over his shoulder. "His route will be through the labyrinth."

Spalko, in the labyrinth with his small party, was becoming more and more apprehensive with every twist and turn they were forced to make. The labyrinth was the only logical approach for an assault on the monastery, which meant they might very well be walking into a trap.

He glanced down, saw the ball of twine was two-thirds behind them. They must be at or near the center of the monastery by now; the trail of twine assured him that the labyrinth hadn't taken them in a circle. At each branching, he believed that he'd chosen well.

He turned to Zina, said under his breath, "I smell an ambush. I want you to stay here in reserve." He patted her backpack. "If we run into trouble, you know what to do."

Zina nodded, and the three men moved off in a half-crouch. They had only just disappeared when she heard machine-pistol fire coming in quick bursts. Quickly she opened her backpack, drew out a canister of tear gas, headed off after them, following the trail of the twine.

She smelled the stench of cordite before she turned the second corner. She peeked around the corner, saw one of their unit sprawled on the ground in a pool of blood. Spalko and the other man were pinned down by gunfire. From her vantage point, she could tell that it was coming from two different directions.

Pulling the pin on the canister, she tossed it over Spalko's head. It struck the ground, then rolled to the left, exploding in a soft hiss. Spalko had slapped his man's back, and they retreated out of the spread of the gas.

They could hear coughing and retching. By this time they'd all donned their gas masks and were ready to mount a second attack. Spalko rolled another canister to their right, cutting short the gunfire directed at them, but not, regrettably, before his second man caught three bullets in the chest and neck. He went down, blood bubbling from between his slack lips.

Spalko and Zina split, one going right, the other left, killing the incapacitated mercenaries—two each—with efficient bursts from their machine-pistols. They both saw the stairway at the same time and made for it.

Sean Keegan grabbed Felix Schiffer even as he shouted orders for his men on the ramparts to abandon their positions and return to the center of the monastery, where he was now dragging his terrified charge.

He'd begun to act the instant he'd caught a whiff of the tear gas seeping up from the labyrinth below. Moments later he heard the resumption of gunfire, then a deathly ringing silence. Seeing his two men rush in, he directed them toward the stone staircase that led down to where he'd deployed the rest of his men to ambush Spalko.

Keegan had for years been employed by the IRA before going out on his own as a mercenary-for-hire, so he was well acquainted with situations where he was outmanned and outgunned. In fact, he relished such situations, saw them as challenges to overcome.

But there was smoke now in the monastery proper, great billowing wafts of it, and now a hail of machine-gun fire coming out of it. His men had no chance; they were mowed down before they had a chance even to identify their killers.

Keegan didn't wait to identify them either. Hauling on Dr. Schiffer, he took them through the warren of small, dark, stifling rooms, looking for a way out.

As they had planned, Spalko and Zina separated the moment they emerged from the dense clouds of the smoke bomb they had tossed out the door at the head of the stairs they had climbed. Spalko went methodically through the rooms while Zina looked for a door to the outside.

It was Spalko who saw Schiffer and Keegan first, and he called to them, only to be greeted with a burst of gunfire, obliging him to duck behind a heavy wooden chest.

"You've no hope of getting out of this alive," he called to the mercenary. "I don't want you; I want Schiffer."

"It's the same thing," Keegan shouted back. "I was given a commission; I intend to carry it out."

"To what purpose?" Spalko said. "Your employer, László Molnar, is dead. So is János Vadas."

"I don't believe you," Keegan responded. Schiffer was whimpering and he shushed him.

"How d'you think I found you?" Spalko went on. "I ground it out of Molnar. Come on. You know he's the only one who knew you were here."

Silence.

"They're all dead now," Spalko said, inching forward. "Who'll pay the last of your commission? Hand over Schiffer and I'll pay you whatever you're owed, plus a bonus. How does that sound?"

Keegan was about to answer, when Zina, having come at him from the opposite direction, put a bullet in the back of his head.

The resulting explosion of blood and gore made Dr. Schiffer whimper like a whipped dog. Then, with his last protector pitched over, he saw Stepan Spalko advancing toward him. He turned and ran right into Zina's arms.

"There's nowhere to go, Felix," Spalko said. "You see that now, don't you?"

Schiffer stared wide-eyed at Zina. He began to gibber, and she put a hand to his head, stroking his hair back from his damp forehead as if he were a child ill with fever.

"You were mine once," Spalko said as he stepped over Keegan's corpse. "And you're mine again." From out of his backpack he took two items. They were made of surgical steel, glass and titanium.

"Oh, God!" The groan from Schiffer was as heartfelt as it was involuntary.

Zina smiled at Schiffer, kissed him on both cheeks as if they were good friends reunited after a long absence. At once, he burst into tears.

Spalko, enjoying the effect the NX 20 diffuser had on its inventor, said, "This is the way the two halves fit together, isn't it, Felix?" Whole, the NX 20 was no larger than the automatic weapon slung across Spalko's back. "Now that I've got a proper payload, you'll teach me the proper use of it."

"No," Schiffer said in a quavery voice. "No, no, no!"

"Don't you worry about a thing," Zina whispered as Spalko took hold of the back of Dr. Schiffer's neck, sending yet another spasm of terror through the scientist's frame. "You're in the best of hands now."

The flight of stairs was short, but, for Bourne, descending them was more painful than he had expected. With every step he took, the trauma he'd received from the blow above his ribs sent jolts of agony through him. What he needed was a hot bath and some sleep, two things he couldn't yet afford.

Back in Annaka's apartment, he showed her the top of the piano bench and she swore under her breath. Together they moved it beneath the light fixture and he stood on it.

"You see?"

She shook her head. "I haven't the slightest idea what's going on."

He went to the escritoire, scribbled on a pad: *Do you have a ladder?*

She looked at him oddly but nodded.

Go get it, he wrote.

When she brought it back into the living room, he climbed it high enough to look into the shallow frosted-glass bowl of the light fixture. And, sure enough, there it was. Carefully, he reached in, plucked up the tiny item between his fingertips. He climbed down and showed it to her in the palm of his hand.

"What—?" She broke off at the emphatic shake of his head.

"Do you have a pair of pliers?" he asked.

Again, the curious look as she opened the door of a shallow closet. She handed him the pliers. He put the tiny square between the ribbed ends, squeezed. The square shattered.

"It's a miniature electronic transmitter," he said.

"What?" Curiosity had turned to bewilderment.

"That's why the man on the roof broke in here, to plant this in the light fixture. He was listening as well as looking."

She looked around the cozy room and shivered. "Dear God, I'll never again feel the same way about this place." Then she turned to Bourne. "What does he *want*? Why try to record our every move?" Then she snorted. "It's Dr. Schiffer, isn't it?"

"It may be," Bourne said, "I don't know." All at once, he became dizzy and, near to blacking out, half-fell, half-sat on the sofa.

Annaka hurried to the bathroom to get him disinfectant and some bandages. He put his head back against the cushions, clearing his mind of everything that had just happened. He had to center himself, maintain his concentration, keeping his eye firmly fixed on what had to be done next.

Annaka returned from the bathroom carrying a tray on which were a shallow porcelain bowl of hot water, a sponge, some towels, an ice pack, a bottle of disinfectant and a glass of water.

"Jason?"

He opened his eyes.

She gave him the glass of water, and when he had drained it, she handed him the ice pack. "Your cheek is starting to swell."

He put the pack against his face, felt the pain slowly recede into numbness. But when he took a quick breath, his side seized up as he twisted to put the empty glass on a side table. He turned back slowly, stiffly. He was thinking of Joshua, who had been resurrected in his mind if not in reality. Maybe that was why he was so filled with blind rage at Khan, for Khan had raised the specter of the awful past, thrusting into the light a ghost so dear to David Webb he had haunted him in both his personalities.

Watching Annaka as she cleaned his face of dried blood, he recalled their brief exchange at the café when he brought up the subject of her father and she had broken down, and yet he knew that he had it pursue it. He was a father who'd violently lost his family. She was a daughter who'd violently lost her father.

"Annaka," he began gently, "I know it's a painful subject for you, but I'd very much like to know about your father." He felt her stiffen, plowed on. "Can you talk about him?"

"What d'you want to know? How he and Alexsei met, I suppose."

She concentrated on what she was doing, but he wondered whether she was deliberately not meeting his gaze.

"I was thinking more along the lines of your relationship with him."

A shadow flickered across her face. "That's an odd—and intimate—question to ask."

"It's my past, you see . . ." Bourne's voice trailed off. He was unable either to lie or to tell the full truth.

"The one you remember only in glimmers." She nodded. "I see." When she wrung out the sponge, the water in the bowl turned pink. "Ah, well, János Vadas was the perfect father. He changed me when I was an infant, read to me at night, sang to me when I was ill. He was there for all my birthdays and special occasions. Honestly, I don't know how he managed it." She wrung out the sponge a second time; he'd begun bleeding again. "I came first. Always. And he never grew tired of telling me how much he loved me."

"What a lucky child you were."

"Luckier than any of my friends, luckier than anyone I know." She was concentrating harder than ever, trying to get the bleeding to stop.

Bourne had sunk into a state of semi-trance, thinking about Joshua—about the rest of his first family—and all the things he would never get to do with them, all the many tiny moments you noted and remembered as your child grew up.

At length, she stanched the flow of blood and now took a peek under the ice pack. Her expression didn't betray what she saw. She sat back on her haunches, hands resting in her lap.

"I think you should take off your jacket and shirt."

He stared at her.

"So we can take a look at your ribs. I saw you wince when you twisted to put the glass down."

She held out her hand and he dropped the ice pack into it. She juggled it a little. "This needs a refill."

When she returned, he was naked to the waist. A frighteningly large red welt on his left side was already puffed up and very tender as his fingertips probed it.

"My God, you need an ice *bath*," she exclaimed.

"At least nothing's broken."

She tossed him the ice pack. He gasped involuntarily as he put it against the swelling. She returned to her haunches, her gaze roving over him once again. He wished he knew what she was thinking.

"I suppose you can't help remembering the son who was killed so young."

He gritted his teeth. "It's just that . . . The man on the roof—the one spying on us—has been following me all the way from the States. He says he wants to kill me, but I know he's lying. He wants me to lead him to someone, that's why he's been spying on us."

Annaka's expression darkened. "Who does he want to get to?"

"A man named Spalko."

She registered surprise. "Stepan Spalko?"

"That's right. Do you know him?"

"Of course I know of him," she said. "Everyone in Hungary does. He's the head of Humanistas, Ltd., the worldwide relief organization." She frowned. "Jason, now I'm truly worried. This man's dangerous. If he's trying to get to Mr. Spalko, we should contact the authorities."

He shook his head. "What would we tell them? That we think a man we know only as Khan wants to contact Stepan Spalko? We don't even know why. And what d'you think they'll say? Why doesn't this Khan just pick up the telephone and call him?"

"Then we should at least call someone at Humanistas."

"Annaka, until I know what's going on, I don't want to contact anyone. It'll only muddy waters that are already clouded with questions for which I don't have any answers."

He rose, made his way to the escritoire, sat down in front of her laptop. "I told you I had an idea. Is it okay if I use your computer?"

"By all means," she said, rising.

As Bourne turned on the machine, she gathered up the bowl, sponge and other paraphernalia, padded into the kitchen. He heard the sound of running water as he went online. He accessed the U.S. Government net, went from site to site, and by the time she returned, he'd found the one he needed.

The Agency had a whole raft of public sites, accessible to anyone with an Internet connection, but there were a dozen other sites, encrypted, password protected, that were part of the CIA's fabled intranet.

Annaka registered his extreme concentration. "What is it?" She came around and stood behind him. In a moment, her eyes opened wide. "What the hell are you doing?"

"Just what it looks like," Bourne said, "I'm hacking into the CIA main database."

"But how d'you—"

"Don't ask," Bourne said as his fingers flew over the keyboard. "Trust me, you don't want to know."

Alex Conklin had always known the way through the front door, but that was because he'd had the updated ciphers delivered to him at six A.M. every Monday morning. It had been Deron, the artist and master forger, who'd taught Bourne the fine art of hacking into U.S Government databases. In his business, it was a necessary skill.

The problem was that the CIA firewall—the software program designed to keep their data secure—was a particular bitch. In addition to its keyword changing every week, it had a floating algorithm tied into the keyword. But Deron had shown Bourne the way to fool the system into thinking you had the keyword when you didn't, so that the program itself would supply it for you.

The way to attack the firewall was through the algorithm, which was a derivation of the core algorithm that encrypted the CIA's central files. Bourne knew this formula because Deron had made him memorize it.

Bourne navigated to the CIA site, where a window popped up in which he was asked to type the current keyword. In this, he typed in the algorithm, which contained a much larger string of numbers and letters than the box was designed to take. On the other hand, after the first three sets of the components, the underlying program recognized it for what it was, and for a moment it was stymied. The trick, Deron had said, was to complete the algorithm before the program figured out what you were doing and shut down, denying you access. The formula string was very long; there was no room for error or even for an instant's hesitation, and Bourne began to sweat because he couldn't believe the software could remain frozen for this long.

In the end, however, he finished entering the algorithm without the program shutting down. The window disappeared, the screen changed.

"I'm inside," Bourne said.

"Pure alchemy," Annaka whispered, fascinated.

Bourne was navigating to the Tactical Non-Lethal Weapons Directorate site. He plugged in Schiffer's name but was disappointed in the sparse material that came up. Nothing on what Schiffer was working on, nothing about his background. In fact, if Bourne didn't know better, he could believe that Dr. Felix Schiffer was a minor scientist of no import whatsoever to the TNLWD.

There was another possibility. He used the back-channel hack that Deron had made him memorize, the same one Conklin had used to keep tabs on events occurring behind the scenes at the Department of Defense.

Once in, he went to the DARPA site and navigated to the Archives. Lucky for him the government computer jockeys were notoriously slow at cleaning out old files. There was Schiffer's, which contained some background. He was MIT-trained, was given his own lab right out of grad school by one of the large pharmaceutical firms. He lasted there less than a year, but when he left, he took with him another of their scientists, Dr. Peter Sido, with whom he worked for five years before being recruited by the government and entering DARPA. No explanation was given for his giving up a private position to go into the public sector, but some scientists were like that. They were as unfit for living in society as many prisoners who, when they'd served their time, committed another crime the minute they hit the street, simply to be sent back into a clearly defined world where everything was taken care of for them.

Bourne read on and discovered that Schiffer had been attached to the Defense Sciences Office which, ominously, trafficked in bio-weapons systems. In his time at DARPA, Dr. Schiffer had been working in a way to biologically "cleanse" a room infected with anthrax.

Bourne paged through, but he couldn't find any more details. What bothered Bourne was that this piece of information wouldn't account for Conklin's intense interest.

Annaka looked over his shoulder. "Is there any clue we could use to find out where Dr. Schiffer might be hiding?"

"I don't think so, no."

"All right then." She squeezed his shoulders. "The cupboard's bare and we both need to eat something."

"I think I'd rather stay here, if you don't mind, rest up a bit."

"You're right. You're in no shape to wander outside." She smiled as she drew on her coat. "I'll just pop around the corner, get us some food. Anything you particularly want?"

He shook his head, watched her head for the door. "Annaka, be careful."

She turned, pulled her gun partway out of her bag. "Don't worry, I'll be fine." She opened the door. "See you in a few minutes."

He heard her depart, but he'd already returned his attention to the computer screen. He felt his heart rate increase and tried to calm himself, without success. Even full of intent, he hesitated. He knew he had to go on, but he also recognized that he was terrified.

Watching his hands as if they belong to someone else, he spent the next five minutes hacking his way through the U.S. Army firewall. At one point, he hit a glitch. The military IT team had upgraded the firewall recently, adding a third layer Deron either hadn't told him about or, more likely, hadn't yet seen. His fingers rose up like Annaka's over the piano keyboard and for a moment they hesitated. It was not too late to turn back, he told himself, there'd be no shame in doing that. For years he'd felt that anything to do with his first family, including the record of them held in the U.S. Army databanks was for him strictly off-limits. He was already tortured enough by their deaths, haunted by the racking guilt that he'd been unable to save them, that he'd been safe at a meeting while the diving jet sent its killing bullets into them. He couldn't help torturing himself anew, conjuring up their last terror-filled minutes. Dao, a child of war, would, of course, have heard the jet engines droning lazily in the hot summer sky. At first she wouldn't have seen it coming out of the white sun, but when its roar grew closer, when its metal bulk became larger than the sun, she would've known. Even while horror gripped her heart, she would've tried to gather her children to her in a vain attempt to protect them from the bullets that would have already begun to pock the surface of the muddy river. *"Joshua! Alyssa! Come to me!"* she would've screamed, as if she could save them from what was to come.

Bourne, sitting in front of Annaka's computer, became aware that he was weeping. For a moment he allowed the tears to flow freely as they hadn't done for so many years. Then he shook himself, wiped his cheeks with his sleeve and, before he had a chance to change his mind, got on with the business at hand.

He found a work-around for the final level of the firewall, and five minutes after beginning the excruciating work, he was logged in. At once, before his nerve could fail again, he navigated to the Death Record Archives, typed in the names and date of death in the required data fields for Dao Webb, Alyssa Webb, Joshua Webb. He stared at the names, thinking, *This was my family, flesh-and-blood human beings who laughed and cried, and who once held me, who called me "Darling" and "Daddy."* Now what were they? Names on a computer screen. Statistics in a databank. His heart was breaking and he felt again that touch of madness that had afflicted him in the first aftermath of their deaths. *I can't feel this again,* he thought. *It'll tear me apart.* Full of a sorrow he found unsupportable, he punched the "Enter" key. He had no other choice; he could not go back. Never go back, that had been his motto from the moment Alex Conklin had recruited him, turned him into another David Webb and then into Jason Bourne. Then why was it he could still hear their voices? *"Darling, I've missed you!" "Daddy, you're home!"*

These memories, reaching across the permeable barrier of time, had ensnared them in their web, which was why he did not at first react to what had come up on the screen. He stared at it for several minutes without seeing the terrible anomaly.

He saw in horrifying detail what he'd hoped he'd never see, the photos of his beloved wife Dao, shoulders and chest riddled with bullets, her face grotesquely disfigured by the traumatic wounds. On the second page he saw the photos of Alyssa, her poor body and her head even more disfigured because of their vulnerability, their smaller size. He sat, paralyzed with grief and horror, at what lay before him. He had to go on. One page left, one last set of photos to complete the tragedy.

He scrolled to the third page, bracing himself for the photos of Joshua. Only there weren't any.

Stupefied, he did nothing for a moment. At first, he thought there had been a computer glitch, that he'd been inadvertently directed to another page in the Archives. But, no, there was the name: Joshua Webb. But below it were words that seared through Bourne's consciousness like a hot needle. "Three articles of clothing, listed below, one shoe, partial (sole and heel missing) found ten meters from the corpses of Dao and Alyssa Webb. After an hour's search, Joshua Webb declared dead. NBF."

NBF. The Army acronym screamed out to him. No Body Found. Bourne was gripped by an icy cold. They searched for Joshua for an hour—*only* an hour? And why hadn't they told him? He'd buried three coffins, his mind excoriated with grief, remorse, and guilt. And all the while they knew, the bastards *knew!* He sat back. His face was white, his hands trembling. In his heart, he felt a rage he could not contain.

He thought of Joshua; he thought of Khan.

His mind was ablaze, overcome by the horror of the terrible possibility that he'd buried from the moment he'd seen the carved stone Buddha around Khan's neck: What if Khan really was Joshua? If so, he'd become a killing machine, a monster. Bourne knew only too well how easy it was to find the path to madness and killing in the jungles of Southeast Asia. But there was, of course, another possibility, one his mind quite naturally gravitated toward and held onto: that the plot to plant Joshua was far more wide-ranging and complex than he'd at first considered. If so, if these records were forged, the conspiracy went all the way up to the highest levels of American government. But, oddly, filling his mind with the usual conspiratorial suspicions only increased his sense of dislocation.

In his mind's eye, he saw Khan holding out the carved stone Buddha, heard him say, *"You gave this one to me—yes, you did. And then you abandoned me to die . . ."*

Abruptly, Bourne's gorge rose into his throat and, with his stomach rebelling madly, he launched himself off the sofa, across the room, and, ignoring the pain, ran to the bathroom, where he vomited every last thing left inside him.

In the OpSit room deep in the bowels of CIA HQ, the duty officer, watching a computer screen, picked up the phone and dialed a specific number. He waited a moment while an automated voice said, "Speak." The DO asked for the DCI. His voice was analyzed, matched against the list of duty officers. The call was switched, a male voice said, "Hold, please." A moment later the clear baritone of the DCI came on the line.

"I thought you should know, sir, that an internal alarm has been tripped. Someone got through the military firewall and accessed death records for the following personnel: Dao Webb, Alyssa Webb, Joshua Webb."

There was a short, unpleasant pause. "Webb, son. You're sure it's *Webb.*"

The sudden urgency in the DCI's voice brought out the sweat on the young duty officer's face. "Yessir."

"Where's this hacker located?"

"Budapest, sir."

"Did the alarm do its job? Did it capture the full IP address?"

"Yessir. 106–108 Fo utca."

In his office the DCI smiled grimly. Totally by coincidence, he'd been leafing through Martin Lindros' latest report. It seemed as if the Frogs had now sifted through all the remains of the accident that was supposed to have killed Jason Bourne without finding a trace of human remains. Not even a molar. So there'd been no definitive confirmation that, despite the Quai d'Orsay officer's eyewitness account, Bourne was actually dead. The DCI's hand clenched into a fist and pounded the desk in anger. Bourne had eluded them again. But despite his ire and frustration, part of him wasn't all that surprised. After all, Bourne had been trained by the best spook the Agency had ever produced. How many times had Alex Conklin faked his own death in the field, though perhaps never in such spectacular fashion.

Of course, the DCI thought, it was always possible that someone other than Jason Bourne had hacked through the U.S. Army firewall in order to get at the moldy death records of a woman and her two children who weren't even military personnel and who were known to only a small handful of people still living. But what were the odds?

No, he thought now with mounting excitement, Bourne hadn't perished in that explosion outside Paris; he was alive and well in Budapest—why there?—and for once he'd made a mistake they could capitalize on. Why he was interested in the death records of his first family the DCI had no idea, nor did he care beyond the fact that Bourne's inquisitiveness had opened the door for finally fulfilling the sanction.

The DCI reached for the phone. He could have assigned the task to a subordinate, but he wanted to feel the joy of ordering this particular sanction himself. He dialed an overseas number, thinking, *I've got you now, you sonuvabitch.*

CHAPTER TWENTY

For a city founded in the late nineteenth century as a British railroad camp on the Mombasa-to-Uganda line, Nairobi had a depressingly banal skyline filled with sleek modern high-rises. It lay on a flat plain, grasslands that for many years had been the home to the Masai before the coming of Western civilization. It was currently the fastest-growing city in East Africa and, as such, was subject to the usual growing pains as well as the disorienting sight of the old and the new, vast wealth and abject poverty uncomfortably rubbing flanks until sparks flew, tempers flared, and calm needed to be restored. With unemployment high, riots were commonplace as well as late-night muggings, especially in and around Uhuru Park to the west of City Center.

None of these inconveniences were of any interest to the party just arriving from Wilson Airport in a pair of armored limousines, although the occupants noted the signs warning of violence and the private security guards that patrolled City Center and west, where government ministries and foreign embassies resided, as well as along the fringes of Latema and River Roads. They passed along the edge of the bazaar, where virtually every sort of surplus war materiel, from flame-throwers to tanks to shoulder-mounted ground-to-air missile launchers were on display for sale next to cheap gingham dresses and woven textiles in colorful tribal patterns.

Spalko was in the lead limousine with Hasan Arsenov. Behind them, in the second car, sat Zina and Magomet and Akhmet, two of Arsenov's most senior lieutenants. These men hadn't bothered to shave their thick curling beards. They wore the traditional black outfits and stared at Zina's Western clothes with stupefaction. She smiled at them, studying their expressions carefully for any sign of change.

"Everything's in readiness, Shaykh," Arsenov said. "My people are perfectly trained and prepared. They are fluent in Icelandic; they have memorized both the hotel's schematics and the procedures you outlined. They await only my final order of commencement."

Spalko, staring out at the passing Nairobi parade of natives and foreigners stained red by the setting sun, smiled, if only to himself. "Do I detect a note of skepticism in your voice?"

"If you do," Arsenov said quickly, "it's only from my acute sense of anticipation. I've been waiting all my life for the chance to be free of the Russian yoke. My people have been outcasts too long; they've been waiting for centuries to be welcomed into the community of Islam."

Spalko nodded abstractedly. For him, Arsenov's opinion had already become irrelevant; the moment he was thrown to the wolves he'd cease to exist altogether.

That evening the five of them convened in a private dining room Spalko had booked on the top floor of the 360 Hotel on Kenyatta Avenue. It, like their rooms, had a view over the city to Nairobi National Park, stocked with giraffes, wildebeest, Thomson's gazelles and rhinos—as well as lions, leopards and water buffalo. During the dinner there was no talk of business, no hint at all as to their purpose here.

After the plates had been cleared, it was a different story. A team from Humanistas, Ltd., that had preceded them to Nairobi had set up a computer-based audiovideo hookup, which was wheeled into the room. A screen was deployed and Spalko commenced to give a Powerpoint presentation, showing the coast of Iceland, the city of Reykjavik and its environs, then aerial views of the Oskjuhlid Hotel, followed by photos outside and inside the hotel. "There's the HVAC system, which as you can see here and here has been fitted with state-of-the-art motion detectors as well as infrared heat sensors," he said. "And here's the control panel, which like every system in the hotel has a security override, electrical in nature but with battery backups." He continued, running through the plan in the most minute detail, beginning with the moment they arrived and ending with the moment they left. Everything had been planned for; everything was in readiness.

"Tomorrow morning at sunrise," he said, standing, and the others stood with him. "*La illaha ill Allah.*"

"*La illaha ill Allah,*" the others chorused in solemn reply.

Late at night Spalko lay in bed smoking. One lamp was on, but he was still able to see the glittering lights of the city and, beyond, the forested darkness of the wildlife park. He appeared lost in thought, but in reality he had cleared his mind. He was waiting.

Akhmed heard the distant roaring of the animals and could not sleep. He sat up in bed, rubbed his eyes with the heels of his hands. It was unusual for him not to sleep soundly and he wasn't certain what to do. For a time he lay back down, but he was awake now and, aware of the pounding of his heart, his eyes would not close.

He thought of the impending day and the full flower of its promise. Allah will that it be the start of a new dawn for us, he prayed.

Sighing, he sat up, swung his legs over the side of the bed and rose. He pulled on the odd Western trousers and shirt, wondering if he'd ever get used to them. Allah grant not.

He was just opening the door to his room when he saw Zina passing by. She walked with an uncanny grace, moving silently, her hips swaying provocatively. Often, he'd licked his lips when she passed near him and he'd find himself trying to inhale as much of her scent as he could.

He peered out. She was headed away from her room; he wondered where she was going. A moment later he had his answer. His eyes opened wide as she rapped softly on the Shaykh's door, which opened to reveal the Shakyh. Perhaps he had summoned her for some lapse in discipline Akhmed was not aware of.

Then she said in a tone of voice he'd never heard her use before, "Hasan's asleep," and he understood everything.

When the soft knock sounded on his door, Spalko turned, stubbed out his cigarette, then rose, padded across the large room and opened the door.

Zina stood in the hallway. "Hasan's asleep," she said as if she was required to explain her presence.

Without a word, Spalko stepped back, and she came in, closing the door softly. He grabbed her, then spun her onto the bed. Within moments she was crying out, her bare flesh slick with their fluids. Their lovemaking contained a certain wildness, as if they had come at last to the end of the world. And when it was over, it wasn't over at all, for she lay astride him, stroking and caressing him, whispering her desires in the most explicit terms until, inflamed, he took her again.

Afterward she lay entwined with him, smoke curling from her half-open lips. The lamp was off, and solely by the pinpoint lights of the Nairobi night, she held him in her gaze. Ever since he had first touched her, she had longed to know him. She knew nothing of his background—to her knowledge, no one did. If he would talk to her, if he would tell her the little secrets of his life, she'd know that he was bound to her as she was bound to him.

She ran her fingertip around the shell of his ear, across the unnaturally smooth skin of his cheek. "I want to know what happened," she said softly.

Spalko's eyes came slowly back into focus. "It was a long time ago."

"All the more reason to tell me."

He turned his head, stared into her eyes. "Do you really want to know?"

"Very much, yes."

He took a breath, let it out. "In those days, my younger brother and I were living in Moscow. He was always getting into trouble, not that he could help it; he had an addict's disposition."

"Drugs?"

"Praise Allah, no. In his case, it was gambling. He couldn't stop betting, even when he'd run out of money. He'd borrow from me, and of course I'd always give him the money because he'd spin a story I chose to believe."

He turned in her arms, shook out a cigarette, lit it. "Anyway, there came a time when the plausibility of the stories faltered, or possibly even I could no longer afford to believe him. In any event, I said, 'No more,' believing, again foolishly as it turned out, that he'd stop." He drew smoke deep into his lungs, let it out with a hiss. "But he didn't. So what d'you suppose he did? He went to the last people he should've approached, because they were the only ones who'd lend him money."

"The mob."

He nodded. "That's right. He took the money from them knowing that if he lost he'd never be able to pay them back. He knew what they'd do to him, but as I said, he couldn't help himself. He bet and, as almost always happened, he lost."

"And?" She was on tenterhooks, begging him to go on.

"They waited for him to pay them back, and when he didn't, they came after him."

Spalko stared at the glowing end of his cigarette. The windows were open. Over the low noise of the traffic and the clattering of the palm fronds, now and again came an animal's booming roar or unearthly howl.

"At first they gave him a beating," he said, his voice barely above a whisper. "Nothing too severe because at that point they still assumed he'd come up with the money. When they realized he had nothing and could get nothing, they pursued him in earnest, shot him in the street like a dog."

He was finished with his cigarette, but he let the butt burn down to where he gripped it between two fingers. He seemed to have forgotten all about it. Beside him, Zina said not a word, so held in thrall was she by his story.

"Six months went by," he said, flicking the butt across the room and out the window. "I did my homework; I paid the people who needed to be paid, and at last I got my chance. It happened that the boss who'd ordered my brother killed went to the barbershop at the Metropole Hotel every week."

"Don't tell me," Zina said, "you posed as his barber, and when he sat in your chair, you slit his throat with a straight razor."

He stared at her for a moment, then he broke into a laugh. "That's very good, very cinematic." He shook his head. "But in real life it wouldn't work. The boss had used the same barber for fifteen years and in all that time he'd never accepted a substitute." He leaned in, kissed her on the mouth. "Don't be disappointed; take it as a lesson and learn from it." He slipped his arm around her, drew her close against him. Somewhere in the park a leopard yowled.

"No, I waited until he was freshly shaved and barbered, relaxed from these tender ministrations. I waited for him in the street outside the Metropole, a place so public only a madman would choose it. When he came out, I shot him and his bodyguards dead."

"And then you escaped."

"In a sense," he said. "That day I escaped, but six months later, in another city in another country a Molotov cocktail was thrown at me from a passing car."

She tenderly ran her fingers over his plasticized flesh. "I like you this way, imperfect. The pain you endured makes you . . . heroic."

Spalko said nothing, and at length he felt her breathing deepen as she drifted off to sleep. Of course, not a word he'd said was true, though he had to admit it made a good story—very cinematic! The truth—what was the truth? He scarcely knew anymore; he'd spent so much time carefully constructing his elaborate facade that there were days when he became lost in his own fiction. In any event, he'd never reveal the truth to anyone else because it would put him at a disadvantage. When people knew you, they thought they owned you—that the truth you had shared with them in a moment of weakness they called intimacy would bind you to them.

In this Zina was like all the rest, and he found the bitter rind of disappointment in his mouth. But then he was always being disappointed by others. They simply weren't in his sphere; they couldn't understand the nuances of the world as he did.

They were amusing for a while, but only for a while. He took this thought with him down into the bottomless chasm of a deep and untroubled sleep, and when he awoke, Zina was gone, returned to the side of the unsuspecting Hasan Arsenov.

At dawn, the five of them piled into a brace of Range Rovers, which had been provisioned and were driven by members of the Humanistas team, and headed south out of the city toward the great unwashed slum that extended like an festering canker on the flank of Nairobi. No one spoke and they had eaten only lightly, for a pall of hideous tension gripped them all, even Spalko.

Though the morning was clear, a toxic haze hung low over the sprawling slum, ready evidence of the lack of proper sanitation and the ever-present specter of cholera. There were ramshackle structures, mean tin and cardboard huts, some wooden ones, as well as squat concrete buildings that could have been mistaken for bunkers except for the zigzag lines of laundry strung outside, flapping in the gritty air. As well, there were mounds of bulldozed earth, raw and enigmatic until the passing party saw the scorched and charcoaled remains of fire-gutted dwellings, shoes with their soles burned off, tatters of a blue dress. These few artifacts, evidence of recent history, which was all that existed here, lent a particularly forlorn aspect to the ugliness of the grinding poverty. If there was a life to be had here, it was fitful, chaotic, dismal beyond either word or thought. All were struck by the sense of a terminal night that existed here even in the light of a new morning. There was a fatedness to the sprawl that made them recall the bazaar, the black market nature of the city's economy they felt was in some obscure way responsible for the depressing landscape through which they crawled, slowed by the thick crowds that overflowed the cracked sidewalks out into the rutted dirt streets. Traffic lights didn't exist, even if they had, the party would have been stopped by hordes of stinking beggars or merchants hawking their pathetic wares.

At length they arrived at more or less the center of the slum, where they entered a gutted two-story building reeking of smoke. Ash was everywhere inside, white and soft as ground bones. The drivers brought in the provisions, which were contained in what appeared to be two rectangular steamer trucks.

Inside were silver-skinned HAZMAT suits which, at Spalko's direction, they donned. The suits contained their own self-contained breathing systems. Spalko then removed the NX 20 from its case inside one of the trunks, carefully fitted the two pieces together as the four Chechen rebels gathered around to watch. Handing it to Hasan Arsenov for a moment, Spalko drew out the small, heavy box given to him by Dr. Peter Sido. With great care, he unlocked it. They all stared down at the glass vial. It was so small, so deadly. Their breathing slowed, grew labored, as if they were already afraid to draw breath.

Spalko directed Arsenov to hold the NX 20 at arm's length. He flipped open a titanium panel on top, placed the vial into the loading chamber. The NX 20 couldn't be fired yet, he explained. Dr. Schiffer had built in a number of safeguards against accidental or premature dispersal. He pointed out the airtight seal that, with the chamber full, would be activated when he closed and locked the top panel. He did this now, then he took the NX 20 from Arsenov and led them up the interior flight of stairs, still standing, despite the ravages of the fire, only because it was made of concrete.

On the second floor they crowded against a window. Like all the others in the building, its glass had been shattered; all that was left was the frame. Through it, they watched the halt and the lame, the famine-stricken, the diseased. Flies buzzed, a three-legged dog squatted and defecated in an open-air market where used goods were piled in the dust. A child ran naked through the street, crying. An old woman hunching along, hawked and spat.

These sights were of only peripheral interest to the party. They were studying Spalko's every move, listening to his every word with a concentration that bordered on the compulsive. The mathematical precision of the weapon worked like a magical counter-spell to the disease that seemed to have conjured itself into the air.

Spalko showed them the two triggers on the NX 20—a small one just forward of the larger one. The small one, he told them, injected the payload from the loading chamber into the firing chamber. Once that, too, was sealed by pressing this button, here, on the left side of weapon, the NX 20 was ready to be fired. He pulled the small trigger, then pressed the button, and could feel within the weapon a slight stirring, the first intimation of death.

The muzzle of the thing was blunt and ugly, but its bluntness was practical as well. Unlike conventional weapons, the NX 20 needed only to be aimed in the most general way, he pointed out. He stuck the muzzle through the window. They all held their breath as his finger curled around the large trigger.

Outside, life went on in its random, disorderly fashion. A young man held a bowl of maize-meal porridge under his chin, scooping up the glop with the first two fingers of his right hand while a group of half-starved people watched with unnaturally large eyes. An impossibly thin girl on a bicycle passed by and a pair of toothless old men stared at the packed earth of the street as if reading there the sad story of their lives.

It was no more than a soft hiss, at least that was how it sounded to each of them secure and safe inside their HAZMAT suits. There was, otherwise, no outward sign of the dispersal. This was as Dr. Schiffer had predicted.

The party watched tensely as the seconds ticked by with agonizing slowness. Every sense seemed heightened. They heard the sonorous tolling of their own pulse in their ears, felt the heavy beat of their hearts. They found that they were holding their breath.

Dr. Schiffer had said that within three minutes they would see the first signs that the disperser had worked properly. It was more or less the last thing he'd said before Spalko and Zina had dropped his near-lifeless body down into the labyrinth.

Spalko, who'd been following the second hand of his watch as it swept toward the three-minute mark, now looked up. He was riveted by what he saw. A dozen people had dropped before the first scream sounded. It was quickly choked off, but others took up the ululating cry, only to drop, writhing, in the street. Chaos and silence as death crept outward in a gathering spiral. There was no hiding from it, no way to avoid it, and no one escaped, even those who tried to run.

He signed to the Chechens and they followed him down the concrete stairs. The drivers were ready and waiting as Spalko broke down the NX 20. The moment he stowed it, they snapped closed the trunks, brought them out to the waiting Range Rovers.

The party took a tour of the street, then the adjacent ones. They walked four blocks in every direction, always seeing the same result. Death and dying, more death and dying. They returned to the vehicles, the taste of triumph in their mouths. The Range Rovers started up the moment they were settled and took them over the entire area of the half-mile-square radius Dr. Schiffer had told Spalko was the NX 20's dispersal range. Spalko was gratified to see that the doctor had neither lied nor exaggerated.

By the time the payload had run its course an hour from now, how many people would be dead or dying? he wondered. He'd stopped counting after a thousand, but he guessed it would be three times that amount, perhaps as much as five times.

Before they left the city of the dead, he gave the order and his drivers started the fires, using a potent accelerant. Immediately, sheets of flame flicked skyward, spreading quickly.

The fire was good to see. It would cover what had happened here this morning, for no one must know, not, at least until after their mission at the Reykjavik summit was completed.

In just forty-eight hours it would be, Spalko thought, exultant. Nothing could stop them.

Now the world is mine.

BOOK THREE

CHAPTER TWENTY-ONE

"I think there may be internal bleeding," Annaka said, looking again at the deeply discolored swelling of Bourne's side. "We've got to get you to the hospital."

"You must be joking," he said. Indeed, the pain was much worse; every time he breathed, he felt as if a couple of ribs had been staved in. But a trip to the hospital was out of the question; he was a wanted man.

"All right," she conceded. "A doctor, then." And raised a hand, anticipating his objection. "My father's friend, Istvan, is discreet. My father used him from time to time without consequence."

Bourne shook his head, said, "Go to a pharmacy if you must, nothing more."

Before he had a chance to change his mind, Annaka grabbed her coat and purse, promising to be back shortly.

In a way he was glad to be rid of her temporarily, he needed to be alone with his thoughts. Curled up on the sofa, he drew the eiderdown closer around him. His mind seemed to be on fire. He was convinced that Dr. Schiffer was the key. He had to find him, for once he did, he'd find the person who had ordered Alex and Mo's murders, the person who had set him up. The problem was Bourne was quite certain he didn't have much time left. Schiffer had been missing for some time now. Molnar had been dead two days. If, as Bourne feared, he'd disclosed Schiffer's whereabouts under articulated interrogation, then Bourne would have to assume that Schiffer was by now in enemy hands, which would mean that the enemy also had in his possession whatever it was that Schiffer had invented, some sort of biological weapon, code-named NX 20, to which Leonard Fine, Conklin's conduit, had reacted so strongly when he'd mentioned it.

Who *was* the enemy? The only name he had was Stepan Spalko, an internationally renowned humanitarian. And yet, according to Khan, Spalko was the man who had ordered the murders of Alex and Mo and had set

Bourne up as the murderer. Khan could be lying, and why not? If he wanted to get to Spalko for his own reasons, he'd hardly announce them to Bourne. Khan!

The very thought of him caused Bourne to be flooded with unwanted emotion. With effort, he concentrated on his rage against his own government. They'd lied to him—colluded in a coverup to keep him from the truth. Why? What were they trying to hide? Did they believe that Joshua might be alive? If so, why wouldn't they want him to know? *What was it they were doing?* He pressed his hands to his head. His vision seemed to lose its perspective—things that had seemed close at hand a moment ago now appeared far away. He thought he might be losing his mind. With an inarticulate cry, he threw the eiderdown off him and rose, ignoring the flash of pain in his side as he stalked to where he'd hidden his ceramic gun beneath his jacket. He took it up in his hand. Unlike the reassuring heft of a steel gun, this was as light as a feather. He held it by the grips, curled his forefinger through the trigger guard. He stared at it a long time, as if through sheer force of will he could conjure up the officials buried deep inside the military responsible for deciding not to tell him that they'd never found Joshua's body, deciding it was simply easier to declare that he'd been killed when they didn't know for a fact if he was actually dead or alive.

Slowly the pain returned, a universe of agony with every breath he took, forcing him to return to the sofa, where he once again wrapped himself in the eiderdown. And in the quiet of the apartment, the thought, unbidden, came again: What if Khan was telling the truth—what if he was Joshua? And the answer, terrible and unalterable: Then he was an assassin, a brutal murderer without remorse or guilt, utterly disconnected from any human emotion.

All at once Jason Bourne put his head down, as close to tears as he'd ever been since Alex Conklin had created him decades ago.

When Kevin McColl had been assigned the Bourne sanction, he'd been on top of Ilona, a young Hungarian woman of his acquaintance, as uninhibited as she was athletic. She could do wonderful things with her legs, was, in fact, doing them when the call came in.

As it happened, he and Ilona were in the Kiraly Turkish Baths on Fo utca. It being Saturday, a woman's day, she'd had to sneak him in, which, he had to admit, had been part of the excitement. Like everyone else in his position, he'd very quickly gotten used to living beyond the law—to *being* the law.

With a grunt of frustration, he unwound himself from her and picked up his cell phone. There was no question of not answering it when it rang it was for a sanction. He listened without comment to the voice of the DCI on the other end of the line. He'd have to go now. The sanction was urgent, the target within range.

And so, as he wistfully watched the gleam of Ilona's sweat-slicked skin in the jewel-toned light reflected off the mosaic tiles, he began to dress. He was a huge man, with the physique of a Midwestern football lineman and a flat imperturbable face. He was obsessed with weight training, and it showed. His muscles rippled with every move he made.

"I'm not finished," Ilona said, her huge dark eyes drinking him in.

"Neither am I," McColl said, leaving her where she lay.

Two jets stood on the tarmac of Nairobi's Nelson Airport. Both belonged to Stepan Spalko; both had the logo of Humanistas, Ltd. on fuselage and tail. Spalko had flown in from Budapest on the first one. The second had been used by his Humanistas support staff, who were now inside the jet that would return him to Budapest. The other jet would be taking Arsenov and Zina to Iceland where they'd be rendezvousing with the rest of the terrorist cadre flying in from Chechnya by way of Helsinki.

Spalko stood facing Arsenov. Zina was a pace behind Arsenov's left shoulder. He, no doubt, thought her position one of deference, but Spalko knew better. Her eyes smoldered as she drank in the Shaykh.

"You've lived up to the letter of your promise, Shaykh," Arsenov said. "The weapon will bring us victory in Reykjavik, of that there can be no question."

Spalko nodded. "Soon you'll have everything that's due you."

"The depth of our gratitude seems quite inadequate."

"You don't give yourself enough credit, Hasan." Spalko drew out a leather briefcase, unlocked it. "Passports, ID tags, maps, diagrams, the latest photos, everything you need." He handed over the contents. "The rendezvous with the boat will be at three-hundred hours tomorrow." He looked at Arsenov. "May Allah lend you strength and courage. May Allah guide your mailed fist."

As Arsenov turned away, preoccupied with his precious cargo, Zina said, "May our next meeting lead to a great future, Shaykh."

Spalko smiled. "The past will die," he said, speaking volumes with his eyes, "in order to make way for that great future."

Zina, laughing to herself in silent pleasure, followed Hasan Arsenov as he mounted the metal ladder into the jet.

Spalko watched the door close behind them, then he crossed to his jet, waiting patiently on the tarmac. He pulled out his cell phone, dialed a number and, when he heard the familiar voice on the other end of the line, said without preamble, "The progress Bourne has been making is an ominous development. I can no longer afford to have Khan kill Bourne in a public way—yes, I know, *if* he ever meant to kill Bourne. Khan's a curious creature, a puzzle I've never been able to solve. But now that he's become unpredictable, I've got to assume he's following his own agenda. If Bourne dies now, Khan will fade into the woodwork and not even I will be able to find him. Nothing must interfere with what will take place in two days' time. Do I make myself clear? Good. Now, listen. There's only one way to neutralize them both."

McColl had received not only Annaka Vadas' name and address—by an extraordinary stroke of luck, just four blocks north of the baths—but also her photo via a jpg file downloaded to his cell phone. As a result, he had no trouble recognizing her when she came out of the entrance to 106–108 Fo utca. He was immediately stirred by her beauty, the authoritative manner of her gait. He watched as she put away her cell phone, unlocked a blue Skoda and slid in behind the wheel.

Just before Annaka inserted her key into the ignition slot, Khan rose from the backseat of the car and said, "I should tell Bourne everything."

She started but made no attempt to turn around; she was that well trained. Staring at him in the rear-view mirror, she replied shortly, "Tell him what? You don't know anything."

"I know enough. I know you're the one who brought the police to Molnar's apartment. I know why you did that. Bourne was getting too close to the truth, wasn't he, getting too close to finding out that Spalko was the one who'd set him up. I'd already told him, but it seems he doesn't believe anything I say."

"Why should he? You have no credibility with him. He's convinced himself you're part of a vast plot to manipulate him."

Khan whipped a steely hand over the seatback, gripping her arm, which had slowly moved while she spoke. "Don't do that." He took her purse, opened it, removed the gun. "You tried to kill me once. Believe me, you won't get a second chance."

She stared at his reflected image. Inside her was a constellation of emotions. "You think I'm lying to you about Jason, but I'm not."

"What I'd like to know," he said easily, ignoring her comment, "was how you convinced him you loved your father when, really, you hated his guts."

She sat mute, breathing slowly, trying to gather her wits. She knew she was in an extremely perilous situation. The question was how was she going to extricate herself.

"How you must've rejoiced when he was shot to death," Khan continued, "though, knowing you as I do, you probably wished you'd been able to shoot him yourself."

"If you're going to kill me," she said tersely, "do it now and spare me your useless chatter."

With a move like a cobra, he leaned forward, grabbed her by her throat, and at last she looked alarmed, which was, after all, the first thing he was after. "I don't intend to spare you anything, Annaka. What did you spare me when you had the chance?"

"I didn't think I needed to baby you."

"You rarely thought when we were together," he said, "at least, not about me."

Her smile was cold. "Oh, I thought about you constantly."

"And repeated every one of those thoughts to Stepan Spalko." His hand tightened on her throat, rattling her head from side to side. "Isn't that right?"

"Why ask me when you already know the answer?" she said a little breathlessly.

"How long has he been playing me?"

Annaka closed her eyes for a moment. "From the beginning."

Khan ground his teeth in fury. "What's his game? What does he want from me?"

"That I don't know." She made a wheezing noise as he squeezed so hard he cut off all air to her windpipe. When he released his grip sufficiently, she said in a thin voice, "Hurt me all you want, you'll still get the same answer, because it's the truth."

"The truth!" He laughed derisively. "You wouldn't know the truth if it bit you." Nevertheless, he believed her, and was disgusted by her uselessness. "What's your business with Bourne?"

"Keeping him away from Stepan."

He nodded, recalling his conversation with Spalko. "That makes sense."

The lie had come easily to her lips. It had the ring of truth not only because she'd had a lifetime of practice but because up until this last call from Spalko it *had* been the truth. Spalko's plans had changed, and now that she'd had time to think it through, it suited her new purpose to tell this to Khan. Perhaps it was fortuitous that he'd come upon her like this, but only if she managed to get out of the encounter alive.

"Where's Spalko now?" he asked her. "Here in Budapest?"

"Actually, he's on his way back from Nairobi."

Khan was surprised. "What was he doing in Nairobi?"

She laughed, but with his fingers painfully gripping her throat, it sounded more like a dry cough. "D'you really think he'd tell me? You know how secretive he is."

He put his lips against her ear. "I know how secretive *we* used to be, Annaka—only it wasn't secretive at all, was it?"

Her eyes engaged his in the mirror. "I didn't tell him everything." How strange it was not to be looking at him directly. "Some things I kept for myself."

Khan's lips curled in contempt. "You don't actually expect me to believe that."

"Believe what you want," she said flatly, "you always have."

He shook her again. "Meaning?"

She gasped and bit her lower lip. "I never understood the depth of my hatred for my father until I spent time with you." He let up on his grip and she swallowed convulsively. "But you with your unswerving enmity toward your father, you showed me the light; you showed me how to bide my time, to savor the thought of revenge. And you're right, when he was shot, I felt the bitterness of not having done it myself."

Though he had no intention of showing it, what she said shook him. Up until a moment ago, he'd had no idea he'd revealed so much of himself to her. He felt ashamed and resentful that she'd been able to get so far under his skin without him being aware of it.

"We were together a year," he said, "a lifetime for people like us."

"Thirteen months, twenty-one days, six hours," she said. "I remember the precise moment I walked out on you because it was then I knew I couldn't control you as Stepan wanted me to."

"And why was that?" His voice was casual, even though his interest was anything but.

Her eyes had engaged his again, refused to let them go. "Because," she said, "when I was with you, I could no longer control myself."

Was she telling the truth or was she playing him again? Khan, so certain about everything until Jason Bourne had come back into his life, didn't know. Once again he felt ashamed and resentful, even a bit frightened that his vaunted powers of observation and instinct were failing him. Despite his best efforts, emotion had entered the picture, spreading its toxic haze over his mind, clouding his judgment, becalming him on an indistinct sea. He could feel his desire for her rising more strongly than it ever had before. He wanted her so badly that he couldn't help but press his lips against the precious skin at the nape of her neck.

And in so doing he missed the shadow's sudden fall into the interior of the Skoda, the shadow marked by Annaka, who shifted her gaze, saw the burly American wrench open the rear door and bring down the butt end of his gun onto the back of Khan's skull.

Khan's grip relaxed, his hand dropping away as he keeled over onto the backseat, unconscious.

"Hello, Ms. Vadas," the burly American said in perfectly inflected Hungarian. He smiled as he swept up her gun into his huge hand. "My name's McColl, but I'd be obliged if you called me Kevin."

Zina dreamed of an orange sky, beneath which a modern-day horde—an army of Chechens brandishing NX 20s—descended from the Caucuses onto the steppes of Russia to lay waste to their bedeviling nemesis. But such was the power of Spalko's experiment that for her it obliterated time. She was back again, a child in her parents' miserable shell-shocked hovel, her mother staring at her from out of her ruined face, saying, "*I can't get up. Even for our water. I can't go on. . . .*"

But someone had to go on. She was then fifteen, the oldest of the four children. When her mother's father-in-law came, he took only her brother Kanti, the male heir of the clan; the Russians had either killed the others, including his own sons, or had sent them away to the dreaded camps in Pobedinskoe and Krasnaya Turbina.

After that, she took over her mother's chores, collecting metal and water. But at night, exhausted as she was, sleep escaped her, fleeing from the vision of Kanti's tear-streaked face, his terror at leaving his family, everything he'd known.

Three times a week she slipped away crossing terrain littered with unexploded landmines in order to see Kanti, to kiss his pale cheeks and give him news of home. One day she arrived to find her grandfather dead. Of Kanti there was no sign. The Russian Special Forces had come through in a sweep, killing her grandfather and taking her brother to Krasnaya Turbina.

She'd spent the next six months trying to find news of Kanti, but she was young and inexperienced in these matters. Besides, without money she could find no one willing to talk. Three years later, her mother dead, her sisters in foster homes, she joined the rebel forces. She hadn't chosen an easy path: She'd had to endure male intimidation; she'd had to learn to be meek and subservient, to identify what she had then thought of as her meager resources and husband them. But she had always been exceptionally clever and this made her a quick learner of physical skills. It also provided her with a springboard from which to discover how the power game was played. Unlike a man, who rose through the ranks by intimidation, she was obliged to use the physical assets she was born with. A year after enduring the hardships of one handler after another, she managed to convince her controller to mount a night-time raid on Krasnaya Turbina.

This was the sole reason she had joined the rebels, had put herself through hell, but she was frankly terrified of what she might find. And yet she found nothing, no evidence of her brother's whereabouts. It was as if Kanti had simply ceased to exist.

Zina awoke with a gasp. She sat up, looked around, realized that she was in Spalko's jet on the way to Iceland. In her mind's eye, still half in its dream-state, she saw Kanti's tear-streaked face, smelled the acrid stench of lye coming from the killing pits at Krasnaya Turbina. She put her head down. It was the uncertainty that ate at her. If she knew he was dead, she could perhaps put her guilt to rest. But if, by some miracle of chance, he was still alive, she would never know, couldn't come to his rescue, save him from the terrors to which the Russians continued to subject him.

Aware of someone approaching, she looked up. It was Magomet, one of the two lieutenants Hasan had brought with him to Nairobi to bear witness to the gateway to their freedom. Akhmed, the other lieutenant, was studiously ignoring her as he had since he'd seen her comfortable in Western dress. Magomet, a bear of a man with eyes the color of Turkish coffee and a long curling beard he combed with his fingers when he was anxious, stood slightly bent, leaning against the seatback.

"Is everything in order, Zina?" he asked.

Her eyes searched first for Hasan, found him asleep. Then she curved her lips in the ghost of a smile. "I was dreaming of our coming triumph."

"It'll be magnificent, won't it? Vindication at last! Our day in the sun!"

She could tell that he was dying to sit next to her, so she said nothing; he would have to be content with her not shooing him away. She stretched, arching her breasts, watching with amusement as his eyes opened slightly. *All that's missing is his tongue hanging out,* she thought.

"Would you like some coffee?" he said.

"I suppose I wouldn't mind." She kept her voice carefully neutral, knowing that he was questing for hints. Her status, heightened by the important task the Shaykh had given her, the trust implicit in what he'd asked of her, was clearly not lost on him, as it was on Akhmed, who, like most Chechen males, saw her only as an inferior female. For a moment, then, her nerve failed her as she considered the enormous cultural barrier she was attempting to attack. But a moment's clear-eyed concentration returned her to her normal state. The plan she'd formulated with the Shaykh's instigation was sound; it would work—she knew it as surely as she drew breath. Now, as Magomet turned to go, she spoke up in furtherance of that plan. "And while you're in the galley," she said, "bring yourself a cup as well."

When he returned, she took the coffee from him, sipped it without inviting him to sit. He stood, his elbows on the seatback, holding his cup between his hands.

"Tell me," Magomet said, "what's he like?"

"The Shaykh? Haven't you asked Hasan?"

"Hasan Arsenov says nothing."

"Perhaps," she said, looking at Magomet over the rim of her cup, "he jealously guards his favored status."

"Do you?"

Zina laughed softly. "No. I don't mind sharing." She sipped more coffee. "The Shaykh's a visionary. He sees the world not as it is but as it will be a year from now, five years! It's quite astonishing to be around him, a man who's so in control of every aspect of his self, a man who commands so much power across the globe."

Magomet made a sound of relief. "Then we're truly saved."

"Yes, saved." Zina put aside her cup, produced a straight razor and cream she'd found in the well-equipped toilet. "Come sit down here, opposite me."

Magomet hesitated only an instant. When he sat, he was so close their knees touched.

"You can't deplane in Iceland looking like that, you know."

He watched her from out of his dark eyes as his fingers combed through his beard. Without taking her eyes off his, Zina grasped his hand in hers, drew it away from his beard. Then she opened the razor, applied cream to his right cheek. The blade scraped against his flesh. Magomet trembled a little, then, as she began to shear him, his eyes closed.

At some point she became aware that Akhmed was sitting up, watching her. By this time, half of Magomet's face was clean-shaven. She continued what she was doing as Akhmed rose and approached her. He said nothing but stared in disbelief as Magomet's beard was peeled away and his face was slowly revealed.

At length he cleared his throat, said to her in a soft voice, "Do you think I could be next?"

"I wouldn't have expected this guy to be carrying such a mediocre gun," Kevin McColl said as he hauled Annaka out of the Skoda. He made a noise of contempt as he stowed it away.

Annaka went meekly enough, happy that he'd mistaken her gun for

Khan's. She stood on the sidewalk beneath the sullen sky of afternoon, her head bowed, eyes lowered, a secret smile lighting her up inside. Like many men, he couldn't fathom that she'd carry a weapon, let alone might know how to use it. What he didn't know would certainly hurt him—she'd make sure of it.

"First of all, I want to assure you that nothing will happen to you. All you have to do is answer my questions truthfully and obey my commands to the letter." He used the pad of his thumb on a minor nerve bundle on the inside of her elbow. Just enough to let her know that he was deadly serious. "Do we understand each other?"

She nodded and cried out briefly as he bore down harder on the nerves.

"I expect you to answer when I ask you a question."

She said, "I understand, yes."

"Good." He took her into the shadows of the entrance to 106–108 Fo utca. "I'm looking for Jason Bourne. Where is he?"

"I don't know."

Her knees buckled in pain as he did something terrible to the inside of her elbow.

"Shall we try it again?" he said. "Where's Jason Bourne?"

"Upstairs," she said as tears rolled down her cheeks. "In my apartment."

His grip on her loosened noticeably. "See how easy that was? No fuss, no muss. Now, let's you and me go on up."

They went inside and she used her key. She turned on the light and they went up the wide staircase. When they reached the fourth floor, McColl reined her in. "Hear me now," he said softly. "As far as you're concerned, nothing's wrong. Got me?"

She almost nodded, caught herself and said, "Yes."

He pulled her back against him hard. "Give him any warning sign and I'll gut you like a large-mouth bass." He shoved her forward. "Okay. Get on with it."

She walked to her door, put her key in the lock and opened it. She saw to her right that Jason was slumped on the sofa, his eyes half closed.

Bourne looked up. "I thought you were—"

At that instant McColl shoved her, raised his gun. "Daddy's home!" he cried as he aimed the gun at the recumbent figure and pulled the trigger.

CHAPTER TWENTY-TWO

Annaka, who'd been biding her time, waiting for McColl's first move, drove the point of her cocked elbow into his arm, deflecting his aim. As a result, the bullet entered the wall above Bourne's head where it met the ceiling.

McColl bellowed in rage, reached out with his left hand even as he was swinging his right arm down to aim again at his recumbent target. His fingers sank into Annaka's hair, grabbed tight, jerked her back off her feet. At that moment Bourne brought his ceramic gun from beneath the eiderdown. He wanted to shoot the intruder in the chest, but Annaka was in the way. Altering his aim, he shot the intruder through the meat of his gun arm. The gun fell to the carpet, blood splattered from the wound, and Annaka screamed as the intruder dragged her back against his chest as a shield.

Bourne was up on one knee, the muzzle of his gun roaming, as the intruder, with Annaka braced against him, backed toward the open door.

"This isn't over, not by a long shot," he said, his gaze on Bourne. "I've never lost a sanction and I don't intend to start now." With that ominous pronouncement, he picked Annaka up and hurled her at Bourne.

Bourne, off the sofa, caught Annaka before she had a chance to smash into the side of it. He whirled her around, then sprinted through the open doorway in time to see the elevator door closing. He took the stairs, limping a little. His side felt as if it were on fire and his legs were weak. His breathing became labored and he wanted to stop, if only to be able to get enough oxygen in his lungs, but he kept going, taking the stairs two and three at a time. Rounding the first-floor landing, his left foot slipped on the edge of a tread and he went down, half-falling, half-sliding down the rest of the flight. He groaned as he rose, slammed through the door into the lobby. There was blood on the marble floor but no assassin. He took a step into the lobby, and his legs collapsed out from under him. He sat there, half-stunned, his gun in one hand, the other lying palm up on his thigh. His eyes were glazed with pain and it seemed to him as if he'd forgotten how to breathe.

I've got to go after the bastard, he thought. But there was a tremendous noise in his head that he eventually identified as the thudding of his heart working overtime. For the moment, at least, he was incapable of movement. He had just enough time, before Annaka arrived, to reflect that his staged death hadn't fooled the Agency for long.

When she saw him, her face turned white with concern. "Jason!" She knelt beside him, her arm around him.

"Help me up," he said.

She took his weight with her canted hip. "Where is he? Where did he go?"

He should've been able to answer her. Christ, he thought, maybe she was right, maybe he really did need to see a doctor.

Perhaps it was the venom in his heart that had pulled Khan back from unconsciousness so quickly. In any case, he was up and out of the Skoda within minutes of the attack. His head hurt, to be sure, but it was his ego that had taken the brunt of the attack. He replayed the whole sorry scene in his mind, knew with a certainty that caused a sinking feeling in his stomach that it was only his foolish and dangerous feelings for Annaka that had made him vulnerable.

What more proof did he need that emotional attachment was to be shunned at all costs? It had cost him dearly with his parents and, again, with Richard Wick, and now most recently with Annaka, who from the first had betrayed him to Stepan Spalko.

And what of Spalko? *"We're far from strangers. We share secrets of the most intimate nature,"* he'd said that night in Grozny. *"I'd like to think we're more than businessman and client."*

Like Richard Wick, he'd offered to take Khan in, claimed he wanted to be his friend, to make him part of a hidden—and somehow intimate— world. *"You owe your impeccable reputation in no small part to the commissions I've given you."* As if Spalko, like Wick, believed he was Khan's benefactor. These people were under the misapprehension that they lived on a higher plane, that they belonged to the elite. Like Wick, Spalko had lied to Khan so that he could use him for his own purposes.

What had Spalko wanted from him? It almost didn't matter; he was past caring. All he wanted was his pound of flesh from Stepan Spalko, a reckoning that would set past injustices to rights. Nothing less than Spalko's death would assuage him now. Spalko would be his first and last commission from himself.

It was then, crouched in the shadows of a doorway, unconsciously massaging the back of his head where a lump had already been raised, that he heard her voice. It rose from the deep, from the shadows in which he sat, dropping down through the depths, pulled under the purling waves.

"Lee-Lee," he whispered. "Lee-Lee!"

It was her voice he heard calling to him. He knew what she wanted; she wanted him to join her in the drowned depths. He put his aching head in his hands and a terrible sob escaped his lips like the last bubble of air from his lungs. Lee-Lee. He hadn't thought of her in so long—or had he? He'd dreamed about her almost every night; it had taken him this long to realize it. Why? What was different now that she should come to him so strongly after such a long time gone?

It was then he heard the slam of the front door and his head came up in time for him to see the big man racing out of the entrance to 106–108 Fo utca. He was grasping one hand with the other, and by the trail of blood behind him Khan figured that he'd run into Jason Bourne. A small smile crept across his face, for he knew this must be the man who'd attacked him.

Khan felt an immediate urge to kill him, but with an effort he gained control and came up with a better idea. Leaving the shadows, he followed the figure as he fled down Fo utca.

Dohány Synagogue was the largest synagogue in Europe. On its western side, the massive structure had an intricate Byzantine brickwork facade in blue, red and yellow, the heraldic colors of Budapest. Crowning the entrance was a large stained-glass window. Above this impressive sight rose two Moorish polygonal towers topped by striking copper and gilt cupolas.

"I'll go in and get him," Annaka said as they got out of her Skoda. Istvan's service had tried to direct her to a covering doctor, but she'd insisted that she needed to see Dr. Ambrus, that she was an old family friend, and at length they'd directed her here. "The fewer people who see you like this, the better."

Bourne agreed. "Listen, Annaka, I'm beginning to lose count of the times you've saved my life."

She looked at him and smiled. "Then stop counting."

"The man who assaulted you."

"Kevin McColl."

"He's an Agency specialist." There was no need for Bourne to have to tell her what sort of specialist McColl was. Yet another thing he liked about her. "You handled him well."

"Until he used me as a shield," she said bitterly. "I should never have allowed—"

"We got out of it. That's all that matters."

"But he's still at large, and his threat—"

"The next time I'll be ready for him."

The small smile returned to her face. She directed him to the courtyard in the rear of the synagogue, where she told him he could wait for them without fear of running into anyone.

Istvan Ambrus, the doctor of János Vadas' acquaintance, was inside at service, but he was amenable enough when Annaka went in and told him of the emergency.

"Of course, I'm pleased to help you in any way I can, Annaka," he said as he rose from his seat and walked with her through the magnificent chandeliered interior. Behind them was the great five-thousand-tube organ, highly unusual in a Jewish house of worship, on whose keyboard the great composers Franz Liszt and Camille Saint-Saens had once played.

"Your father's death has hit us all very hard." He took her hand, squeezed it briefly. He had the blunt, strong fingers of a surgeon or a bricklayer. "How are you holding up, my dear?"

"As well as can be expected," she said softly, leading him outside.

Bourne was sitting in the courtyard under whose earth lay the corpses of five thousand Jews who had perished in the brutal winter of 1944–45, when Adolph Eichmann turned the synagogue into a concentration point from which he sent ten times that number to camps where they were exterminated. The courtyard, contained between the arches of the inner loggia, was filled with pale memorial stones through which dark-green ivy crept. The trunks of the trees with which it had been planted were similarly wound with the vines. A cold wind ruffled the leaves, a sound that in this place could have been mistaken for distant voices.

It was difficult to sit here and not think of the dead and of the terrible suffering that had gone on here during that dark time. He wondered whether another dark time was gathering itself to overwhelm them once again. He looked up from his contemplation to see Annaka in the company of a round-faced, dapper individual with a pencil mustache and apple cheeks. He was dressed in a brown three-piece suit. The shoes on his small feet were highly polished.

"So you're the disaster in question," he said after Annaka had made the introductions, assuring him that Bourne could speak their native tongue. "No, don't get up," he went on as he sat down beside Bourne and began his examination. "Well, sir, I don't believe Annaka's description did your injuries justice. You look like you've been put through a wurst-grinder."

"That's just how I feel, Doctor." Bourne winced despite himself as Dr. Ambrus' fingers probed a particularly painful spot.

"As I walked out into the courtyard, I saw you deep in thought," Dr. Ambrus said in a conversational tone. "In a sense, this is a terrible place, this courtyard, reminding us of those we've lost and, in a larger sense, what humanity as a whole lost during the Holocaust." His fingers were surprisingly light as well as agile as they roamed over the tender flesh of Bourne's side. "But the history of that time isn't all so grim, you know. Just before Eichmann and his staff marched in, several priests helped the rabbi remove the twenty-seven scrolls of the Torah from the Ark inside the synagogue. They took them, these priests, and buried them in a Christian cemetery, where they remained safe from the Nazis until after the war was ended." He smiled thinly. "So what does this tell us? There remains the potential for light even in the darkest places. Compassion can come from the most unexpected places. And you have two cracked ribs."

He rose now. "Come. I have at my house all the equipment necessary to bind you up. In a matter of just a week or so the pain will recede, and you'll be on the mend." He waggled a thick forefinger. "But in the interim you must promise me you'll rest. No strenuous exercise for you. In fact, no exercise at all would be best."

"I can't promise you that, Doctor."

Dr. Ambrus sighed as he shot Annaka a quick glance. "Now why doesn't that surprise me?"

Bourne got to his feet. "In fact, I'm very much afraid I'm going to have to do everything you've just warned me against, in which case I've got to ask you to do what you can in order to protect the damaged ribs."

"How about a suit of armor?" Dr. Ambrus chuckled at his own joke, but his amusement quickly dropped away as he saw the expression on Bourne's face. "Good God, man, what do you expect to be going up against?"

"If I could tell you," Bourne said bleakly, "I imagine we'd all be better off."

Though clearly taken aback, Dr. Ambrus was as good as his word, leading them to his house in the Buda Hills where he had a small examining room where others might have had a study. Outside the window were climbing roses, but the geranium pots were still bare, awaiting warmer weather. Inside, were cream walls, white moldings, and on top of the cabinets, framed snapshots of Dr. Ambrus' wife and his two sons.

Dr. Ambrus sat Bourne down on the table, humming to himself as he went methodically through his cabinets, picking out one item here, two more there. Returning to his patient who he'd bade strip to the waist, he swung an armatured light around, snapped it on the field of battle. Then he went to work binding Bourne's ribs tightly in three different layers of material—cotton, spandex and a rubberlike material he said contained Kevlar.

"Better than that no one could do," he declared when he was finished.

"I can't breathe," Bourne gasped.

"Good, that means the pain will be kept to a minimum." He rattled a small brown plastic bottle. "I'd give you some painkillers, but for a man such as yourself—um, no, I think not. The drug will interfere with your senses, your reflexes will be off, and the next time I see you, you might be on a slab."

Bourne smiled at the attempt at humor. "I'll do my best to spare you that shock." Bourne dug in a pocket. "How much do I owe you?"

Dr. Ambrus raised his hands. "Please."

"How to thank you, then, Istvan?" Annaka said.

"Just to see you again, my dear, is payment enough." Dr. Ambrus took her face in his hands, kissed her on first one cheek, then the other. "Promise me you'll come to dinner one night soon. Bela misses you as much as I. Come, my dear. Come. She'll make you her goulash, which you loved as a child."

"I promise, Istvan. Soon."

Content at last with this promise of payment, Dr. Ambrus let them go.

CHAPTER TWENTY-THREE

"Something needs to be done about Randy Driver," Lindros said.

The DCI finished signing a set of papers, pushing them into his outbox before looking up. "I heard he gave you a sound tongue-lashing."

"I don't understand. Is this a source of amusement for you, sir?"

"Indulge me, Martin," he said with a smirk he refused to hide. "I have few sources of entertainment these days."

The sun-dazzle that had all afternoon spun off the statue of the three Revolutionary War soldiers outside the window was gone, making the bronze figures appear weary in the shadows shrouding them. The fragile light of another spring day had all too quickly passed into night.

"I want him taken care of. I want access—"

The DCI's face darkened. " 'I want, I want'—what are you, a three-year-old?"

"You put me in charge of the investigation into Conklin's and Panov's murders. I'm only doing what you asked."

"Investigation?" The DCI's eyes sparked with anger. "There is no investigation. I told you in no uncertain terms, Martin, that I wanted an end to this. The bleeding is killing us with the bitch-woman. I want it cauterized so it can be forgotten. The last thing I need is for you to be running all over the Beltway, throwing your weight around like a bull in a china shop." He waved a hand to stave off his deputy's protestations. "Hang Harris, hang him high and loud enough for the National Security Advisor to be certain we know what we're doing."

"If you say so, sir, but with all due respect that would be just about the worst mistake we could make right now." As the DCI stared open-mouth at him, he spun across the desk the computer printout Harris had sent over.

"What is this?" the DCI said. He liked a precis of everything he was given before he had a chance to read it.

"It's part of the electronic record of a ring of Russians providing people with illegal handguns. The gun used to murder Conklin and Panov is there. It was falsely registered to Webb. This proves Webb was set up, that he didn't murder his two best friends."

The DCI had begun reading the printout, and now his thick white brows furrowed. "Martin, this proves nothing."

"Again, with all due respect, sir, I don't see how you can ignore the facts that are right in front of you."

The DCI sighed, pushed the printout away from him as he sat back in his chair. "You know, Martin, I've trained you well. But it occurs to me now that you still have a great deal to learn." He pointed a forefinger at the paper lying on his desk. "This tells me that the gun Jason Bourne used to shoot Alex and Mo Panov was paid for via a wire transfer from Budapest. Bourne has I don't know how many bank accounts overseas, in Zurich and Geneva mostly, but I don't see why he wouldn't have one in Budapest as well." He grunted. "It's a clever trick, one of so many taught to him by Alex himself."

Lindros' heart had plummeted to his shoes. "So you don't think—"

"You want me to take this so-called evidence to the bitch-woman?" The DCI shook his head. "She'd shove it back down my throat."

Of course, the first thing that had entered the Old Man's mind was that Bourne had hacked into the U.S. Government database from Budapest, which was why he himself had activated Kevin McColl. No point telling Martin that; he'd only get himself all het up. No, the DCI thought obstinately, the money for the murder weapon had originated in Budapest and that was where Bourne had fled. Further damning evidence of his guilt.

Lindros broke in on his musing. "So you won't authorize going back to Driver—"

"Martin, it's coming up on seven-thirty and my stomach has started to rumble." The DCI stood. "To show you that there's no hard feelings, I want you to join me for dinner."

The Occidental Grill was an insider restaurant at which the DCI had his own table. It was for civilians and low-grade government employees to stand on lines, not for him. In this arena his power rose out of the shadow world he inhabited, made itself known to all of Washington. There were precious few inside the Beltway who possessed this status. After a difficult day, there was nothing like using it.

They valet-parked and mounted the long flight of granite steps to the restaurant. Inside, they went down a narrow passageway hung with photos of the presidents as well as other famous political personages who had dined at the grill. As he always did, the DCI paused in front of the photo of J. Edgar Hoover and his ever-constant shadow, Clyde Tolson. The DCI's eyes bored into the photo of the two men as if he had the power to expunge by fire this duo from the pantheon on the wall of greats.

"I distinctly remember the moment we intercepted the Hoover memo exhorting his senior officers to find the link that tied Martin Luther King, Jr., and the Communist Party to the anti–Vietnam War demonstrations." He shook his head. "What a world I've been a party to."

"It's history, sir."

"Ignominious history, Martin."

With that pronouncement, he passed through the half-glass doors into the restaurant itself. The room was all wooden booths, cut-glass partitions and mirrored bar. As usual, there was a line, which the DCI navigated like the Queen Mary sailing through a flotilla of motorboats. He stopped in front of the podium, which was presided over by an elegant silver-haired maître d'.

At the DCI's approach, the man turned with a brace of long menus clutched to his breast. "Director!" His eyes opened wide. There was an odd paleness to his usually florid skin. "We had no idea that you'd be dining with us tonight."

"Since when do you need advance notice, Jack?" The DCI said.

"May I suggest a drink at the bar, Director? I have your favorite sour mash."

The DCI patted his stomach. "I'm hungry, Jack. We'll dispense with the bar and go straight to my table."

The maître d' looked distinctly uncomfortable. "Please give me a moment, Director," he said, hurrying away.

"What the hell's the matter with him?" muttered the DCI with some annoyance.

Lindros had already taken a look at the DCI's corner table, saw that it was occupied, and blanched. The DCI saw his expression and he whirled, peering through the throng of waiters and patrons at his beloved table, where the power seat reserved for him was now occupied by Roberta Alonzo-Ortiz, National Security Advisor of the United States. She was deep in conversation with two senators from the Foreign Intelligence Services Committee.

"I'll kill her, Martin. So help me God, I'll rend the bitch-woman limb from limb."

At that moment the maître d', clearly sweating inside his collar, returned. "We have a nice table all set up for you, Director, a table for four, just for you gentlemen. And the drinks're on the house, all right?"

The DCI bit back his rage. "It's quite all right," he said, aware that he was unable to rid himself of his high color. "Lead on, Jack."

The maître d' took them on a route that didn't pass his old table, and the DCI was grateful to Jack for that.

"I told her, Director," the maître d' said almost under his breath. "I made it quite clear that that particular corner table was yours, but she insisted. She wouldn't take no for an answer. What could I do? I'll have the drinks over in just a minute." Jack said all this in a rush as he seated them, presenting the food and wine menus. "Is there anything else I can do, Director?"

"No, thank you, Jack." The DCI picked up his menu.

A moment later a burly waiter with muttonchop sideburns brought two glasses of sour mash, along with the bottle and a carafe of water.

"Compliments of the maître d'," he said.

If Lindros had been under any illusion that the DCI was calm, he was disabused of that notion the moment the Old Man took up his glass to sip his sour mash. His hand shook, and now Lindros could see that his eyes were glazed with rage.

Lindros saw his opening and, like the fine tactician he was, took it. "The National Security Advisor wants the double murders attended to and swept away with as little fuss as possible. But if the basic assumption that underlies this reasoning—mainly that Jason Bourne is responsible—is untrue, then everything else falls apart, including the NSA's extremely vocal position."

The DCI looked up. He stared shrewdly at his deputy. "I know you, Martin. You already have some plan in mind, don't you?"

"Yessir, I do, and if I'm right, we'll make the NSA look like fools. But for that to happen, I need Randy Driver's full and complete cooperation."

The waiter appeared with the chopped salads.

The DCI waited until they were alone and poured them both more sour mash. With a tight smile, he said, "This business with Randy Driver—you believe it's necessary?"

"More than necessary, sir. It's vital."

"Vital, eh?" The DCI tucked into his salad, looked at the resulting piece of glistening tomato impaled on the tines of his fork. "I'll sign the paperwork first thing tomorrow."

"Thank you, sir."

The DCI frowned, his gaze sought out that of his deputy, held it captive. "Only one way to thank me, Martin, bring me the ammunition I need to put the bitch-woman in her place."

The advantage of having a girl in every port, McColl knew, was that he always had a place to hole up. There was, of course, an Agency safe house in Budapest—in fact, there were several, but with his bleeding arm he had no intention of showing up in an official residence and thereby announcing to his superiors his failure to satisfy the sanction the DCI himself had given him. In his section of the Agency, results were the only thing that mattered.

Ilona was home when, wounded arm at his side, he stumbled up to her door. As always, she was ready for action. He, for once, wasn't, he had business to attend to first. He sent her to make him something to eat—something proteinaceous, he told her, for he needed to regain his strength. Then he went into her bathroom, stripped to the waist, and washed off the blood from his right arm. Then he poured hydrogen peroxide over the wound. The searing pain shot up and down his arm and made his legs tremble so that he was obliged to sit for a moment on the closed toilet lid in order to collect himself. In a moment the pain had subsided to a deep throbbing and he was able to assess the damage done him. The good news was that the wound was clean; the bullet had gone cleanly through the muscle of his arm and exited. Leaning over so that he could rest his elbow on the edge of the sink, he poured more hydrogen peroxide on the wound, whistled softly through his bared teeth. Then he rose, rifled through the cabinets without finding any sterile cotton pads. He did find, under the sink, a roll of duct tape. Using a pair of cuticle scissors, he cut off a length, wrapped it tightly around the wound.

When he returned, Ilona had his meal prepared. He sat, wolfing down the food without tasting it. It was hot and nourishing, which was all he cared about. She stood behind him as he ate, massaging the bunched muscles of his shoulders.

"You're so tense," she said. She was small and slender with flashing eyes, a ready smile, and curves in all the right places. "What did you do after you left me at the baths? You were so relaxed then."

"Work," he said laconically. He knew by experience that it wasn't politic to ignore her questions, though he had very little desire for small talk. He needed to gather his thoughts, plan for the second, and final, assault on Jason Bourne. "I've told you my work is stressful."

Her talented fingers continued to knead the tension out of him. "I wish you'd quit then."

"I love what I do," he said, pushing his empty plate away. "I'd never quit."

"And still you're sullen." She came around, held out her hand. "Then come to bed now. Let me make it better."

"You go," he said. "Wait for me there. I've some business calls to make. When I'm finished, I'll be all yours."

Morning came in a bevy of shouts to the small, anonymous room in a cheap hotel. The sounds of Budapest stirring penetrated the thin walls as if they were gauze, goading Annaka from her fitful sleep. For a time she lay immobile in the grayish morning illumination, side by side with Bourne on the double bed. At length she turned her head, stared at him.

How her life had changed since she'd met him on the steps of Matthias Church! Her father was dead and now she couldn't return to her own apartment because its location was known to both Khan and the CIA. In truth, there wasn't much about her apartment she'd miss, except for her piano. The pang of yearning she felt for it was akin to what she'd read identical twins experienced when they were separated by a great distance.

And what of Bourne, what did she feel for him? It was difficult for her to tell, since from an early age a certain switch had been thrown inside her that had turned off the spigot of emotion. The mechanism, a form of self-preservation instinct, was a complete mystery, even to experts who purported to study such phenomena. It was buried so deeply inside her mind that she could never reach it—another aspect of its preservation of the self.

As in everything else, she'd lied to Khan when she'd told him that she couldn't control herself around him. She'd walked out on him because Stepan had ordered her to leave. She hadn't minded; in fact, she'd rather relished the look on Khan's face when she'd told him it was over. She'd hurt him, which she liked. At the same time she saw that he'd cared for her, and she was curious about this, not understanding it herself. Of course, long ago and far away she'd cared about her mother, but of what use had that emotion been? Her mother had failed to protect her; worse, she'd died.

Slowly, carefully, she inched away from Bourne until finally she turned and rose. She was reaching for her coat when Bourne, rising from deep sleep to immediate wakefulness, spoke her name softly.

Annaka started, turned. "I thought you were fast asleep. Did I wake you?"

Bourne watched her, unblinking. "Where are you going?"

"I . . . we need new clothes."

He struggled to sit up.

"How are you feeling?"

"I'm fine," he said. He was in no mood for receiving sympathy. "Besides clothes, we both need disguises."

"We?"

"McColl knew who you were, that means he'd been sent a photo of you."

"But why?" She shook her head. "How did the CIA know you and I were together?"

"They didn't—at least, they couldn't be sure," he said. "I've been thinking, and the only way they could've made you was through your computer's IP address. I must've set off an internal alarm when I hacked into the government's intranet."

"God in heaven." She slipped into her coat. "Still, it's far safer for me out on the streets than it would be for you."

"Do you know a shop that sells theatrical makeup?"

"There's a district not far from here. Yes, I'm sure I can find a place."

Bourne grabbed a pad and the stub of a pencil off the desk and made a hurried list. "This is what I'll need for both of us," he said. "I've also written down my shirt, neck and waist sizes. Do you have enough money? I have plenty but it's in American dollars."

She shook her head. "Too dangerous. I'd have to go to a bank and change it into Hungarian forint, and that might be noticed. There are ATM's all over the city."

"Be careful," he warned.

"Don't worry." She glanced at the list he'd made. "I should be back in a couple of hours. Until then, don't leave the room."

She descended in the tiny creaking elevator. Save for the day clerk behind the desk, the commensurately tiny lobby was deserted. He lifted his head from his newspaper, glanced at her with bored eyes before returning to his reading. She went out into bustling Budapest. The presence of Kevin McColl, a complicating factor, made her uneasy, but Stepan reassured her when she telephoned him with the news. She'd been updating him when she'd telephoned him from her apartment every time she'd run the water in the kitchen.

As she entered the flow of pedestrian traffic, she glanced at her watch. It was just after ten. She had coffee and a sweet roll at a corner café, then proceeded on to an ATM about two-thirds of the way to the shopping district toward which she was headed. She slipped in her debit card, withdrew the maximum amount, put the wad of bills in her purse and, with Bourne's list in hand, set out to shop.

Across town, Kevin McColl strode into the branch of the Budapest Bank that handled Annaka Vadas' account. He flashed his credentials and, in due course, was admitted to the glass-enclosed office of the branch manager, a well-dressed man in a conservatively cut suit. They shook hands as they introduced themselves and the manager indicated that McColl sit in the upholstered chair facing him.

The manager steepled his fingers and said, "How can I be of assistance, Mr. McColl?"

"We're looking for an international fugitive," McColl began.

"Ah, and why isn't Interpol involved?"

"They are," McColl said, "as well as the Quai d'Orsay in Paris, which was this fugitive's last stop before coming here to Budapest."

"And the name of this wanted man?"

McColl produced the CIA flyer, which he unfolded and set on the desk in front of the manager.

The bank manager adjusted his glasses as he scanned the flyer. "Ah, yes, Jason Bourne. I watch CNN." He glanced up over the gold rim of his glasses. "You say he's here in Budapest."

"We've got a confirmed sighting."

The bank manager set the flyer aside. "And how may I help?"

"He was in the company of one of your depositors. Annaka Vadas."

"Really?" The bank manager frowned. "Her father was killed—shot dead two days ago. Do you think the fugitive murdered him?"

"It's entirely possible." McColl held tight rein on his impatience. "I would appreciate your help in finding out if Ms. Vadas has used an ATM anytime in the last twenty-four hours."

"I understand." The bank manager nodded sagely. "The fugitive needs money. He might force her to get it for him."

"Precisely." Anything, McColl thought, to get this guy to move off the dime.

The bank manager swiveled around, began to type on his computer keyboard. "Let's see then. Ah, yes, here she is. Annaka Vadas." He shook his head. "Such a tragedy. And now to be subjected to this."

He was staring at his computer screen when a chirp sounded. "It seems you were right, Mr. McColl. Annaka Vadas' PIN number was used at an ATM less than a half hour ago."

"Address," McColl said, leaning forward.

The manager wrote the address down on a sheet of notepaper, handed it to McColl, who was up and on his way with a "Thank you" thrown over his shoulder.

Bourne, down in the lobby of the hotel, asked the clerk for directions to the nearest public Internet access point. He walked the twelve blocks to AMI Internet Café at 40 Váci utca. Inside, it was smoky and crowded, people sitting at computer stations, smoking as they read e-mail, did research or simply surfed the Web. He ordered a double-espresso and a buttered roll from a spike-haired young woman, who handed him a time-stamped slip of paper with the number of his station on it and directed him to a free computer that was already logged onto the Internet.

He sat down and began his work. In the "Search" field, he typed in the name of Peter Sido, Dr. Schiffer's former partner, but found nothing. That, in itself, was both odd and suspicious. If Sido was a scientist of any note at all—which Bourne had to assume he was if he'd worked with Felix

Schiffer—then chances were he'd be *somewhere* on the Web. The fact that he wasn't caused Bourne to consider the fact that his "absence" was deliberate. He'd have to try another path.

There was something about the name Sido that rang a bell in his linguist's brain. Was it Russian in origin? Slavic? He searched these language sites but came up blank. On a hunch he switched to a site on the Magyar language, and there it was.

It turned out that Hungarian family names—what Hungarians called bynames—most always meant something. For instance, they could be patronymic, meaning they used the father's name, or they could be locative, identifying where the person came from. Their family name could also tell you their profession—interestingly, he noted that Vadas meant hunter. Or *what* they were. Sido was the Hungarian word for Jew.

So Peter Sido was a Hungarian, just like Vadas. Conklin had chosen Vadas to work with. Coincidence? Bourne didn't believe in coincidences. There was a connection; he could sense it. Which opened up the following line of thought: All the world-class hospitals and research facilities in Hungary were in Budapest. Could Sido be here?

Bourne's hands flew over the keyboard, accessing the on-line Budapest phone directory. And there he found a Dr. Peter Sido. He noted the address and phone number, then logged off, paid for his time on-line and took his double espresso and roll to the café section, where he sat at a corner table away from other patrons. He chomped on his roll while he took out his cell phone and dialed Sido's number. He sipped his double espresso. After several rings, a female voice answered.

"Hello," Bourne said in a cheerful voice, "Mrs. Sido?"

"Yes?"

He hung up without responding, wolfed down the rest of his breakfast while waiting for the taxi he'd called for. One eye on the front door, he scrutinized everyone who walked in, on the lookout for McColl or any other Agency operative who might have been sent into the field. Certain that he was unobserved, he went out into the street to meet the taxi. He gave the driver Dr. Peter Sido's address and not more than twenty minutes later, the taxi drew up in front of a small house with a stone facade, a tiny garden in front, and miniature iron balconies projecting from each story.

He climbed the steps and knocked. The front door was opened by a rather rotund woman of middle years with soft brown eyes and a ready smile. She had brown hair, pulled back in a bun, and was stylishly dressed.

"Mrs. Sido? Dr. Peter Sido's wife?"

"That's right." She gazed at him inquiringly. "May I help you?"

"My name is David Schiffer."

"Yes?"

He smiled winningly. "Felix Schiffer's cousin, Mrs. Sido."

"I'm sorry," Peter Sido's wife said, "but Felix never mentioned you."

Bourne was prepared for this. He chuckled. "That's not surprising. You see, we lost touch with each other. I'm only now just returned from Australia."

"Australia! My word!" She stepped aside. "Well, do come in, please. You must think me rude."

"Not at all," Bourne said. "Simply surprised, as anyone would be."

She showed him into a small sitting room, comfortably, if darkly, furnished and bade him make himself at home. The air smelled of yeast and sugar. When he was seated in an over-upholstered chair, she said, "Would you like coffee or tea? I have some stollen. I baked it this morning."

"Stollen, a favorite of mine," he said. "And only coffee will do with stollen. Thank you."

She chuckled and headed for the kitchen. "Are you sure you're not part Hungarian, Mr. Schiffer?"

"Please call me David," he said, rising and following her. Not knowing the family background, he was on shaky ground when it came to the Schiffers. "Is there something I can help you with?"

"Why, thank you, David. And you must call me Eszti." She pointed at a covered cake platter. "Why don't you cut us each a piece?"

On the refrigerator door, he saw among several family snapshots, one of a young woman, very pretty, alone. Her hand was pressed to the top of her Scottish tam and her long dark hair was windblown. Behind her was the Tower of London.

"Your daughter?" Bourne said.

Eszti Sido glanced up and smiled. "Yes, Roza, my youngest. She's at school in London. Cambridge," she said with understandable pride. "My other daughters—there they are with their families—are both happily married, thank God. Roza's the ambitious one." She smiled shyly. "Shall I tell you a secret, David? I love all my children, but Roza is my favorite—Peter's too. I think he sees something of himself in her. She loves the sciences."

Several more minutes of bustling around the kitchen brought a carafe of coffee and plates of stollen on a tray, which Bourne carried back into the sitting room.

"So you're Felix's cousin," she said when they were both settled, he on the chair, she on the sofa. Between them was a low table on which Bourne had placed the tray.

"Yes, and I'm eager for news of Felix," Bourne said as she poured the coffee. "But, you see, I can't find him, and I thought . . . well, I was hoping your husband could help me out."

"I don't think he knows where Felix is." Eszti Sido handed him the coffee and a plate of stollen. "I don't mean to alarm you, David, but he's been quite upset lately. Though they hadn't officially worked together for some time, they'd had a long-distance correspondence going recently." She stirred cream into her coffee. "They never stopped being good friends, you see."

"So this recent correspondence was of a personal nature," Bourne said.

"I don't know about that." Eszti frowned. "I gathered that it had something to do with their work."

"You wouldn't know what, would you, Eszti? I've come a long way to find my cousin, and, frankly, I've begun to worry a little. Anything you or your husband could tell me, anything at all would be of great help."

"Of course, David, I understand completely." She took a dainty bite of her stollen. "I imagine Peter would be quite happy to see you. At the moment, though, he's at work."

"D'you think I could have his phone number?"

"Oh, that won't do you any good. Peter never answers his phone at work. You'll have to go to the Eurocenter Bio-I Clinic at 75 Hattyu utca. When you do, you'll first go through a metal detector, after which you'll be stopped at the front desk. Because of the work they do there, they're exceptionally security conscious. They require special ID tags to get into his section, white for visitors, green for resident doctors, blue for assistants and support staff."

"Thank you for the information, Eszti. May I inquire as to what your husband specializes in?"

"You mean Felix never told you?"

Bourne, sipping his delicious coffee, swallowed. "As I'm sure you know, Felix is a secretive person, he never spoke to me about his work."

"Quite so." Eszti Sido laughed. "Peter's just the same and, considering the frightening field he's in, it's just as well. I'm sure if I knew what he was into, I'd have nightmares. You see, he's an epidemiologist."

Bourne's heart skipped a beat. "Frightening, you say. He must work with some nasty bugs then. Anthrax, pneumonic plague, Argentinian hemorrhagic fever . . ."

Eszti Sido's face clouded over. "Oh dear, oh dear, please!" She waved a pudgy-fingered hand. "Those are just the things I know Peter works with but don't want to know about."

"I apologize." Bourne leaned forward, poured her more coffee, for which she thanked him in relief.

She sat back, sipping her coffee, her eyes turned inward. "You know, David, now that I think about it, there was an evening not long ago when Peter came home in a high state of excitement. So much so, in fact, that for once he forgot himself and mentioned something to me. I was cooking dinner and he was unusually late and I was having to juggle six things at once—a roast, you know, doesn't like to be overcooked, so I'd taken it out, then put it back when Peter finally walked through the door. I wasn't happy with him that night, I can tell you." She sipped again. "Now, where was I?"

"Dr. Sido came home very excited," Bourne prompted.

"Ah, yes, just so." She took up a tiny piece of the stollen between her fingers. "He'd been in contact with Felix, he said, who'd had some sort of breakthrough with the—*thing*—he'd been working on for more than two years."

Bourne's mouth was dry. It seemed odd to him that the fate of the world now lay with a housewife with whom he was cozily sharing coffee and homemade pastry. "Did your husband tell you what it was?"

"Of course he did!" Eszti Sido said with gusto. "That was the reason he was so exercised. It was a biochemical disperser—whatever that is. According to Peter, what was so extraordinary about it was that it was portable. It could be carried in an acoustic guitar case, he said." Her kind eyes gazed at him. "Isn't that an interesting image to use for a scientific thingy?"

"Interesting, indeed," Bourne said, his mind furiously clicking into place pieces of the jigsaw puzzle the pursuit of which had more than once almost gotten him killed.

He rose. "Eszti, I'm afraid I must be going. Thank you so much for your time and your hospitality. Everything was delicious—*especially* the stollen."

She blushed, smiling warmly as she saw him to the door. "Do come again, David, under happier circumstances."

"I will," he assured her.

Out on the street, he paused. Eszti Sido's information confirmed both his suspicions and his worst fears. The reason everyone wanted to get their hands on Dr. Schiffer was that he had indeed created a portable means of dispersing chemical and biological pathogens. In a big city such as New York or Moscow, that would mean thousands of deaths with no means to save anyone within the radius of the dispersion. A truly terrifying scenario, one that would come true unless he could find Dr. Schiffer. If anyone knew, it would be Peter Sido. The mere fact that he'd become agitated of late confirmed that theory.

There was no doubt that he needed to see Dr. Peter Sido, the sooner the better.

"You realize you're just asking for trouble," Feyd al-Saoud said.

"I know that," Jamie Hull replied. "But Boris forced it on me. You know he's a sonuvabitch as well as I do."

"First of all," Feyd al-Saoud said evenly, "if you insist on calling him Boris, there can be no further discussion. You're doomed to a blood feud." He spread his hands. "Perhaps it's my failing, Mr. Hull, so I would ask you to explain to me why you'd want to further complicate an assignment that's already taxing all our security skills."

The two agents were inspecting the Oskjuhlid Hotel's HVAC system in which they'd installed both heat-sensitive infrared and motion detectors. This foray was quite apart from the daily inspection of the summit's forum HVAC the three agents undertook as a team.

In a little over eight hours the first contingent of the negotiating parties would arrive. Twelve hours after that, the leaders would present themselves and the summit would begin. There was absolutely no margin for error for any of them, including Boris Illyich Karpov.

"You mean you *don't* think he's a sonuvabitch?" Hull said.

Feyd al-Saoud checked a branching against the schematic he seemed to carry with him at all times. "Frankly, I've had other things on my mind." Satisfied that the junction was secure, Feyd al-Saoud moved on.

"Okay, let's cut to the chase."

Feyd al-Saoud turned to him. "I beg your pardon?"

"What I was thinking was that you and I make a good team. We get along well. When it comes to security, we're on the same page."

"What you mean is, I follow your orders well."

Hull looked hurt. "Did I say that?"

"Mr. Hull, you didn't have to. You, like most Americans, are quite transparent. If you're not in complete control, you tend to either get angry or sulk."

Hull felt himself flooding with resentment. "We're not children!" he cried.

"On the contrary," Feyd al-Saoud said equably, "there are times when you remind me of my six-year-old son."

Hull wanted to pull his Glock 31 .357 mm and shove its muzzle in the Arab's face. Where did he get off talking to a representative of the U.S. Government like that? It was like spitting on the flag, for Christ's sake! But what good would a show of force do him now? No, much as he hated to admit it, he needed to go another way.

"So what d'you say?" he said as equably as he could.

Feyd al-Saoud appeared unmoved. "In all honesty, I'd prefer to see you and Mr. Karpov work out your differences together."

Hull shook his head. "Ain't gonna happen, my friend, you know that as well as I do."

Unfortunately, Feyd al-Saoud did know that. Both Hull and Karpov were entrenched in their mutual enmity. The best that could be hoped for now was that they'd confine hostilities to taking the occasional potshot at each other without an escalation into all-out war.

"I think I could best serve you both by maintaining a neutral position," he said now. "If I don't, who's going to keep the two of you from rending each other limb from limb?"

After purchasing everything Bourne needed, Annaka left the men's clothes shop. As she headed toward the theatrical district, she saw the reflection of movement behind her in the shop window. She didn't hesitate or even break stride but slowed her pace enough so that as she strolled she confirmed that she was being followed. As casually as she could, she crossed the street, paused in front of a shop window. In it she recognized the image of Kevin McColl as he crossed the street behind her, ostensibly heading toward a café on the corner of the block. She knew that she had to lose him before she reached the area of theatrical makeup shops.

Making sure he couldn't see, she pulled out her cell phone, dialed Bourne's number.

"Jason," she said softly, "McColl's picked me up."

"Where are you now?" he said.

"The beginning of Váci utca."

"I'm not far away."

"I thought you weren't going to leave the hotel. What've you been doing?"

"I've discovered a lead," he said.

"Really?" Her heart beat fast. Had he found out about Stepan? "What is it?"

"First, we've got to deal with McColl. I want you to go to 75 Hattyu utca. Wait for me at the front desk." He continued, giving her details of what she was to do.

She listened intently, then said, "Jason, are you sure you're up to this?"

"Just do what I tell you," he said sternly, "and everything will be fine."

She disconnected and called a taxi. When it came, she got in and gave the driver the address Bourne had made her repeat back to him. As they drove off, she looked around but didn't see McColl, though she was certain he'd been following her. A moment later a battered dark-green Opel threaded its way through traffic, wedging itself behind her taxi. Annaka, peering into the driver's off-side mirror, recognized the hulking figure behind the wheel of the Opel, and her lips curled in a secret smile. Kevin McColl had taken the bait; now if only Bourne's plan would work.

Stepan Spalko, newly returned to the Humanistas Ltd. headquarters in Budapest, was monitoring the international clandestine service cipher traffic for news on the summit when his cell phone rang.

"What is it?" he said tersely.

"I'm on my way to meet Bourne at 75 Hattyu utca," Annaka said.

Spalko turned and walked away from where his technicians were sitting at their deciphering workstations. "He's sending you to the Eurocenter Bio-I Clinic," he said. "He knows about Peter Sido."

"He said he had an exciting new lead, but he wouldn't tell me what it was."

"The man's relentless," Spalko said. "I'll take care of Sido, but you can't let him anywhere near his office."

"I understand that," Annaka said. "In any event, Bourne's attention is initially going to be directed toward the American CIA agent who's been shadowing him."

"I don't want Bourne killed, Annaka. He's far too valuable to me alive—at least for the moment." Spalko's mind was sorting through possibilities, discarding them one by one until he arrived at his desired conclusion. "Leave everything else to me."

Annaka, in the speeding taxi, nodded. "You can count on me, Stepan."

"I know that."

Annaka stared out the window at passing Budapest. "I never thanked you for killing my father."

"It was a long time coming."

"Khan thinks I'm angry because I didn't get to do it myself."

"Is he right?"

There were tears in Annaka's eyes and with some annoyance she wiped them away. "He was my father, Stepan. Whatever he did . . . still, he was my father. He raised me."

"Poorly, Annaka. He never really knew how to be a father to you."

She thought about the lies she'd told Bourne without an iota of compunction, the idealized childhood she'd wished for herself. Her father had never read to her at night or changed her; he'd never once come to one of her graduations—it seemed he was always far away; and as for birthdays, he'd never remembered. Another tear, escaping her vigilance, crawled down her cheek and, at the corner of her mouth, she tasted its salt as if it were the bitterness of memory.

She tossed her head. "A child can never fully condemn her father, it seems."

"I did mine."

"That was different," she said. "And, anyway, I know how you felt about my mother."

"I loved her, yes." In his mind Spalko conjured up an image of Sasa

Vadas: her large, luminous eyes, her creamy skin, the full bow of her mouth when that slow smile brought you close to her heart. "She was completely unique, a special creature, a princess as her name suggested."

"She was as much your family as she was mine," Annaka said. "She saw right through you, Stepan. In her heart she felt the tragedies you'd suffered without you having to tell her a thing."

"I waited a long time to take my revenge on your father, Annaka, but I never would've done it if I didn't know it was what you wanted, too."

Annaka laughed, now fully back to herself. The brief emotional wallow she'd fallen into disgusted her. "You don't expect me to believe that, do you, Stepan?"

"Now, Annaka—"

"Remember who you're trying to con. I know you, you killed him when it served your purpose. And you were right, he would've told Bourne everything and Bourne would've wasted no time coming after you with everything he had. That I'd wanted my father dead, too, was mere coincidence."

"Now you're underestimating your importance to me."

"That may or may not be true, Stepan, but it doesn't matter to me. I wouldn't know how to form an emotional attachment even if I wanted to try."

Martin Lindros presented his official papers to Randy Driver, Director of the Tactical Non-Lethal Weapons Directorate in person. Driver, who was staring at Lindros as if he had a chance of intimidating him, took the papers without comment and dropped them on his desk.

He was standing as a marine would stand, straight-spined, gut in, muscles taut, as if he were about to go into battle. His close-set blue eyes seemed almost crossed, such was his concentration. A slight antiseptic scent lingered in the white-metal office, as if he'd seen fit to fumigate the place in anticipation of Lindros' arrival.

"I see you've been a busy little beaver since last we met," he said, looking at no one in particular. Apparently, he'd realized that he wouldn't be able to intimidate Lindros simply with his stare. He was moving on to verbal intimidation.

"I'm always busy," Lindros said. "You just forced me into make-work."

"Happy am I." Driver's face fairly creaked with the tightness of his smile.

Lindros shifted from one foot to the other. "Why do you see me as the enemy?"

"Possibly because you *are* the enemy." Driver finally sat down behind his smoked-glass and stainless-steel desk. "What else would you call someone who comes in here wanting to dig up my backyard?"

"I'm only investigating—"

"Don't give that bullshit, Lindros!" Driver had leaped up, his face livid. "I can smell a witch-hunt at a hundred paces! You're the Old Man's bloodhound. You can't fool me. This isn't about Alex Conklin's murder."

"And why would you think that?"

"Because this investigation is about *me!*"

Now Lindros was really interested. Aware that Driver had given him the advantage, he seized it with a knowing smile. "Now why would we want to investigate you, Randy?" He'd chosen his words with care, using "we" to tell Driver that he was operating with the full force of the DCI behind him and his first name to unnerve him.

"You already know why, damnit!" Driver stormed, falling into the trap Lindros had set for him. "You must've known the first time you ambled in here. I could see it on your face when you asked to talk to Felix Schiffer."

"I wanted to give you the chance to come clean before I went to the DCI." Lindros was having fun following the path Driver was laying out, even though he had no idea where it was leading. On the other hand, he had to be careful. One false move on his part, one mistake and Driver would realize his ignorance and, likely as not, clam up, waiting for advice from his lawyer. "It's not too late for you to do so now."

Driver stared at him for a moment, before pressing the heel of his hand to his damp forehead. He slumped a little before falling back into his mesh chair.

"Christ Almighty, what a mess," he mumbled. As if having received a devastating body blow, all the wind had gone out of him. He looked around at the Rothko prints on the wall, as if they might be doorways through which he could flee. At last, finally resigned to his fate, he let his gaze return to the man standing patiently in front of him.

He gestured. "Sit down, Deputy Director." His voice was sad. When Lindros had taken his seat, he said, "It started with Alex Conklin. Well, it always started with Alex, didn't it?" He sighed, as if all at once overcome by nostalgia. "Almost two years ago Alex came to me with a proposition. He'd befriended a scientist at DARPA; the connection was coincidental, though, to tell you the truth, Alex networked with so many people I doubt if anything in his life was coincidence. I imagine you've worked out that the scientist in question was Felix Schiffer."

He paused for a moment. "I'm dying for a cigar. D'you mind?"

"Knock yourself out," Lindros said. So that explained the smell: air freshener. The building, like all government facilities, was supposed to be smoke-free.

"Care to join me?" Driver asked. "They were a present from Alex."

When Lindros declined, Driver pulled out a drawer, extracted a cigar from a humidor, went through the complex ritual of lighting up. Lindros understood; he was calming his nerves. He sniffed as the first puff of blue smoke wafted through the room. It was a Cuban.

"Alex came to see me," Driver continued. "No, that's not quite accurate—he took me out to dinner. He told me he'd met this guy who worked at DARPA. Felix Schiffer. He hated the military types there and wanted out. Would I help his friend?"

"And you agreed," Lindros said, "just like that?"

"Of course, I did. General Baker, the head of DARPA, had poached one of our guys last year." Driver took a puff on his cigar. "Payback's a bitch. I leaped at the chance to stick it to that uptight asshole Baker."

Lindros stirred. "When Conklin came to you, did he tell you what Schiffer was working on at DARPA?"

"Sure. Schiffer's field was pushing around airborne particulates. He was working on methods to clear indoor areas infected with biologicals."

Lindros sat up. "Like anthrax?"

Driver nodded. "That's right."

"How far along was he?"

"At DARPA?" Driver shrugged. "I wouldn't know."

"But surely you'd gotten updates on his work after he came to work for you."

Driver glared at him, then pressed some keys on his computer terminal. He swivelled the screen around so they could see.

Lindros leaned forward. "Looks like gibberish to me, but then I'm no scientist."

Driver stared at the end of his cigar as if now, at the moment of truth, he couldn't bring himself to look at Lindros. "It *is* gibberish, more or less."

Lindros froze. "What the hell d'you mean?"

Driver was still staring with fascination at the end of his cigar. "This couldn't be what Schiffer had been working on because it makes no sense."

Lindros shook his head. "I don't understand."

Driver sighed. "It's possible that Schiffer isn't much of a particulate expert."

Lindros, who had begun feeling a ball of icy terror form in his gut, said, "There's another possibility, isn't there?"

"Well, yes, now that you mention it." Driver ran his tongue around his lips. "It's possible that Schiffer was working on something else entirely that he wanted neither DARPA nor us to know about."

Lindros looked perplexed. "Why haven't you asked Dr. Schiffer about this?"

"I'd very much like to," Driver said. "The trouble is I don't know where Felix Schiffer is."

"If you don't," Lindros said angrily, "who the hell does?"

"Alex was the only one who knew."

"Jesus H. Christ, Alex Conklin's dead!" Lindros rose and, leaning forward, swiped the cigar out of Driver's mouth. "Randy, how long has Dr. Schiffer been missing?"

Driver closed his eyes. "Six weeks."

Now Lindros understood. This was why Driver had been so hostile when he'd first come to him; he was terrified that the Agency suspected his egregious breach of security. He said now, "How on earth did you allow this to happen?"

Driver's blue gaze rested on him for a moment. "It was Alex. I trusted him. Why wouldn't I? I knew him for years—he was an Agency legend, for Christ's sake. And then what does he up and do? He disappears Schiffer."

Driver stared at the cigar on the floor as if it had become a malignant object. "He used me, Lindros, played me like a fiddle. He didn't want Schiffer in my directorate, he didn't want us, the Agency, to have him. He wanted to get him away from DARPA so he could disappear him."

"Why?" Lindros said. "Why would he do that?"

"I don't know. I wish to God I did."

The pain in Driver's voice was palpable, and for the first time since they'd met, Lindros felt sorry for him. Everything he'd ever heard about Alexander Conklin had turned out to be true. He was the master manipulator, the keeper of all the dark secrets, the agent who trusted no one—no one save Jason Bourne, his protégé. Fleetingly, he wondered what this turn of events was going to do to the DCI. He and Conklin had been close friends for decades; they'd grown up together in the Agency—it was their life. They'd relied on each other, trusted each other, and now this bitterest blow. Conklin had breached just about every major Agency protocol to get what he wanted: Dr. Felix Schiffer. He'd screwed not only Randy Driver but the Agency itself. How was he ever going to protect the Old Man from this news? Lindros wondered. But, even as he thought this, he knew that he had a more pressing problem to deal with.

"Obviously, Conklin knew what Schiffer was really working on and wanted it," Lindros said. "But what the hell was it?"

Driver looked at him helplessly.

Stepan Spalko was standing in the center of Kapisztrán tér, within shouting distance of his waiting limo. Above him rose the Mary Magdalene Tower, all that was left of the thirteenth-century Franciscan church, whose nave and chancel were destroyed by Nazi bombs during World War II. As he waited, he felt a gust of chill wind raise the hem of his black coat, insinuating itself against his skin.

Spalko glanced at his watch. Sido was late. Long ago, he'd trained himself not to worry, but such was the significance of this meeting that he couldn't help but experience a twinge of anxiety. At the top of the tower, the twenty-four-piece glockenspiel sounded fifteen minutes after the hour. Sido was *very* late.

Spalko, watching the crowds ebb and flow, was just about to break protocol and call Sido on the cell phone he'd given him when he saw the scientist hurrying toward him from the opposite side of the tower. He was carrying something that looked like a jeweler's sample case.

"You're late," Spalko said shortly.

"I know, but it couldn't be helped." Dr. Sido wiped his forehead with the sleeve of his overcoat. "I had trouble getting the item out of storage. There was staff inside and I had to wait until the cold room was empty so as not to arouse—"

"Not here, Doctor!"

Spalko, who wanted to hit him for talking about their business in public, took Sido firmly by the elbow and all but frog-marched him deep into the desolate shadows thrown by the rather forbidding baroque stone tower.

"You've forgotten to watch your tongue around outsiders, Peter," Spalko said. "We're part of an elite group, you and I. I've told you that."

"I know," Dr. Sido said nervously, "but I find it difficult to—"

"You don't find it difficult to take my money, do you?"

Sido's eyes slipped away. "Here's the product," he said. "It's everything you asked for and more." He held out the case. "But let's get this over and done with quickly. I have to get back to the lab. I was in the middle of a crucial chemical calculation when you called."

Spalko pushed Sido's hand away. "You hold onto that, Peter, at least for a little while longer."

Sido's spectacles flashed. "But you said you needed it now—immediately. As I told you, once put in the portable case, the material is alive for only forty-eight hours."

"I haven't forgotten."

"Stepan, I'm at a loss. I took a great risk in bringing it out of the clinic during working hours. Now I must get back or—"

Spalko smiled and, at the same time, tightened his grip on Sido's elbow. "You're not going back, Peter."

"What?"

"I apologize for not mentioning it before, but, well, for the amount of money I'm paying you, I want more than the product. I want you."

Dr. Sido shook his head. "But that's quite impossible. You know that!"

"Nothing is impossible, Peter, you know that."

"Well, this is," Dr. Sido said adamantly.

With a charming smile, Spalko produced a snapshot from inside his overcoat. "What do they say about a picture's worth?" he said, handing it over.

Dr. Sido stared at it and swallowed convulsively. "Where did you get this photo of my daughter?"

Spalko's smile stayed firmly in place. "One of my people took it, Peter. Look at the date."

"It was taken yesterday." A sudden spasm overtook him and he tore the photo into pieces. "One can do anything with a photographic image these days," he said stonily.

"How true," Spalko said. "But I assure you this one wasn't doctored."

"Liar! I'm leaving!" Dr. Sido said. "Let go of me."

Spalko did as the doctor asked, but as Sido started to walk away, he said, "Wouldn't you like to talk with Roza, Peter?" He held out a cell phone. "I mean right now?"

Dr. Sido halted in midstep. Then he turned to face Spalko. His face was dark with anger and barely suppressed fear. "You said you were Felix's friend; I thought you were *my* friend."

Spalko continued to hold out the phone. "Roza would like to speak to you. If you walk away now . . ." He shrugged. His silence was its own threat.

Slowly, heavily, Dr. Sido came back. He took the cell phone in his free hand, put it up to his ear. He found that his heart was beating so loudly he could scarcely think. "Roza?"

"Daddy? Daddy! Where am I? What's happening?"

The panic in his daughter's voice sent a lance of terror through Sido. He could never remember being so afraid.

"Darling, what's going on?"

"Men came to my room, they took me, I don't know where, they put a hood over my head, they—"

"That's enough," Spalko said, taking the phone from Dr. Sido's nerveless fingers. He cut the connection, put the phone away.

"What have you done to her?" Dr. Sido's voice shook with the force of the emotions running through him.

"Nothing yet," Spalko said easily. "And nothing will happen to her, Peter, as long as you obey me."

Dr. Sido swallowed as Spalko resumed possession of him. "Where . . . where are we going?"

"We're taking a trip," Spalko said, guiding Dr. Sido toward the waiting limo. "Just think of it as a vacation, Peter. A well-deserved vacation."

CHAPTER TWENTY-FOUR

The Eurocenter Bio-I Clinic was housed in a modern stone building the color of lead. Bourne entered with the quick authoritative strides of someone who knew where he was going and why.

The interior of the clinic spoke of money, a great deal of it. The lobby was marble-clad. Classical-looking columns were interspersed with bronze statuary. Along the walls were arched niches in which resided the busts of the historical demigods of biology, chemistry, microbiology and epidemiology. The ugly metal detector was particularly offensive in this tranquil and monied setting. Beyond the skeletal structure was a high bank behind which sat three harried-looking attendants.

Bourne passed through the metal detector without incident, his ceramic gun going entirely unnoticed. At the front desk, he was all business.

"Alexander Conklin to see Dr. Peter Sido," he said so crisply that it was akin to being an order.

"ID, please, Mr. Conklin," said one of the three female attendants, unconsciously responding and snapping to.

Bourne handed over his false passport, which the attendant glanced at it, looking at Bourne's face only long enough to make visual confirmation before returning it to Bourne. She handed over a white plastic tag. "Please wear this at all times, Mr. Conklin." Such was Bourne's tone and demeanor that she failed to ask if Sido was expecting him, taking it for granted that "Mr. Conklin" had an interview with Dr. Sido. She provided the new visitor with directions and Bourne set off.

"They require special ID tags to get into his section, white for visitors, green for resident doctors, blue for assistants and support staff," Eszti Sido had told him, so his immediate task was to find a likely member of the staff.

On his way to the Epidemiological Wing, he passed four men, none of whom were the right somatotype. He needed someone who was more or less his size. Along the way he tried every door that wasn't marked as an office or lab, looking for storage rooms and the like, places that would be infrequently visited by the medical staff. He was unconcerned with members of the cleaning crew, since it was likely that they wouldn't be in until the evening.

At length he saw coming toward him a man in a white lab coat of more or less his height and weight. He wore a green ID tag that identified him as Dr. Lenz Morintz.

"Excuse me, Dr. Morintz," Bourne said with a deprecating smile, "I wonder if you could direct me to the Microbiological Wing. I seem to have lost my way."

"Indeed you have," Dr. Morintz said. "You're headed straight for the Epidemiological Wing."

"Oh, dear," Bourne said, "I really have got myself turned around."

"Not to worry," Dr. Morintz said. "Here's all you have to do."

As he turned to point Bourne in the right direction, Bourne chopped down with the edge of his hand and the bacteriologist collapsed. Bourne caught him before he could hit the floor. Standing him more or less upright, he half-carried, half-dragged the doctor back to the nearest storage room, ignoring the searing pain from his cracked ribs.

Inside, Bourne turned on the light, took off his jacket, and stuffed it into a corner. Then he stripped Dr. Morintz of his lab coat and ID. Using some spare surgical tape, he bound the doctor's hands behind his back, taped his ankles tightly, and wrapped a final piece across his mouth. Then he dragged the body into a corner, stashing it behind a couple of large cartons. He returned to the door, turned off the light and went out into the corridor.

For a time after she arrived at the Eurocenter Bio-I Clinic, Annaka sat in the taxi while the meter ran. Stepan had made it abundantly clear that they were now entering the mission's final phase. Every decision they made, every move they took, was of critical importance. Any mistake now could lead to disaster. Bourne or Khan. She didn't know which was the greater wild card, which one presented the greatest danger. Of the two, Bourne was the more stable, but Khan was without compunction. His similarity to her was an irony she couldn't afford to ignore.

And yet it had occurred to her most recently that there were more differences that she'd once imagined. For a start, he hadn't been able to bring himself to kill Jason Bourne, despite his stated desire to do so. And then, just as startlingly, there was his lapse in her Skoda when he'd leaned down to kiss the nape of her neck. From the moment she'd walked out on him she'd wondered whether what he'd felt for her had been genuine. Now she knew. Khan could feel; he could, if given enough incentive, forge emotional attachments. Frankly, she'd never have believed it of him, not with his background.

"Miss?" the taxi driver's query broke into her thoughts. "Are you meeting someone here or is there somewhere else you want me to take you?"

Annaka leaned forward, pressing a wad of bills into his hand. "This will be fine here."

Still she didn't move, but she looked around, wondering where Kevin McColl was. It was easy for Stepan sitting safe in his office at Humanistas to tell her not to worry about the CIA agent, but she was in the field with a capable and dangerous assassin and the severely wounded man he was determined to kill. When the bullets began to fly, she was the one who was going to be in the line of fire.

She got out at last, her agitation causing her to look up and down the block for the battered green Opel before she caught herself and with a grunt of irritation went through the front door of the clinic.

Inside, the setup was just as Bourne had described it to her. She wondered where he'd gotten his information in such short order. She had to hand it to him; he had a remarkable ability for ferreting out information.

Passing through the metal detector, she was stopped on the other side, was asked to open her purse so the officer could peer through its contents. Following Bourne's instructions to the letter, she approached the high marble bank, smiled at one of the three attendants who looked up long enough to acknowledge her presence.

"My name is Annaka Vadas," she said. "I'm waiting for a friend."

The attendant nodded, went back to her work. The two others were either on the phone or inputting data into a computer workstation. Another phone rang and the woman who'd smiled at Annaka, picked up the receiver, spoke into it for a moment, then, astonishingly, beckoned her over.

When Annaka approached the bank, the attendant said, "Miss Vadas. Dr. Morintz is expecting you." She glanced briefly at Annaka's driver's license, then handed her a white plastic ID tag. "Please wear that at all times, Miss Vadas. The doctor is waiting for you in his laboratory."

She pointed the way and Annaka, baffled, followed her direction down a corridor. At the first T-junction, she turned left and ran right into a man in a white lab coat.

"Oh, excuse me! What . . . ?" She'd looked up to see Jason Bourne's face. On his lab coat was a green plastic ID tag with the name Dr. Lenz Morintz printed on it, and she started to laugh. "Oh, I see, a pleasure to meet you, Dr. Morintz." She squinted. "Even though you don't look all that much like your photo."

"You know how those cheap cameras are," Bourne said, taking her by the elbow and leading her back to the corner she'd just turned. "They never do you justice." Peering around the corner, he said, "Here comes the CIA, right on schedule."

Annaka saw Kevin McColl showing his credentials to one of the attendants. "How'd he get his gun past the metal detector?" she asked.

"He didn't," Bourne said. "Why d'you think I directed you here?"

Despite herself, she looked at him with admiration. "A trap. McColl's here without a gun." He was clever indeed, and this realization caused her a spark of concern. She hoped Stepan knew what he was doing.

"Look, I discovered that Schiffer's former partner, Peter Sido, works here. If anyone knows where Schiffer is, it's Sido. We need to speak with him, but first we've got to take care of McColl once and for all. Are you ready?"

Annaka took a second look at McColl and, shuddering, nodded in assent.

Khan had used a taxi to tail the battered green Opel; he hadn't wanted to use the rental Skoda in case it had been made. He waited for Kevin McColl to pull into a parking space, then he had the taxi go past, and when the CIA agent got out of his Opel, he paid the driver and started after the other on foot.

Last evening, following McColl from Annaka's, he had called Ethan Hearn and read him off the license plate of the green Opel. Within the hour Hearn had gotten him the name and number of the rental car location McColl had used. Posing as an Interpol agent, he'd obtained from the suitably cowed attendant, McColl's name and address in the States. He hadn't left a local address, but as it had turned out, with typical American arrogance, he'd used his real name. It had been a simple matter, then, for Khan to call another number, where a contact of his in Berlin had run McColl's name through his data banks and come up with CIA.

Up ahead, McColl turned the corner onto Hattyu utca, entering a modern gray stone building at 75 that had more than a passing resemblance to a medieval fortress. It was fortunate that Khan waited a moment, as was his habit, because just then McColl ducked out. Khan watched him, curious, as he went to a trash bin. Looking around to make sure no one was paying him any attention, he drew out his gun, placed it quickly and carefully into the bin.

Khan waited until McColl had returned inside, then continued on, passing through the steel and glass door into the lobby. There, he observed McColl throwing around his Agency credentials. Observing the metal detector, Khan realized why McColl had gotten rid of his weapon. Was it coincidence or had Bourne set a trap for him? It's what Khan himself would've done.

As McColl was given an ID tag and went down the corridor, Khan passed through the metal detector, showed the Interpol ID he'd picked up in Paris. This, of course, alarmed the attendant, especially after seeing the Agency man, and she wondered aloud whether she should either alert the clinic's security or call the police, but Khan calmly assured her that they were on the same case and were only here for interview purposes. Any interruption in that process, he warned her sternly, could only lead to unforseen complications, which he knew she didn't want. Still slightly nervous, she nodded and waved him through.

Kevin McColl saw Annaka Vadas up ahead and knew that Bourne had to be close by. He was certain she hadn't made him, but in any event he fingered the small plastic square attached to the wristband of his watch. Inside was a length of nylon line retracted onto a tiny reel hidden within the plastic housing. He'd have preferred to complete the Bourne sanction with a gun because it was quick and clean. The human body, no matter how powerful, couldn't fight off a bullet to the heart or lungs or brain. Other methods using surprise and brute force, which the presence of the metal detector was forcing him into using, took longer and were more often than not messy. He understood the increased risk, as well as the possibility that he would have to kill Annaka Vadas as well. That thought alone caused him a pang of regret. She was a handsome, sexy woman; it went against the grain to kill such beauty.

He saw her now, headed he was quite sure toward a rendezvous with Jason Bourne; there was no other reason he could imagine for her to be here. He hung back, tapping the plastic square lying against the inside of his wrist as he waited for his opportunity.

From his position inside a supply room, Bourne saw Annaka pass by. She knew precisely where he was, but to her credit she didn't even turn her head a fraction as she passed his vantage point. His keen ears detected McColl's tread before he even came into view. Everyone had a way of walking, a certain stride that unless they deliberately altered it became unmistakable. McColl's was heavy and solid, ominous, without doubt the gait of a professional stalker.

The primary issue here, Bourne knew, was timing. If he moved too quickly, McColl would see him and react, negating the element of surprise. If he waited too long, he'd be forced to take a couple of steps to catch up to him and would risk McColl hearing him. But Bourne had taken the measure of McColl's strides and so was able to accurately anticipate when the CIA assassin would be in just the right spot. He pushed from his mind the aches and pains in his body, most especially his cracked ribs. He had no idea what a handicap they would place on him, but he had to be confident in the triple binding Dr. Ambrus had used to protect them.

He could see Kevin McColl now, large and dangerous. Just as the agent passed the partly open door to the supply room, Bourne leaped out and delivered a massive two-handed blow to McColl's right kidney. The agent's body canted over toward Bourne, who grabbed him and began to drag him into the supply room.

But McColl whirled and, with a grimace of pain, exploded a massive fist into Bourne's chest. Pain pinwheeled and, as Bourne staggered back, McColl drew out the nylon line, lunging at Bourne's neck. Bourne used the edge of his hand to land two fierce blows that must have caused McColl a great deal of pain. Still, he came on with reddened eyes and a grim determination. He looped the nylon line around Bourne's neck, pulled so tight that for the first instant Bourne was lifted off his feet.

Bourne fought for breath, which only allowed McColl to tighten the line further. Then Bourne realized his mistake. He ceased to worry about breathing, concentrating on freeing himself. His knee came up, making sharp contact with McColl's genitals. All the breath went out of McColl, and for an instant his grip loosened enough for Bourne to get two fingers between the nylon line and the flesh of his throat.

McColl, though, was a bull of a man, and he recovered more quickly than Bourne could've imagined. With a grunt of rage, he drew all his energy into his arms, jerking the nylon line more tightly than ever. But Bourne had managed to gain the advantage he needed, and his two fingers curled, twisting as the line tightened, and it snapped just as a powerful fish can exert enough torque to break the line on which it's caught.

Bourne used the hand that had been at his neck to strike out and up, catching McColl under the jaw. McColl's head snapped back against the doorjamb, but as Bourne closed with him, he used his elbows, spinning Bourne into the supply room. McColl came after him, snatched up a box cutter, swung with it, slicing through the lab coat. Another swipe and, though Bourne leaped back, the blade cut into his shirt so that it hung open, revealing his bound ribs.

A grin of triumph lit up McColl's face. He knew a vulnerability when he saw it, and he went after it. Switching the box cutter to his left hand, he feinted with it, then lowered a massive blow toward Bourne's rib cage. Bourne wasn't fooled and was able to block the blow with his forearm.

Now McColl saw his opening and swung in with the box cutter, directly toward Bourne's exposed neck.

Having heard the first sounds of engagement, Annaka had turned, but she'd immediately spotted two doctors coming toward the junction in the corridor beyond which Bourne and McColl were locked together. Neatly interposing herself between them and the doctors, she asked the doctors a barrage of questions, all the while moving them along until they were past the junction.

Extricating herself as quickly as she could, she hurried back. By that time she saw that Bourne was in trouble. Remembering Stepan's admonishment to keep Bourne alive, she rushed back down the corridor. By the time she arrived, the two combatants were already inside the supply room. She swung in through the open door just in time to see McColl's vicious attack at Bourne's neck.

She hurled herself at him, knocking him off stride just enough so that the box cutter blade, flashing in the light, flew by Bourne's neck, sparking off the metal corner of a shelf stanchion. McColl, aware of her now in the periphery of his vision, whirled, his left elbow high and cocked, and he smashed it back into her throat.

Annaka gagged, reflexively grabbed at her neck as she began to sink down onto her knees. McColl came at her with the box cutter, slashing at her coat. Bourne took the length of nylon still gripped in one hand and lashed it around McColl's neck from behind.

McColl arched back, but instead of grasping for his throat, he jammed an elbow into Bourne's cracked ribs. Bourne saw stars, but still he held on, inching McColl backward, away from Annaka, hearing his heels dragging on the floor tiles as McColl flailed at his ribs with ever-increasing desperation.

The blood pooled in McColl's head, the cords stood out on the sides of his neck like taut ropes, and soon thereafter, his eyes began to bulge in their sockets. Blood vessels burst in his nose and cheeks and his lips pulled back from his pallid gums. His swollen tongue swirled around his gasping mouth, and still he had it in him to deliver one last blow to Bourne's side. Bourne winced, his grip faltered slightly, and McColl began to regain his balance.

That's when Annaka recklessly kicked him in the stomach. McColl grabbed her raised knee and, twisting violently, brought her back against him. His left arm whipped around her neck, the heel of his right hand positioned itself against the side of her head. He was about to break her neck.

Khan, observing all this from the vantage point of the small darkened office across and slightly down the corridor, watched Bourne, at great risk to himself, let go of the nylon cord he'd so expertly wrapped around McColl's neck. He slammed the assassin's head against a shelf, then drove a thumb into his eye.

McColl, about to scream, found Bourne's forearm between his jaws, and so the sound rattled in his lungs, dying inside him. He kicked out and flailed, refusing to die or even to go down. Bourne withdrew his ceramic gun, smashed the butt into the soft spot over McColl's left ear. Now he was on his knees, his head shaking, his hands moving to press themselves tightly to his ruined eye. But it was only a ruse. He used his hands to trip Annaka, to bring her down to his level. His murderous hands grasped her, and Bourne, without any other recourse, pressed the muzzle of the gun against McColl's flesh and pulled the trigger.

There was very little noise, but the hole in McColl's neck was impressive. Even dead, McColl wouldn't let go of Annaka, and Bourne, putting away the gun, was obliged to pry his fingers one by one off her flesh.

Bourne reached down, pulled her up, but Khan could see his grimace, saw one hand press against his side. Those ribs. Were they bruised, broken, or something in between? he wondered.

Khan moved back into the shadows of the empty office. He'd caused that injury. He could remember in vivid detail the power he'd put behind the blow, the feel of his hand as it made contact, the almost electric jarring that had passed through him, as if from Bourne. But, curiously, the feeling of hot satisfaction never materialized. Instead, he was forced to admire the strength and tenacity of the man to hold on, to continue his titanic struggle with McColl, despite the beating he was taking in his most vulnerable spot.

Why was he even thinking these thoughts? he asked himself angrily. Bourne had done nothing but reject him. In the face of mounting evidence, he adamantly refused to believe that Khan was his son. What did that say about him? For whatever reason, he'd chosen to believe that his son was dead. Didn't that mean that he'd never wanted him in the first place?

"The support staff arrived just a few hours ago," Jamie Hull said to the DCI over their secure video linkup. "We've familiarized them with everything. All that's lacking is the principals."

"The president's in the air even as we speak," the DCI said as he waved Martin Lindros to a seat. "In approximately five hours, twenty minutes from now, the President of the United States will be on Icelandic soil. I hope to Christ you're ready for him."

"Absolutely I am, sir. We all are."

"Excellent." But his frown deepened as he glanced down at the notes on his desktop. "Give me an update on how you're handling Comrade Karpov?"

"Not to worry," Hull said. "I have the Boris situation under control."

"That's a relief. Relations between the president and his Russian counterpart are strained as it is. You've no idea what blood, sweat and tears it took to persuade Aleksandr Yevtushenko to come to the table. Can you imagine the blowup if he hears you and his top security man are ready to slit each other's throats?"

"It'll never happen, sir."

"Damned straight," the DCI growled. "Keep me informed 24-7."

"Will do, sir," Hull said, signing off.

The DCI swiveled around, ran his hand through his shock of white hair. "We're in the final stretch, Martin. Does it pain you as much as it pains me to be stuck here behind a desk while Hull is taking care of business in the field?"

"It does, indeed, sir." Lindros, keeping his secret close to the vest for all this time, almost lost his nerve then, but duty won out over compassion. He didn't want to wound the Old Man, no matter how badly he'd been treated recently.

He cleared his throat. "Sir, I've just come from seeing Randy Driver."

"And?"

Lindros took a deep breath and told the Old Man what Driver had confessed, that Conklin had brought Dr. Felix Schiffer over to the Agency from DARPA for his own dark and unknown reasons, that he had deliberately "disappeared" Schiffer and that now that Conklin was dead no one knew where Schiffer was.

The Old Man's fist slammed down on his desk. "Sweet Christ, to have one of our directorate scientists gone missing with the summit about to start is a catastrophe of the first rank. If the bitch-woman should get wind of this, it'll be my ass in a sling, no ifs, ands or buts."

For a moment nothing stirred in the vast corner office. The photos of world leaders past and present looked back at the two men with mute rebuke.

At last the DCI stirred. "Are you saying that Alex Conklin stole a scientist out from under DOD's nose and stashed him with us so he could whisk him away to God knows where and for what unknown purpose?"

Lindros, folding his hands in his lap, said nothing, but he knew better than to move his gaze away from the Old Man's.

"Well, that's . . . I mean to say, we don't do that in the Agency, and most especially Alexander Conklin wouldn't do that. He would be breaking every rule in the playbook."

Lindros stirred, thinking of his research in the top-secret Four-Zero Archives. "He did it often enough in the field, sir. You know that."

Indeed, the DCI did, only too well. "This is different," he protested. "This happened here at home. It's a personal affront to the Agency, and to me." The Old Man shook his craggy head. "I refuse to believe it, Martin. Goddammit, there must be another explanation!"

Lindros held firm. "You know there isn't. I'm truly sorry to have been the one to bring you this news, sir."

At that moment the Old Man's secretary entered the room, handed him a slip of paper, and went out. The DCI unfolded the note.

"Your wife would like to speak with you," he read. *"She says it's important."*

He crumpled the note, then looked up. "Of course there's another explanation. Jason Bourne."

"Sir?"

The DCI looked straight at Lindros and said bleakly, "This is Bourne's doing, not Alex's. It's the only explanation that makes sense."

"For the record, I think you're wrong, sir," Lindros said, gathering himself for the uphill battle. "With all due respect, I think you've allowed your personal friendship with Alex Conklin to cloud your judgment. After studying the Four-Zero files, I believe that no one alive was closer to Conklin than Jason Bourne, even you."

A Cheshire cat smile spread across the DCI's face. "Oh, you're right about that one, Martin. And it's because Bourne knew Alex so well that he was able to capitalize on Alex's involvement with this Dr. Schiffer. Believe me, Bourne smelled something and he went after it."

"There's no proof—"

"Ah, but there is." The DCI shifted in his chair. "As it happens, I know where Bourne is."

"Sir?" Lindros fairly goggled at him.

"106–108 Fo utca," the DCI read off a slip of paper. "That's in Budapest." The DCI threw his deputy a hard look. "Didn't you tell me that the gun used to murder Alex and Mo Panov was paid for out of an account in Budapest?"

Lindros' heart contracted. "Yes, sir."

The DCI nodded. "That's why I gave this address to Kevin McColl."

Lindros' face went white. "Oh, Christ. I want to talk to McColl."

"I feel your pain, Martin, really I do." The DCI nodded toward the phone. "Call him if you like, but you know McColl's record for efficiency. Chances are Bourne is already dead."

Bourne kicked the door to the supply room closed, stripped off the bloody lab coat. He was about to drop it over the corpse of Kevin McColl when he noticed a small LED light blinking at McColl's hip. His cell phone. Squatting down, he picked it out of its plastic holster, opened it up. He saw the number and knew who was calling. Rage filled his heart.

Opening the connection, he said to the DCI, "Keep this up and you'll be paying the undertakers overtime."

"Bourne!" Lindros cried. "Wait!"

But he didn't wait. Instead, he threw the cell phone so hard against the wall it split open like an oyster.

Annaka watched him carefully. "An old enemy?"

"An old fool," Bourne growled, retrieving his leather jacket. He grunted involuntarily as the pain struck him a hammer blow.

"It appears that McColl gave you quite a beating," Annaka said.

Bourne slipped on his jacket with its white visitor's ID tag in order to cover his slit shirt. His mind was completely focused on finding Dr. Sido. "And what about you? How badly did McColl hurt you?"

She refused to rub the red welt at her throat. "Don't worry about me."

"We won't worry about each other, then," Bourne said as he took a bottle of cleaner from the shelf and, using a rag, wiped the blood stains off her coat as best he could. "We've got to get to Dr. Sido as quickly as possible. Dr. Morintz is bound to be missed sooner or later."

"Where's Sido?"

"In the Epidemiological Wing." He gestured. "Come on."

He peered around the doorjamb, checking to make sure no one was around. As they emerged into the corridor, he registered that an office door across the way was partially open. He took a step toward it but heard voices approaching from that direction and he hurried them away. He needed a moment to reorient himself, then he took them through a set of swinging doors into the Epidemiological Wing.

"Sido's in 902," he said, scanning the numbers on the doors they passed.

The wing was in actuality a square with an open space in its center. Doors to labs and offices were set at intervals along the four walls, the only exception being a barred metal exit door, locked from the outside which was in the center of the far wall. Obviously the Epidemiological Wing was at the back of the clinic because it was clear from the markings on the small storerooms to either side that the door was used to remove hazardous medical waste.

"There's his lab," Bourne said, hurrying ahead.

Annaka, just behind him, saw the fire alarm box on the wall ahead of her, precisely where Stepan said it would be. As she came abreast of it, she lifted the glass. Bourne was knocking on the door to Sido's lab. Receiving no answer, he opened the door. Just as he stepped into Dr. Sido's lab, Annaka pulled down the handle and the fire alarm went off.

The wing was suddenly filled with people. Three members of the clinic's security force appeared; it was obvious that these were extremely efficient people. Bourne, desperate now, looked around Sido's empty office. He noticed a mug half-filled with coffee, the computer screen lit with a screen saver. He pressed the "Escape" key, and the upper part of the screen filled with a complex chemical equation. The lower half had the following legend: "Product must be kept at −32 degrees Celsius as it is extremely fragile. Heat of any kind renders it instantly inert." Through the mounting chaos, Bourne was thinking furiously. Though Dr. Sido wasn't here, he had been here not long ago. All evidence pointed to him having left in a hurry.

At that moment Annaka rushed in and pulled at him. "Jason, the clinic's security is asking questions, checking everyone's ID. We've got to get out of here now." She led him to the doorway. "If we can make it to the rear exit, we can escape that way."

Out in the open space of the wing, chaos reigned. The alarm had triggered sprays of water. As there was a great deal of flammable material in the labs, including oxygen tanks, the staff was understandably panicking. Security, trying to get a grip on who was present, was having to deal with calming the clinic's personnel.

Bourne and Annaka were heading toward the metal exit door when Bourne saw Khan working his way through the stampeding crowd toward them. Bourne grabbed Annaka, interposed himself between her and the oncoming Khan. What was Khan's intention, he wondered. Did he mean to kill them or to intercept them? Did he expect Bourne to tell him everything he'd discovered about Felix Schiffer and the biochemical diffuser? But no, there was something different about Khan's expression, some clockwork calculation that was missing.

"Listen to me!" Khan said, trying to make himself heard above the noise. "Bourne, you've got to listen to me!"

But Bourne, herding Annaka, had reached the metal exit door and, crashing through it, hurtled into the alley behind the clinic, where a HAZ-MAT truck was parked. Six men armed with machine-guns stood in front of it. Bourne, instantly recognizing it as a trap, turned and instinctively shouted at Khan, who was coming on behind him.

Annaka, swinging around, saw Khan at last and ordered two of the men to open fire. But Khan, heeding Bourne's warning, leaped aside a split-second before the hail of bullets mowed down the clinic's security detail that had come to investigate. Now all hell broke loose inside the clinic, as staff ran, screaming, through the swinging doors, down the corridor toward the front entrance.

Two of the men grabbed Bourne from behind. He whirled, engaging them.

"Find him," he heard Annaka shout. "Find Khan and kill him!"

"Annaka, what—"

Bourne, stunned, watched the pair that had fired race past him, leaping over the wreckage of the bullet-ridden bodies.

Bourne, pushing himself to action, smashed one man in the face, putting him down, but another took his place.

"Careful," Annaka warned. "He's got a gun!"

One of the men shackled Bourne's arms behind his back while a second scrabbled for the weapon. He wrestled free, chopped down hard, breaking his would-be captor's nose. Blood gushed and the man fell back, his hands cupping the center of his ruined face.

"What the hell are you doing?"

Then Annaka, armed with a machine pistol, stepped in, slammed him hard with its thick butt in his cracked ribs. All the breath went out of him and he canted over, losing his balance. His knees were like rubber and the agony that racked him was for a moment unbearable. Then they'd grabbed hold of him. One man punched him in the side of the head. Bourne sagged again in their arms.

The two men returned from their recon of the clinic wing. "No sign of him," they reported to Annaka.

"No matter," she said, and pointed to the man writhing on the ground. "Get him into the vehicle. Hurry now!"

She turned back to Bourne, saw the man with the broken nose was pressing a gun to the side of Bourne's head. His eyes blazed with fury and he seemed intent on pulling the trigger.

Annaka said calmly but firmly. "Put the gun down. He's to be taken alive." She stared at him, not moving a muscle. "Spalko's orders. You know that." At length the man put the gun up.

"All right," she said. "Into the truck."

Bourne stared at her, his mind was ablaze with her betrayal.

Smirking, Annaka held out a hand and one of the men handed her a hypodermic filled with a clear liquid. With a swift and sure motion, she emptied the hypodermic into Bourne's vein, and slowly his eyes lost focus.

CHAPTER TWENTY-FIVE

Hasan Arsenov had put Zina in charge of the physical aspect of the cadre, as if she were a stylist. She took her orders seriously as she always did, though not without a private snicker of cynicism. Like a planet to a sun, she was aligned with the Shaykh now. As was her way, she had mentally and emotionally removed herself from Hasan's orbit. It had begun that night in Budapest—though, in truth, the seeds must have been planted earlier—and had come to fruition under the burning sun of Crete. She clove to their time together on the Mediterranean island as if it were her own private legend, one she shared only with him. They'd been—what?—Theseus and Ariadne. The Shaykh had recounted the myth of the Minotaur's terrible life and bloody death to her. Together, she and the Shaykh had entered a real-life labyrinth and triumphed. In the fever of these newly precious memories, it never occurred to her that this was a Western myth in which she had inserted herself, that in aligning herself with Stepan Spalko, she had moved away from Islam, which had nurtured her, raised her like a second mother, had been her succor, her only solace in the dark days of the Russian occupation. It never occurred to her that to embrace one, she had to let go of the other. And even if it had, with her cynic's nature, she might have made the same choice.

Because of her knowledge and diligence the men of the cadre that arrived in twilit Keflavik Airport were clean-shaven, barbered in the European style, dressed in dark Western business suits, so bland they made themselves virtually anonymous. The women were without traditional *khidzhab*, the scarf that covered their faces. Their bare faces were made up in the European style and they were clothed in sleek Parisian fashions. They passed through Immigration without incident, using the false identities and forged French passports Spalko had provided.

Now, as Arsenov had ordered, they were careful to speak only Icelandic, even when they were alone together. At one of the rental companies counters in the terminal, Arsenov rented one car and three vans for the cadre, which was composed of six men and four women. While Arsenov and Zina took the car into Reykjavik, the rest of the cadre drove the vans south of the city to the town of Hafnarfjördur, the oldest trading port in Iceland, where Spalko had rented a large clapboard house on a cliff overlooking the harbor. The colorful village of small, quaint clapboard houses was surrounded on the land side by lava flows, filled with mist and a sense of being lost in time. It was possible to imagine among the brightly painted fishing boats lying side by side in the harbor war-shield-bedecked Viking longships readying themselves for their next bloody campaign.

Arsenov and Zina drove through Reykjavik, familiarizing themselves with the streets they'd previously seen only on maps, getting a sense of traffic and travel patterns. The city was picturesque, built on a peninsula so that it was possible to see the white snow-encrusted mountains or the piercing blue-black North Atlantic ocean from almost any place you stood. The island itself was created from the shift of tectonic plates as the American and Eurasian landmasses pulled apart. Because of the relative youth of the island, the crust was thinner than on either of the surrounding continents, which accounted for the remarkable abundance of geothermal activity used to heat Icelandic homes. The entire city was connected to the Reykjavik Energy hot water pipeline.

In City Centre, they cruised past the modern and peculiarly unsettling Hallgrimskirkja Church, looking like a rocket ship out of science fiction. It was by far the tallest structure in what was otherwise a low-rise city. They found the health services building and drove from there to the Oskjuhlid Hotel.

"You're sure this is the route they'll take?" Zina said.

"Absolutely." Arsenov nodded. "It's the shortest way and they'll want to get to the hotel as quickly as possible."

The hotel's periphery was teeming with American, Arab and Russian security.

"They've turned it into a fortress," Zina said.

"Just as the Shaykh's photos showed us," Arsenov replied with a small smile. "How much personnel they have makes no difference to us."

They parked and went from shop to shop, making their various purchases. Arsenov had been far happier inside the metal shell of their rented
car. Mingling with the crowds, he was acutely aware of his own alienness.
How different these slim, light-skinned, blue-eyed people were! With his
black hair and eyes, his big bones and swarthy skin, he felt as graceless as a
Neanderthal among Cro-Magnons. Zina, he discovered, had no such difficulties. She took to new places, new people, new ideas with a frightening
zeal. He worried about her, worried about her influence on the children
they would one day have.

Twenty minutes after the operation at the rear of the Eurocenter Bio-I
Clinic, Khan still wondered when he'd ever felt more strongly the urge to
retaliate against an enemy. Even though he'd been outmanned and outgunned, even though the rational part of his mind—usually so in control
of every action he took—understood all too well the foolhardiness of
launching a counterattack against the men Spalko had sent to get him and
Jason Bourne, another part of him had been determined to fight back.
Strangely, it was Bourne's warning that had brought out in him the irra-
tional desire to hurl himself into the pitched battle and rend Spalko's men
limb from limb. It was a feeling that came from the very core of him, and
so powerful was it that it had taken all his rational willpower to pull back,
to hide from the men Annaka had sent in to find him. He could have taken
those two down, but of what use would it have been? Annaka would only
have sent more of them in for him.

He was sitting in Grendel, a café about a mile from the clinic, which was
now crawling with police and, probably, Interpol agents. He sipped at his
double espresso and thought about the primal feeling in which he still felt
gripped. Once again, he saw the look of concern on Jason Bourne's face
when he saw Khan about to step into the trap in which he was already ensnared. As if he'd been more concerned with keeping Khan out of danger
than with his own safety. But that was impossible, wasn't it?

Khan was not in the habit of replaying recent scenarios, but he found
himself doing so now. As Bourne and Annaka had headed for the exit, he'd
tried to warn Bourne about her, but he'd been too late. What had motivated
him to do that? Certainly, he hadn't planned on it. It was a spur-of-the-

moment decision. Or was it? He recalled, with a vividness he found unsettling, his feeling when he'd seen the damage he'd done to Bourne's ribs. Had it been remorse? Impossible!

It was maddening. The thought would not let him be: the moment when Bourne had made the choice between staying safe behind the deadly creature McColl had become or putting himself in harm's way in order to protect Annaka. Up until that moment, he'd been trying to reconcile the notion of David Webb, college professor, being Jason Bourne, international assassin, of being in his line of work. But no assassin he could think of would have endangered himself to protect Annaka.

Who, then, was Jason Bourne?

He shook his head, annoyed at himself. This was a question, though maddening, that he needed to put aside for the time being. At last he understood why Spalko had called him while he was in Paris. He'd been given a test and, to Spalko's way of thinking, he'd failed. Spalko now thought of Khan as an imminent threat to him, just as he thought of Bourne as a threat. For Khan, Spalko had become the enemy. All his life, Khan had only one way of dealing with enemies: He eliminated them. He was very well aware of the danger; he welcomed it as a challenge. Spalko was certain he could defeat Khan. How could Spalko know that that arrogance would only make him burn all the brighter?

Khan drained his small cup and, flipping open his cell phone, punched in a number.

"I was just about to call you but I wanted to wait until I was out of the building," Ethan Hearn said. "Something's up."

Khan checked his watch. It wasn't yet five. "What, exactly?"

"About two minutes ago I saw a HAZMAT truck approaching and I got down to the basement in time to see two men and a woman bringing a man in on a stretcher."

"That woman will be Annaka Vadas," Khan said.

"She's quite the stunner."

"Listen to me, Ethan," Khan said forcefully, "if you run into her, be very careful. She's as dangerous as they come."

"Too bad," Hearn mused.

"No one saw you?" Khan wanted to get him off the subject of Annaka Vadas.

"No," Hearn said. "I was quite careful about that."

"Good." Khan thought a moment. "Can you find out where they took this man? I mean the exact location?"

"I already know. I watched the elevator when they took him up. He's somewhere on the fourth floor. That's Spalko's personal level; it's accessed only with a magnetic key."

"Can you get it?" Khan asked.

"Impossible. He keeps it on his person at all times."

"I'll have to find another way," Khan said.

"I thought magnetic keys were foolproof."

Khan laughed shortly. "Only a fool believes that. There's always a way into a locked room, Ethan, just as there's always a way out."

Khan rose, threw some money on the table, and walked out of the café. Right now he was loath to stay in one place for too long. "Speaking of which, I need a way into Humanistas."

"There are any number—"

"I have reason to believe Spalko is expecting me." Khan crossed the street, his eyes alert for anyone who might be watching him.

"That's a completely different story," Hearn said. There was a pause as he considered the problem, then: "Wait a minute, hang on. Let me look in my PDA. I might have something.

"Okay, I'm back." Hearn gave a little laugh. "I *do* have something, and I think you're going to like it.

Arsenov and Zina arrived at the house ninety minutes after the others. By that time, the cadre had changed into jeans and workshirts and had pulled the van into the large garage. While the women took charge of the bags of food Arsenov and Zina had bought, the men opened the box of hand weapons waiting for them and helped set up the spray-painters.

Arsenov took out the photos Spalko had given him and they set about spray-painting the van the proper color of an official government vehicle. While the van was drying, they drove the second van into the garage. Using a stencil, they spray-painted *Hafnarfjördur Fine Fruits & Vegetables* onto both sides of the vehicle.

Then they went into the house, which was already perfumed by the meal the women had prepared. Before sitting down to eat, they commenced their prayers. Zina, excitement buzzing through her like an electrical current, was barely present, praying to Allah by rote while she thought of the Shaykh and her role in the triumph that was now only a day away.

At dinner the conversation was spirited, a flux of tension and anticipation animating them. Arsenov, who normally frowned on such loose behavior, allowed this outlet for their nerves, but only for a contained amount of time. Leaving the women to clean up, he led the men back down to the garage, where they applied the official decals and markings to the sides and front of the van. They drove that outside, brought the third one in, spray-painted it the colors of Reykjavik Energy.

Afterward they were all exhausted and ready for sleep, for they would be rising very early. Still, Arsenov made them run through their parts of the plan, insisting they speak Icelandic. He wanted to see what effect mental fatigue would have on them. Not that he doubted them. All of his nine compatriots had long ago proven themselves to him. They were physically strong, mentally tough and, perhaps most important of all, completely without remorse or compunction. However, none of them had ever been involved in an operation of this size, scope or global ramifications; without the NX 20 they'd never had the wherewithal. And so it was particularly satisfying to watch them dredge up the necessary reserves of energy and stamina to run through their roles with flawless precision.

He congratulated them and then, as if they were his blood children, said to them with great love and affection in his heart, *"La illaha ill Allah."*

"La illaha ill Allah," they chorused in unison with such love burning in their eyes that Arsenov was moved close to tears. In this moment, as they searched one another's faces, the enormity of the task set before them was brought home to them. For Arsenov's part, he saw them all—his family—gathered together in a strange and forbidding land, on the brink of the most glorious moment their people would ever witness. Never had his sense of the future burned so brilliantly, never had his sense of purpose—the righteousness—of their cause been made so manifest to him. He was grateful for the presence of all of them.

As Zina was about to go upstairs, he put a hand on her arm, but as the others passed her, glancing at them, she shook her head. "I have to help them with the peroxide," she said, and he let her go.

"May Allah grant you a peaceful sleep," she said softly, mounting the stairs.

Later, Arsenov lay in bed unable, as usual, to sleep. Across from him, in the other narrow bed, Akhmed snored with the noise of a buzzsaw. A light wind ruffled the curtains of the open window; as a youth, Arsenov had grown used to the cold; now he liked it. He stared up at the ceiling, thinking as he always did in the dark hours of Khalid Murat, of his betrayal of his mentor and his friend. Despite the necessity of the assassination, his personal disloyalty continued to eat at him. And there was the wound in his leg, a pain no matter how well it was healing that acted as a goad. In the end he'd failed Khalid Murat, and nothing he could do now could change that fact.

He rose, went into the hallway and padded silently down the stairs. He'd slept in his clothes, as he always did. He went out into the chill night air, extracting a cigarette and lighting it. Low on the horizon a bloated moon sailed through the star-spangled sky. There were no trees; he heard no insects.

As he walked farther away from the house, his seething mind began to clear, to calm itself. Perhaps, after he'd finished the cigarette he'd even be able to catch a few hours of sleep before the three-thirty rendezvous with Spalko's boat.

He had almost finished his cigarette and was about to turn around when he heard the whisper of low voices. Startled, he drew his gun and looked around. The voices, drifting on the night air, were coming from behind a pair of enormous boulders that rose up like the horns of a monster from the top of the cliff's face.

Dropping his cigarette and grinding its lit end into the ground, he moved toward the rock formation. Though he used caution, he was fully prepared to empty his weapon into the hearts of whoever was spying on them.

But as he peered around the curving face of the rock, it wasn't infidels he saw but Zina. She was talking in low tones to another, larger figure, but from his angle Arsenov could not tell who it was. He moved slightly, drawing closer. He couldn't hear their words, but even before he noticed Zina's hand on the other's arm, he had recognized the voice she used when she was set on seducing him.

He pressed his fist to his temple as if to stop the sudden throbbing in his head. He wanted to scream as he watched the fingers of Zina's hand draw up into what looked to him like spider's legs, her nails scoring the forearm of . . . who was it she was trying to seduce? His jealousy goaded him to action. At the risk of being seen, he moved farther, part of him entering the moonlight, until the face of Magomet came into view.

Blind rage gripped him; he was shaking all over. He thought of his mentor. What would Khalid Murat have done? he asked himself. Doubtless, he would have confronted the pair, heard their separate explanations of what they were doing and then made his judgment accordingly.

Arsenov stood up to his full height and, advancing on the pair, held his right arm out straight in front of him. Magomet, who was more or less turned facing him, saw him and abruptly stepped back, severing the hold Zina had on him. His mouth opened wide, but in his shock and terror, nothing came out.

"Magomet, what is it?" Zina said and, turning, saw Arsenov advancing on them.

"Hasan, no!" she cried just as Arsenov pulled the trigger.

The bullet entered Magomet's open mouth and blew the back of his head off. He was thrown backward in a welter of blood and brains.

Arsenov turned the gun on Zina. Yes, he thought, Khalid Murat would surely have handled the situation differently, but Khalid Murat was dead and he, Hasan Arsenov, the architect of Murat's demise, was alive and in charge, and this was why. It was a new world.

"Now you," he said.

Staring into his black eyes, she knew that he wanted her to grovel, to get down on her knees and beg him for mercy. He could care less about any explanation she might give him. She knew that he was beyond reason; at this moment he wouldn't know the truth from a clever concoction. She also knew that giving him what he wanted at the moment he wanted it was a trap, a slippery slope once embarked upon impossible to get off. There was only one way to stop him in his tracks.

Her eyes blazed. "Stop it!" she ordered. "Right now!" Reaching out, she closed her fingers around the barrel of the gun, drew it upward so that it was no longer pointed at her head. She risked a quick glance at the dead Magomet. That was a mistake she wouldn't make twice.

"What's come over you?" she said. "So close to our shared goal, have you lost your mind?"

She was clever to have reminded Arsenov of their reason for being in Reykjavik. For the moment, his devotion to her had blinded him to the larger goal. All he'd reacted to was her voice and her hand on Magomet's arm.

With a ragged motion, he put the gun away.

"Now what will we do?" she said. "Who'll take over Magomet's responsibilities?"

"You caused this," he said with disgust. "You figure it out."

"Hasan." She knew better than to try to touch him at this moment or even to come closer than she already was. "You are our leader. It's your decision and yours alone."

He looked around, as if just coming out of a trance. "I suspect our neighbors will assume the report of the gunshot was merely a truck backfiring." He stared at her. "Why were you out here with him?"

"I was trying to dissuade him from the path he'd chosen," Zina said carefully. "Something happened to him when I shaved his beard on the plane. He made overtures."

Arsenov's eyes blazed anew. "And what was your response?"

"What d'you imagine it was, Hasan?" she said, her hard voice matching his. "Are you saying that you don't trust me?"

"I saw your hand on him, your fingers. . . ." He could not go on.

"Hasan, look at me." She reached out. "Please look at me."

He turned slowly, reluctantly, and elation rose inside her. She had him; despite her error in judgment, she still had him.

Breathing an inaudible sigh of relief, she said, "The situation required some delicacy. Surely you can understand that. If I turned him down flat, if I was cold to him, if I angered him, I was afraid of a reprisal. I was afraid his anger would impair his use to us." Her eyes held his. "Hasan, I was thinking of the reason we're here. That's my only focus now, as it should be yours."

He stood immobile for long moments, absorbing her words. The hiss and suck of the waves spending themselves against the cliffs far below seemed unnaturally loud. Then, abruptly, he nodded and the incident was swept away. That was his way.

"All that remains is to dispose of Magomet."

"We'll wrap him up and take him with us to the rendezvous. The boat crew can dispose of him in deep water."

Arsenov laughed. "Zina, really, you're the most pragmatic female I know."

Bourne awoke to find himself strapped into what appeared to be a dentist's chair. He looked around the black concrete room, saw the large drain in the center of the white tile floor, the hose coiled on the wall, the tiered cart beside the chair on which were arrayed ranks of gleaming stainless-steel implements, all, it seemed, designed to inflict agonizing damage to the human body, and was not reassured. He tried to move his wrists and ankles, but the wide leather straps were secured, he noted, with the same buckles used on straitjackets.

"You can't get out," Annaka said, coming around from behind him. "It's useless to try."

Bourne stared at her for a moment, as if he was struggling to bring her into focus. She was dressed in white leather pants and a black sleeveless silk blouse with a plunging neckline, an outfit she never would have worn while she was playing the role of the innocent classical pianist and devoted daughter. He cursed himself for being gulled by her initial antipathy toward him. He should've known better. She was too available, too conveniently knowledgeable about Molnar's building. Hindsight was useless, however, and he put aside his disappointment in himself and applied himself to the difficult situation at hand.

"What an actress you turned out to be," he said.

A slow smile broadened her lips, and when she parted them slightly, he could see her white, even teeth. "Not only with you but with Khan." She drew up the single chair in the room and sat down close beside him. "You see, I know him well, your son. Oh, yes, I know, Jason. I know more than you think, much more than you do." She gave a little laugh, a tinkling, bell-like sound of pure delight as she drank in the expression on Bourne's face. "For a long time Khan didn't know whether you were alive or dead. Indeed, he made a number of attempts to find you, always unsuccessful—your CIA had done an excellent job of hiding you—until Stepan helped him. But even before he knew you were, in fact, alive, he'd spent all his idle hours concocting elaborate ways in which he'd seek his revenge on you." She nodded. "Yes, Jason, his hatred for you was all-encompassing." Putting her elbows on her knees, she leaned toward him. "How does that make you feel?"

"I applaud your performances." Despite the potent emotions she had dredged from him, he was determined not to rise outwardly to her bait.

Annaka made a moue. "I'm a woman of many talents."

"And as many loyalties, it seems." He shook his head. "Did our saving each other's lives mean nothing to you?"

She sat back up, her manner brisk now, almost businesslike. "You and I can agree on these things, at least. Often life and death are the only things that matter."

"Then free me," he said.

"Yes, I've fallen head over heels for you, Jason." She laughed. "That's not the way things work in real life. I saved you for one reason only: Stepan."

His brow was furrowed in concentration. "How can you let this happen?"

"How can I not? I have a history with Stepan. For a time he was the only friend my mother had."

Bourne was surprised. "Spalko and your mother knew each other?"

Annaka nodded. Now that he was bound and presented no danger to her, she seemed to want to talk. Bourne was rightfully suspicious of this.

"He met her after my father had her sent away," Annaka continued.

"Sent away where?" Bourne was intrigued despite himself. She could charm the venom out of a snake.

"To a sanatorium." Annaka's eyes darkened, revealing in a flash a trace of genuine feeling. "He had her committed. It wasn't difficult; she was physically frail, unable to fight him. In those days . . . yes, it was still possible."

"Why would he do such a thing? I don't believe you," Bourne said flatly.

"I don't care whether you believe me or not." She contemplated him for a moment with the disturbing aspect of a reptile. Then, possibly because she needed to, she went on. "She'd become an inconvenience. His mistress demanded it of him; in this he was abominably weak." The outpouring of naked hatred had transformed her face into an ugly mask, and Bourne understood that, at last, she had unleashed the truth about her past. "He never knew that I'd discovered the truth, and I never let on. *Never*." She tossed her head. "Anyway, Stepan was visiting the same asylum. In those days, he went to see his brother . . . the brother who'd tried to kill him."

Bourne stared at her, dumbfounded. He realized that he had no idea whether she was lying or telling the truth. He had been correct about one aspect of her, at least—she *was* at war. The parts she played so masterfully were her offensives, her raiding parties into enemy territory. He looked into her implacable eyes and knew that there was something monstrous about the way she chose to manipulate those she had drawn close to her.

She leaned in, took his chin between her thumb and fingers. "You haven't seen Stepan, have you? He's had extensive plastic surgery on the right side of his face and neck. What he tells people about it varies, but the truth is, his brother threw gasoline on him and then put a lighter to his face."

Bourne couldn't help but react. "My God. Why?"

She shrugged. "Who knows? The brother's dangerously insane. Stepan knew it, so for that matter did his father, but he refused to acknowledge it until it was too late. And even afterward, he continued to defend the boy, insisting that it was a tragic accident."

"All this might be true," he said. "But even if it is, it doesn't excuse you conspiring against your own father."

She laughed. "How can you, of all people, say that, when you and Khan have tried to kill each other? Such fury in two men, my God!"

"He came after me. I only defended myself."

"But he hates you, Jason, with a passion I've rarely seen. He hates you just as much as I hated my father. And d'you know why? Because you abandoned him as my father abandoned my mother."

"You're talking as if he's really my son," Bourne spat.

"Oh, yes, that's right, you've convinced yourself that he isn't. That's convenient, isn't it? That way you don't have to think about how you left him to die in the jungle."

"But I didn't!" Bourne knew he shouldn't let her drag him into this emotionally charged subject, but he couldn't help himself. "I was told he was dead. I had no idea he might've survived. That's what I discovered when I was inside government database."

"Did you stay around to look, to check? No, you buried your family without even looking in the coffins! If you had, you would've seen that your son wasn't there. No, you coward, you fled the country instead."

Bourne tried to pull himself out of his bonds. "That's rich, you lecturing me on family!"

"That's quite enough." Stepan Spalko had entered the room with the perfect timing of a ringmaster. "I have more important matters to discuss with Mr. Bourne than family sagas."

Annaka obediently stood up. She patted Bourne's cheek. "Don't look so sullen, Jason. You're not the first man I've fooled, and you won't be the last."

"No," he said. "Spalko will be the last."

"Annaka, leave us now," Spalko said, adjusting his butcher's apron with hands covered in Latex gloves. The apron was clean and well pressed. As yet, there wasn't a spot of blood on it.

As Annaka departed, Bourne turned his attention to the man who, according to Khan, had engineered the murders of Alex and Mo. "And you don't distrust her, not even a little?"

"Yes, she's an excellent liar." He chuckled. "And I know a thing or two about lying." He crossed to the cart, eyed with the connoisseur's intensity the implements arrayed there. "I suppose it's natural to think that because she betrayed you, she'd do the same to me." He turned, the light reflecting off the unnaturally smooth skin on the side of his face and neck. "Or are you trying to drive a wedge between us? That would be standard operating procedure for an operative of your high caliber." He shrugged and picked up an implement, twirled it between his fingers. "Mr. Bourne, what I'm interested in is how much you've discovered about Dr. Schiffer and his little invention."

"Where's Felix Schiffer?"

"You can't help him, Mr. Bourne, even if you could manage the impossible and free yourself. He outlived his usefulness and now he's beyond anyone's power to resurrect."

"You killed him," Bourne said, "just as you killed Alex Conklin and Mo Panov."

Spalko shrugged. "Conklin took Dr. Schiffer away from me when I needed him the most. I got Schiffer back, of course. I always get what I want. But Conklin had to pay for thinking he could oppose me with impunity."

"And Panov?"

"He was in the wrong place at the wrong time," Spalko said. "It's as simple as that."

Bourne thought of all the good Mo Panov had done in his life and felt overwhelmed by the uselessness of his death. "How can you talk about the taking of two men's lives as if it was as simple as snapping your fingers?"

"Because it was, Mr. Bourne." Spalko laughed. "And by tomorrow the taking of those two men's lives will be as nothing to what's coming."

Bourne tried not to look at the glinting implement. Instead, what came into his mind was an image of László Molnar's blue-white body stuffed into his own refrigerator. He'd seen first-hand the damage these tools of Spalko's could inflict.

Because he was face to face with the fact that Spalko had been responsible for Molnar's torture and death, he knew that everything Khan had told him about this man was true. And if Khan had told the truth about Spalko, was it not possible that he'd been telling the truth all along, that he was, in fact, Joshua Webb, Bourne's own son? The facts were mounting, the truth was before him, and Bourne felt its crushing weight as if it were a mountain on his shoulders. He couldn't bear to look at . . . what?

It didn't matter now because Spalko had begun wielding his instruments of pain. "Again, I'll ask you what you know about Dr. Schiffer's invention."

Bourne stared past Spalko. At the blank concrete wall.

"You've chosen not to answer me," Spalko said. "I applaud your courage." He smiled charmingly. "And pity the futility of your gesture."

He applied the whorled end of the implement to Bourne's flesh.

CHAPTER TWENTY-SIX

Khan went into Houdini, a magic and logic games shop at 87 Vaci utca building. The walls and display cabinets of the smallish boutique were crammed with magic tricks, brain teasers and mazes of all kinds, shapes and descriptions, old and new. Children of all ages, their mothers or fathers in tow, prowled the aisles, pointing and staring wide-eyed at that fantastic wares.

Khan approached one of the harried salespeople and told her he wanted to see Oszkar. She asked him his name, then picked up a phone and dialed an interior extension. She spoke into the receiver for a moment, then directed Khan to the back of the store.

He passed through a door at the rear of the shop into a tiny vestibule lit by one bare bulb. The walls were of an indeterminate color; the air smelled of boiled cabbage. He went up an iron circular staircase to the office on the second floor. It was lined with books—mostly first-edition volumes on magic, biographies and autobiographies of famous magicians and escape artists. An autographed photo of Harry Houdini hung on the wall over an antique oak rolltop desk. The old Persian carpet was still on the plank floor, still in desperate need of cleaning, and the huge, thronelike high-backed armchair still sat in its place of honor facing the desk.

Oszkar sat in exactly the same position he'd been in a year ago when Khan last had occasion to visit him. He was a pear-shaped man of middle years with huge side whiskers and a bulbous nose. He rose when he saw Khan and, grinning, came around from behind the desk and shook his hand.

"Welcome back," he said, gesturing for Khan to take a seat. "What can I do for you?"

Khan told his contact what he needed. Oszkar wrote as Khan spoke, from time to time nodding to himself.

Then he looked up. "Is that all?" He seemed disappointed; he loved nothing better than being challenged.

"Not quite," Khan said. "There's the matter of a magnetic lock."

"Now we're talking!" Oszkar was beaming now. He rubbed his hands together as he rose. "Come with me, my friend."

He led Khan into a wallpapered hallway lit by what appeared to be gaslamps. He had a way of waddling when he walked, comical as a penguin, but when you saw him escape from three pairs of handcuffs in under ninety seconds, you were exposed to a whole new meaning of the word finesse.

He opened a door and walked into his workshop—a large space evenly divided into areas by workbenches and metal counters. He directed Khan over to one, where he commenced to rummage through a vertical stack of drawers. At length he brought out a small black and chrome square.

"All mag locks work off current, you know that, right?" When Khan nodded, he continued. "And they're all fail-safe, meaning they need a constant power supply to work. Anyone who installs one of these knows that if you cut the current, the lock will open, so there's certain to be a backup power supply, possibly even two, if the subject's paranoid enough."

"This one is," Khan assured him.

"Very well then." Oszkar nodded. "So forget about cutting the power supply—it'll take you too long, and even if you had the time you still might not be able to cut the power to all the backups." He held up a forefinger. "But, what's not so commonly known is that all magnetic locks work off DC current, so . . ." He rummaged around again, held up another object. "What you need is a portable AC power supply with enough juice to zap the mag lock."

Khan took the power pack in his hand. It was heavier than it looked. "How is it going to work?"

"Imagine a lightning strike on an electrical system." Oszkar tapped the power supply. "This baby will scramble the DC current long enough for you to open the door, but it won't short it out completely. Eventually, it'll cycle back on again and the lock will reestablish itself."

"How long will I have?" Khan asked.

"That depends on the make and model of the mag lock." Oszkar shrugged his meaty shoulders. "The best guess I can give you is fifteen minutes, maybe twenty, but no more than that."

"Can't I just zap it again?"

Oszkar shook his head. "Chances are good you'll freeze the mag into its locked position, and then you'd have to take the entire door down in order to get out." He laughed, clapped Khan on the back. "Not to worry, I have faith in you."

Khan looked at him askance. "Since when did you have faith in anything?"

"Quite right." Oszkar handed him a small zippered leather case. "Tricks of the trade always trump faith."

At precisely two-fifteen in the morning, local Icelandic time, Arsenov and Zina placed the carefully wrapped body of Magomet into one of the vans and drove down the coast farther south toward an out-of-the-way cove. Arsenov was behind the wheel. Periodically, Zina, studying a detailed map, gave him directions.

"I sense the nervousness in the others," he said after a time. "It's more than simple anticipation."

"We're on more than a simple mission, Hasan."

He glanced at her. "Sometimes I wonder whether icewater runs in your veins."

She put a smile on her face as she briefly squeezed his leg. "You know very well what runs in my veins."

He nodded. "That I do." He had to admit that, as much as he was driven by his desire to lead his people, he was happiest being with Zina. He longed for a time when the war would be over, when he could shed his rebel's guise and be a husband to her, a father to their children.

"Zina," he said as they turned off the road and jounced down the rutted path that descended off the cliff face to their destination, "we've never talked about us."

"What d'you mean?" Of course she knew very well what he meant and tried to push away the sudden dread that constricted her. "Of course we have."

The way had become steeper and he slowed the van. Zina could see the last turn in the path; beyond that was the rocky cove and the restless North Atlantic.

"Not about our future, our marriage, the children we'll have one day. What better time to pledge our love for each other."

It was then that she fully understood how intuitive the Shaykh really was. For by his own words, Hasan Arsenov had condemned himself. He was afraid to die. She heard it in his choice of words, if not in his voice or in his eyes.

She saw his doubts, now, about her. If there was one thing she'd learned since joining the rebels, it was that doubt undermined initiative, determination, most especially action. Because of the extreme tension and anxiety, perhaps, he had exposed himself, and his weakness was as repugnant to her as it had been to the Shaykh. Hasan's doubts about her were sure to infect his thinking. She'd made a terrible blunder in seeking so quickly to enlist Magomet, but she was so very eager to embrace the Shaykh's future. Still, judging by Hasan's violent reaction, his doubts about her must have begun earlier. Did he think that he could no longer trust her?

They had arrived at the rendezvous point fifteen minutes ahead of schedule. She turned and took his face in her hands. Tenderly, she said, "Hasan, long have we walked side by side in the shadow of death. We have survived through the will of Allah, but also because of our unswerving devotion to one another." She leaned over and kissed him. "So now we pledge ourselves to one another, because we desire death in the path of Allah more than our enemies desire life."

Arsenov closed his eyes for a moment. This was what he'd wanted from her, what he'd been afraid she'd never give him. It was why, he realized now, he'd jumped to an ugly conclusion when he'd seen her with Magomet.

"In Allah's eyes, under Allah's hand, in Allah's heart," he said in a form of benediction.

They embraced, but Zina was, of course, far away across the North Atlantic. She was wondering what the Shaykh was doing at this very moment. She longed to see his face, to be near him. Soon, she told herself. Soon enough everything she wanted would be hers.

Sometime later they got out of the van and stood watching on the shore, hearing the waves rumble and spend themselves against the shingle. The moon had already gone down in the short span of darkness this far north. In another half hour it would grow light and another long day would dawn. They were in more or less the center of the cove, its arms extended on either side so that the tide was stymied, the waves made small and robbed of their usual peril. A chill wind off the black water made Zina shiver, but Arsenov embraced it.

They saw the sweep of the light then, blinking on and off three times. The boat had arrived. Arsenov switched on the flashlight, returning the signal. Faintly, they could see the fishing boat running no lights, nosing in. They went to the back of the van and, together, brought their burden down to the tide line.

"Won't they be surprised to see you again," Arsenov said.

"They're the Shaykh's men, nothing surprises them," Zina replied, acutely aware that according to the story the Shaykh told Hasan she was supposed to have met this crew. Of course, the Shaykh would have already apprised them of that fact.

Arsenov switched on his flashlight again and they saw heading toward them an oared boat, heavily laden, lying low in the water. There were two men and a stack of crates; there would be more crates on the fishing boat. Arsenov glanced at his watch; he hoped they could finish before first light.

The two men nosed the prow of the rowboat up onto the shingle and got out. They didn't waste time with introductions, but as they had been ordered to do, they treated Zina as if she was known to them.

With great efficiency, the four of them offloaded the crates, piling them up neatly in the back of the van. Arsenov heard a sound, turned and saw that a second rowboat had pulled up onto the shingle and knew then that they'd beat the dawn.

They loaded Magomet's corpse onto the first rowboat, now otherwise empty, and Zina gave the crew members the order to dump it when they were in the deepest water. They obeyed her without question, which pleased Arsenov. Obviously, she'd made an impression on them when she'd supervised the delivery of the cargo to them.

In short order, then, the six of them moved the rest of the crates into the van. Then the men returned to their boats as silently as they had disembarked from them and, with a push from Arsenov and Zina, began their return journey to the fishing boat.

Arsenov and Zina looked at each other. With the arrival of the cargo, the mission had suddenly taken on a reality it hadn't had before.

"Can you feel it, Zina?" Arsenov said as he put his hand on one of the crates. "Can you feel the death waiting there?"

She put her hand over his. "What I feel is victory."

They drove back to the base where they were met by the other members of the cadre, who through the judicious application of peroxide dye and colored contact lenses had now been utterly transformed. Nothing was said concerning the death of Magomet. He had come to a bad end and this close to their mission none of them wanted to know the details—they had more important things on their minds.

Carefully, the crates were unloaded and opened, revealing compact machine pistols, packs of C4 plastique explosive, HAZMAT suits. Another crate, smaller than the others, contained scallions, bagged, bedded in shaved ice. Arsenov gestured to Akhmed, who donned Latex gloves and removed the crate of scallions to the van that had printed on it *Hafnarfjördur Fine Fruits & Vegetables.* Then the blond and blue-eyed Akhmed climbed into the van and drove off.

The last crate was left for Arsenov and Zina to open. It contained the NX 20. Together, they looked at it, the two halves lying innocently inside their molded foam bed, and thought of what they'd been witness to in Nairobi. Arsenov looked at his watch. "Very soon now the Shaykh will arrive with the payload."

The final preparations had begun.

Just after nine A.M., a van from Fontana Department Store pulled up at the service entrance on the basement level of Humanistas, Ltd. where it was halted by a pair of security guards. One of them consulted his daily work sheet and even though he saw on it a delivery from Fontana for Ethan Hearn's office, he asked to see the bill of lading. When the driver complied, the guard told him to open the back of the van. The guard climbed in, checked off each item on the list, then he and his partner opened every carton, checking the two chairs, credenza, cabinet and sofa bed. All the doors on the credenza and cabinet were opened, the interiors inspected, the pillows on the sofa and chairs lifted. Finding everything in order, the security guards handed back the bill of lading and gave the driver and his delivery partner directions to Ethan Hearn's office.

The driver parked near the elevator and he and his partner unloaded the furniture. It took them four trips to get everything up to the sixth floor, where Hearn was waiting for them. He was only too pleased to show them where he wanted each piece of furniture, and they were just as pleased to receive the generous gratuity he handed them when their task was completed.

After they left, Hearn closed the door and began to transfer the stacks of files that had built up beside his desk into the cabinet in alphabetical order. The hush of a well-run office fell over the room. After a time, Hearn rose and went to the door. Opening it, he found himself face to face with the woman who had accompanied the man on the stretcher into the building late yesterday.

"You're Ethan Hearn?" When he nodded, she held out a hand. "Annaka Vadas."

He took her hand briefly, noting that it was firm and dry. He recalled Khan's warning and he put an innocently quizzical look on his face. "Do we know each other?"

"I'm a friend of Stepan's." Her smile was dazzling. "Do you mind if I come in, or were you just leaving?"

"I do have an appointment in"—he glanced at his watch—"a little while."

"I won't take up much of your time." She walked to the sofa bed and sat, crossing her legs. Her expression, as she stared up at Hearn, was alert and expectant.

He sat in his chair and swiveled it around to face her. "How may I help you, Ms. Vadas?"

"I think you've got it wrong," she said brightly. "The question is how may I help you?"

He shook his head. "I don't think I understand."

She looked around the office, humming to herself. Then she leaned forward, her elbows on her knee. "Oh, but I think you do, Ethan." That smile again. "You see, I know something about you even Stepan doesn't."

He stitched that quizzical look back onto his face, spread his hands in a gesture of helplessness.

"You're trying too hard," she said shortly. "I know you're working for someone else as well as for Stepan."

"I don't—"

But she'd put a forefinger across his lips. "I saw you yesterday in the garage. You couldn't have been there for your health, and even if you were, you were far too interested in the proceedings."

He was too stunned even to formulate a denial. And what was the point? he asked himself. She'd made him, even though he thought he'd been so very careful. He stared at her. She was, indeed, beautiful, but she was even more formidable.

She cocked her head. "It isn't Interpol you work for—you don't have their habits. CIA, no, I don't think so. Stepan would know if the Americans were trying to penetrate his organization. So who then, hmm?"

Hearn wouldn't say; he couldn't. He was only terrified that she already knew—that she knew everything.

"Don't look so ashen, Ethan." Annaka rose. "I don't care, really. I simply want an insurance policy in case things turn sour here. That insurance policy is you. For now, let's just call your treachery our little secret."

She had crossed the room and gone out the door before Hearn could think of a reply. He sat for a moment, immobile with shock. Then, at last he got up and opened the door, looking this way and that up and down the corridor to make certain she was really gone.

Then he closed the door, walked over to the sofa bed and said, "All clear."

The cushions lifted up and he put them on the wall-to-wall carpet. When the plywood panels that covered the bed mechanism began to stir, he reached down and lifted them out.

Underneath, instead of the mattress and bed frame, lay Khan.

Hearn realized that he was sweating. "I know you warned me, but—"

"Quiet." Khan climbed out of the space that was no larger than a coffin. Hearn cowered, but Khan had more important things on his mind than corporal punishment. "Just make sure you don't make the same mistake twice."

Khan walked to the door, put his ear against it. All that could be discerned was the background hum of the offices on the floor. He was dressed in black trousers, shoes, shirt and waist-length jacket. To Hearn, he looked a good deal bulkier in the upper body than he had the last time they'd met.

"Put the sofa bed back together," Khan ordered, "then return to work as if nothing had happened. You have a meeting soon? Make sure you go to it and that you're not late. It's imperative that everything appear normal."

Hearn nodded, dropping the plywood panels into the well of the sofa bed, then replacing the cushions. "We're on the sixth floor," he said. "Your target's on the fourth floor."

"Let's see the schematics."

Hearn sat down at his computer terminal and brought up the schematics for the building.

"Let me see the fourth floor," Khan said, bending over his shoulder.

When Hearn brought it up, Khan studied it carefully. "What's this?" he asked, pointing.

"I don't know." Hearn tried zooming in. "It looks like blank space."

"Or," Khan said, "it could be a room adjacent to Spalko's bedroom suite."

"Except there isn't a way in or out," Hearn pointed out.

"Interesting. I wonder if Mr. Spalko made some alterations his architects knew nothing about."

Having memorized the floor plan, Khan turned away. He'd gotten all he could from the schematic; now he needed to see the place for himself. At the door he turned back to Hearn. "Remember. Get to your appointment on time."

"What about you?" Heard said. "You can't get in there."

Khan shook his head. "The less you know, the better."

The flags were out in the endless Icelandic morning, filled with brilliant sunshine and the mineral scent of the thermal springs. The elaborate aluminum scaffold of a large dais had been set up and wired for sound at one end of Keflavik Airport, which Jamie Hull, Boris Illyich Karpov and Feyd al-Saoud had determined was the most secure space on the grounds. None of them, even Comrade Boris, it seemed, was happy about their respective leaders appearing in such a public forum, but in this all the heads of state were of a like mind. It was imperative, they felt, not only to show their solidarity in a public manner but also to show their lack of fear. They all knew the risk of assassination when they took their positions, were acutely aware of how that risk had escalated exponentially when they had agreed to the summit. But they all knew the risk of death was a component of their work. If you set out to change the world, inevitably there would be those who would stand in your way.

And so on this morning of the start of the summit, the flags of the United States, Russia and the four most influential Islamic nations rippled and cracked in the biting wind, the front of the dais had been draped with the carefully fought-over logo of the summit, armored security was in place around the perimeter, snipers placed high up at every possible strategic sight line. The press had come from every nation in the world; they had been required to show up two hours in advance of the press conference. Journalists had been methodically screened, their credentials checked, their fingerprints taken and scanned through various databases. Photographers had been warned not to load their cameras ahead of time because they needed to be X-rayed on site, each film cannister examined, every one of the photographers themselves observed while they loaded their cameras. As for cell phones, they were confiscated, meticulously tagged and kept outside the perimeter, to be retrieved at the end of the press conference by their respective owners. No detail had been overlooked.

As the president of the United States made his appearance, Jamie Hull was at his side, along with a brace of Secret Service agents. Hull was in constant contact with every member of his contingent as well as the other two heads of security via an electronic earbud. Just behind the U.S. president came Aleksandr Yevtushenko, president of Russia, accompanied by Boris and a cadre of grim-faced FSB agents. Behind him were the leaders of the four Islamic states, with the respective heads of their security services.

The crowd as well as the press surged forward only to be kept back from the front of the dais the dignitaries had now mounted. The microphones were tested, the television cameras went live. The U.S. president took the microphone first. He was a tall, handsome man with a prominent nose and the eyes of a watchdog.

"My fellow citizens of the world," he began in the strong, declarative voice honed at many a successful primary race, smoothed of any remaining rough edges by numerous press conferences and richly burnished by intimate speeches in the Rose Garden and at Camp David, "this is a great day for world peace and for the international fight for justice and freedom against the forces of violence and terrorism.

"Today, we once again stand at a crossroads in the history of the world. Will we allow all of humankind to be plunged into the darkness of fear and

neverending war or will we band together to strike at the heart of our enemies wherever they may hide?

"The forces of terrorism are arrayed against us. And make no mistake,
terrorism is a modern-day hydra, a beast of many heads. We have no illusions about the difficult road ahead of us, but we will not be deterred in
our desire to move forward in a single concerted effort. Only united can
we destroy the many-headed beast. Only united do we stand a chance of
making our world a safe place for each and every citizen."

At the end of the president's speech there was great applause. Then he
yielded the microphone to the Russian president, who said more or less the
same things, also to great applause. The four Arab leaders spoke one by
one, and though their words were more circumspect, they too reiterated
the burning need for a united effort at stamping out terrorism once and
for all.

A short question and answer period ensued, after which the six men
stood side by side for their photo op. It was an impressive sight, made even
more memorable when they grasped one another's hands and raised their
arms aloft in an unprecedented display of solidarity between the West and
the East.

As the crowd slowly filed out, the mood was jubilant. And even the most
jaded journalists and photographers agreed that the summit had gotten off
to a sterling start.

"Do you realize that I'm on my third pair of Latex gloves?"

Stepan Spalko was at the scarred and blood-stained table, sitting on the
chair Annaka had used the day before. In front of him was a bacon, lettuce
and tomato sandwich, for which he'd developed a taste during his long
convalescence between operations in the United States. The sandwich was
on a plate of fine bone china, and at his right hand was a stemmed glass of
finest crystal filled with a vintage Bordeaux.

"No matter. The hour grows late." He tapped the crystal of the chro-
nometer on his wrist. "It occurs to me now, Mr. Bourne, that my marvelous
entertainment is at an end. I must tell you what a wonderful night you've
provided me." He barked a laugh. "Which is more than I did for you, I
daresay."

His sandwich had been cut into two equal triangles, exactly to his specifications. He picked one up and bit into it, chewed slowly and luxuriously. "You know, Mr. Bourne, a bacon, lettuce and tomato sandwich is no good unless the bacon had been freshly cooked and, if possible, thickly sliced."

He swallowed, put down the sandwich and, grasping the crystal glass, swirled a measure of Bordeaux around in his mouth. Then he pushed back his chair, rose and went over to where Jason Bourne sat strapped into the dentist's chair. His head was lolled on his chest and there were blood spatters in a two-foot radius around him.

Spalko used a knuckle to lift Bourne's head. His eyes, dulled with endless pain, were sunken into dark circles and his face appeared drained of blood. "Before I go, I must tell you the irony of it all. The hour of my triumph is upon us. It doesn't matter what you know. It doesn't matter whether you talked or not now. All that matters is that I have you here, safe and unable to act against me in any way." He laughed. "What a terrible price you've paid for your silence. And for what, Mr. Bourne? Nothing!"

Khan saw the guard standing in the corridor beside the elevator and went cautiously back down toward the door to the staircase. Through the wire-mesh reinforced glass panel he could see a pair of armed guards talking and smoking in the stairwell. Every fifteen seconds one or the other would glance out through the glass panel, checking the sixth-floor corridor. The stairs were too well defended.

He reversed himself. Striding down the corridor at a normal and relaxed pace, he drew the air gun he purchased from Oszkar and held it at his side. The instant the guard saw him, Khan raised the air gun, shot a dart into his neck. The man collapsed where he stood, rendered unconscious by the chemical in the dart's tip.

Khan broke into a run. He began to drag the guard into the men's room when the door opened and a second guard appeared, his machine pistol aimed at Khan's chest.

"Hold it right there," he said. "Throw down your weapon and let me see your empty hands."

Khan did as he was ordered. As he held out his hands for the guard to inspect, he touched a hidden spring-loaded sheath attached to the inner side of his wrist. The guard clapped one hand to his throat. The dart felt like an insect bite. But all at once he found that he couldn't see. That was the last thought he had before he, too, sank into unconsciousness.

Khan dragged both bodies into the men's room, then hit the call button on the wall panel. A moment later the two sets of doors opened as the elevator cab arrived. He got in and pressed the button for the fourth floor. The elevator began to descend, but as it passed the fifth floor, it jolted to a halt, hanging suspended. He pressed several floor buttons to no avail. The elevator was stuck, no doubt deliberately so. He knew he had very little time to escape from the trap Spalko had set for him.

Climbing up onto the handrail that ran around the cab, he stretched upward toward the maintenance hatch. He was about to open it when he stopped and peered more closely. What was that metallic glint? He took out the mini-light from the kit Oszkar had given him, shone it on the screw in the farthest corner. There was a bit of copper wire wrapped around it. It was booby-trapped! Khan knew that the moment he tried to take off the hatch it would detonate a charge placed on top of the cab.

At that moment, a lurch dislodged him from his perch and the elevator cab, shuddering, began to plummet down the shaft.

Spalko's phone rang and he stepped out of the interrogation room. Sunlight spilled through the windows of his bedroom as he walked into it, feeling the warmth on his face.

"Yes?"

A voice spoke in his ear, the words accelerating his pulse. He was here! Khan was here! His hand clenched into a fist. He had them both now. His work here was almost done. He ordered his men onto the third floor, then called the main security desk and ordered them to begin a fire drill that would in short order evacuate all normal Humanistas personnel from the building. Within twenty seconds, the fire alarm shrilled and all through the building, men and women left their offices and proceeded in an orderly fashion to the stairwells, where they were escorted out onto the street. By this time Spalko had called his driver and his pilot, telling the latter to ready the jet that had been waiting for him in the Humanistas hangar at

Ferihegy Airport. Per his instructions, it had already been fueled and inspected, a flight plan logged in with the tower.

There was one more call he needed to make before he returned to Jason Bourne.

"Khan's in the building," he said when Annaka answered the phone. "He's trapped in the elevator and I've sent men to deal with him if he manages to escape, but you know him better than anyone." He grunted at her response. "What you're saying isn't a surprise. Deal with it as you see fit."

Khan hit the Emergency Stop button with the heel of his hand, but nothing happened, the elevator continued its precipitous descent. With one of the tools from Oszkar's kit, he quickly pried open the display panel. Inside was a nest of wires, but he immediately saw that the wires to the emergency break had been disconnected. Deftly, he fitted them back into their receptacles, and at once with a squeal of sparking metal the elevator cab lurched to a halt as the emergency brake kicked in. As the cab hung, stalled, between the third and fourth floors, Khan continued to work on the wiring with a breathless intensity.

On the third floor Spalko's armed men reached the outer elevator doors. Employing a fire key, they manually pried open the doors, exposing the shaft. Just above them, they could see the bottom of the stalled elevator cab. They had their orders; they knew what to do. Aiming their machine pistols, they opened fire in a massed fusillade that chewed up the bottom third of the elevator cab. No one could survive such massed firepower.

Khan, spreadeagled, hands and feet pressed hard against the walls of the elevator shaft's setback, watched the lower part of the cab fall away. He was protected from the ricochet of bullets both by the doors of the cab and by the shaft itself. He'd rewired the panel to allow him to open the cab doors just enough to squeeze out. He'd been squirming into position in the setback, climbing to approximately the height of the cab's top when the hail of automatic fire began.

Now, in the echoing aftermath of the percussion, he heard a buzzing as of a swarm of bees loosed from their hive. Looking up, he saw a pair of rappeling lines snaking down from the top of the shaft. Moments later two heavily armed guards in riot gear came down the lines, hand over hand.

One of them saw him and swung his machine pistol toward him. Khan fired his air gun, and the guard's weapon dropped from his numbed fingers. As the second guard aimed his weapon, Khan leaped out, grabbed hold of the unconscious man, who by dint of his rappeling harness was held fast to the line. The second guard, faceless and anonymous in his riot helmet, fired at Khan, who swung his line companion around, using his body as a shield to stop the bullets. He kicked out, snapping the machine pistol out of the second guard's grasp.

They both landed atop the elevator cab together. The small pale square of deadly C4 explosive was taped to the center of the maintenance hatch where it had been hastily wired to set the booby trap. Khan could see that the screws had been loosened; if either of them inadvertently struck the hatch plate, dislodging it even a little, the entire cab would be blown to pieces.

Khan squeezed the trigger on his air gun, but the guard, who had seen how he'd incapacitated his partner, dived out of the way, rolled and kicked upward, knocking the weapon out of Khan's grasp. At the same time he grabbed his partner's machine pistol. Khan trod down hard on his hand, grinding with his heel in an attempt to dislodge the weapon from the guard's grip. But now there were bursts of automatic fire from the guards on the third floor, who were firing up the shaft.

The guard, taking advantage of the distraction, smashed Khan's leg sideways and wrested the machine pistol from him. As he fired, Khan leaped off the cab, sliding down the side of the shaft to the place where the emergency brake was extended. Moving back from the hail of gunfire, he worked on the brake mechanism. The guard on the roof of the cab had followed his progress and was now stretched out on his belly, aiming the machine pistol at Khan. As he began firing, Khan was able to release the emergency brake mechanism. The elevator cab plunged down the shaft, taking the shocked guard with it.

Khan leaped for the nearest rappeling rope and clambered up it. He reached the fourth floor and was applying the AC current to the magnetic lock when the elevator cab impacted with the bottom of the shaft in the sub-basement. The shock dislodged the maintenance hatch and the C4 detonated. The explosion shot up the shaft just as the mag lock circuit was disrupted and Khan tumbled through the door.

The fourth-floor vestibule was clad entirely in café-au-lait marble. Frosted-glass sconces provided soft indirect lighting. As Khan picked himself up, he saw Annaka not five yards from him, fleeing down the hall. Clearly, she was surprised and, quite possibly, he thought, not a little frightened. Obviously, neither she nor Spalko had counted on him making it to the fourth floor. He laughed silently as he set off in pursuit. He couldn't blame them; it was quite a feat he'd performed.

Up ahead, Annaka went through a door. As she slammed it shut behind her, Khan heard the lock click into place. He knew he needed to get to Bourne and Spalko, but Annaka had become a wild card he couldn't afford to ignore. He had a set of picks out even as he reached the locked door. Inserting one, he finessed out the grooves of the tumbler. It took him less than fifteen seconds to open the door, hardly time enough for Annaka to have made it to the other side of the room. She threw him a frightened glance over her shoulder before she slammed the door shut behind her.

In retrospect, he should have been warned by her expression. Annaka never showed fear. He was, however, alerted by the ominous room, which was small and square, as featureless as it was windowless. It appeared unfinished, freshly painted a dead white, even the wide, carved moldings. There was no furniture, nothing at all in the space. But his alarm arrived too late, for the soft hiss had already begun. Peering up, he saw the vents high in the walls, from which a gas was being discharged. Holding his breath, he went to the far door. He picked the lock, but still the door wouldn't open. It must be bolted from the outside, he thought, as he ran back to the door through which he'd entered the room. He turned the knob only to find that it, too, had been bolted from the outside.

The gas was starting to permeate the barred room. He was neatly trapped.

Next to the crumb-spattered bone china plate and the stemmed glass in which remained the dregs of the Bordeaux, Stepan Spalko had arrayed the items he had taken from Bourne: the ceramic gun, Conklin's cell phone, the wad of money and the switchblade knife.

Bourne, battered and bloody, had been deep in delta meditation for hours now, first to survive the waves of agony that had rippled through his body at every new twist and jab of Spalko's implements, then to protect and conserve his inner core of energy, and finally to throw off the debilitating effects of the torture and to build up his strength.

Thoughts of Marie, Alison and Jamie flickered through his emptied mind like fitful flames, but what had come to him most vividly was his years in sun-drenched Phnom Penh. His mind, calmed to the point of complete tranquility, resurrected Dao, Alyssa and Joshua. He was tossing a baseball to Joshua, showing him how to use the glove he'd brought from the States, when Joshua turned to him and said, *"Why did you try to replicate us? Why didn't you save us?"* He became confused for a moment, until he saw Khan's face hanging in his mind like a full moon in a starless sky. Khan opened his mouth and said, *"You tried to replicate Joshua and Alyssa. You even used the same first letters in their names."*

He wanted to rise out of his enforced meditation, to abandon the fortress he'd erected to protect himself against the worst of the ravages Spalko was visiting upon him, anything to get away from the accusatory face, the crushing guilt.

Guilt.

It was his own guilt that he'd been running away from. Ever since Khan had told him who he really was, he'd run from the truth, just as he'd run from Phnom Penh as fast as he could. He thought he'd been running away from the tragedy that had befallen him, but the truth was he'd run from the burden of his unsupportable guilt. He hadn't been there to protect his family when they'd needed him the most. Slamming the door on the truth, he'd fled.

God help him, in this he was, as Annaka had said, a coward.

As Bourne's watched out of bloodshot eyes, Spalko pocketed the money and took up the gun. "I've used you to keep the hounds of the world's intelligence organizations off my trail. In this you've served me well." He leveled the gun at Bourne, aiming for a spot just above and between his eyes. "But, sadly, your use to me is at an end." His finger tightened on the trigger.

At that moment Annaka came into the room. "Khan made it onto the floor," she said.

Despite himself, Spalko registered surprise. "I heard the explosion. He wasn't killed by it?"

"He somehow managed to crash the elevator. It exploded in the sub-basement."

"Luckily, the latest delivery of weapons was shipped out." At last he turned his gaze on her. "Where's Khan now?"

"He's trapped in the locked room. It's time to leave."

Spalko nodded. She'd been dead on when it came to Khan's skills. He'd been right to encourage the liaison between them. Duplicitous creature that she was, she's gotten to know Khan better than he himself could've hoped to. Still, he stared at Bourne, certain his business with him was not yet finished.

"Stepan." Annaka put a hand on his arm. "The plane is waiting. We need time to leave the building unseen. The fire-circuits have been activated and all the oxygen has been pumped out of the elevator shaft so there's no chance of major damage. Still, there must be flames in the lobby and the fire wagons will be here if they're not already."

She'd thought of everything. Spalko looked at her admiringly. Then, without any warning, he swept the hand that held Bourne's ceramic gun in an arc, slamming the barrel into the side of Bourne's head.

"I'll just take this as a souvenir of our first and last encounter."

Then he and Annaka left the room.

Khan, down on his belly, dug furiously, using a small crowbar from the tools he'd requested from Oszkar, at a section of the molding. His eyes burned and teared from the gas, and his lungs were near to bursting from lack of oxygen. He had only a few more seconds left before he passed out and his autonomous nervous system took over, allowing the gas into his system.

But now he'd pried off a section of the molding and immediately he could feel the draft of cool air coming from outside the room he was in. He stuck his nose into the vent he'd made, breathed in the fresh air. Then, taking a deep breath, he quickly set up the small charge of C4 Oszkar had provided. This, above all the items on his list, had told Oszkar the extent of the danger he was heading into, prompting the contact to give Khan the escape kit as added protection.

Putting his nose into the vent, Khan took another deep breath, then he replaced it with the packet of C4, wedging it as far in as he was able. Scrambling to the opposite side of the room, he pressed the remote.

The resulting explosion brought down a section of the wall as it blew a hole right through it. Without waiting for the plastic and wood dust to settle, Khan leaped though the wall into Stepan Spalko's bedroom.

Sunlight slanted through the windows, and the Danube glittered below. Khan threw open all the windows in order to dissipate whatever leakage of gas found its way in. At once he could hear sirens, and glancing down, he saw the fire trucks and the police cars, the frenzied activity on street level. He stepped back from the windows, looked around, orienting himself to the architectural plans Hearn had brought up on his computer screen.

He turned to where the blank space had been, saw the gleaming wooden wall panels. Pressing his ear to each panel in turn, he rapped with his knuckles. In this way the third panel from the left revealed itself as a door. He pressed against the left side of the panel and it swung inward.

Khan stepped into the room of black concrete and white tiles. It stank of sweat and blood. He found himself facing a bloody, battered Jason Bourne. He stared at Bourne, strapped into the dentist's chair, blood spatters in a circle around him. Bourne was bare to the waist. His arms, shoulders, chest and back were a welter of puffy wounds and blistered flesh. The two outer layers that wrapped his ribs had been stripped away, but the underlayer was still intact.

Bourne's head swung around and regarded Khan with the look of a wounded bull, bloody but unbowed.

"I heard the second explosion," Bourne said, in a reedy voice. "I thought you had been killed."

"Disappointed?" Khan bared his teeth. "Where is he? Where's Spalko?"

"I'm afraid you're too late on that score," Bourne said. "He's gone, and Annaka Vadas with him."

"She was working for him all along," Khan said. "I tried to warn you at the clinic, but you didn't want to listen."

Bourne sighed, closed his eyes against the sharp rebuke. "I didn't have time."

"You never seem to have time to listen."

Khan approached Bourne. His throat seemed constricted. He knew that he should go after Spalko, but something rooted him to the spot. He stared at the damage Spalko had wrought.

Bourne said, "Will you kill me now." It was not a question, more a statement of fact.

Khan knew that he would never have a better chance. The dark thing inside him that he had nurtured, that had become his only companion, which daily feasted on his hate, and which daily had spewed its poison back out into his system, refused to die. It wanted to kill Bourne, and it almost took possession of him then. Almost. He felt the impulse coming up from his lower belly into his arm, but it had bypassed his heart and so fell short of impelling him to action.

Abruptly, he turned on his heel and went back into Spalko's luxe bedroom. In a moment he'd returned with a glass of water and a handful of items he'd scavenged from the bathroom. He held the glass to Bourne's mouth, tipping it slowly until it had been drained. As if of their own volition, his hands unstrapped the buckles, freeing Bourne's wrists and ankles.

Bourne's eyes watched him as he went about cleaning and disinfecting the wounds. Bourne didn't lift his hands from the arms of the chair. In a sense, he felt more completely paralyzed now than he had while restrained. He stared hard at Khan, scrutinizing every curve and angle, every feature of his face. Did he see Dao's mouth, his own nose? Or was it all an illusion? If this was his son, he needed to know; he needed to understand what had happened. But he still felt an undercurrent of uncertainty, a ripple of fear. The possibility that he was confronting his own son after so many years of believing him dead was too much for him. On the other hand, the silence into which they had now been plunged was intolerable. And so he fell back to the one neutral topic he knew was of extreme interest to both of them.

"You wanted to know what Spalko was up to," he said, breathing slowly and deeply as each shock of the disinfectant sent bolts of pain through him. "He's stolen a weapon invented by Felix Schiffer—a portable bio-diffuser. Somehow Spalko has coerced Peter Sido—an epidemiologist working at the clinic—to provide him with the payload."

Khan dropped the blood-soaked piece of gauze, picked up a clean one. "Which is?"

"Anthrax, a designer hemorrhagic fever, I don't know. The only thing for certain is that it's quite lethal."

Khan continued to clean Bourne's wounds. The floor was now littered with bloody bits of gauze. "Why are you telling me this now?" he said with undisguised suspicion.

"Because I know what Spalko means to do with this weapon."

Khan looked up from his work.

Bourne found it physically painful to look into Khan's eyes. Taking a deep breath, he plowed on. "Spalko's on a very tight time constraint. He needed to get moving now."

"The terrorism summit in Reykjavik."

Bourne nodded. "It's the only possibility that makes sense."

Khan stood up, rinsing off his hands at the hose. He watched the pink water swirl through the huge grate. "That is, if I believe you."

"I'm going after them," Bourne said. "After putting the pieces together, I finally realized that Conklin had taken Schiffer and hidden him with Vadas and Molnar because he'd learned of Spalko's threat. I got the code name for the bio-diffuser—NX 20—from a pad in Conklin's house."

"And so Conklin was murdered for it." Khan nodded. "Why didn't he go to the Agency with his information? Surely, the CIA as a whole would've been better equipped to handle the threat to Dr. Schiffer."

"There could be many reasons," Bourne said. "He didn't think he'd be believed, given Spalko's reputation as a humanitarian. He didn't have enough time; his intel wasn't concrete enough for the Agency's bureaucracy to move on it quickly enough. Also, it wasn't Alex's way. He hated sharing secrets."

Bourne rose slowly and painfully, one hand supporting himself on the back of the chair. His legs felt like rubber from having been in one position for so long. "Spalko killed Schiffer, and I have to assume that he has Dr. Sido, alive or dead. I've got to stop him from killing everyone at the summit."

Khan turned and handed Bourne the cell phone. "Here. Call the Agency."

"Do you think they'd believe me? As far as the Agency's concerned, I murdered Conklin and Panov in the house in Manassas."

"I'll do it then. Even the bureaucracy of the CIA has to take seriously an anonymous call that threatens the life of the president of the United States."

Bourne shook his head. "The head of American security is a man named Jamie Hull. He'd be sure to find a way to screw up the intel." His eyes gleamed. They'd already lost most of their dullness. "That leaves only one other option, but I don't think I can do it alone."

"Judging by the look of you," Khan said, "you can't do it at all."

Bourne forced himself to look Khan in the eye. "All the more reason, then, for you to join me."

"You're insane!"

Bourne inured himself to the rising hostility. "You want Spalko as badly as I do. Where's the downside?"

"*All* I see is downside." Khan sneered. "Look at you! You're a mess."

Bourne had detached himself from the chair and was walking around the room, stretching his muscles, gaining strength and confidence in his body with every stride he took. Khan saw this and was, frankly, astonished.

Bourne turned to him and said, "I promise not to make you do all the heavy lifting."

Khan didn't reject the offer out of hand. Instead, he made a grudging concession, not at all certain why he was doing it. "The first thing we have to do is get out of here safely."

"I know," Bourne said, "you managed to start a fire and now the building is swarming with firemen and, no doubt, the police."

"I wouldn't be here if I hadn't started that fire."

Bourne could see that his light bantering wasn't easing the tension. If anything, it was doing the opposite. They didn't know how to talk to each other. He wondered whether they ever would. "Thank you for rescuing me," he said.

Khan wouldn't meet his eye. "Don't flatter yourself. I came here to kill Spalko."

"At last," Bourne said, "something to thank Stepan Spalko for."

Khan shook his head. "This can't work. I don't trust you and I know you don't trust me."

"I'm willing to try," Bourne said. "Whatever's between us, this is far bigger."

"Don't tell me what to think," Khan said shortly. "I don't need you for that; I never did." He managed to raise his head and look at Bourne. "All right, here's how it goes. I'll agree to work together with you on one condition. You find us a way out of here."

"Done." Bourne's smile confounded Khan. "Unlike you, I've had a great many hours to think about escaping from this room. I had assumed that even if I somehow managed to free myself from the chair, I wouldn't get far using conventional methods. At the time I was quite unable to go up against a squadron of Spalko's guards. So I came up with another solution."

Khan's expression registered annoyance. He hated that this man knew more than he did. "Which is?"

Bourne nodded in the direction of the grate.

"The drain?" Khan said incredulously.

"Why not?" Bourne knelt beside the grate. "The diameter is large enough to get through." He gestured as he snapped open the switchblade and inserted the blade between the grate and its flush housing. "Why don't you give me a hand?"

As Khan knelt on the opposite side of the grate, Bourne used the knifeblade to raise it slightly. Khan lifted it up. Putting aside the switchblade, Bourne joined him and, together, they heaved the grate all the way up.

Khan could see Bourne wince with the effort. At that moment an eerie sensation rose in him, both strange and familiar, a kind of pride he was able to identify only at length and with considerable pain. It was an emotion he'd felt when he was a boy, before he'd wandered in shock, lost and abandoned, out of Phnom Penh. Since then, he'd so successfully walled it off that it hadn't been a problem for him. Until now.

They rolled the grate aside and Bourne took up some of the bloody bandage that Spalko had ripped off him and wrapped his cell phone. Then he put it and the closed switchblade in his pocket. "Who'll go first?" he asked.

Khan shrugged, giving no sign that he was in any way impressed. He had a good idea where the drain led, and he believed Bourne did, too. "It's your idea."

Bourne levered himself into the circular hole. "Wait ten seconds, then follow me down," he said just before he vanished from sight.

Annaka was elated. As they sped toward the airport in Spalko's armor-plated limousine, she knew no one and nothing could stop them. Her last-minute ploy with Ethan Hearn hadn't been necessary, as it turned out, but she didn't regret the overture. It always paid to err on the side of caution, and at the time she'd decided to confront Hearn, Spalko's fate seemed to have hung in the balance. Looking over at him now, she knew that she never should have doubted him. He had the courage, skills and worldwide resources to pull off anything, even this audacious power coup. She had to admit that when he'd first told her what he planned, she'd been skeptical, and she'd remained so until he had engineered their successful emergence on the other side of the Danube through an old air-raid tunnel he'd discovered when he'd bought the building. When he'd started to renovate it, he'd successfully erased any notation of it from the architectural plans so that it remained, up until the moment he'd shown it to her, his personal secret.

The limo and driver had been waiting for them on the far side in the fiery glow of the late afternoon sunshine, and now they were speeding along the motorway toward Ferihegy Airport. She moved closer to Stepan, and when his charismatic face turned toward her, she took his hand briefly in hers. He'd stripped off the bloody butcher's apron and the Latex gloves somewhere in the tunnel. He wore jeans, a crisp white shirt and loafers. You'd never know he'd been up all night.

He smiled. "I think a glass of champagne is called for, don't you?"

She laughed. "You think of everything, Stepan."

He indicated the flutes sitting in their niches on the inside panel of her door. They were crystal, not plastic. As she leaned forward to take them, he removed a split of champagne from a refrigerated compartment. Outside, the high-rises on either side of the motorway sped by, reflecting the orb of the lowering sun.

Spalko ripped off the foil, popped the cork and poured the foaming champagne into first one flute, then the other. He put down the bottle and they clinked glasses in a silent toast. They sipped together and she looked into his eyes. They were like brother and sister, closer even because neither carried with them the baggage of sibling rivalry. Of all the men she had known, she reflected, Stepan came closest to fulfilling her desires. Not that she'd ever longed for a mate. As a girl, a father would have suited her, but it was not to be. Instead, she'd chosen Stepan, strong, competent, invincible. He was everything a daughter would want from her father.

The high-rises were becoming less numerous as they passed through the outermost ring of the city. The light continued to lower as the sun set. The sky was high and ruddy and there was very little wind, conditions ripe for a perfect takeoff.

"How about a little music," Spalko said, "to go with our champagne moment?" His hand was raised to the multi-CD player embedded over his head. "What would please you most? Bach? Beethoven? No, of course. Chopin."

He chose the corresponding CD and his forefinger pressed a button. But instead of the lyrical melody typical of her favorite composer, she heard her own voice:

"It isn't Interpol you work for—you don't have their habits. CIA, no, I don't think so. Stepan would know if the Americans were trying to penetrate his organization. So who then, hmm?"

Annaka, her flute halfway to her partly open lips, froze.

"Don't look so ashen, Ethan."

She saw, to her horror, Stepan grinning at her over the rim of his flute.

"I don't care, really. I simply want an insurance policy in case things turn sour here. That insurance policy is you."

Spalko's finger hit the "Stop" button, and save for the muffled thrumming of the limo's powerful engine, silence overtook them.

"I imagine you're wondering how I came by your treachery."

Annaka found that she had temporarily lost the ability to speak. Her mind was frozen in place at the precise moment Stepan had very kindly asked her what music would please her most. More than anything in the world, she wanted to go back to that moment. Her shocked mind could only reflect on the split in her reality that had opened up like a yawning abyss at her feet. There was only her perfect life before Spalko had played the digital recording and the disaster it had become after he'd played it.

Was Stepan still smiling that awful crocodile smile? She found that she was having difficulty focusing. Without thinking, she swiped at her eyes.

"My God, Annaka, are those genuine tears?" Spalko shook his head ruefully. "You've disappointed me, Annaka, though, to be perfectly honest, I'd been wondering when you'd betray me. On that point, your Mr. Bourne was quite correct."

"Stepan, I—" She stopped of her own accord. She hadn't recognized her own voice, and the last thing she would do was beg. Her life was miserable enough as it was.

He was holding something up between thumb and finger, a tiny disk, smaller even than a watch battery. "An electronic listening device planted in Hearn's office." He laughed shortly. "The irony is that I didn't particularly suspect him. One of these is in every new employee's office, at least for the first six months." He pocketed the disk with the flourish of a magician. "Bad luck for you, Annaka. Good luck for me."

Swallowing the rest of his champagne, he set the flute down. She still hadn't moved. Her back was straight, her right elbow cocked. Her fingers surrounded the rim of the flute's flared bottom.

He looked at her tenderly. "You know, Annaka, if you were anyone else, you'd be dead by now. But we share a history, we share a mother, if you want to stretch a definition to its limit." He cocked his head, putting the surface of his face in the last of the afternoon's light. The side of his face that was as poreless as plastic shone like the glass windows of the high-rises that were now far behind them. Very little in the way of habitation lay before them until they turned into the airport proper.

"I love you, Annaka." One hand held her by her waist. "I love you in a way I could never love anyone else." The bullet from Bourne's gun made surprisingly little noise. Annaka's torso was thrown back into his welcoming arm and her head came up all at once. He could feel the tremor run through her and knew that the bullet must have lodged near her heart. His eyes never left hers. "It really is a pity, isn't it?"

He felt the heat of her running over his hand, down onto the leather seat as her blood pooled. Her eyes seemed to be smiling, but there was no expression anywhere else on her face. Even at the point of death, he reflected, she had no fear. Well, that was something, wasn't it?

"Is everything all right, Mr. Spalko?" his driver asked from up front.

"It is now," Stepan Spalko said.

CHAPTER TWENTY-SEVEN

The Danube was cold and dark. The grievously injured Bourne hit the river-water first, where the drain emptied out, but it was Khan who had difficulty. The extreme chill of the water was of no import to him, but the darkness brought to him the nightmarish horror of his recurring dream.

The shock of the water, the surface so distant above his head, caused him to feel as if his ankle was tied to the white semi-decomposed body, spinning slowly below him in the depth. Lee-Lee was calling to him, Lee-Lee wanted him to join her. . . .

He felt himself tumbling into darkness, even deeper water. And then, quite suddenly and terrifyingly, he was being pulled. By Lee-Lee? he wondered in a panic.

All at once he felt the warmth of another body, large and, despite its wounds, still immensely powerful. He felt Bourne's arm circle his waist, the surge of Bourne's legs as he kicked them out of the swift current into which Khan had fallen, driving them upward toward the surface.

Khan seemed to be crying, or at least crying out, but when they breached the surface and made for the far shore, Khan struck out, as if he wanted nothing more than to punish Bourne, to beat him senseless. But all he could manage at the moment was to tear the encircling arm from around his waist and glare at Bourne as they pulled themselves against the stone embankment.

"What did you think you were doing?" Khan said. "You almost caused me to drown!"

Bourne opened his mouth to answer him, but apparently thought better of it. Instead, he pointed downriver to where a vertical iron rose out of the water. Across the deep blue water of the Danube, fire trucks, ambulances and police cars still ringed the Humanistas, Ltd., building. Crowds had joined the knots of evacuated employees, surging like surf along the sidewalks, spilling through the streets, hanging out windows, craning their necks for a better angle. Boats sailing up and down the river were converging on the spot and even though members of the police force waved them away, the passengers rushed to the railing to get a closer look at what they thought might be a disaster in the making. But they were too late. It appeared that whatever fires had been started by the explosion in the elevator shaft had been extinguished.

Bourne and Khan, sticking to the shadows of the embankment, made their way to the ladder, which they climbed as quickly as they could. Lucky for them, all eyes were on the commotion at the Humanistas, Ltd., building. Several yards away, a section of the embankment was under repair and they were able to crawl into the sheltering shadows below street level but above the water-line, where the concrete had become undermined and was now shored up with pillars of heavy timber.

"Give me your phone," Khan said. "Mine's waterlogged."

Bourne unwrapped Conklin's cell phone and handed it over.

Khan dialed Oszkar's cell phone and, when he reached him, told him where they were and what they required. He listened for a moment and then said to Bourne.

"Oszkar, my contact here in Budapest, is chartering us a flight. And he's getting you some antibiotics."

Bourne nodded. "Now let's see how good he really is. Tell him we need the schematics for the Oskjuhlid Hotel in Reykjavik."

Khan glared at him and for a moment Bourne was afraid that he was going to hang up simply out of spite. He bit his lip. He'd have to remember to talk to Khan in a less confrontational manner.

Khan told Oszkar what they needed. "It'll take about an hour," he said.

"He didn't say 'impossible'?" Bourne said.

"Oszkar never says 'impossible.'"

"My contacts couldn't have done better."

A chill and fitful wind had sprung up, forcing them to move farther into their makeshift cave. Bourne took the opportunity to assess the damage Spalko had inflicted on him; Khan had done well in ministering to the punctures, which were numerous on his arms, chest and legs. Khan still had on his jacket. He now took it off and shook it out. As he did so, Bourne saw that the inside was composed of a number of pockets, all of which looked filled.

"What d'you have in there?" he asked.

"Tricks of the trade," Khan said unhelpfully. He retreated into his own world by using Bourne's cell phone.

"Ethan, it's me," he said.

"Is everything all right?"

"That depends," Hearn said. "In the mêlé, I discovered that my office was bugged."

"Does Spalko know who you work for?"

"I never mentioned your name. Anyway, mostly my calls to you were out of the office."

"Still, it would be wise for you to leave."

"My thoughts exactly," Hearn said. "I'm happy to hear your voice. After the explosions I didn't know what to think."

"Have a little faith," Khan said. "How much d'you have on him?"

"Enough."

"Take everything you have and get out now. I will have my revenge on him no matter what happens."

He heard Hearn take a breath, "What's that supposed to mean?"

"It means I want a backup. If for some reason you can't get the material to me, I want you to contact—hold on a moment." He turned to Bourne and said, "Is there someone at the Agency who can be trusted with intel on Spalko?"

Bourne shook his head, then immediately reconsidered. He thought about what Conklin had told him about the Deputy Director—that he was not only fair-minded but that he was his own man. "Martin Lindros," he said.

Khan nodded and repeated the name to Hearn, then he closed the connection and handed back the phone.

Bourne felt in a quandary. He wanted to find some way to connect with Khan, but he didn't know how. Finally, he hit upon the idea of asking him how he had reached the interrogation room. He felt a relief when Khan began to talk. He told Bourne about hiding in the sofa, the explosion in the elevator shaft and his escape from the bolted room. He did not, however, mention Annaka's treachery.

Bourne listened with mounting fascination, but even so, part of him remained detached, as if this conversation was happening to someone else. He was shying away from Khan; the psychic wounds were too raw. He recognized that in his present debilitated state, he was as yet mentally unprepared to tackle the questions and doubts that flooded him. And so the two of them talked fitfully and awkwardly, always skirting the central issue that lay between them like a castle that could be sieged but not taken.

An hour later Oszkar arrived in his company van with towels and blankets and new clothes, along with an antibiotic for Bourne. He gave them a Thermos of hot coffee to drink. They climbed into the backseat, and while they changed, he bundled up their torn and sodden clothes, all except Khan's remarkable jacket. Then he gave them bottled water and food, which they wolfed down.

If he was surprised at the sight of Bourne's wounds, he didn't show it, and Khan assumed that he'd worked out that the assault had been a success. He presented Bourne with a lightweight laptop computer.

"The schematics for every system and subsystem in the hotel have been downloaded to the hard drive," he said, "as well as maps of Reykjavik and the surrounding area and some basic information I thought might come in handy."

"I'm impressed." Bourne said this to Oszkar, but he meant it for Khan, too.

Martin Lindros got the call just after eleven A.M. Eastern Daylight Time. He jumped into his car and made the fifteen-minute drive to George Washington Hospital in just under eight minutes. Detective Harry Harris was in the E.R. Lindros used his credentials to cut through the red tape so that one of the harried residents took him over to the bed. Lindros pulled aside the curtain that ran around three sides of the emergency room station, pulled it shut behind him.

"What the hell happened to you?" he said.

Harris eyed him as best he could from his propped-up position on the bed. His face was puffy and discolored. His upper lip was split and there was a gash under his left eye that had been stitched.

"I got fired—that's what happened."

Lindros shook his head. "I don't understand."

"The National Security Advisor called my boss. Directly. Herself. She demanded I be fired. Dismissed without compensation or pension. This is what he told me when he summoned me to his office yesterday."

Lindros' hands curled into fists. "And then?"

"What d'you mean? He fired my ass. Disgraced me after the spotless career I've had."

"I mean," Lindros said, "how did you wind up here?"

"Oh, that." Harris turned his head to one side, looking at nothing. "I got drunk, I guess."

"You guess?"

Harris turned back to him, his eyes blazing. "I got very drunk, okay? I think it was the least I deserved."

"But you got more than that."

"Yah. There was an argument with a couple of bikers, if I remember right, which escalated into something of a brawl."

"I suppose you think you deserved to get beaten to a pulp."

Harris said nothing.

Lindros passed a hand across his face. "I know I promised you I'd take care of this, Harry. I thought I had it under control, even the DCI had come around, more or less. I just didn't figure on the NSA making a preemptive strike."

"Fuck her," Harris said. "Fuck everyone." He laughed bitterly. "It's like my ma used to say, 'No good deed goes unpunished.'"

"Look, Harry, I never would've cracked this Schiffer thing without you. I'm not going to abandon you now. I'll get you out of this."

"Yeah? I'd like the fuck to know how."

"As Hannibal, one of my military icons, once famously said, 'We will either find a way or make one.'"

When they were ready, Oszkar drove them to the airport. Bourne, whose body was racked with pain, was happy to let someone else drive. Still, he remained on operational alert. He was pleased to see that Oszkar was using his mirrors to check for tags. No one appeared to be following them.

Up ahead, he could see the airport's control tower, and a moment later

Oszkar turned off the motorway. There were no cops in sight. Nothing seemed out of place. Still, he could feel the vibrations start up inside him.

No one came for them as they cruised through the airport roads, heading toward the charter services airfield. The aircraft was waiting, ready and fueled. They got out of the van. Before he left, Bourne gripped Oszkar's hand. "Thanks again."

"No problem," Oszkar said with a smile. "It all goes on the bill."

He drove off and they went up the stairs and into the aircraft.

The pilot welcomed them aboard, then pulled up the stairs and closed and locked the door. Bourne told him their destination and five minutes later they were taxiing down the runway, lifting off for their two-hour, ten-minute flight to Reykjavik.

"We'll be coming up on the fishing boat in three minutes," the pilot said.

Spalko adjusted the electronic earbud, picked up Sido's refrigerated box and went to the rear of the plane and shrugged himself into the harness. As he tightened the cinches, he stared at the back of Peter Sido's head. Sido was handcuffed to his seat. One of Spalko's armed men was in the seat next to him.

"You know where to take him," he said softly to the pilot.

"Yessir. It won't be anywhere near Greenland."

Spalko went to the rear doorway, signaled to his man, who rose and walked back up the narrow aisle to join him.

"Are you all right for fuel?"

"Yessir," the pilot answered. "My calculation's right on the money."

Spalko peered out the small round window in the door. They were lower now, the North Atlantic blue-black, the wave crests a sure sign of its vaunted turbulence.

"Thirty seconds, sir," the pilot said. "There's a pretty stiff wind from the north-northeast. Sixteen knots."

"Roger that." Spalko could feel the slowing of their airspeed. He was wearing a 7-mm survival dry suit under his clothes. Unlike a diver's wet suit, which relied on a thin layer of water between the body and the neoprene suit to keep body temperature up, this was sealed at the feet and the

wrists to keep the water out. Inside the trilaminate shell he wore a Thermal
Protection System Thinsulate undersuit for added protection against the
cold. Still, unless he timed his landing perfectly, the impact of the freezing
water could paralyze him and even with the protection of the suit that
would prove fatal. Nothing could go wrong. He attached the box to his left
wrist with a locking chain and drew on his dry gloves.

"Fifteen seconds," the pilot said. "Wind constant."

Good, no gusts, Spalko thought. He nodded to his man, who pulled
down on the huge lever and swung open the door. The howling of the wind
filled the interior of the aircraft. There was nothing below him but thirteen
thousand feet of air, and then the ocean, which would be as hard as concrete if he hit it at the rate of free fall.

"Go!" the pilot said.

Spalko jumped. There was a rushing in his ears, the wind against his
face. He arched his body. Within eleven seconds he was falling at 110 miles
per hour, terminal velocity. And yet he didn't feel as if he was falling.
Rather, the sensation was one of something softly pressing against him.

He looked down, saw the fishing boat and, using the air pressure, moved
himself horizontally to compensate for the sixteen-knot north-by-
northeast wind. Aligning himself, he checked his wrist altimeter. At twenty-
five hundred feet he pulled the rip cord, felt the gentle tug at his shoulders,
the soft rustle of nylon as the canopy deployed above him. All at once the
ten square feet of air resistance his body had provided had been transformed into 250 square feet of drag. He was now descending at a leisurely
sixteen feet per second.

Above him was the luminous bowl of the sky; below him spread the
vastness of the North Atlantic, restless, heaving, sheened to beaten brass by
the late afternoon sunlight. He saw the fishing boat bobbing and, far off,
the jutting curve of the Icelandic peninsula upon which Reykjavik was
built. The wind was a constant tug, and for a time he was busy compensat-
ing by repeatedly flaring the canopy. He breathed deeply, relishing the pil-
lowy sensation of the drop.

He seemed suspended, then in a shell of endless blue he thought of the
meticulous planning, the years of hard work, maneuvering and manipulation by which he'd reached this point, what he'd come to view as the pinna-
cle of his life. He thought of his year in America, in tropical Miami, the

painful procedures to remake and remodel his ruined face. He had to admit that he'd enjoyed telling Annaka the story of his fictional brother, but then again, how else would he have explained his presence in the asylum? He could never tell her that he was having a passionate affair with her mother. It was a simple matter to bribe the doctors and nurses into giving him private time with their patient. How utterly corrupt human beings are, he reflected. Much of his success had been built on taking advantage of that principle.

What an amazing woman Sasa had been! He'd never met her like before or since. Quite naturally, he'd made the assumption that Annaka would be like her mother. Of course, he'd been much younger then and his foolishness could be forgiven.

What would Annaka have thought, he wondered now, if he'd told her the truth, that years ago he'd slaved for a crime boss, a vindictive, sadistic monster who'd sent him out on a vendetta knowing full well that it could be a trap. It was—and Spalko's face was the result of it. He'd gotten his revenge on Vladimir, but not in the heroic manner he'd painted for Zina. It was shameful what he'd done, but in those days he'd lacked the power to act on his own. But not now.

He was more than five hundred feet in the air when the wind abruptly reversed itself. He began to sail away from the boat, and he worked the canopy to minimize the effect. Still, he was unable to reverse his course. Below him, he could see the flash of reflection on board the fishing boat and knew that the crew was carefully monitoring his descent. The boat began to move with him.

The horizon was higher, and now the ocean was coming up fast, filling the entire world as his perspective changed. The wind suddenly died, and he came down, flaring his canopy at just the right instant, making his landing as soft as possible.

His legs went in first and then he was under the water. Even mentally prepared as he was, the shock of the freezing water struck a hammerblow that drove all the breath from him. The weight of the refrigerated box pulled him quickly under, but he compensated with powerful, practiced scissor-kicks. He surfaced with a swing of his head and took a deep breath while he shed his harness.

He could hear the grinding churn of the fishing boat's engines echoing in the deep, and without even bothering to look, he struck out in that direction. The swells were so high and the current so swift that he soon abandoned the notion of swimming as futile. By the time the boat came alongside, he was near to being spent. Without the protection of the dry suit, he knew he would have gone into hypothermia by now.

A crew member threw him a line and a rope ladder was cast over the side. He grabbed the line and held on with all his strength as they pulled him to the side where the ladder hung down. He climbed up it, the ocean a constant drag on him until the very last instant.

A strong hand reached down, helping him over the side. He looked up, saw a face with piercing blue eyes and thick blond hair.

"*La illaha ill Allah.*" Hasan Arsenov said. "Welcome aboard, Shaykh," Spalko stood back while crew members wrapped him in absorbent blankets. "*La illaha ill Allah,*" he replied. "I almost didn't recognize you."

"When I first looked at myself in the mirror after I'd bleached my hair," Arsenov said, "I didn't either."

Spalko peered at the terrorist leader's face. "How do the contact lenses feel?"

"None of us have had a problem." Arsenov could not take his eyes off the metal box the Shaykh was holding. "It's here."

Spalko nodded. He glanced over Arsenov's shoulder and saw Zina standing in the last of the sunlight. Her golden hair streamed out behind her and her cobalt eyes watched his with an avid intensity.

"Head for shore," Spalko told the crew. "I want to change into dry clothes."

He went below into the forward cabin, where clothes had been neatly stacked on a berth. A pair of sturdy black shoes were on the deck beneath. He unlocked the box and set it on the berth. As he stripped off his sopping clothes and peeled off the dry suit, he glanced at his wrist to see how badly the cuff had abraded his skin. Then he rubbed his palms together until he'd returned full circulation to his hands.

While his back was turned, the door opened and just as quickly closed. He did not turn around, did not need to see who'd entered the cabin.

"Let me warm you up," Zina said in honeyed tones.

A moment later he felt the press of her breasts, the heat from her loins against his back and buttocks. The exhilaration of the jump was still running high through him. It had been heightened by the final denouement to his long relationship with Annaka Vadas, making Zina's advance irresistible.

He turned, sat back on the edge of the berth and allowed her to climb all over him. She was like an animal in heat. He saw the glitter of her eyes, heard the guttural sounds he pulled from her belly. She had lost herself in him, and he was for the moment satisfied.

Approximately ninety minutes later Jamie Hull was below street level, checking the security at the Oskjuhlid Hotel's delivery entrance when he caught sight of Comrade Boris. The Russian security chief evinced surprise at Hull's presence, but Hull wasn't fooled. He'd had a feeling that Boris had been shadowing him of late, but maybe he was just being paranoid. Not that he wouldn't be justified. All the principals were in the hotel. Tomorrow morning at eight A.M. the summit would begin and the time of maximum risk would be upon him. He dreaded the thought that somehow Comrade Boris had gotten wind of what Feyd al-Saoud had discovered, what he and the Arab security chief had concocted.

And so as not to let Comrade Boris get an inkling of the dread in his heart, he put a smile on his face, preparing himself to eat a bite or two of American crow if he had to. Anything now to keep Comrade Boris in the dark.

"Working overtime, I see, my good Mr. Hull," Karpov said in his booming announcer's voice. "No rest for the weary, eh?"

"Time enough for rest when the summit's concluded and our job is done."

"But our job is never done." Karpov, Hull saw, was wearing one of his very bad serge suits. It looked more like a suit of armor than anything in the least bit fashionable. "No matter how much we accomplish, there is always more to do. That's one of the charms of what we do, no?"

Hull felt himself wanting to say no just to be argumentative, but he bit his tongue instead.

"And how is security here?" Karpov was looking around with his beady raven's eyes. "Up to your high American standards, one hopes?"

"I've only just begun."

"Then you'll welcome some help, no? Two heads are better than one, four eyes are better than two."

Hull was abruptly weary. He could no longer remember how long he'd been here in this godforsaken country or when he'd last had a decent night's sleep. Not even a single tree to tell you what time of year it was! A kind of disorientation had set in, the sort from which first-time submariners were said sometimes to suffer.

Hull watched the security team stop a food service truck, question the driver and climb into the back to check its load. He could find no fault with either the procedure or the methodology.

"Don't you find this place depressing?" he asked Boris.

"Depressing? This is a fucking wonderland, my friend," Karpov boomed. "Spend a winter in Siberia if you want a definition of depressing."

Hull frowned. "You were sent to Siberia?"

Karpov laughed. "Yes, but not in the way you think. I was operational up there several years ago when the tension with China was at its peak. You know, secret military maneuverings, clandestine intelligence gathering, all in the darkest, coldest place you can imagine." Karpov grunted. "Or, being American, I suppose you're incapable of imagining such a thing."

Hull kept the smile stitched to his face, but it cost him in both pent-up anger and self-esteem. Happily, another van was rolling in, the food service vehicle having passed muster. This one was from Reykjavik Energy. For some reason, it seemed to have piqued Comrade Boris' interest, and Hull followed him over to where the van was stopped. Inside were two uniformed men.

Karpov took the call sheet the driver had dutifully handed over to one of the security personnel, glanced down at it. "What's this all about?" he said in his typically overaggressive manner.

"Quarterly geothermal checkup," the driver said blandly.

"This has to be done now?" Karpov glared at the blond driver.

"Yes, sir. Our system is interconnected throughout the city. If we don't perform periodic maintenance, we put the entire network at risk."

"Well, we can't have that," Hull said. He nodded to one of the security men. "Check inside. If it's all clear, let them through."

He walked away from the van and Karpov followed.

"You don't like this work," Karpov said, "do you?"

Forgetting himself for a moment, Hull turned on his heel and confronted the Russian. "I like it just fine." Then he remembered, and grinned boyishly. "Nah, you're right. I'd much rather be using my more, shall we say, physical skills."

Karpov nodded, apparently mollified. "I understand. There's no feeling like a good kill."

"Exactly," Hull said, warming to his task. "Take this newest sanction, for instance. What I wouldn't give to be the one to find Jason Bourne and put a bullet through his brain."

Karpov's caterpillar eyebrows lifted. "For you, this sanction sounds personal. You should beware such emotionalism, my friend. It clouds good judgment."

"Fuck that," Hull said. "Bourne had what I wanted most, what I should've had."

Karpov considered for a moment. "It seems that I've misjudged you, my good friend Mr. Hull. It seems that you're more of a warrior than I thought." He clapped the American on the back. "What d'you say to trading war stories over a bottle of vodka?"

"I think that sounds doable," Hull said, as the Reykjavik Energy van rolled inside the hotel.

Stepan Spalko, in a Reykjavik Energy uniform, colored contact lenses in his eyes and a piece of molded Latex making his nose wide and ugly, stepped out of the van and told the driver to wait. With a work order on a clipboard in one hand and a small toolbox in the other, he went through the labyrinth in the hotel's belly. The plan of the hotel floated in his mind like a three-dimensional overlay. He knew his way around the vast complex better than many of the employees whose work confined them to a single area.

It took him twelve minutes to reach the section of the hotel that housed the space that would serve as the summit's venue. In that time, he was stopped four times by security guards even though he was wearing his ID clipped to his overalls. He took the stairs, went down three levels belowground, where he was stopped once again. He was near enough to a thermal heat junction to make his presence there plausible. Still, he was near enough to the HVAC substation that the guard insisted on accompanying him.

Spalko stopped at an electrical junction box and opened it. He could feel the guard's scrutiny like a hand at his throat.

"You've been here how long?" he said in Icelandic as he opened the box he was carrying.

"D'you speak Russian, maybe?" the guard replied.

"As a matter of fact, I do." Spalko rummaged around in the box. "You've been here, what, two weeks now?"

"Three," the guard admitted.

"And in all that time, have you seen anything of my wonderful Iceland?" He found what he wanted in among all the junk and palmed it. "Do you know anything about it?"

The Russian shook his head, which was Spalko's cue to launch into his discourse. "Well, let me enlighten you then. Iceland is an island of 103,000 square kilometers at an average height of 500 meters above sea level. Its highest peak, Hvannadalshnúkur, rises to 2.119 meters and over 11 percent of the country is covered by glaciers, including Vatnajökull, the largest in Europe. We're governed by the Althing, whose 63 members are elected every four—"

His voice died out as the guard, unutterably bored by the guidebook babble, turned his back and moved away. Instantly he got to work, taking the small disk and pressing it against two sets of wires until he was sure its four contacts had penetrated the insulation.

"All done here," he said, slamming the junction box closed.

"Now where? The thermal housing?" the guard said, clearly hoping this stint would be over soon.

"Nah," Spalko said. "I've got to check in with my boss first. I'm off to the van." He waved as he left, but the guard was already walking in the other direction.

Spalko returned to the van, climbed in, and there he sat next to the driver until a security guard wandered up.

"Okay, guys, what's up?"

"We're finished here for the time being." Spalko smiled winningly as he made some meaningless marks on his bogus worksheet. He checked his watch. "Hey, we were here longer than I thought. Thanks for checking up."

"Hey, it's my job."

As the driver turned on the ignition and put the van in gear, Spalko said, "Here's the value of making a dry run. We'll have precisely thirty minutes before they come looking for us."

The chartered jet flung itself through the sky. Across from Bourne sat Khan, staring straight ahead, looking, it seemed, at nothing. Bourne closed his eyes. The overhead lights had been turned off. A few reading lights cast oval pools of illumination in the dark. In an hour they'd be touching down at Keflavik Airport.

Bourne sat very still. He wanted to put his head in his hands and weep bitter tears for the sins of the past, but with Khan across the aisle he couldn't show anything that might be misinterpreted as weakness. The tentative detente they'd managed to achieve seemed as fragile as an eggshell. There were so many things that had the potential to crush it. Emotions churned in his chest, making it difficult to breathe. The pain he felt all through his tortured body was as nothing compared to the anguish that threatened to rend his heart asunder. He grasped the armrests so hard that his knuckles cracked. He knew he had to gain control of himself, just as he knew that he couldn't sit in his seat a moment longer.

He rose and, like a sleepwalker, slipped across the aisle and lowered himself into the seat next to Khan. The young man did not in any way register the fact of Bourne's presence. He might have been deep in meditation, save for the rapid rate of his breathing.

With his heart hammering painfully against his cracked ribs, Bourne said softly, "If you're my son, I want to know it. If you really are Joshua, I *need* to know it."

"In other words, you don't believe me."

"I *want* to believe you," Bourne said, trying to ignore the by-now familiar knife-edge of Khan's voice. "Surely you must know that."

"When it comes to you, I know less than nothing." Khan turned to him, the hammer of his rage all in his face. "Don't you remember me at all?"

"Joshua was six, just a child." Bourne felt his emotions rising again, ready to choke him. "And then some years ago I suffered amnesia."

"Amnesia?" This revelation seemed to startle Khan.

Bourne told him what had happened. "I remember little of my life as Jason Bourne before that time," he concluded, "and virtually nothing about my life as David Webb, except when now and again a scent or the sound of a voice dislodges something and I recall a fragment. But that's all it is, discontinuous from a whole that's forever lost to me."

Bourne tried to find Khan's dark eyes in the low light, searched for the hint of an expression, even the barest clue as to what Khan might be thinking or feeling. "It's true. We're complete strangers to each other. So before we go on . . ." He broke off, for the moment unable to continue. Then he steeled himself, forcing himself to speak because the silence that was so quick to build between them was worse than the explosion that would surely come. "Try to understand. I need some tangible proof, something irrefutable."

"Fuck you!"

Khan stood up, about to step over Bourne into the aisle, but again, as in Spalko's interrogation room, something held him fast. And then, unbidden, he heard Bourne's voice in his head, spoken on a rooftop in Budapest: *"That's your plan, isn't it? This whole sick story about you being Joshua. . . . I won't lead you to this Spalko or whoever it is you're planning to get to. I won't be anyone's cat's-paw again."*

Khan gripped the carved stone Buddha around his neck and sat back down. They'd both been Stepan Spalko's cat's-paws. It was Spalko who'd brought them together and now, ironically, it was their shared enmity of Spalko that might conceivably keep them together, at least for the time being.

"There *is* something," he said in a voice he barely recognizable. "A recurring nightmare I have of being underwater. I'm being drowned, pulled deeper because I'm tied to her dead body. She's calling to me, I hear her voice calling to me, or else it's my voice calling to her."

Bourne recalled Khan's thrashing in the Danube, the panic that had swirled him deeper into the pull of the current. "What does the voice say?"

"It's *my* voice. I'm saying 'Lee-Lee, Lee-Lee.'"

Bourne felt his heart skip a beat, for up from the depths of his own damaged memory swam Lee-Lee. For one precious moment only he could see her oval face with his light eyes and Dao's straight black hair. "Oh, God," Bourne whispered. "Lee-Lee was Joshua's nickname for Alyssa. No one else called her that. No one else but Dao knew."

Lee-Lee.

"One of the powerful memories of those days that, with a great deal of help, I've been able to recall is how your sister looked up to you," Bourne went on. "She'd always wanted to be close to you. At night, when she went through a bout of night-terrors, you were the only one who could calm her down. You called her Lee-Lee and she called you Joshy."

My sister, yes. Lee-Lee. Khan closed his eyes and immediately he was under the murky water of the river in Phnom Penh. Half-drowned, in shock, he'd seen her tumbling toward him the shot-up corpse of his little sister. Lee-Lee. Four years old. Dead. Her light eyes—their Daddy's eyes—staring sightlessly at him, accusingly. *Why you?* she seemed to say. *Why was it you and not me?* But he knew that was his own guilt talking. If Lee-Lee could have spoken, she would've said, *I'm glad you didn't die, Joshy. I'm so happy one of us stayed to be with Daddy.*

Khan put his hand to his face, turned away toward the Perspex window. He wanted to die, he wished he *had* died in the river, that it had been Lee-Lee who'd survived. He couldn't stand this life one second more. There was, after all, nothing left for him. In death, at least, he would join her. . . .

"Khan."

It was Bourne's voice. But he couldn't face him, couldn't even look him in the eye. He hated him and he loved him. He couldn't understand how this could be; he was ill equipped to deal with this emotional anomaly. With a strangled sound, he rose and pushed past him, staggering up to the front of the aircraft where he wouldn't have to see Bourne.

With an inexpressible sorrow, Bourne watched his son go. It took an enormous effort to rein in the impulse to pull him back, to put his arms around him and hug him to his chest. He sensed that would be the worst thing he could do now, that, given Khan's history, it might lead to renewed violence between them.

He had no illusions. They both had a hard road to travel before they could accept each other as family. It could even be an impossible task. But because he wasn't in the habit of thinking anything was impossible, he set that frightening thought aside.

In a rush of anguish he realized at last why he'd spent so much time denying that Khan might, in fact, be his son. Annaka, damn her, had nailed it perfectly.

At that moment he looked up. Khan was standing over him, his hands gripping the seatback in front of him as if for dear life.

"You said that you just found out that I was MIA."

Bourne nodded.

"How long did they look for me?" Khan said.

"You know I can't answer that. No one can." Bourne had lied on instinct. There was nothing to be gained and much to be lost by telling Khan that the authorities had only searched for one hour. He was acutely conscious of wanting to protect his son from the truth.

An ominous stillness had come over Khan, as if he were preparing for an act of terrible consequence. "Why didn't *you* check?"

Bourne heard the accusatory tone and sat as if poleaxed. His blood ran cold. Ever since it became clear that Khan could be Joshua, he'd been asking himself the same question.

"I was half-mad with grief," he said, "but I don't think now that's a good enough excuse. I couldn't face the fact that I'd failed you all as a father."

Something in Khan's face shifted, showing what was akin to a spasm of pain, as an ominous thought wormed its way up to the surface. "You must've had . . . difficulties when you and my mother were together in Phnom Penh."

"What d'you mean?" Bourne, alarmed by Khan's expression, responded in a tone that was perhaps sharper than in ought to have been.

"You know. Didn't you hear it from your colleagues because you were married to a Thai?"

"I loved Dao with all my heart."

"Marie isn't Thai, is she?"

"Khan, we don't choose whom we fall in love with."

There was a short pause, and then, into the charged silence that had sprung up between them, Khan said, as casually as if it were an afterthought, "And then there was the matter of your two mixed-race children."

"I never saw it that way," Bourne said flatly. His heart was breaking, for he heard the silent cry that underlay this line of questioning. "I loved Dao, I loved you and Alyssa. My God, you were all my life. In the weeks and months afterward, I nearly lost my mind. I was devastated, uncertain whether or not I wanted to go on. If not for meeting Alex Conklin, I might not have. Even so, it took years of agonizingly hard work to recover sufficiently."

He fell silent for a moment, listening to them both breathe. Then he took a deep breath and said, "What I've always believed, always struggled with is that I should've been there to protect you."

Khan regarded him for a long time, but the tension had been broken, some Rubicon had been crossed. "If you'd been there, you would've been killed, too."

He turned away without another word, and as he did so, Bourne saw Dao in his eyes and knew that in some profound way the world had changed.

CHAPTER TWENTY-EIGHT

Reykjavik, like any other civilized place on earth, had its fair share of fast food restaurants. Each day these establishments as well as the more upscale restaurants received shipments of fresh meats, fish, vegetables and fruit. Hafnarfjördur Fine Fruits & Vegetables was one of the main suppliers to the fast-food industry in Reykjavik. The company's van that had pulled up to the Kebab Höllin in City Centre early that morning with a delivery of leaf lettuce, pearl onions and scallions was one of many that had fanned out through the city on their daily rounds. The crucial difference was that, unlike all the others, this particular van had not been dispatched by Hafnarfjördur Fine Fruits & Vegetables.

By early evening all three sites of the Landspitali University Hospital were besieged by people who were increasingly ill. Doctors admitted these patients in alarming numbers even as they ran tests on their blood. By dinnertime the results confirmed that the city had a virulent outbreak of hepatitis A on its hands.

Health department officials frenziedly went to work to deal with the burgeoning crisis. Their job was hampered by several important factors: the quickness and severity of the onset of the particularly virulent strain of the virus, the complexities associated with trying to track which foodstuffs might be involved and where its source might be, and unspoken but much on their minds was the intense worldwide spotlight trained on Reykjavik by the international summit. High on their list of suspect foods were scallions, the culprits in the recent outbreaks of hepatitis A in the United States, but scallions were fairly ubiquitous in the local fast food chains, and of course they couldn't rule out meats or fish.

They worked into the twilit night, interviewing the owners of every company that specialized in fresh vegetables, sending their own staff out to inspect the warehouses, storage containers and vans of each firm, including Hafnarfjördur Fine Fruits & Vegetables. However, much to their surprise and dismay, they found nothing amiss, and as the hours swept by, they were forced to admit that they were no closer to finding the source of the outbreak than when they had started.

Accordingly, just after nine P.M., health department officials went public with their findings. Reykjavik was under a hepatitis A alert. Because they hadn't yet found the source of the infection, they put the city under quarantine. Over all their heads was the specter of a full-blown epidemic, something they could not afford with the terrorism summit beginning and the entire world's attention focused on the capital. In their television and radio interviews, the officials sought to reassure an uneasy public that they were taking every measure to gain control over the virus. To that end, they said repeatedly, the department was devoting its entire staff to the ongoing safety of the public at large.

It was just before ten P.M. when Jamie Hull walked down the hotel corridor to the president's suite in a high state of agitation. First, there was the sudden outbreak of hepatitis A to worry about. Then he was summoned to an unscheduled briefing with the president.

He looked around and saw the Secret Service men who were guarding the president. Farther down the corridor were the Russian FSB and Arab security guarding their leaders, who, for the sake of security and the ease of housing their staffs, had been assigned to one wing of the hotel.

He went through the door guarded by a pair of Secret Service guards, huge and impassive as sphinxes, and into the suite. The president was prowling restlessly back and forth, dictating to a pair of his speechwriters as the press secretary looked on, scribbling hurried notes on a tablet computer. Three more Secret Service men stood by. They were keeping the president away from the windows.

He cooled his heels without protest until the president dismissed the press people, and like mice, they scurried off to another room.

"Jamie," the president said with a big smile and an extended hand. "Good of you to come." He squeezed Hull's hand, gestured for him to sit, then took a seat across from him.

"Jamie, I'm counting on you to help bring this summit off without a hitch," he said.

"Sir, I can assure you that I have everything under control."

"Even Karpov?"

"Sir?"

The president smiled. "I heard that you and Mr. Karpov have been going at it pretty good."

Hull swallowed hard, wondering if he'd been brought in to be fired. "There was some minor friction," he said tentatively, "but that's all in the past."

"I'm glad to hear it," the president said. "I'm having enough difficulties with Aleksandr Yevtushenko as it is. I don't need him pissed off at me over a slight to his number-one security chief." He slapped his thighs and rose. "Well, showtime is eight o'clock this morning. There's still a lot to prepare for." He stuck out his hand as Hull rose. "Jamie, no one knows better than I how perilous this situation might become. But I think we're agreed that there's no turning back now."

Outside in the corridor Hull's cell phone rang.

"Jamie, where are you?" the DCI barked in his ear.

"I just came out of a briefing with the president. He was pleased to hear that I have everything under control, including Comrade Karpov."

But instead of sounding pleased, the DCI forged on in a tense urgent tone. "Jamie, listen to me carefully. There's another aspect to this situation, which is given strictly on a need-to-know basis."

Hull automatically looked around and walked quickly out of earshot of the Secret Service guards. "I appreciate your confidence in me, sir."

"It concerns Jason Bourne," the DCI said. "He wasn't killed in Paris."

"What?" For a moment Hull lost his composure. "Bourne's *alive*?"

"Alive and kicking."

"Jamie, just so we're on the same page, this call, this conversation, never happened. If you ever mention it to anyone, I'll deny it ever took place and I'll have your ass in a sling, are we clear?"

"Perfectly sir."

"I have no idea what Bourne is going to do next, but I always believed that he was heading your way. He may or may not have killed Alex Conklin and Mo Panov, but he sure as hell killed Kevin McColl."

"Jesus. I knew McColl, sir."

"We all did, Jamie." The Old Man cleared his throat. "We can't allow that act to go unpunished."

All at once Hull's rage vanished, to be replaced by a sense of high elation. "Leave it to me."

"Use caution, Jamie. Your first order of business is keeping the president safe."

"I understand, sir. Absolutely. But you can be sure that if Jason Bourne shows up, he won't leave the hotel."

"Well, I trust he will," the Old Man said. "Feet first."

Two members of the Chechen cadre were waiting in front of the Reykjavik Energy van when the health services vehicle, dispatched to the Oskjuhlid Hotel, came around the corner. The van was parked crosswise in the street and they had placed orange plastic work cones around and seemed hard at work.

The health services vehicle came to an abrupt halt.

"What are you doing?" one of the health services people said. "This is an emergency."

"Fuck you, little man!" one of the Chechen answered in Icelandic.

"What did you say?" The irate health services worker climbed out of his vehicle.

"Are you blind? We have important work here," the Chechen said. "Use another fucking route."

Sensing a situation that could turn ugly, the second man got out of the health services vehicle. Arsenov and Zina, armed and intent, emerged from the back of the Reykjavik Energy van and herded the suddenly cowed health services workers into the van.

Arsenov and Zina and one other member of the cadre arrived at the delivery entrance to the Oskjuhlid Hotel in the hijacked vehicle. The other Chechen had taken the Reykjavik Energy van to pick up Spalko and the remainder of the cadre.

They were dressed as government employees and presented the health department ID tags that Spalko had procured at great expense to the security detail on duty. When queried, Arsenov spoke in Icelandic, then changed to halting English when the American and Arab security people couldn't understand him. He said that they had been sent to ensure that the hotel kitchen was free of hepatitis A. No one—least of all the various security teams—wanted any of the dignitaries to come down with the dread virus. With all due dispatch, they were admitted and directed to the kitchen. This was where the cadre member went, but Arsenov and Zina had other destinations in mind.

Bourne and Khan were still scrutinizing the schematics of the various Oskjuhlid Hotel subsystems when the pilot announced that they were landing at Keflavík Field. Bourne, who had been pacing back and forth while Khan sat with the laptop, reluctantly took his seat. His body ached horribly, which the aircraft's cramped seating had only exacerbated. He'd tried to put on hold the feelings that had come up in connection with finding his son. Their conversations were awkward enough as it was, and he had the distinct impression that Khan would instinctively shy away from any strong emotion he might show.

The process of working toward a reconciliation was immensely difficult for both of them. Still, he suspected, it was worse for Khan. What a son needed from his father was far more complex than what a father needed from his son in order to love him unconditionally.

Bourne had to admit that he was afraid of Khan, not only of what had been done to him, of what he had become, but of his prowess, his cleverness and ingenuity. How he had escaped from the bolted room was a marvel in and of itself.

And there was something else as well, a stumbling block to their accepting each other and perhaps eventually reconciling, which dwarfed all the other obstacles. In order to accept Bourne, Khan had to give up everything his life had been.

In this Bourne was correct. Ever since Bourne had sat down next to him on the park bench in Old Town Alexandria, Khan had been a man at war with himself. He still was, the only difference being that now the war was in the open. As if staring into a rear-view mirror, Khan could see all the opportunities he'd had to kill Bourne, but it was only now that he understood that his decision not to take them had been deliberate. He couldn't harm Bourne, but he couldn't open his heart to him either. He remembered the desperate urge he'd felt to launch himself at Spalko's men at the rear of the clinic in Budapest. The only thing that had stopped him was Bourne's warning. At the time he'd put his feelings down to his desire for revenge against Spalko. But now he knew that it stemmed from another emotion entirely: the devotion one family member has for another.

And yet, to his shame, he realized that he was afraid of Bourne. He was a fearsome man in strength, endurance and intellect. Being near him, Khan felt somehow diminished, as if whatever he'd managed to accomplish in his life was as dust.

With a roll, a bump and a brief squeal of rubber, they were down and taxiing off the active runway toward the far end of the airport, where all private aircraft were directed. Khan was up and heading down the aisle to the door before they had come to a halt.

"Let's go," he said. "Spalko already has at least a three-hour start on us."

But Bourne had also risen and was standing in the aisle to oppose him.

"There's no telling what's waiting for us out there. I'll go out first."

Immediately, Khan's anger, so near the surface, flared. "I told you once—don't tell me what to do! I have my own mind; I make my own decisions. I always have and I always will."

"You're right. I'm not trying to take anything away from you," Bourne said with his heart in his mouth. This stranger was his son. Everything he said or did around him would have exaggerated consequences for some time to come. "But consider, up until now you've been alone."

"And whose fault d'you think that is?"

It was difficult not to take offense, but Bourne did his best to defuse the accusation. "There's no point in talking of blame," he said equally. "Now we're working together."

"So I should just concede control to you?" Khan answered hotly. "Why? D'you for a minute think you've earned it?"

They were almost to the terminal. He could see just how fragile their detente was.

"It would be foolish to believe that I've earned anything with you." He glanced out the window at the bright lights of the terminal. "I was thinking that if there's a problem—if we're walking into some kind of trap—I'd rather it be me than you who—"

"Have you not listened to anything I've told you?" Khan said as he shouldered past Bourne. "Have you discounted everything I've done?"

By this time the pilot had appeared. "Open the door," Khan ordered him brusquely. "And stay onboard."

The pilot dutifully opened the door and dropped the stairs down to the tarmac.

Bourne took one step down the aisle. "Khan—"

But the glare from his son stopped him in his tracks. He watched from the Perspex window as Khan went down the stairs and was met by an Immigration official. He saw Khan show him a passport, then point to the aircraft. The immigration official stamped Khan's passport and nodded.

Khan turned and trotted up the steps. When he came down the aisle, he withdrew a pair of handcuffs from under his jacket, slapped them on Bourne and then on himself.

"My name is Khan LeMarc and I'm a deputy inspector for Interpol." Khan took the laptop under his arm and began to lead Bourne back down the aisle. "You're my prisoner."

"What's my name?" Bourne said.

"You?" Khan pushed him out the door, following closely behind. "You're Jason Bourne, wanted for murder by the CIA, the Quai d'Orsay and Interpol. It's the only way he'd admit you to Iceland without a passport. Anyway, he, like every other official on the planet, has read the CIA circular."

The Immigration official stood back, giving them a wide berth as they walked past him. Khan unlocked the cuffs as soon as they were through the terminal. Out front, they got into the first taxi in the queue and gave the driver an address that was within a half-mile of the Oskjuhlid Hotel.

Spalko, the refrigerated box between his legs, sat in the passenger's seat of the Reykjavik Energy van as the Chechen rebel drove through the streets of City Centre toward the Oskjuhlid Hotel. His cell phone rang and he opened it. It wasn't good news.

"Sir, we were successful in closing off the interrogation room before the police or firemen entered the building," his head of security said from Budapest. "However, we've just completed an exhaustive sweep of the entire building without finding a sign of either Bourne or Khan."

"How is that possible?" Spalko said. "One was strapped down and the other was trapped in a room filled with gas."

"There was an explosion," his security chief said, and he went on to describe in detail what they'd found.

"Goddammit!" In a rare display of anger Spalko slammed his fist against the console of the van.

"We're expanding the search perimeter."

"Don't bother," Spalko said shortly. "I know where they are."

Bourne and Khan walked toward the hotel.

"How are you feeling?" Khan asked.

"I'm fine," Bourne replied a little too quickly.

Khan glanced at him. "Not even stiff and sore?"

"All right, I'm stiff and sore," Bourne conceded.

"The antibiotics Oszkar brought you are state of the art."

"Don't worry," Bourne said. "I'm taking them."

"What makes you think I'm worried?" Khan pointed. "Take a look at that."

The perimeter of the hotel was cordoned off by the local police. Two checkpoints manned both by police and by security personnel of various nationalities were the only ways in and out. As they watched, a Reykjavik Energy van pulled up to the checkpoint at the rear of the hotel.

"That's the only way we're going to get in," Khan said.

"Well, it's one way," Bourne said. As the van went through the checkpoint, he saw a pair of hotel employees walking out from behind it.

Bourne glanced at Khan, who nodded. He'd seen them, too. "What d'you think?" Bourne said.

"Going off-duty, I'd say," Khan replied.

"That was my thought."

The hotel employees were talking animatedly to each other and paused only long enough to show their IDs as they went through the checkpoint. Normally, they would have driven into and out of the hotel, using the underground car park, but since the security services had arrived, all hotel personnel were obliged to park on the streets surrounding the hotel.

They shadowed the two men as they turned down a side street, out of sight of the police and guards. Waiting until they neared their cars, they took them down from behind, silently and swiftly. Using the keys, they opened the trunks, placed the unconscious bodies inside, taking the hotel IDs before slamming the trunks closed.

Five minutes later they appeared at the other checkpoint in the front of the hotel so as not to come into contact with the policeman and security people who had checked the two hotel workers as they'd walked out.

They passed through the security ring without incident. At last they were inside the Oskjuhlid Hotel.

The time had come to sever Arsenov, Stepan Spalko thought. The moment had long been brewing, ever since he found that he could no longer bear Arsenov's weakness. Arsenov had once said to him, "I'm no terrorist. All I want is for my people to receive their due." Such a childish belief was a fatal flaw. Arsenov could delude himself all he wanted, but the truth was that whether he was asking for money, for prisoners returned, or for his land back, he was marked a terrorist by his methodology not by his aims. He killed people if he didn't get what he wanted. He targeted enemies and civilians—men, women, children—it made no difference to him. What he was sowing was terror; what he would reap was death.

Accordingly, Spalko ordered him to take Akhmed, Karim, and one of the females down to the substation of the HVAC system that supplied the air to the summit's forum. This was a slight change in plan. Magomet had been assigned to go with the three others. But Magomet was dead, and since it had been Arsenov who had killed him, he accepted it without question or complaint. In any event, they were now on a strict timetable.

"We have precisely thirty minutes from the moment we arrived in the Reykjavik Energy van," he said. "After that, as we know from the last time, security will come to check up on us." He consulted his watch. "Which means we now have twenty-four minutes to accomplish our mission."

As Arsenov left with Akhmed and the other cadre members, Spalko pulled Zina aside. "You understand that this will be the last time you see him alive."

She nodded her blond head.

"You have no misgivings?"

"On the contrary, it'll be a relief," she replied.

Spalko nodded. "Come on." He hurried them down the corridor. "There's no time to waste."

Hasan Arsenov took immediate control of his little group. They had a vital function to perform, and he would make certain they performed it. They turned the corner and saw the security guard at his post near the large air discharge grille.

Without breaking stride, they came toward him.

"Hold it right there," he said, bringing his machine pistol off his chest.

They stopped in front of him. "We're from Reykjavik Energy," Arsenov said in Icelandic and then, in response to the guard's blank look, repeated it in English.

The guard frowned. "There're no heat vents here."

"I know," Akhmed said, grabbing the machine pistol with one hand and slamming the guard's head against the wall with the other.

The guard started to go down and Akhmed hit him again, this time with the butt of his own machine pistol.

"Give me a hand here," Arsenov said, digging his fingers into the air discharge grille. Karim and the female pitched in, but Akhmed kept smashing the butt of his weapon into the guard, even after it was clear that he was unconscious and likely to stay that way for some time.

"Akhmed, give me the weapon!"

Akhmed tossed the machine pistol to Arsenov, then began kicking the fallen guard in the face. Blood was flowing and there was death in the air.

Arsenov forcibly dragged Akhmed away from the security guard. "When I give you an order, you'll obey it or, by Allah, I'll break your neck."

Akhmed, his chest heaving, glared at Arsenov.

"We're on a schedule," Arsenov said fiercely. "You don't have time to indulge yourself."

Akhmed bared his teeth and laughed. Shrugging off Arsenov's grip, he went to help Karim take off the grille. They shoved the guard into the air shaft, then, one by one, they crawled in after him. Akhmed, the last in, pulled the grille back in place.

They were obliged to crawl over the guard. As Arsenov did so, he pressed his fingers to the carotid artery. "Dead," he said.

"So what?" Akhmed said belligerently. "Before the morning's over, they'll all be dead."

On hands and knees, they crawled along the shaft until they came to the junction. Directly ahead of them was a vertical shaft. They deployed their rappeling gear. Placing the aluminum bar across the top of the vertical shaft, they belayed the rope and let it uncoil into the space below them. Taking the lead, Arsenov wrapped the rope around his left thigh and over his right. Moving hand under hand, he descended down the shaft at a steady pace. By the small shivering of the line, he became aware when each member of the cadre began to rappel down after him.

Just above the first junction box, Arsenov stopped. Flicking on a mini-flashlight, he played its concentrated beam over the wall of the shaft, illuminating the vertical lines of trunk cables and electric lines. In the middle of the tangle, something new gleamed.

"Heat sensor," he called up.

Karim, the electronics expert, was just above him. While Arsenov played his flashlight onto the wall, the man took out pliers and a length of wire with alligator clips on either end. Climbing carefully over Arsenov, he kept going until he hung just above the outer range of the detector. Kicking out with one foot, he swung toward the wall, grabbed a trunk cable and held on. His fingers picked through the nest of wires, cut one, to which he attached one alligator clip. Then he stripped the insulation off the middle of another wire and attached the other alligator clip to it.

"All clear," he said softly.

He moved down into the range of the sensor, but there was no alarm. He'd successfully bypassed the circuit. So far as the sensor knew, nothing was amiss.

Karim made way for Arsenov, who led them down to the bottom of the shaft. They were in range of the heart of the summit forum's HVAC subsystem.

"Our objective is the summit forum's HVAC subsystem," Bourne said as he and Khan hurried through the lobby. Khan carried the laptop they'd gotten from Oszkar under his arm. "That's the logical place for them to activate the diffuser."

At this hour of the night, the lobby, vast, high-ceilinged and cold, was deserted save for various security and hotel personnel. The dignitaries were in their suites, either sleeping or prepping for the start of the summit, which was only hours away.

"Security has undoubtedly come to the same conclusion," Khan said, "which means that we'll be all right until we get near the substation's hub, then they're going to want to know what we're doing in that area."

"I've been thinking about that," Bourne said. "It's time we used my condition to our advantage."

They went through the main section of the hotel without incident and passed through a decorative inner courtyard of geometric gravel paths, sheared evergreen shrubs, and futuristic-looking stone benches. On the other side was the forum section. Inside, they went down three flights of stairs. Khan activated the laptop and they checked the schematics, reassuring themselves that they were on the right level.

"This way," Khan said, closing the computer as they moved off.

But they'd gotten only a hundred feet from the stairwell when a harsh voice said, "Take another step and you're both dead men."

At the bottom of the vertical air shaft, the Chechen rebels waited, crouched, anxious, their nerves strained to the breaking point. They had been awaiting this moment for months. They were primed, aching to move forward. They shivered as much from the unbearable anticipation as from the chill air, which had grown colder the deeper they went below the hotel. They had only to crawl along a short horizontal shaft to get to the HVAC relays, but they were separated from their objective by the security personnel in the corridor outside by the grillwork. Until the guards moved off on their rounds, they were at bay.

Ahkmed checked his watch and saw that they had fourteen minutes to complete their mission and return to the van. Beads of sweat stood out on his forehead and, gathering in his armpits, ran down his side, prickling his skin. His mouth was dry and his breathing shallow. It was always this way on the cusp of a mission. His heart beat fast and his entire body vibrated.

He was still seething from Arsenov's rebuke, which had come in front of the others and so was doubly offensive. As he listened, his ears straining, he stared at Arsenov, contempt in his heart. After that night in Nairobi, he'd lost all respect for Arsenov, not only because he was being cuckolded but because he had no idea. Akhmed's thick lips curled into a smile. It felt good to have this power over Arsenov.

At last he heard the voices receding. He sprang forward, eager now to meet his destiny, but Arsenov's powerful arm checked him painfully.

"Not yet." Arsenov's eyes glowered.

"They've moved off," Akhmed said. "We're wasting time."

"We go when I give the orders."

This further affront was too much for Akhmed. He spat, his contempt on his face. "Why should I follow your orders? Why should any of us? You cannot even keep your woman in her place."

Arsenov lunged at Akhmed and for a moment they grappled indecisively. The others stood by, terrified to interfere.

"I'll tolerate no more of your insolence," Arsenov said. "You'll follow my orders or I'll see you dead."

"Kill me then," Akhmed said. "But know this: In Nairobi on the night before the demonstration, Zina entered the Shaykh's room while you were asleep."

"Liar!" Arsenov said, thinking of the pledge he and Zina had made to each other at the cove. "Zina would never betray me."

"Think of where my room was, Arsenov. You made the assignments. I saw her with my own eyes."

Arsenov's eyes glowed with enmity, but he let Akhmed go. "I would kill you now except that we all have vital roles to play in the mission." He gestured to the others. "Let's get on with it."

Karim, the electronics expert, went first, then the female and Akhmed, while Arsenov brought up the rear. Soon enough Karim lifted a hand, bringing them to a halt.

Arsenov heard his soft voice float back to them. "Motion sensor."

He saw Karim crouching down, preparing his equipment. He was grateful for the presence of this man. How many bombs had Karim constructed for them over the years? All had worked flawlessly; he never made a mistake.

As before, Karim drew out a length of wire with the alligator clips at either end. With his pliers in one hand, he searched out the proper electrical wires, isolating them, cutting into one and applying an alligator clip to the bare copper end. Then, as before, he stripped away the insulation from the second wire and attached the other alligator clip, creating the bypass loop.

"All clear," Karim said, and they moved forward into range of the motion sensor.

The alarm went off, shrilling through the corridor, bringing the security guards running, their machine pistols at the ready.

"Karim!" Arsenov cried.

"It's a trap!" Karim wailed. "Someone crossed the wires!"

Moments before, Bourne and Khan turned slowly to confront the American security guard. He was dressed in army fatigues and riot gear. He came a step closer, peering at their ID tags. He relaxed somewhat, putting the machine pistol up, but the deep frown didn't leave his face.

"What are you guys doing down here?"

"Maintenance checks," Bourne said. He remembered the Reykjavik Energy truck he'd seen entering the hotel as well as something in the material Oszkar had downloaded to the laptop. "The thermal heating system's gone offline. We're supposed to be helping the people the energy company sent over."

"You're in the wrong section," the guard said, pointing. "You need to go back the way you came, make a left, then left again."

"Thanks," Khan said. "I guess we got turned around. We're not normally in this section."

As they turned to leave, Bourne's legs went out from under him. He gave a deep groan and fell.

"What the hell!" the guard said.

Khan knelt beside Bourne, opened his shirt.

"Jesus Christ," the guard said, leaning over to stare at Bourne's wounded torso, "what the hell happened to him?"

Khan reached up, jerked down hard on the front of the guard's uniform, slamming the side of his head into the concrete floor. As Bourne rose, Khan stripped the clothes off the guard.

"He's more your size than mine," Khan said, handing Bourne the fatigues.

Bourne climbed into the guard's uniform while Khan dragged the unconscious form into the shadows.

At that moment the motion sensor alarm screamed and they took off toward the substation at a run.

The security guards were well trained, and, commendably, the Americans and Arabs who were on duty this shift worked together flawlessly. Each kind of sensor had a different-sounding alarm, so they knew immediately that the motion sensor had been tripped and precisely where it was. They were on hair-trigger alert and, this close to the summit, were under orders to shoot first and ask questions later.

As they ran, they opened fire, raking the grillwork with automatic fire. Half of them emptied their magazines into the suspect area. The other half stood back in reserve while the others used crowbars to pry off the ruined grilles. They found three bodies, two men and a woman. One of the Americans notified Hull and one of the Arabs contacted Feyd al-Saoud.

By this time, more security personnel from other sectors on the floor had converged on the site to offer added support.

Two of the personnel held in reserve climbed into the air shaft, and when it was determined that no other hostiles were in evidence, they secured the area. Others dragged the three chewed-up corpses out of the air shaft, along with Karim's paraphernalia for bypassing sensors and what at first glance looked like a time bomb.

Jamie Hull and Feyd al-Saoud arrived almost at the same time. Hull took one look at the situation and called his chief of staff via the wireless network.

"As of this moment, we're on red alert. There's been a breach of security. We have three hostiles down, repeat, three hostiles down. Put the entire hotel on absolute lockdown, no one in or out of the premises." He continued to bark orders, moving his men into the planned position for a red alert. Then he contacted the Secret Service, who were with the president and his staff in the dignitary wing.

Feyd al-Saoud had squatted down and was studying the corpses. The bodies were pretty well shot up, but their faces, though blood-streaked, were intact. He took out a pen flash, shone it on one of the faces. Then he reached out, put his forefinger against the eye of one of the males. His fingertip came away blue; the corpse's iris was dark brown.

One of the FSB men must have contacted Karpov because the Alpha Unit commander appeared at an ungainly lope. He was out of breath and Feyd al-Saoud guessed that he'd run all the way.

He and Hull briefed the Russian on what had happened. He held up his fingertip. "They're wearing colored contacts—and look here, they've dyed their hair to pass for Icelanders."

Karpov's face was grim. "I know this one," he said, kicking one of the male corpses. "His name's Akhmed. He's one of Hasan Arsenov's top lieutenants."

"The Chechen terrorist leader?" Hull said. "You'd better inform your president, Boris."

Karpov stood up, fists on hips. "What I want to know is where's Arsenov?"

"I would say that we're too late," Khan said from behind a metal column, as he watched the arrival of the two security chiefs, "except that I don't see Spalko."

"It's possible that he wouldn't put himself at risk by coming to the hotel," Bourne said.

Khan shook his head. "I know him. He's both an egotist and a perfectionist. No, he's here somewhere."

"But not here, obviously," Bourne said thoughtfully. He was watching the Russian jogging up to Jamie Hull and the Arab security chief. There was something vaguely familiar about that flat, brutal face, the beetling brow and caterpillar eyebrows. When he heard the other's voice, he said, "I know that man. The Russian."

"No surprise there. I recognize him, too," Khan said. "Boris Illyich Karpov, head of the FSB's elite Alpha Unit."

"No, I mean I *know* him."

"How? Where?"

"I don't know," Bourne said. "Is he friend or foe?" He beat his fists against his forehead. "If only I could remember."

Khan turned to him and clearly saw the anguish that racked him. He felt a dangerous urge to grasp Bourne's shoulder and reassure him. Dangerous because he didn't know where the gesture would lead or even what it would mean. He felt the further disintegration of his life that had begun the moment Bourne sat down beside him and spoke to him. *"Who are you?"* he had said. At the time, Khan had known the answer to that question; now he wasn't sure. Could it be that everything he'd believed, or thought he'd believed, was a lie?

Khan took refuge from these deeply disturbing thoughts by cleaving to what he and Bourne knew best. "I'm bothered by that object," he said. "It's a time bomb. You said that Spalko was planning to use Dr. Schiffer's bio-diffuser."

Bourne nodded. "I'd say that this was a classic diversion, except for the fact that it's now just past midnight. The summit isn't scheduled to begin for another eight hours."

"That's why they've used a time bomb."

"Yes, but why set it now, so far in advance?" Bourne said.

"Less security," Khan pointed out.

"True, but there's also more chance of its being discovered during one of security's periodic sweeps." Bourne shook his head. "No, we're missing something, I know it. Spalko has something else in mind. But what?"

Spalko, Zina and the remainder of the cadre had reached their objective. Here, far from the section of the hotel housing the summit's forum, security, though tight, had gaps in it that Spalko was able to exploit. Though there were many security people, they couldn't be everywhere at once, and so by taking out two guards, Spalko and his team were soon in position.

They were three levels below the street in a huge concrete windowless space, completely enclosed save for a single open doorway. Masses of huge black pipes ran through the concrete wall on the far side of the space, each labeled with the section of the hotel it served.

The cadre now broke out their HAZMAT suits and put them on, carefully sealing them. Two of the Chechen females went into the passage to stand guard just outside the doorway, and a male rebel backed them up inside.

Spalko opened the larger of the two metal containers he carried. Inside was the NX 20. He carefully fitted the two halves together, checking that all the fittings were securely fastened. He handed it to Zina while he unlocked the refrigerated container Peter Sido had provided. The glass vial it contained was small, almost minuscule. Even after they had seen its effect in Nairobi, it was difficult to believe that such a small amount of the virus could be lethal to so many people.

As he'd done in Nairobi, he opened the loading chamber on the diffuser and placed the vial into it. He closed and locked the chamber, took the NX 20 from Zina's arms and curled his finger around the smaller of the two triggers. Once he squeezed it, the virus, still sealed in its special vial, would be injected into the firing chamber. After that, all that was required was for him to press the button on the left side of the stock, which would lock the firing chamber, and, when it was aimed correctly, pull the main trigger.

He cradled the bio-diffuser in his arms as Zina had done. This weapon needed to be given the proper respect, even from him.

He looked into Zina's eyes, which were shining with her love for him and her patriot's zeal. "Now we wait," he said, "for the sensor alarm."

They heard it then, the sound faint but its vibrations unmistakable, magnified by the bare concrete corridors. The Shaykh and Zina smiled into each other's faces. He could feel the tension come into the room, fueled by righteous anger and an expectation of redemption long denied.

"Our moment is at hand," he said, and they all heard him, all reacted. He could almost hear their ululation of victory begin.

With the unstoppable force of destiny propelling him forward, the Shaykh pulled the small trigger, and with an ominous whisper, the payload clicked home into the firing chamber, where it rested, waiting for the moment of its release.

CHAPTER TWENTY-NINE

"They're all Chechens, isn't that right, Boris?" Hull said.

Karpov nodded. "All, according to the records, members of Hasan Arsenov terrorist group."

"This is a coup for the good guys," Hull exulted.

Feyd al-Saoud, shivering in the damp and chill, said, "With the amount of C4 in that time bomb, they would've taken out almost the entire weight-bearing substructure. The forum above would've collapsed of its own weight, killing everyone inside."

"Lucky for us they tripped the motion sensor," Hull said.

As the minutes passed, Karpov's frown had grown only deeper as he echoed Bourne's query, "Why set the bomb so far in advance? I think we had a good chance of finding it before the summit started."

Feyd al-Saoud turned to one of his men. "Is there some way to turn up the heat down here? We're going to be here for some time and I'm already freezing."

"That's it!" Bourne said, turning to Khan. He took his laptop, turned it on, scrolling through the schematics until he found the one he wanted. He traced a route from where they were back toward the main section of the hotel. Snapping the computer closed, he said, "Come on! Let's go!"

"Where are we headed?" Khan asked as they made their way through the maze of the sublevel.

"Think about it. We saw a Reykjavik Energy van pull into the hotel; the entire hotel is heated by the thermal system that services the city as a whole."

"That's why Spalko sent those Chechens to the HVAC subsystem now," Khan said as they raced around a corner. "They were never meant to succeed in planting the bomb. We were right, it *was* a diversion, but not for later this morning when the summit is scheduled to start. He's going to activate the bio-diffuser now!"

"Right," Bourne said. "Not through the HVAC subsystem. His target is the main thermal heating system. At this time of night all the dignitaries are in their rooms, right where he's going to release the virus."

"Someone coming," one of the female Chechens said.

"Kill them," the Shaykh commanded.

"But it's Hasan Arsenov!" cried the other female guard.

Spalko and Zina exchanged a bewildered look. What had gone wrong? The sensor had been tripped, the alarm had gone off, and shortly thereafter they'd heard the satisfying bursts of automatic gunfire. How had Arsenov escaped?

"I said kill him!" Spalko shouted.

What haunted Arsenov, what had made him turn tail at the instant he smelled the trap, thus saving himself from the sudden death suffered by his compatriots, was the terror that had been lurking inside him, the thing that had given him nightmares for the past week. He had told himself that it was his guilt at having betrayed Khalid Murat—a hero's guilt at having made the hard choice that would save his people. But the truth of the matter was his terror had to do with Zina. He had not been able to admit to seeing her withdrawal, gradual but inexorable, her emotional distance that, in retrospect, had become glacial. She had been slipping away from him for some time, though even up to a few moments ago he had refused to believe it. But now Akhmed's revelation had thrown it into the light of consciousness. She had lived behind a glass wall, always keeping part of herself aloof and hidden. He couldn't touch that part of her, and it seemed to him now that the harder he'd tried, the further away she pulled herself.

Zina didn't love him—he wondered now whether she ever had. Even if their mission was a complete success, there would be no life with her, no children they could share together. What a farce their last intimate conversation had been!

All at once, he was overcome by shame. He was a coward—he loved her more than he loved his freedom, for without her he knew there would be no freedom for him. In the wake of her betrayal, victory would be like ashes in his mouth.

Now, as he pounded down the cold corridor toward the thermal heating station, he saw one of his own people raise her machine pistol as if she was going to shoot him. Perhaps in the HAZMAT suit she couldn't tell who was coming toward her.

"Wait! Don't shoot!" he cried. "It's Hasan Arsenov!"

A bullet from her opening volley struck him in the left arm, and half in shock, he spun around, diving around a corner, away from the deadly spray of ricocheting bullets.

In the abrupt frenzy of the present, there was no more time for questions or speculation. He heard renewed gunfire but not in his direction. Peering around the corner, he saw that the two females had turned their backs to him and, crouched, were firing at two figures as they advanced down the passageway.

Arsenov rose and, taking advantage of the diversion, headed for the doorway to the thermal heating station.

Spalko heard the gunfire and said, "Zina, that can't be just Arsenov."

Zina swung her machine pistol around, nodded to the guard, who threw her a second one.

Behind them, Spalko went over to the wall of thermal heating pipes. Each one had a valve and, beside it, a gauge that showed the pressure. He found the pipe that corresponded to the dignitaries' wing, began to unscrew the valve.

Hasan Arsenov knew that he'd been meant to die with the others in the HVAC substation. *"It's a trap! Someone crossed the wires!"* Karim had wailed just before he'd died. Spalko had crossed the wires; he'd needed not simply a diversion, as he'd told them, but scapegoats—targets of enough importance that their deaths would occupy the security for a sufficient amount of time for Spalko to reach the real objective and release the virus. Spalko had tricked him and, Arsenov was quite certain now, Zina had conspired with him.

How quickly love turned rancid, its transformation into hate occurring in no more time than it takes a heart to beat. Now they had turned against him, all his compatriots, the men and women he'd fought alongside, whom he'd laughed and cried with, prayed to Allah with, who had the same goals as he did. Chechens! All corrupted now by Stepan Spalko's power and poisonous charm.

In the end Khalid Murat had been right about everything. He hadn't trusted Spalko; he wouldn't have followed him into this folly. Once, Arsenov had accused him of being an old man, of being too cautious, of not understanding the new world that lay before them. But now he knew what Khalid Murat had surely known: that that new world was nothing more than a self-serving illusion created by the man who called himself the Shaykh. Arsenov had believed this pipe dream because he'd wanted to believe it. Spalko had preyed upon that weakness. But no more! Arsenov vowed. No more! If he was to die today, it would be on his own terms, not as a sheep to the slaughter of Spalko's making.

He pressed himself against the edge of the doorway, took a deep breath and when he let it out, he somersaulted past the open doorway. The resulting hail of automatic fire told him all he needed to know. Rolling, he kept to the concrete floor, wriggling on his stomach into the opening. He saw the guard, his machine pistol aimed at waist height, and shot him four times in the chest.

When Bourne saw the two terrorists in HAZMAT suits behind a concrete column, firing their machine pistols in alternate bursts, his blood ran cold. He and Khan took cover around the corner of a T-junction and he fired back.

"Spalko's in that room with the bio-weapon," Bourne said. "We've got to get in there now."

"Not unless those two run out of ammo." Khan was looking around behind them. "Do you remember the schematics? Remember what's in the ceiling?"

Bourne, continuing to fire, nodded.

"There's an access panel back about twenty feet. I need a boost."

Bourne got off one more burst before retreating with Khan.

"Will you be able to see anything up there?" he asked.

Khan nodded, indicating his miraculous jacket. "I've got a pen light, among other things, up my sleeve."

Tucking the machine pistol under his arm, Bourne laced his fingers together for Khan to put his foot in. His bones seemed to crack with the weight and the strained muscles in his shoulder seemed to catch fire.

Then Khan slid the panel off and had hoisted himself the rest of the way into the access hatch.

"Time," Bourne said.

"Fifteen seconds," Khan replied, disappearing.

Bourne turned. He counted to ten, then turned the corner, his machine pistol blazing. But almost immediately he stopped. He could feel his heart pounding painfully against his ribs. The two Chechens had taken off their HAZMAT suits. They had emerged from behind the column and now stood facing him. He saw that they were female and that around their waists were a series of linked packets filled with C4 explosive.

"Good Christ," Bourne said. "Khan! They're wearing suicide belts!"

At that moment they were plunged into darkness. Khan, in the electrical conduit above his head, had cut the wires.

Arsenov was up and sprinting forward the moment after he fired. He ran into the station, grabbed the guard before he fell. Two other figures were in the room: Spalko and Zina. Using the dead guard as a shield, he fired at the target with a machine pistol in each hand. Zina! But she had squeezed the triggers and even as she staggered back, hit, the massed fury of the automatic fire blew right through the guard's body.

Arsenov's eyes opened wide as he felt the searing pain in his chest, and then an odd kind of numbness. The lights winked out and he lay on the floor, the breath rattling in his blood-filled lungs. As if in a dream, he heard Zina screaming, and he wept for all the dreams he'd had, for a future that would now never come. With a sigh, life left him as it had come upon him, in hardship and brutality and pain.

———

A terrible, deathly silence had descended on the passage. Time seemed to have stopped. Bourne, his gun aimed into the darkness, heard the soft, shallow breathing of the human bombs. He could feel their fear as well as their determination. If they sensed him take a step toward them, if they became aware of Khan moving in the electrical conduit, they would surely detonate the explosives strapped around their waists.

Then, because he was listening for it, he heard the very faint double tap above his head, the sound, swiftly diminishing, of Khan moving in the electrical conduit. He knew there was an access panel more or less where the doorway to the thermal heating station was, and he had an idea what Khan was going to try. It would require nerves of steel and a very steady hand from both of them. The AR-15 he carried was short-barreled, but it made up for any slight inaccuracy with its awesome firepower. It used .223-caliber ammo which it spit out with a muzzle velocity in excess of 2400 feet per second. He wriggled silently closer, then, aware of a slight shifting ahead of him in the darkness, he froze. His heart was in his throat. Had he heard something, a sibilance, a whisper, footsteps? Utter silence now. He held his breath and concentrated on sighting down the barrel of the AR-15.

Where was Spalko? Had he loaded the bio-weapon yet? Would he stay to finish the mission or would he cut and run? Knowing he had no answers, he put these terrifying questions aside. *Concentrate*, he berated himself. *Relax now, breathe deeply and evenly as you move into alpha rhythm, as you become one with the weapon.*

He saw it then. Khan's penlight flash, the beam illuminating a woman's face, blinding her. There was no time to consider or to think. His finger had been curled on the trigger and now instinct flowed naturally and instantaneously into action. The muzzle flash lit up the corridor, and he watched the woman's head disintegrate in a welter of blood, bone and brains.

He was up then, running forward, looking for the other woman. Then the lights blinked on and he saw the second human bomb, lying beside the other one, her throat slit. An instant later, Khan dropped down from the open access hatch and together they entered the thermal heating station.

Moments before, in the darkness that smelled of cordite and blood and death, Spalko had dropped to his knees, searching blindly for Zina. The darkness had defeated him. Without light, he was unable to make the delicate connection between the muzzle of the NX 20 and the valve into the thermal heating system.

His arm extended, he felt along the floor. He hadn't been paying attention to her, wasn't certain of her position, and in any case, she had moved the moment Arsenov had burst through the doorway. It had been clever of him to use the human shield, but Zina was cleverer still and she had killed him. But she was still alive. He had heard her scream.

Now he waited, knowing that the human bombs he had primed would protect him from whoever was out there. Bourne? Khan? He was ashamed to realize that he was afraid of the unknown presence in the passage. Whoever it was had seen through his diversion, had followed his own reasoning regarding the vulnerability of the thermal heating system. There was a rising panic in him, alleviated for the moment when he heard Zina suck in a ragged breath. Quickly he crawled through a pool of sticky blood to where she lay.

Her hair was wet and stringy as he kissed her cheek. "Beautiful Zina," he whispered in her ear. "Powerful Zina."

He felt a kind of spasm pass through her and his heart constricted in fear. "Zina, don't die. You can't die." Then he tasted the salty wetness running down her cheek and knew that she was weeping. Her breast rose and fell irregularly with her silent sobs.

"Zina"—he kissed away her tears—"you must be strong, now more than ever before." He embraced her tenderly and felt her arms slowly come around him.

"This is the moment of our greatest triumph." He drew away and pressed the NX 20 into her embrace. "Yes, yes, I choose you to fire the weapon, to bring the future to fruition."

She couldn't speak. It was all she could do to keep the breath sawing in and out of her lungs. Once again he cursed the darkness, for he couldn't see her eyes, couldn't be certain that he had her. He had to take the chance, however. He took her hands and placed the left one on the barrel of the bio-diffuser, the right one at the guard on the stock. He placed her forefinger on the main trigger.

"All you need do is squeeze," he whispered in her ear. "But not yet, not yet. I need time."

Yes, time was what he needed in order to escape. He was trapped in the darkness, the one contingency for which he hadn't been prepared. And now he couldn't even take the NX 20 with him. He'd have to run and run hard, a condition that Schiffer had made clear, the weapon once loaded was not designed to handle. The payload and its container were far too fragile.

"Zina, you'll do this, won't you?" He kissed her cheek. "You have enough strength inside you, I know you do." She was trying to say something, but he put a hand over her mouth, afraid that his unknown pursuers outside would hear her strangled cry. "I'll be close by, Zina. Remember that."

Then so slowly and gently that it was imperceptible to her impaired senses, he slithered away. Turning, at last, from her, he stumbled over Arsenov's corpse and his HAZMAT suit ripped. For a moment his new-found terror returned as he imagined himself being trapped in here when Zina pulled the trigger, the virus seeping into the rent, infecting him. In his mind's eye, the city of the dead he had created in Nairobi bloomed in all its vivid, gruesome detail.

Then he'd regained his composure and he stripped off the encumbering suit altogether. Silent as a cat, he made his way to the doorway, swung out into the passage. At once the human bombs became aware of him and shifted slightly, tensing.

"*La illaha ill Allah,*" he whispered.

"*La illaha ill Allah,*" they whispered in return.

Then, in the darkness, he stole away.

They both saw it at once, the blunt, ugly snout of Dr. Felix Schiffer's bio-diffuser pointed at them. Bourne and Khan froze.

"Spalko's gone. There's his HAZMAT suit," Bourne said. "This station has only one entrance." He thought of the movement he'd detected, the whisper, the sound of furtive footfalls he thought he'd heard. "He must've slipped out in the darkness."

"I know this one," Khan said. "It's Hasan Arsenov, but this other, the female holding the weapon, I don't know."

The female terrorist lay half-propped up on the corpse of another terrorist. How she had managed to drag herself into this position neither of them could say. She was very badly wounded, possibly fatally, though from this distance it was impossible to say for sure. She looked at them from a world filled with pain and, Bourne was quite certain, something else that went beyond mere physical hurt.

Khan had taken a Kalishnikov from one of the human bombs outside and he aimed it now at the female. "There's no way out for you," he said.

Bourne, who had been watching only her eyes, stepped forward and pushed the Kalishnikov down. "There's always a way out," he said.

Then he squatted down so that he was at the other's level. Without taking his gaze from her, he said, "Can you speak? Can you tell me your name?"

For a moment there was only silence, and Bourne had to force himself to keep his gaze on her face, not to look at her finger curled and tense on the trigger.

At length her lips opened and began to tremble. Her teeth chattered and a tear slipped free, rolling down her stained cheek.

"What d'you care what her name is?" Khan's voice was filled with contempt. "She's not human; she's been turned into a machine of destruction."

"Khan, some might say the same of you." Bourne's voice was so gentle it was clear that what he said wasn't a rebuke, merely a truth that might not have occurred to his son.

He turned his attention back to the terrorist. "It's important that you tell me your name, isn't it?"

Her lips opened and with a great effort, she said in a voice somewhere between a rattle and a gurgle, "Zina."

"Well, Zina, we're at the endgame," Bourne said. "There's nothing left now, except death and life. By the looks of things, it appears as if you've already chosen death. If you pull the trigger, you'll be sent to heaven and in glory will become a *houri*. But I wonder whether that will happen. What is it that you'll be leaving behind? Dead compatriots, at least one of whom you've shot yourself. And then there's Stepan Spalko. Where has he gone, I wonder. No matter. What's important is that at the crucial moment, he abandoned you.

"He's left you to die, Zina, while he's cut and run. So I guess you have to ask yourself if you pull that trigger, will you go to your glory or will you be cast down, found wanting by Mounkir and Nekir, the Questioners. Given your life, Zina, when they ask you 'Who is thy creator? Who is thy Prophet?' will you be able to answer them? Only the righteous remember, Zina, you know that."

Zina was openly weeping now. But her breast was heaving strangely and Bourne was afraid that a sudden spasm would cause her to pull the trigger in reflex. If he was going to reach her, it had to be now.

"If you pull that trigger, if you choose death, you won't be able to answer them. You know that. You've been abandoned and betrayed, Zina, by those closest to you. And, in turn, you've betrayed them. But it's not too late. There can be redemption; there's always a way out."

At the moment Khan realized that Bourne was talking as much to him as he was to Zina; he experienced a feeling not unlike an electrical shock. This feeling raced through his body until it sparked both his extremities and his brain. He felt himself stripped naked, revealed at last, and he was terrified of nothing more or less than himself—his own true authentic self that he had buried so many years ago in the jungle of Southeast Asia. It was so long ago that he couldn't remember exactly where or when he'd done it. The truth was that he was a stranger to himself. He hated his father for leading him to that truth, but he could no longer deny that he loved him for it, too.

He knelt, then, beside the man he knew to be his father, and putting the Kalishnikov down where Zina could see it, he extended a hand toward her.

"He's right," Khan said in an altogether different voice from the one he normally used. "There is a way to make up for your past sins, for the murders you've committed, for the betrayals to those who've loved you without, perhaps, you even knowing."

He moved forward inch by inch until his hand closed over hers. Slowly and gently he pried her forefinger away from the trigger. She let go then and allowed him to take the weapon from her useless embrace.

"Thank you, Zina," Bourne said. "Khan will take care of you now." He rose, and giving his son's shoulder a brief squeeze, he turned and went swiftly and silently down the passage after Spalko.

CHAPTER THIRTY

Stepan Spalko sprinted down the bare concrete passage, Bourne's ceramic gun at the ready. He knew that all the gunfire would bring the security people into the main section of the hotel. Up ahead, he saw the Saudi security chief, Feyd al-Saoud, and two of his men. He ducked out of sight. They hadn't seen him yet and he used this element of surprise, waiting for them to come closer, then shooting them before they had time to react.

For a breathless moment he stood over the downed men. Feyd al-Saoud groaned and Spalko shot him at close range in the forehead. The Saudi security chief flopped once and was still. Quickly Spalko took the ID tags off one of his men, changed into the man's uniform and got rid of his colored contact lenses. As he did so, his thoughts turned inexorably to Zina. She had been fearless, true enough, but the ardor of her loyalty to him had been her fatal flaw. She had protected him from everyone—especially Arsenov. She'd enjoyed that, he could tell. But it struck him that her true passion was for him. It was this love, the repugnant weakness of sacrifice, that had driven him to abandon her.

Swift footfalls behind him brought him back to the present, and he hurried on. The fateful meeting with the Arabs had been a two-edged sword, for while it had provided him with a ready means of disguise, it had slowed him down, and now as he threw a glance over his shoulder, he saw a figure in security fatigues and cursed mightily. He felt like Ahab, who pursued his nemesis until, in an utterly unexpected reversal, his nemesis had come after him. The man in the security fatigues was Jason Bourne.

Bourne saw Spalko, now in an Arab security uniform, open a door and vanish into a stairwell. He leaped over the bodies of the men Spalko had just killed and headed after him. He emerged into the chaos of the lobby.

Just a short time ago, when he and Khan had entered the hotel, this vast glassed-in space was tense but hushed, almost deserted. Now it was a welter of security personnel running to and fro. Some were rounding up the hotel personnel, sorting them into groups, depending on their jobs and where they had just been inside the premises. Others had already begun the laborious and time-consuming process of questioning the staff. Each individual had to account for every moment of his whereabouts over the course of the last two days. Still others were on their way down to the subbasement or were being deployed by wireless network to other areas of the hotel. Everyone was hustling; no one had time to question the two men who, one after the other, crossed through the mob scene toward the front door.

It was ironic to watch Spalko walking among them, blending in, becoming one of them. Briefly, Bourne considered trying to alert those around him but immediately thought better of it. Spalko would no doubt call his bluff—it was Bourne who was the internationally wanted murderer still under a CIA sanction. Spalko, of course, knew this, being the clever architect of Bourne's dangerous predicament. And as he followed Spalko out of the front doors, he realized something else. *We're both the same now,* he thought, *both chameleons employing the same marking in order to keep our true identities from being revealed to those around us.* It was odd and disquieting to realize that at the moment this international security force was as much his enemy as it was Spalko's.

The moment he was outside, Bourne realized that the hotel was in absolute lockdown. He watched with fascinated dread as Spalko boldly made his way to the security services car park. Although it was within the limits of the lockdown cordon, it was deserted, as even security personnel weren't allowed in or out.

Bourne went after him but almost immediately lost him in the ranks of vehicles. He broke into a run. There was a shout from behind him. He pulled open the door of the first vehicle he came to—an American Jeep. Yanking out the plastic panel on the bottom of the steering column, he fumbled for the wires. Just then another engine fired up and he saw Spalko in the car he'd stolen, wheeling out of the car park.

There were more shouts now and the pounding of boots against pavement. Several shots were fired. Bourne, concentrating on what needed to be done, got the wires stripped and braided together. The Jeep's engine coughed to life, and he put it in gear. Then with a hard squeal of tires, he turned out of the car park and accelerated through the security checkpoint.

The night was moonless but, then again, it wasn't really night. An insipid darkness lay over Reykjavik as the sun, hanging just below the horizon, turned the sky the color of an oystershell. As Bourne followed Spalko's twists and turns through the city, he realized that Spalko was heading south.

This was something of a surprise, for he'd expected Spalko to make for the airport. Surely he had an escape plan and just as surely it involved an aircraft. But the more Bourne thought about it, the less surprised he was. He was getting to know his adversary better now. Already he understood that Spalko never took the logical way in or out of a situation. His mind was unique, involved as it was in puzzle-logic. He was a man of feints and twists, someone who liked to trap his opponent rather than kill him outright.

So. Keflavik was out. Too obvious and, as Spalko would undoubtedly have foreseen, too well guarded for him to use as an escape route. Bourne oriented himself to the map he'd studied on Oszkar's laptop. What lay south of the city? Hafnarfjördur, a fishing village too small to land the kind of aircraft Spalko would use. The coast! They were on an island, after all. Spalko was going to escape via boat.

At this time of night there was little traffic, especially after they left the city behind them. The roads became narrower, winding through the hillsides that fronted the landward side of the sea cliffs. As Spalko's car went around a particularly sharp curve, Bourne dropped back. Turning off his headlights, he accelerated around the turn. He could see Spalko's vehicle up ahead, but he hoped that Spalko, peering into his rear-view mirror, wouldn't be able to see him. It was a risk, losing sight of the car every time they went around a turn, but Bourne didn't see that he had any alternative. He had to make Spalko believe he'd lost his pursuer.

The utter lack of trees lent the landscape a certain gravity and, with the blue ice mountains as backdrop, a sense of eternal winter as well, made all the more eerie by the intermittent swaths of verdant green. The sky was immense and, in the long false-dawn, filled with the black shapes of shorebirds, soaring and swooping. Seeing them, Bourne felt a certain freedom from his entombment in the death-laden bowels of the hotel. Despite the chill, he rolled down the windows and breathed deeply of the fresh salt-laced air. A sweet smell rose to his nostrils as he flashed past the rolling, flower-dotted carpet of a meadow.

The road narrowed further as it turned toward the sea. Bourne descended through a lushly foliated glen and then zoomed around another curve. The road steepened in its switchback descent of the cliff face. He saw Spalko, then lost him again as another curve loomed. He made the turn and saw the North Atlantic low and spangled dully in the slate-gray dawn.

Spalko's car went around another turn and Bourne followed on. The next turn was so close that the car was already out of sight, and despite the added risk, Bourne pushed the Jeep faster.

He had already committed to the turn when he heard the sound. It was soft and familiar above the flutter of the wind, the noise his ceramic gun made when fired. His front nearside tire blew and he slewed around. He caught a glimpse of Spalko, gun in hand, running to where he'd left his car. Then his view changed, and he was too busy trying to get the Jeep under control as it skidded perilously close to the seaside edge of the road.

He downshifted into neutral, but it wasn't enough. He needed to turn off the ignition, but without the key that was impossible. The rear tires slipped off the road. Bourne unbuckled himself and held on as the Jeep spun off the cliff. It seemed to float, turning over twice. The brash, unmistakable odor of overheated metal came to him, along with the acrid stench of rubber or plastic burning.

He leaped just before the Jeep hit, rolling away as the vehicle bounced off an outcropping of rock and burst open. Flames shot up into the air, and by their light he saw in the cove just below him the fishing boat, nosing in toward the shore.

Spalko drove like a maniac down the road to the dead end at the inner edge of the cove. Throwing a glance back at the flaming Jeep, he said to himself, *To hell with Jason Bourne. He's dead now.* But not, unfortunately, soon forgotten. It was Bourne who had foiled him, and now he had neither the NX 20 nor the Chechens as cat's-paws. So many months of careful planning come to nothing!

He got out of the car and walked across what remained of the wrack-strewn shingle. A rowboat was coming for him, even though it was high tide and the fishing boat was very close to shore. He'd called the captain the moment he'd successfully run the hotel's security checkpoint. Only a skeleton crew of the captain and a mate were onboard. He climbed in as the captain nosed the rowboat onto the shingle, then the mate pushed off with his oar.

Spalko was fuming and not a word was said on the short, unpleasant trip back to the fishing boat. When he was aboard, Spalko said, "Make ready to leave, Captain."

"Begging you pardon, sir," the captain replied, "but what about the rest of the crew?"

Spalko grabbed the captain by his shirtfront. "I gave you an order, Captain. I expect you to carry it out."

"Aye, aye, sir," the captain grumbled with an evil glint in his eye. "But with only the two of us to crew, it'll take a little longer to get under way."

"You'd damn well better get to it then," Spalko told him, as he headed below.

The water was cold as ice, black as the subbasement of the hotel. Bourne knew that he needed to get onboard the fishing boat as quickly as possible. Thirty seconds after he'd pushed out from the shingle, his fingers and toes had started to go numb; thirty seconds after that, he couldn't feel them at all.

The two minutes it took him to reach the boat seemed like the longest in his life. He reached up for an oiled hawser and hauled himself out of the sea. He shivered in the wind, moving hand over hand up the line.

As he went, he experienced an eerie dislocation. With the scent of the sea in his nostrils, the feel of the brine drying on his skin, it seemed to him as if he wasn't in Iceland at all but in Marseilles, that he wasn't climbing onto a fishing boat in pursuit of Stepan Spalko but was clandestinely boarding a pleasure yacht on his way to execute the international assassin for hire, Carlos. For it was in Marseilles that the nightmare had begun, where the pitched battle with Carlos had ended with him being flung overboard, the shock of being shot and almost drowned robbing him of his memory, of his very life.

As he lifted himself over the gunwale onto the deck of the fishing boat, he felt a stab of fear that was almost paralyzing in its intensity. It was in this very same situation that he'd failed. He felt abruptly exposed, as if he wore this failure on his sleeve. He almost faltered then, but into his mind sprang the image of Khan, and he remembered what he'd said to him when they'd first met in that tension-filled setting. *"Who are you?"* Because it occurred to him now that Khan didn't know, and if Bourne wasn't around to help him find out who he was, he'd have no one. He thought of Khan, on his knees in the thermal heating station, and it seemed to him that it wasn't only the Kalishnikov he'd let go of but also, possibly, something of his own inner rage.

Bourne, taking a deep breath, settled his mind on what was before him and crept along the deck. The captain and his mate were busy in the wheelhouse and he encountered little difficulty in rendering them unconscious. There was plenty of rope around and he was in the process of binding their wrists behind their backs when Spalko said from behind him, "I think you'd better find a bit of rope for yourself."

Bourne was crouched down. The two seamen lay on their sides, back to back. Without showing anything to Spalko, Bourne slipped out his switchblade. Immediately, he knew he'd made a fatal mistake. The mate had his back to him, but the captain did not and saw very clearly that he was now armed. His eyes looked into Bourne's but, curiously, he made no sound or movement that would alert Spalko. Instead, he closed his eyes as if in sleep.

"Stand up and turn around," Spalko ordered.

Bourne did as he was told, keeping his right hand hidden behind the outer edge of his thigh. Spalko, in freshly pressed jeans and a black cable-knit turtleneck sweater, stood spread-legged on the deck, Bourne's ceramic gun in his hand. And again Bourne was subjected to the strange sense of dislocation. As with Carlos years ago, Spalko now had the drop on him. All that remained was for Spalko to pull the trigger, for Bourne to be hit and cast into the water. This time, however, in the bone-chilling North Atlantic, there would be no rescue as there had been in the mild Mediterranean waters. He would quickly freeze and drown.

"You simply will not die, will you, Mr. Bourne?"

Bourne dove at Spalko, the switchblade snapping open. Spalko, startled, squeezed the trigger far too late. The bullet sang out over the water as the blade buried itself in his side. He grunted, clubbed the barrel of the gun down onto Bourne's cheek. Blood spurted from both of them. Spalko's left knee buckled, but Bourne crashed to the deck.

Spalko, remembering, kicked him viciously in his cracked ribs, rendering Bourne nearly unconscious. He pulled the switchblade from his side, threw it into the water. Then he bent and dragged Bourne to the gunwale. As Bourne began to stir, Spalko hit him with heel of his hand. Then he hauled him more or less upright and bent him over the side.

Bourne was phasing in and out of consciousness, but the sharp tang of the icy black water brought him around enough to know that he was on the brink of annihilation. It was happening again, just as it had so many years ago. He was in so much pain that he could barely draw breath, but there was life to think of—his life now, not the one that had been taken away from him. He wouldn't let himself be robbed again.

As Spalko exerted himself to heave him over the side, Bourne kicked out with all his might. With a sickening snap, the sole of his shoe connected with Spalko's jaw. Spalko, grabbing his broken jaw, staggered backward, and Bourne ran at him. Spalko had no time to use the gun; Bourne was already inside his guard. He slammed the butt down on Bourne's shoulder, and Bourne staggered as more pain flashed through him.

Then he'd reached up, digging his fingers into the broken bones of Spalko's jaw. Spalko screamed and Bourne wrenched the gun from his grip. He jammed the muzzle underneath Spalko's chin and pulled the trigger.

The sound did not amount to much, but the force of the percussion lifted Spalko bodily off the deck and pitched him over the side. He went into the sea headfirst.

For a moment, as Bourne looked on, he floated facedown, rocked back and forth by the restless waves. Then he went under as if drawn by something huge and immensely potent beneath the sea.

CHAPTER THIRTY-ONE

Martin Lindros spent twenty minutes on the phone with Ethan Hearn. Hearn had much information about the famous Stepan Spalko, all of it such a stunning revelation it took Lindros some time to absorb and accept. In the end, no item was of more interest to him than the one that showed an electronic transfer from one of Spalko's many shell companies in Budapest to buy a gun from a certain illegal Russian-run company operating out of Virginia until Detective Harris had shut them down.

An hour later he had two hard copies printed out from the electronic files Hearn had e-mailed him. He got into his car and headed over to the DCI's town house. Overnight, the Old Man had been stricken with the flu. It must be bad, Lindros thought now, for him to have left the office at all during the crisis at the summit.

His driver stopped the staff car at the high iron gates, leaned out the open window, and pressed the intercom. In the ensuing silence he began to wonder if the Old Man, feeling better, had summarily taken himself back to the office without informing anyone.

Then the querulous voice crackled over the intercom, the driver announced Lindros, and a moment later, the gates swung soundlessly open. The driver pulled the car up and Lindros got out. He rapped on the door with the brass knocker, and when it opened, he saw the DCI, his face wrinkled and his hair disheveled from lying on a pillow. He was wearing striped pajamas over which he'd wrapped a heavy-looking bathrobe. On his bony feet were carpet slippers.

"Come in, Martin. Come in." He turned and left the door open without waiting for Lindros to cross the threshold. Lindros entered, closed the door behind him. The DCI had padded into the study, which was off to the left. There were no lights on; there appeared to be none on in the house at all.

He went into the study, a masculine space with hunter green walls, a cream ceiling, and oversize leather chairs and sofa scattered about. A TV, set into a wall of built-in bookcases, was off. Every other time Lindros had been in this room it had been on, tuned to CNN, either with or without the sound.

The Old Man sat heavily down in his favorite chair. The side table at his right elbow was crammed with a large box of tissues and bottles of aspirin, Tylenol Cold & Sinus, NyQuil, Vicks VapoRub, Coricidin, DayQuil, and Robitussin DM cough syrup.

"What is this, sir?" Lindros said, indicating the small drugstore.

"I didn't know what I'd need," The DCI said, "so I just took everything out of the medicine chest."

Then Lindros saw the bottle of bourbon and the old-fashioned glass, and he frowned. "Sir, what's going on?" He craned his neck to see out the open doorway of the study. "Where's Madeleine?"

"Ah, Madeleine." The Old Man picked up his whiskey glass and slugged some down. "Madeleine has gone to her sister's in Phoenix."

"And left you on your own?" Lindros reached over and turned on a standing lamp, and the DCI blinked owlishly at him. "When will she be back, sir?"

"Hmmm." The DCI said, as if considering his deputy's words. "Well, the thing of it is, Martin, I don't know when she's coming back."

"Sir?" Lindros said with some alarm.

"She's left me. At least that's what I think has happened." The DCI's gaze seemed fixed as he drained his glass of bourbon. He pursed his shining lips as if perplexed. "How does one know these things, really?"

"Haven't the two of you talked?"

"Talked?" The DCI's gaze snapped back into focus. He looked at Lindros for a moment. "No. We haven't spoken about it at all."

"Then how do you know?"

"You think I'm making it up, tempest in a rotunda, eh?" The DCI's eyes came alive for an instant and all at once his voice was clotted with barely suppressed emotion. "But there are things of hers that're gone, you see—personal things, intimate things. The house is goddamned empty without them."

Lindros sat down. "Sir, you have my sympathy, but I have something—"

"Maybe, Martin, she never loved me." The Old Man reached for the bottle. "But how is one to know such a mysterious thing?"

Lindros learned forward, gently took the bourbon from his commander. The DCI didn't seem surprised. "I'll work on it for you, sir, if you'd like."

The DCI nodded vaguely. "All right."

Lindros put the bottle aside. "But for now we have another pressing matter to discuss." He set the file he'd gotten from Ethan Hearn down on the Old Man's side table.

"What is that? I can't read anything now, Martin."

"Then I'll tell you," Lindros said. When he was done, there was a silence that seemed to echo throughout the house.

After a time the Old Man looked at his deputy with watery eyes. "Why'd he do it, Martin? Why did Alex break every rule and steal one of our own people?"

"I think he'd gotten a hint of what was coming, sir. He was frightened of Spalko. As it turned out, with very good reason."

The Old Man sighed and put his head back. "So it wasn't treason, after all."

"No, sir."

"Thank God."

Lindros cleared his throat. "Sir, you must rescind the Bourne sanction at once, and someone's going to have to debrief him."

"Yes, of course. I think you're best equipped to do that, Martin."

"Yes, sir." Lindros stood.

"Where are you going?" The querulousness had returned to the Old Man's voice.

"To the Virginia State Police Commissioner. I have another copy of that file to drop into his lap. I'm going to insist that Detective Harris be reinstated, with a commendation from us. And as for the National Security Advisor herself . . . ?"

The DCI took up the file and stroked it lightly. With this bit of animation, some color returned to his face. "Give me overnight, Martin." Slowly, the old glint was returning to his eyes. "I'll think of something deliciously suitable." He laughed, the first time he'd done so, it seemed, in ages. " 'Let the punishment fit the crime,' eh?"

Khan was with Zina to the end. He'd hidden the NX 20 and its horribly lethal payload. As far as the security people who were swarming all over the thermal heating station were concerned, he was a hero. They knew nothing about the bio-weapon. They knew nothing about him.

It was a curious time for Khan. He held the hand of a dying young woman who couldn't speak, who could barely breathe, and yet who quite clearly didn't want to let him go. Perhaps it was simply that, in the end, she didn't want to die.

After Hull and Karpov realized that she was on the verge of dying and couldn't provide them with information, they lost interest and so they left her alone with Khan. And he, so inured to death, experienced something wholly unexpected. Each breath she took, labored and painful, was a lifetime. He saw this in her eyes which, like her hand, would not let him go. She was drowning in the silence, sinking down into darkness. He couldn't let that happen.

Unbidden, his own pain was brought to the surface by hers, and he spoke to her of his life: of his abandonment, his imprisonment by the Vietnamese gunrunner, the religious conversion forced on him by the missionary, the political brainwashing by his Khmer Rouge interlocutor.

And then, most painful of all, was wrenched out of him his feelings about Lee-Lee. "I had a sister," he said in a thin, reedy voice. "She would've been about your age had she lived. She was two years younger than me, looked up to me, and I—I was her protector. I wanted so much to keep her safe, not only because my parents said I should but because I needed to. My father was away a lot. When we were off playing, who would protect her if not me?" Unaccountably, his eyes felt hot and his vision was blurred. Suffused with shame, he was about to turn away, but he saw something in Zina's eyes, a fierce compassion that served as a lifeline for him, and his shame vanished. He continued then, connected to her on an even more intimate level. "But, in the end, I failed Lee-Lee. My sister was killed along with my mother. I should've been too, but I survived." His hand found its way to the carved stone Buddha, gaining strength from it as he had done so many times before. "For such a long time, I used to wonder, what use was my survival? I had failed her."

When Zina's lips parted slightly, he saw that her teeth were bloody. Her hand, which he held so tightly, squeezed his and he knew that she wanted him to go on. He was not only freeing her from her own agony but he was freeing himself from his own. And the most curious thing was that it worked. Though she couldn't speak, though she was slowly dying, still her brain functioned. She heard what he said, and by her expression, he knew that it meant something to her—he knew that she was transported and that she understood.

"Zina," he said, "in a way, we're kindred spirits. I see myself in you—alienated, abandoned, utterly alone. I know this won't make much sense to you, but my own guilt at my failure to protect my sister made me hate my father beyond reason. All I could see was his abandonment of us—of me." And then, in a moment of astonishing revelation, he realized that he was looking through a glass darkly, that the only way he recognized himself in her was that he had changed. She was, in fact, the way he used to be. It was far easier to plan revenge on his father than to face the full brunt of his own guilt. It was from this knowledge that his desire to help her sprang. He fervently wished that he could rescue her from death.

But he, of all people, understood with uncanny intimacy the coming of death. Its tread, once heard, could not be stopped, even by him. And when the time came, when he heard the tread and saw death's proximity in her eyes, he leaned over and, without being aware of it, smiled down at her reassuringly.

Picking up where Bourne, his father, had left off, he said, "Remember what to tell the Questioners, Zina. 'My God is Allah, my prophet Moham-mad, my religion Islam, and my kibla the Holy Kaaba.'" There seemed so much that she wanted to tell him and could not. "You are righteous, Zina. They will welcome you to glory."

Her eyes flickered once and then, like a flame, the life that animated them was extinguished.

Jamie Hull was waiting for Bourne when he returned to the Oskjuhlid Ho-tel. It had taken Bourne some time to get back there. Twice he was on the verge of passing out and was obliged to turn off the road, sitting with his forehead pressed against the steering wheel, he was in terrible pain, weary beyond thought, still, his will to see Khan again goaded him on. He did not care about security; he didn't care about anything now but being with his son.

At the hotel, after Bourne had briefly recounted Stepan Spalko's role in the assault on the hotel, Hull insisted on taking him to a medic to see to his fresh wounds.

"Spalko's worldwide reputation is such that even after we recover the body and release the evidence, there will be those who will refuse to believe it," Hull responded.

The emergency medic's rooms were filled with casualties lying on hastily erected cots. The more seriously wounded had been driven off by ambulance to the hospital. Then there were the dead, of whom no one yet wished to speak.

"We know your part in this, and I must say we're all grateful," Hull said, as he sat beside Bourne. "The president wants to speak with you, of course, but that will come later."

The medic arrived and started to stitch up Bourne's lacerated cheek.

"This won't heal pretty," she said. "You might want to consult a plastic surgeon."

"It won't be my first scar," Bourne said.

"So I see," she said dryly.

"One thing we found troubling was the presence of HAZMAT suits," Hull continued. "We found no sign of a biological or chemical agent. Did you?"

Bourne had to think fast. He'd left Khan alone with Zina and the bioweapon. A sudden stab of fear struck him. "No. We were as surprised as you were. But, afterward, there was no one left alive to ask."

Hull nodded, and when the medic was finished, he helped Bourne up and out into the corridor. "I know you'd like nothing better than a hot shower and a change of clothes, but it's important that I debrief you immediately." He smiled reassuringly. "It's a matter of national security. My hands are tied. But at least we can do it in a civilized manner over a hot meal, okay?"

Without another word, he delivered a short, sharp kidney punch that dropped Bourne to his knees. As Bourne gasped for breath, Hull drew back his other hand. In it was a push-dagger, the stubby leaflike blade that emerged from between his second and third fingers dark with a substance that was doubtless poisonous.

As he was about to drive it into Bourne's neck, a shot sounded in the corridor. Bourne, released from Hull's grip, slumped against the wall. Turning his head, he took everything in: Hull lying dead on the maroon carpet, the poisoned push-dagger in his hand, and hurrying up on his slightly bandy legs, Boris Illyich Karpov, director of the FSB's Alpha Unit, a silenced pistol in his hand.

"I must admit," Karpov said in Russian, as he helped Bourne to his feet, "I always harbored a secret desire to kill a CIA agent."

"Christ, thanks," Bourne gasped in the same language.

"This was a pleasure, believe me." Karpov stared down at Hull. "The CIA sanction against you has been rescinded, not that it mattered to him. It seems that you still have enemies inside your own Agency."

Bourne took several deep breaths, in itself a terribly painful proposition. He waited for his mind to clear sufficiently. "Karpov, how do I know you?"

The Russian let loose with a booming laugh. "*Gospadin* Bourne, I see the rumors about your memory are true." He put his arm around Bourne's waist, half supporting him. "Do you remember—? No, of course you don't. Well, the truth is, we've met several times. The last time, you saved my life, in fact." He laughed again at Bourne's bewildered expression. "It's a fine tale, my friend. A suitable story to tell over a bottle of vodka. Or maybe two, eh? After a night like this, who knows?"

"I'd be grateful for some vodka," Bourne acknowledged, "but there's someone I need to find first."

"Come," Karpov said, "I'll contact my men to clean up this garbage and we'll do together whatever needs to be done." He grinned hugely, dissolving the brutality of his features. "You stink like a week-old fish, you know that? But what the hell, I'm used to all sorts of foul odors!" He laughed again. "What a pleasure to see you again! One doesn't make friends easily, I've discovered, especially in our line of work. And so we must celebrate this event, this reunion, no?"

"Absolutely."

"And who must you need to find, my good friend Jason Bourne, that you cannot take a hot shower and a well-deserved rest first?"

"A young man named Khan. You've met him, I assume."

"Indeed," Karpov said as he led Bourne down another corridor. "A most remarkable young man. D'you know he never left the dying Chechen's side? And she, for her part, never let go of his hand until the end." He shook his head. "Most extraordinary."

He pursed his ruby lips. "Not that she deserved his attention. What was she, a murderer, a destroyer? You only have to see what they were attempting here to understand what kind of a monster she was."

"And yet," Bourne said, "she needed to hold his hand."

"How he put up with it I'll never know."

"Perhaps he needed something from her, as well." Bourne gave him a look. "Still think she was a monster?"

"Oh, yes," Karpov said, "but then the Chechens have trained me to think that way."

"Nothing changes, does it?" Bourne said.

"Not until we wipe them out." Karpov gave him a sideways glance. "Listen, my idealistic friend, they have said about us what other terrorists have said about you Americans, 'God has declared war on you.' We have learned from bitter experience to take such pronouncements seriously."

As it happened, Karpov knew just where Khan was—in the main restaurant, which was, after a fashion, up and running again with a severely limited menu.

"Spalko's dead," Bourne said to cover the rush of feeling he felt when he saw Khan.

Khan put down his hamburger and studied the stitches on Bourne's swollen cheek. "Are you hurt?"

"More than I already am?" Bourne winced as he sat down. "It's only minor."

Khan nodded but didn't take his eyes off Bourne.

Karpov, sitting down beside Bourne, called out to a passing waiter for a bottle of vodka. "Russian," he said sharply, "not that Polish swill. And bring with it large glasses. We're real men here, a Russian and heroes who are almost as good as Russians!" Then he returned his attention to his companions. "All right, what am I missing?" he said cannily.

"Nothing," Khan and Bourne said together.

"Is that so?" The Russian agent's caterpillar eyebrows lifted. "Well, then, there's nothing left but to drink. *In vino, veritas.* In wine, there is truth, so the ancient Romans believed. And who should disbelieve them? They were damn fine soldiers, the Romans, and they had great generals, but they would've been even better if they'd drunk vodka instead of wine!" He laughed raucously until the other two had no choice but to join in.

The vodka came then, along with water glasses. Karpov waved the waiter away.

"One must open the first bottle oneself," he said. "It's tradition."

"Bullshit," Bourne said, turning to Khan. "It's a habit from the old days when Russian vodka was so poorly refined there was often fuel oil in it."

"Don't listen to him." Karpov pursed his lips, but there was a twinkle in his eye. He filled their glasses and very formally placed them in front of them. "To share a bottle of fine Russian vodka is the very definition of friendship, fuel oil notwithstanding. Because over that bottle of fine Russian vodka we talk of old times, of comrades and enemies who have passed."

He lifted up his glass and they followed suit.

"*Na Sdarovye!*" he cried, taking an enormous swallow.

"*Na Sdarovye!*" they echoed, following suit.

Bourne's eyes watered. The vodka burned all the way down, but in a moment a warmth suffused his stomach, reaching out its fingers to assuage the constant pain he'd been in.

Karpov hunkered down, his face slightly flushed from both the fiery liquor and the simple pleasure of being with friends. "Now we'll get drunk and tell all our secrets. We'll learn what it means to be friends."

He took another huge swallow and said, "I'll begin. Here's my first secret. I know who you are, Khan. Though there's never been a photo taken of you, I know you." He put his finger beside his nose. "I haven't been in the field for twenty years without honing my sixth sense. And knowing this, I steered you away from Hull, who, had he suspected, would surely have arrested you, hero status or no."

Khan shifted slightly. "Why would you do that?"

"Oho, now you would kill me? Here at this amiable table? You think that I kept you isolated for myself? Did I not say that we were friends!" He shook his head. "You've much to learn about friendship, my young friend." He leaned forward. "I kept you safe because of Jason Bourne, who always works alone. You were with him, therefore I knew you were important to him."

He took another slug of vodka and pointed at Bourne. "Your turn, my friend."

Bourne stared down into his vodka. He was acutely aware of Khan's scrutiny. He knew what secret he wanted to divulge, but he was afraid that if he did, Khan would get up and walk away. But a truth was what he needed to tell them. He looked up finally.

"In the end, when I was with Spalko, I almost faltered. Spalko came close to killing me, but the truth is . . . the truth is . . ."

"It will be better for you to say it, yes," Karpov urged.

Bourne took the vodka into his mouth, swallowed the liquid courage down and turned to his son. "I thought of you. I thought if I failed now, if I allowed Spalko to kill me, I wouldn't come back. I couldn't abandon you; I couldn't allow that to happen."

"Good!" Karpov banged his glass on the table. He pointed at Khan. "Now you, my young friend."

In the ensuing silence Bourne felt as if his heart was in danger of stopping. Blood pounded in his head and all the pain of his many wounds, so briefly anesthetized, came flooding back.

"Well," Karpov said, "has the cat got your tongue? Your friends have given themselves up to you, and now they're waiting."

Khan looked straight at the Russian and said, "Boris Illyich Karpov, I'd like to formally introduce myself. My name is Joshua. I'm Jason Bourne's son."

Many hours and liters of vodka later, Bourne and Khan stood together in the subbasement of the Oskjuhlid Hotel. It was musty down there and cold, but all they could smell were vodka fumes. There were bloodstains everywhere.

"I suppose you're wondering what happened to the NX 20," Khan said.

Bourne nodded. "Hull was suspicious of the HAZMAT suits. He said they didn't find any evidence of biological or chemical weapons."

"I hid it," Khan said. "I was waiting for you to come back so that we could destroy it together."

Bourne hesitated for a moment. "You had faith I'd come back."

Khan turned and looked at his father. "It seems that I've newly acquired my faith."

"Or had it restored."

"Don't tell me—"

"I know, I know, I have no business telling you what you think." Bourne ducked his head. "Some acquisitions take more time than others."

Khan moved to where he'd hidden the NX 20, inside a crumbly niche behind a broken block of concrete obscured from view by one of the huge pipes in the thermal power station. "I had to leave Zina for a moment to do it," he said, "but it couldn't be helped." He held it with understandable respect as he handed it over to Bourne. He went and took a small metal box out of the niche. "The vial with the payload is in here."

"We need a fire," Bourne said, thinking of the legend he'd read on Dr. Sido's computer. "Heat will render the payload inert."

The vast hotel kitchen was spotless. Its gleaming stainless-steel surfaces seemed even colder with the absence of personnel. Bourne had moved the skeleton staff out for the time being while he and Khan went over to the huge floor-to-ceiling ovens. They were gas-powered, and Bourne turned them up to the highest level. At once fierce flames shot through the firebrick-lined interior. In less than a minute, it was too hot even to get close to.

They donned HAZMAT suits, broke down the weapon and each one threw one half into the flames. The vial went next.

"It's like a Viking funeral pyre," Bourne said as he watched the NX 20 collapse in on itself. He closed the door and they took off the suits.

Turning to his son, he said, "I've phoned Marie, but I haven't told her about you yet. I was waiting—"

"I'm not going back with you," Khan said.

Bourne chose his next words with great care. "That would not be my choice."

"I know," Khan said. "But I think there was a very good reason you didn't tell your wife about me."

In the silence that abruptly engulfed them, Bourne was gripped by a terrible sorrow. He wanted to look away, to hide what had rushed to his face, but he could not. He was through hiding his emotions from his son and from himself.

"You have Marie, two small children," Khan said. "This is the new life David Webb has made for himself and I'm not a part of it."

Bourne had learned many things in the few days since the first bullet sang its warning song past his ear on campus, not the least of which was when to keep his mouth shut around his son. He'd made up his mind and that was it. Trying to talk him out of his decision would be useless. Worse, it would reawaken the still-latent anger he would carry around with him for some time. An emotion so toxic, so deep-seated, it couldn't be expunged in a matter of days, weeks or even months.

Bourne understood that Khan had made a wise decision. There was still too much pain, the wound still raw, though the bleeding, at least, had been stopped. And as Khan had astutely pointed out, he knew deep down Khan's entry into the life that David Webb had fashioned for himself made no sense at all. Khan *didn't* belong there.

"Perhaps not now, perhaps not ever. But no matter how you feel about me, I want you to know that you have a brother and a sister who deserve to know you and have an older brother in their life. I hope there will come a time when that will happen—for all our sakes."

They walked together to the door and Bourne was very much aware that it was for the last time for many months to come. But not forever, no. This, at least, he had to make known to his son.

He moved forward and took Khan into his embrace. They stood together in silence. Bourne could hear the hiss of the gas jets. Inside the ovens, the fire continued to burn fiercely, annihilating the terrible threat to them all.

Reluctantly, he let Khan go, and for the briefest moment, as he stared into his son's eyes, he saw him as he had been, as a little boy in Phnom Penh with the blazing Asian sun on his face and, in the dappled shadows of the palms just beyond, Dao watching, smiling at them both.

"I'm also Jason Bourne," he said. "That's something you should never forget."

EPILOGUE

When the President of the United States personally opened the double walnut doors to his West Wing study, the DCI felt as if he was being readmitted to the precincts of heaven after cooling his heels in the seventh circle of hell.

The DCI was still suffering from the godawful malady, but with the telephone summons, he'd managed to drag himself out of his leather chair, had showered, shaved and dressed. He had been expecting the call. In fact, after he had his "Eyes Only" report delivered to the president, including all the detailed evidence compiled by Martin Lindros and Detective Harris he'd been mentally waiting for the call. And yet he'd waited in his robe and pajamas, sunk in his chair, listening to the oppressive silence of the house as if, within that void, he could discern the ghost of his wife's voice.

Now, as the president ushered him into the royal blue and gold corner office, he felt the desolation of his house even more keenly. Here was his life—the life he'd painstakingly built for himself over decades of faithful service and convoluted manipulation—here is where he understood the rules and knew how to play them, here and nowhere else.

"Good of you to come," the president said with his high-wattage smile. "It's been too long."

"Thank you, sir," the DCI said. "I was thinking the same thing."

"Take a seat." The president waved him to an upholstered wing-back chair. He was dressed in an impeccably tailored dark-blue suit, white shirt and a red tie with blue polka dots. His cheeks were slightly flushed, as if he'd just come in from running wind sprints. "Coffee?"

"I think I will. Thank you, sir."

At that moment, as if in response to an unheard summons, one of the presidential aides came in with a chased silver tray on which sat an ornate coffee pot and china cups in their delicate saucers. With a little thrill of pleasure, the DCI noted that there were only two cups.

"The NSA will be along presently," the president said, taking a seat opposite the DCI. The flush, the DCI could see now, wasn't from physical exertion but from the full ripening of his power. "But before that, I wanted to thank you personally for your good work these past several days."

The aide handed them their coffee and left, closing the heavy door softly behind him.

"I shudder to think of the dire consequences suffered by the civilized world were it not for your man Bourne."

"Thank you, sir. We never fully believed that he'd murdered Alex Conklin and Dr. Panov," the DCI said with an earnest and thoroughly hypocritical candor, "but we were presented with certain evidence—trumped-up, as it turned out—and we were forced to act on it."

"Of course—I understand." The president dropped two cubes of sugar into his cup and stirred thoughtfully. "All's well that ends well, though in our world—as opposed to Shakespeare's—there are consequences to every action." He sipped his coffee. "Nevertheless, despite the bloodbath, the summit, as you know, went on as scheduled. And it was an unqualified success. In fact, the threat served to bring us more firmly together. All the heads of state—even, thank God, Aleksandr Yevtushenko—could see clearly the fate the world faced if we didn't put aside our own myopic viewpoints and agree to work together. We now have signed, sealed and delivered a practical framework for going forward in a united front against terrorism. Already, the Secretary of State is on his way to the Middle East to begin the next round of talks. Quite an opening salvo across our enemies' bows."

And your reelection is assured, the DCI thought. *Not to mention the legacy of your presidency.*

At the discreet sound of the intercom, the president excused himself, rose and crossed to his desk. He listened for a moment, then looked up. His penetrating gaze rested on the DCI. "I've allowed myself to be cut off from someone who could have provided measured and valuable advice. Rest assured I won't allow that to happen again."

Clearly, the president didn't expect him to respond because he was already saying into the intercom, "Send her in."

The DCI, as emotionally vulnerable as he'd ever been, took a moment to collect himself. He looked about the spacious high-ceilinged room with its cream walls, royal blue carpet, dentiled molding and solid, comfortable furniture. Large oil portraits of several Republican presidents hung above a matching pair of Chippendale cherrywood sideboards. An American flag stood half-furled in a corner. Outside the windows, under a downy white haze, was an expanse of closely mowed lawn above which a cherry tree spread its arching branches. Clusters of pale pink blossoms shivered like bells in the spring breeze.

The door opened and Roberta Alonzo-Ortiz was ushered in. The DCI noted with relish that the president didn't budge from his position behind his desk. He stood still, facing the NSA, and, quite pointedly, didn't ask her to sit down. The NSA was wearing a severely cut black suit, steel-gray silk blouse and practical low-heeled pumps. She appeared ready to attend a funeral, which, the DCI thought with no little glee, was entirely appropriate.

She registered a split-instant's surprise at the DCI's presence. A last spark of enmity glowed in her eyes before they turned inward and she drew her face into a rigid mask. Her complexion appeared oddly mottled, as if in reaction to the obvious effort of stifling her emotions. She didn't address him or otherwise acknowledge his presence.

"Ms. Alonzo-Ortiz, I want you to understand some things so that you can put the events of the last several days into some kind of perspective," the president began in a sonorous voice that brooked no interruption. "While I acceded to the Bourne sanction, I did so strictly on advice from you. I also agreed when you petitioned me for a quick resolution to the murders of Alex Conklin and Morris Panov and, foolishly, followed your judgment in condemning Detective Harry Harris of the Virginia State Police for the debacle beneath Washington Circle.

"All I can say is that I'm profoundly grateful that the sanction wasn't in the end carried out, but I'm appalled at the damage done to the career of a fine detective. Zeal is a commendable trait but not when it overrides the truth, something you swore to uphold when I asked you to come aboard."

Through this speech, he had neither moved nor taken his gaze from her. His expression was carefully neutral, but there was a certain clipped cadence to his words that revealed to the DCI, who after all knew him best, both the depth and the breadth of his anger. This was not a man to be made a fool of, this was not a president to forgive and forget. The DCI had counted on this when he prepared his damning report.

"Ms. Alonzo-Ortiz, my administration has no place for political opportunists—at least, not those who are willing to sacrifice the truth in order to cover their own ass. The truth is, you should've aided in the investigation of the murders instead of trying your best to bury those falsely implicated. If you had, we might have uncovered this terrorist, Stepan Spalko, soon enough to have averted the bloodbath at the summit. As it is, we all owe a debt of gratitude to the DCI, especially you."

At this last, Roberta Alonzo-Ortiz winced, as if the president had dealt her a terrific blow, which, in a sense, he very deliberately had.

He picked up a single sheet of paper off his desk. "Therefore, I accept your letter of resignation and grant your request to return to the private sector, effective immediately."

The former NSA opened her mouth to speak, but the president's laser-like stare froze her in her tracks.

"I wouldn't," he said shortly.

She blanched, nodded slightly in submission, and turned on her heel.

The moment the door closed behind her the DCI took a deep breath. For a moment the president's gaze intersected his and all was revealed. He knew why his Commander-in-Chief had summoned him to witness the NSA's humiliation. It was his way of making an apology. In all his years toiling as a servant of his country, the DCI had never before been apologized to by the president. He was so overcome he had no idea how to respond.

In a daze of euphoria, he rose. The president was already on the phone, his eyes roving elsewhere. For a brief moment, the DCI paused, savoring his moment of triumph. Then he, too, departed the sanctum sanctorum, striding down the hushed corridors of power that he had made his home.

David Webb had finished hanging the multicolored HAPPY BIRTHDAY sign in the living room. Marie was in the kitchen, putting the finishing touches on the chocolate cake she'd baked for Jamie's eleventh birthday. The smells of pizza and chocolate drifted deliciously through the house. He looked around, wondering if there were enough balloons. He counted thirty—surely, that was more than enough.

Though he'd returned to his life as David Webb, his ribs pained him with every breath he took and the rest of his body ached enough for him to know that he was also Jason Bourne and always would be. For so long he'd been terrified each time that side of his personality resurfaced, but now with Joshua's reemergence, everything had changed. He had a compelling reason to become Jason Bourne again.

But not with the CIA. With Alex's death, he was quits with them, even though the DCI himself had asked him to stay, even though he actually liked and respected Martin Lindros, the man responsible for having the sanction against him lifted. It was Lindros who had admitted him to Bethesda Naval Hospital. In between bouts with a team of Agency-vetted specialists, who had seen to Webb's wounds and had carefully examined his cracked ribs, Lindros had debriefed him. The DDCI had made a difficult task almost easy, allowing Webb precious time to sleep and unwind from his arduous trials.

But after three days Webb wanted nothing more than to return to his students, and he needed time with his family, even though there was now an ache in his heart, a certain void given form and shape by Joshua's return. He'd meant to tell Marie about him, had in fact told her every other detail of what had happened while they'd been out of touch. And yet each time he had come to the subject of his other son, his brain shut down. It wasn't that he was afraid of her reaction—he trusted her too much for that. It was his own reaction he was unsure of. After only a week away he felt estranged from Jamie and Alison. He'd completely forgotten Jamie's birthday until Marie had gently reminded him. Like the proverbial line in the sand, he felt a clear demarcation of his life before Joshua's startling appearance and after. There was the darkness of grief and now there was the light of reconnection. There was death and now, miraculously, there was life. He needed to understand the implications of what had happened. How could he share something so monumental with Marie until he understood it himself?

And so, on this, his young son's birthday, his mind was flooded with thoughts of his older son. Where was Joshua? Shortly after he'd heard from Ozskar that Annaka Vadas' body had been found by the side of the motorway leading to Ferihegy Airport, Joshua had slipped away, vanishing as quickly and completely as he had appeared. Had he returned to Budapest to see Annaka one last time? Webb hoped not.

In any case, Karpov had promised to keep his secret, and Webb believed him. He realized that he had no idea where his son lived or even if he had a real home. It was impossible to imagine where Joshua was or what he might now be doing, and this caused a pain in Webb unlike any other. He felt the lack of him as acutely as if he'd lost a limb. There was so much he wanted to say to Joshua, so much time to make up for. It was difficult being patient, painful not even knowing whether Joshua would choose to come to him again.

The party had begun, the twenty or so kids playing and yelling at the tops of their lungs. And there was Jamie in the center of it all, a born leader, a boy others his own age looked up to. His open face, so like Marie's, was shining with happiness. Webb wondered whether he'd ever see such a look of unalloyed pleasure on Joshua's face. Instantly, as if there was a telepathic link between them, Jamie glanced up and, seeing his father's gaze on him, grinned hugely.

Webb, having drawn greeter duty, once again heard the bell ring. He opened the door to find a FedEx agent with a package for him. He signed for it and at once took it down to the basement, where he unlocked a room to which there was only one key. Inside was a portable X-ray machine Conklin had procured for him. All packages coming to the Webbs were, unbeknownst to the children, run through this machine.

Determining it was clean, Webb opened it. Inside were a baseball and two gloves, one for him and the other just the right size for an eleven-year-old. He unfolded the accompanying note, which read, simply:

> For Jamie's birthday
> —Joshua

David Webb stared at the gift, which meant more to him than anyone would ever know. Music drifted down to him from above, along with the intermittent laughter of the children. He thought of Dao and Alyssa and Joshua as they existed in his splintered memory, and this kaleidoscopic image, stimulated by the sharp, earthy scent of the oiled leather, was brought vividly to life. Reaching out, he felt the supple grain of the leather, ran his fingertips over the rawhide stitching. What memories were stirring inside him! His smile, when it came to his face, was bittersweet. He slipped his hand into the larger of the gloves and threw the baseball into the heart of it. Catching it there, he held it as tightly as if it were a will-o'-the-wisp.

He heard a light tread on the top of the stairs, and then Marie's voice calling to him.

"I'll be right up, sweetheart," he said.

He sat very still for some moments longer, allowing the events of the recent past to swirl around him. Then he exhaled deeply and set aside the past. With Jamie's present cradled in the other hand, he mounted the basement stairs and went to rejoin his family.